Get up
with an i...

CW00370329

❄ *Seduced by*
CHRISTMAS

from

SANDRA MARTON
& YVONNE LINDSAY

Two brand-new, sizzling and
glamorous Christmas novels to
heat up the festive season

Get up close and passionate
with sultry, intense, sexy millionaire
this holiday

Seduced by CHRISTMAS

Featuring:

The Sicilian's Christmas Bride
SANDRA MARTON

The Boss's Christmas Seduction
YVONNE LINDSAY

DID YOU PURCHASE THIS BOOK WITHOUT A COVER?

If you did, you should be aware it is **stolen property** as it was reported *unsold and destroyed* by a retailer. Neither the author nor the publisher has received any payment for this book.

All the characters in this book have no existence outside the imagination of the author, and have no relation whatsoever to anyone bearing the same name or names. They are not even distantly inspired by any individual known or unknown to the author, and all the incidents are pure invention.

All Rights Reserved including the right of reproduction in whole or in part in any form. This edition is published by arrangement with Harlequin Enterprises II B.V./S.à.r.l. The text of this publication or any part thereof may not be reproduced or transmitted in any form or by any means, electronic or mechanical, including photocopying, recording, storage in an information retrieval system, or otherwise, without the written permission of the publisher.

This book is sold subject to the condition that it shall not, by way of trade or otherwise, be lent, resold, hired out or otherwise circulated without the prior consent of the publisher in any form of binding or cover other than that in which it is published and without a similar condition including this condition being imposed on the subsequent purchaser.

M&B™ and M&B™ with the Rose Device
are trademarks of the publisher.
Harlequin Mills & Boon Limited, Eton House,
18-24 Paradise Road, Richmond, Surrey TW9 1SR

SEDUCED BY CHRISTMAS © by Harlequin Books S.A. 2007
This collection is first published in Great Britain in 2007

The Sicilian's Christmas Bride © Sandra Myles 2006
The Boss's Christmas Seduction © Yvonne Lindsay 2006

ISBN: 978 0 263 86576 9

24-1107

Harlequin Mills & Boon policy is to use papers that are natural, renewable and recyclable products and made from wood grown in sustainable forests. The logging and manufacturing processes conform to the legal environmental regulations of the country of origin.

Printed and bound in Spain
by Litografía Rosés S.A., Barcelona

The Sicilian's Christmas Bride

SANDRA MARTON

Dear Reader,

Is Christmas your favourite time of year? Do you have warm childhood memories of family gatherings, tinsel and sleigh bells, the excitement of running downstairs to see what wonderful presents Santa left under the tree? Even years later, when we're all grown-up, we think back to Christmas and smile.

But we don't all have those memories.

For Dante Russo, Christmas was just another hard day on the mean streets of Sicily. It still is just another day, even though Dante's life has changed dramatically. He's fabulously wealthy. He's incredibly handsome. He holds a world of power, and he can have any woman he wants.

That woman is Taylor Sommers.

Dante makes her his mistress. He tells himself he'll keep her until he tires of her. Tally tells herself that suits her just fine. Such are the lies we sometimes hide behind to keep our hearts safe.

Their affair ends just before Christmas. Three years go by. Another Christmas is approaching and Dante suddenly realises he's furious. He wants answers. Why did Tally run away from him, three years ago? Tally's defiant. She says he's only angry because she made the first move.

What she doesn't tell him is that she has a secret, one that will change their lives forever.

Come with me on an unforgettable journey as Dante Russo takes the biggest gamble of his life by opening his heart to a woman's love, a child's innocence… and the joyous miracle of Christmas.

Happy holidays!

Love,

Sandra Marton

Sandra Marton wrote her first novel while she was still in primary school. Her doting parents told her she'd be a writer someday and Sandra believed them. In secondary school and college, she wrote dark poetry nobody but her boyfriend understood, though looking back, she suspects he was just being kind. As a wife and mother, she wrote murky short stories in what little spare time she could manage, but not even her boyfriend-turned-husband could pretend to understand those. Sandra tried her hand at other things, among them teaching and serving on the Board of Education in her home town, but the dream of becoming a writer was always in her heart.

At last, Sandra realised she wanted to write books about what all women hope to find: love with that one special man, love that's rich with fire and passion, love that lasts forever. She wrote a novel, her very first, and sold it to Mills & Boon® Modern™. Since then, she's written more than sixty books, all of them featuring sexy, gorgeous, larger-than-life heroes. A four-time RITA® award finalist, she's also received five *Romantic Times Magazine* awards and has been honoured with a Career Achievement Award for Series Romance. Sandra lives with her very own sexy, gorgeous, larger-than-life hero in a sun-filled house on a quiet country lane in the north-eastern United States.

Look out for Sandra Marton's new novel, *The Spanish Prince's Virgin Bride*, which is on sale in December 2007.

Sandra loves to hear from her readers.
You can write to her or visit her at
http://www.sandramarton.com

CHAPTER ONE

THE HOTEL BALLROOM was a Christmas fairyland.

Evergreen garlands hung with silver and gold orna-
ments were draped across the ceiling; elegant white
faux Christmas trees sparkled with tiny gold lights.
Someone said there'd even be a visit from Santa at
midnight, tossing expensive baubles to the well-dressed
and incredibly moneyed crowd.

Nothing could ever compare with New York's first
charity ball of the holiday season.

Dante Russo had seen it all before. The truth was, it
bored the hell out of him. The crowds, the noise, the in-
your-face signs of power and wealth…

But then, for some reason everything bored him lately.

Even—perhaps especially—the high-octane excitement of his current mistress as she clung to his arm.

"Oh, DanteDarling," she kept saying, "oh, oh, oh,
isn't this fabulous?"

That was how she'd taken to addressing him, as if
his name and the supposed-endearment were one
word instead of two. And *fabulous* seemed to be her
favorite adjective tonight. So far, she'd used it to

describe the decorations, the band, their table and the guests.

A month ago, he'd found Charlotte's affectations amusing. Now, he found them almost as irritating as her breathless, little-girl voice.

Dante glanced at his watch. Another hour and he'd make his excuses about an early-morning meeting and leave. She'd protest: it would mean missing Santa's visit. But he'd assure her Santa would bring her something special tomorrow.

A little blue box from Tiffany, delivered to her apartment building not by Saint Nick but by FedEx.

He would see to it the box held something fabulous, Dante thought wryly. Something that would serve not only as a gift to make up for ending the night early but as a goodbye present.

His interest in Charlotte was at an end. He'd sensed it for days. Now, he knew it. He only hoped the breakup would be clean. He always made it clear he wasn't interested in forever, but some women refused to get the message, and—

"DanteDarling?"

He blinked. "Yes, Charlotte?"

"You're not listening!"

"I'm sorry. I, ah, I have a meeting in the morning and—"

"Dennis and Eve were telling everyone about their place in Colorado."

"Yes. Of course. Aspen, isn't it?"

"That's right," Eve said, and sighed wearily. "It's still gorgeous—"

"Fabulous," Charlotte said eagerly.

"But it's not what it used to be. So many people have discovered the town…"

Dante did his best to listen but his attention wandered again. What was the matter with him tonight? He didn't feel like himself at all. Bored or not, he knew better than to let his emotions gain control.

Giving free rein to your feelings was a mistake. It revealed too much, and revealing yourself to others was for fools.

That conviction, bred deep in his Sicilian bones by a childhood of poverty and neglect, had served him well. It had lifted him from the gutters of Palermo to the spires of Manhattan.

At thirty-two, Dante ruled an international empire, owned homes on two continents, owned a Mercedes and a private jet, and had his choice of spectacularly beautiful women.

His money had little to do with that.

He was, as more than one woman had whispered, beautiful. He was tall and leanly muscled, with the hard body of an athlete, the face of Michelangelo's David and the reputation of being as exciting in the bedroom as he was formidable in the boardroom.

In other words, Dante had everything a man could possibly want, including the knowledge that his life could very well have turned out differently. Being aware of that was part of who he was. It helped keep him alert.

Focused.

Everyone said that of him. That he was focused. Tightly so, not just on his business affairs or whatever woman held his interest at the moment but on whatever was happening around him.

Not tonight.

Tonight, he couldn't keep his attention on anything.

He'd already lost interest in the conversation of the others at the table. He took his cue from Charlotte, nodded, smiled, even laughed when it seemed appropriate.

It bothered him that he should be so distracted.

Except, that was the wrong word. What he felt was— What? Restless. As if something was about to happen. Something he wasn't prepared for, which was impossible.

He was always prepared.

Always, he thought… Except for that one time. That one time—

"DanteDarling, you aren't paying attention at all!"

Charlotte was leaning toward him, head tilted at just the right angle to make an offering of her décolletage. She was smiling, but the glint in her eye told him she wasn't happy.

"He's always like this," she said gaily, "when he's planning some devastating business coup." She gave a delicate shudder. "Whatever is it, DanteDarling? Something bloody and awful—and oh, so exciting?"

Everyone laughed politely. So did Dante, but he knew, in that instant, his decision to end things with Charlotte was the right one.

These past couple of weeks, while he'd grown bored she'd grown more demanding. Why hadn't he phoned? Where had he been when she called him? She'd begun using that foolish name for him and now she'd taken to dropping little remarks that made it seem as if she and he were intimate in all the ways he had made clear he never would be.

With any woman. Any woman, even—

"…would love to spend Christmas in Aspen, wouldn't we, DanteDarling?"

Dante forced a smile. "Sorry. I didn't get that."

"Dennis and Eve want us to fly to Aspen," Charlotte purred. "And I accepted."

Dante's eyes met hers. "Did you," he said softly.

"Of course! You know we're going to spend Christmas together. Why on earth would we want to be apart on such a special day?"

"Why, indeed," he said, after a long pause. Then he smiled and rose to his feet. "Would you like to dance, Charlotte?"

Something of what he was thinking must have shown in his face.

"Well—well, not just now. I mean, we should stay here and discuss the party. When to fly out, how long we'll stay—"

Dante took her hand, drew her from her chair and led her from the table. The band was playing a waltz as they stepped onto the dance floor.

"You're angry," she said, her voice affecting that little-girl whisper.

"I'm not angry."

"You are. But it's your own fault. Six weeks, Dante. Six weeks! It's time we took the next step."

"Toward what?" he said, his tone expressionless.

"You know what I mean. A woman expects—"

"You knew what *not* to expect, Charlotte." His mouth thinned; his voice turned cold. "And yet, here you are, making plans without consulting me. Talking as if our arrangement is something it is not." He danced her across the floor and into a corner. "You're right about one thing. It's time we, as you put it, took the next step."

"Are you breaking up with me?" When he didn't answer, two bright spots of color rose in her cheeks. "You bastard!"

"An accurate perception, but it changes nothing. You're a beautiful woman. A charming woman. And a bright one. You knew from the beginning how this would end."

His tone had softened. After all, he had only himself to blame. He should have read the signs, should have realized Charlotte had been making assumptions about the future despite his initial care in making sure she understood they had none. Women seemed to make the same mistake all the time.

Most women, he thought, and a muscle jumped in his cheek.

"I've enjoyed the time we've spent together," he said, forcing his attention back where it belonged.

Charlotte jerked free of his hand. "Don't patronize me!"

"No," he replied, his voice cooling, "certainly not. If you prefer to make a scene, rest assured that I can accommodate you."

Her eyes narrowed. He knew she was weighing her options. An embarrassing public display or a polite goodbye that would make it easy for her to concoct a story to soothe her pride.

"Your choice, *bella*," he said, more softly. "Do we part friends or enemies?"

She hesitated. Then a smile curved her lips. "You can't blame me for trying." Still smiling, she smoothed her palms over the lapels of his dinner jacket. It was a proprietorial gesture and he let her do it; he knew it was for those who might be taking in the entire performance. "But you're cruel, DanteDarling. Otherwise, you wouldn't humiliate me in front of my friends."

"Is that what concerns you?" Dante shrugged. "It's not a problem. We'll go back to our table and finish the evening pleasantly. All right?"

"Yes. That's fine. But Dante?" The tip of her tongue flickered across her lips. "Hear me out, would you?"

"What now?" he said, trying to mask his impatience.

"I know you don't believe in love and forever after, darling. Well, neither do I." She paused. "Still, we could have an interesting life together."

He stared at her in surprise. Was she suggesting marriage? He almost laughed. Still, he supposed he understood. He didn't know Charlotte's exact age but she had to be in her late twenties, old enough to want to find a husband who could support her fondness for expensive living.

As for him, men his age had families. Children to carry forward their names. He had to admit he thought about that from time to time, especially since he'd plucked the name "Russo" from a newspaper article.

Having a child to bear the name was surely a way to legitimatize it.

Charlotte could be the perfect wife. She would demand nothing but his superficial attention and tolerate his occasional affair; she would never interfere in his life. Never fill his head to the exclusion of everything else.

And, just that suddenly, Dante knew what was wrong with him tonight.

A woman had once filled his head to the exclusion of everything else. And, damn her, she was still doing it.

The realization shot through him. He felt his muscles tighten, as if all the adrenaline his body could produce was overwhelming his system.

"Oh, for heaven's sake," Charlotte said, "don't look at me that way! I was only joking."

He knew she hadn't been joking but he decided to go along with it because it gave him something to concentrate on as he walked her back to their table.

Eva greeted them with a coy smile. "Well," she said, "what have you decided? Will we see you in Aspen?"

For a second, he didn't know what she was talking about. His thoughts were sucking him into a place of dark, cold shadows and unwanted memories.

Memories of a woman he thought he'd forgotten.

Then he remembered the gist of the conversation and his promise to Charlotte.

"Sorry," he said politely, "but I'm afraid we can't make it."

Charlotte shot him a grateful look as she took her seat. He squeezed her shoulder.

"I'll be back in a few minutes."

"Going for a cigar?" Dennis said. "Russo? Wait. I'll join you."

But Dante was already making his way through the ballroom, deliberately losing himself in the crowd as he headed for one of the doors. He pushed it open, found himself in a narrow service hallway. A surprised waitress bumped into him, murmured an apology and tried to tell him he'd taken a wrong turn.

He almost told her she was right, except he'd taken that wrong turn three years ago.

He went through another door, then down a short corridor and ended up outside on a docking bay. Once he was sure he was alone, Dante threw back his head and dragged the cold night air deep into his lungs.

Dio, he had to be crazy.

All this time, and she was still there. Taylor Sommers, whom he had not seen in three years, was inside him tonight, probably had been for a very long time. How come he hadn't known it?

You didn't want to know it, a sly voice in his head told him.

A muscle knotted in his jaw.

No, he thought coldly, no. What was inside him was rage. It was one thing not to let your emotions rule you and another to suppress them, which was what he had done since she'd left him.

He'd kept his anger inside, as if doing so would rid him of it. Now, without warning, it had surfaced along with all the memories he'd carefully buried.

Not of Taylor. Not of what it had been like to be with her. Her whispers in bed.

Yes. Dante, yes. When you do that, when you do that...

He groaned at the memory. The need to be inside her had been like a drug. It had brought him close to believing in the ancient superstitions of his people that said a man could be possessed.

He was long past that, had been past it by the time she left him.

It was the rest, what had happened at the end, that

was still with him. Knowing that she believed she'd left him, when it wasn't true.

He had left her.

He'd never had the chance to say, "You made the first move, *cara,* but that's all it was. You ran away before I had a chance to end our affair."

She didn't know that and it drove him crazy. Pathetic, maybe, that it should matter…but it did. Obviously it did, or he wouldn't be standing out here in the cold, glaring at a stack of empty produce cartons and finally admitting that he'd been walking around in a state of smoldering fury since a night like this, precisely like this, late November, cold, snow already in the forecast, when Taylor had left a message on his answering machine.

"Dante," she'd said, "I'm afraid I'll have to cancel our date for tonight. I think I'm coming down with the flu. I'm going to take some aspirin and go to bed. Sorry to inconvenience you."

Sorry to inconvenience you.

For some reason, the oh-so-polite phrase had irritated him. Was *inconvenience* a word for a woman to use to her lover? And what was all that about canceling their date? She was his mistress. They didn't have "dates."

Jaw knotted, he'd reached for the phone to call and tell her that.

But he'd controlled his temper. Actually, there was nothing wrong in what she'd said. *Date* implied that they saw each other when it suited them. When it suited him.

So, why had it pissed him off? Her removed tone. Her impersonal words. And then another possibility had elbowed its way into his brain.

Maybe, he'd thought, *maybe I should call and see if she needs something. A doctor. Some cold tablets.*

Or maybe I should see if she just needs me.

The thought had stunned him. Need? It wasn't a word in his vocabulary. Nor in Taylor's. It was one of the things he admired about her.

So he'd put the phone aside and gone to the party. Not just any party. *This* party. The same charity, the same hotel, the same guests. He'd eaten what might have been the same overdone filet, sipped the same warm champagne, talked some business with the men at his table and danced with the women.

The women had all asked the same question.

"Where's Taylor?"

"She's not feeling well," he'd kept saying, even as it struck him that he was spending an inordinate amount of time explaining the absence of a woman who was not in any way a permanent part of his life. They'd only been together a couple of months.

Six months, he'd suddenly realized. Taylor had been his mistress for six months. How had that happened?

While he'd considered that, one of the women had touched his arm.

"Dante?"

"Yes?"

"If Taylor's ill, she needs to drink lots of liquids."

He'd blinked. Why tell him what his mistress needed to do?

"Water's good, but orange juice is better. Or ginger tea."

"That wonderful chicken soup at the Carnegie Deli,"

another woman said. "And does she have an inhalator? There's that all-night drugstore a few block away…"

Amazing, he'd thought. Everyone assumed that he and Taylor were living together.

They weren't.

"I prefer that you keep your apartment," he'd told her bluntly, at the start of their relationship.

"That's good," she'd said with a little smile, "because I intended to."

Had she told people something else? Had she deliberately made the relationship seem more than it was?

He'd thought back a few weeks to his birthday. He had no idea how she'd known it was his birthday; he'd never mentioned it. Why would he? And yet, when he'd arrived at her apartment to take her to dinner, she'd told him she wanted to stay in.

"I'm going to cook tonight," she'd said with a little smile. "For your birthday."

He made a habit of avoiding these things, a homemade dinner, a quiet evening, but he couldn't see a way to turn her down without seeming rude so he'd accepted her invitation.

To his amazement, he'd enjoyed the evening.

"Pasta Carbonara," she'd said, as she served the meal. "I remember you ordering it at Luigi's and saying how much you liked it." Her cheeks had pinkened. "I just hope my version is half as good."

It was better than good; it was perfect. So was everything else.

The candles. The bottle of his favorite Cabernet. The flowers.

And Taylor.

Taylor, watching him across the table, her green eyes soft with pleasure. Taylor, blushing again when he said the food was delicious. Taylor, bringing out a cake complete with candles. And a familiar blue box. He'd given boxes like that to more women than he could count, but being on the receiving end had been a first.

"I hope you like them," she'd said as he opened the box on a pair of gold cuff links, exactly the kind he'd have chosen for himself.

"Very much," he'd replied, and wondered what she'd say if he told her this was the first birthday cake, the first birthday gift anyone had ever given him in all his life.

He'd blown out the candles. Taken a bite of the cake. Put on the cuff links and felt something he couldn't define…

"Dante?" Taylor had said, her smooth brow furrowing, "what's the matter? If you don't like the cuff links—"

He'd silenced her in midsentence by gathering her in his arms, taking her mouth with his, carrying her to her bed and making love to her.

Sex with her was always incredible. That night…that night, it surpassed anything he'd ever known with her, with any woman. She was tender; she was passionate. She was wild and sweet and, as he threw back his head and emptied himself into her, she cried out his name and wept.

When it was over, she lay beneath him, trembling. Then she'd brought his mouth to hers for a long kiss.

"Don't leave me tonight," she'd whispered. "Dante. Please stay."

He'd never spent the entire night with her. With any woman. But he'd been tempted. Tempted to keep his arms around her warm body. To close her eyes with soft kisses. To fall asleep with her head on his shoulder and wake with her curled against him.

He hadn't, of course.

Spending the night in a woman's bed had shades of meaning beyond what he needed or expected from a relationship.

Two weeks after that, he'd attended this charity ball without her, listened to people urge him to feed his mistress chicken soup…

And everything had clicked into place.

The birthday supper. The fantastic night of sex. The plea that he not leave her afterward.

Taylor was playing him the way a fisherman who's hooked a big one plays a fish. His beautiful, clever mistress was doing her best to settle into his life. She knew it, his acquaintances knew it. The only person who'd been blind to the scheme was him.

"Excuse me," he'd suddenly said to everyone at the table, "but it's getting late."

"Don't forget the chicken soup," a woman called after him.

Dante had instructed his driver to take him to Taylor's apartment. It was time to set things straight. To make sure she still understood their agreement, that the rules hadn't changed simply because their affair had gone on so long.

In fact, perhaps it was time to end the relationship. Not tonight. Not abruptly. He'd simply see her less often. In a few weeks, he'd take her to L'Etoile for dinner, give her a bracelet or a pair of earrings to remember him by and tell her their time together had been fun but—

But Taylor didn't answer the door when he rang—which reminded him that she'd never given him a key. He hadn't given her one to his place, either, but that was different. He never gave his mistresses keys, but they were always eager to give theirs to him.

And it occurred to him again, as it often did, that Taylor wasn't really his mistress. She insisted on paying her own rent, even though most women gladly let him do it.

"I'm not most women," she'd said when he'd tried to insist, and he'd told himself that was good, that he admired her independence.

That night, however, he saw it for what it was. Just another way to heighten his interest, he'd thought coldly, as he rang the bell again.

Still no answer.

His thoughts turned even colder. Was she out with another man?

No. She was sick. He believed that; she'd sounded terrible on the phone when she'd called him earlier, her voice hoarse and raw.

Dante's heart had skittered. Was she lying unconscious behind the locked door? He took the stairs to the super's basement apartment at a gallop when the damned elevator refused to come, awakened the man and bought his cooperation with a fistful of bills.

Together, they'd gone up to Taylor's apartment. Unlocked the door...

And found the place empty.

His mistress was gone.

Her things were gone, too. All that remained was a trace of her scent in the air and a note, a *note,* goddamn her, on the coffee table.

"Thank you for everything," she had written, "it's been fun." Only that, as if their affair had been a game.

And Dante had swallowed the insult. What else could he have done? Hired a detective to find her? That would only have made his humiliation worse.

Three years. Three years, and now, without warning, it had all caught up to him. The embarrassment. The anger...

"Dante?"

He turned around. Charlotte had somehow managed to find him. She stood on the loading dock, wrapped in a velvet cloak he'd bought her, her face pink with anger.

"Here you are," she said sharply.

"Charlotte. My apologies. I, ah, I came out for a breath of air—"

"You said you wouldn't embarrass me."

"Yes. I know. And I won't. I told you, I only stepped outside—"

"You've been gone almost an hour! How dare you make me look foolish to my friends?" Her voice rose. "Who do you think you are?"

Dante's eyes narrowed. He moved toward her, and something dangerous must have shown in his face because she took a quick step back.

"I know exactly who I am," he said softly. "I am Dante Russo, and whoever deals with me should never forget it."

"Dante. I only meant—"

He took her arm, quick-marched her down a set of concrete steps and away from the dock. An alley led to the street where he hailed a cab, handed the driver a hundred-dollar bill and told him Charlotte's address.

He'd left his topcoat inside the hotel but he didn't give a damn. Coats were easy to replace. Pride wasn't.

"Dante," she stammered, "really, I'm sorry—"

So was he, but not for what had just happened. He was sorry he had lived a lie for the past three years.

Taylor Sommers had made a fool of him. Nobody, *nobody* got away with that.

He took his cell phone from his pocket and called his driver. When his Mercedes pulled to the curb, Dante got in the back and pressed another number on the phone. It was late, but his personal attorney answered on the first ring.

He didn't waste time on preliminaries. "I need a private investigator," he said. "No, not first thing Monday. Tomorrow. Have him call me at home."

Three years had gone by. So what? Someone had once said that revenge was a dish best served cold.

A tight smile curved Dante's hard mouth.

He couldn't have agreed more.

IT WAS A LONG WEEKEND.

Charlotte left endless messages on his voice mail. They ranged from weepy to demanding, and he erased them all.

Saturday morning, he heard from the detective his attorney had contacted. The man asked for everything Dante knew about Taylor.

"Her name," he said, "is Taylor Sommers. She lived in the Stanhope, on Gramercy Park. She's an interior decorator."

There was a silence.

"And?" the man said.

"And what? Isn't that enough?"

"Well, I could use the names of her parents. Her friends. Date of birth. Where she grew up. What schools she attended."

"I've told you everything I know," Dante said coldly.

He hung up the phone, then walked through his bedroom and onto the wraparound terrace that surrounded his Central Park West penthouse. It was cold; the wind had a way of whipping around the building at this height. And it had snowed overnight, not heavily, just enough to turn the park a pristine white.

Dante frowned.

The detective had seemed surprised he knew so little about Taylor, but why would he have known more? She pleased his eye; she was passionate and intelligent.

What more would a man want from a woman?

There had been moments, though. Like the time he'd brought her here for a late supper. It had snowed that night, too. He'd excused himself, gone to make a brief but necessary phone call. When he came back, he'd found the terrace door open and Taylor standing out here, just as he was now.

She'd been wearing a silk dress, a little slip of a thing. He'd taken off his jacket, stepped outside and put it around her shoulders.

"What are you doing, *cara?* It's much too cold for you out here."

"I know," she'd answered, snuggling into his jacket and into the curve of his arm, "but it's so beautiful, Dante." She'd turned her face up to his and smiled. "I love nights like this, don't you?"

Cold nights reminded him of the frigid winters in

Palermo, the way he'd padded his shoes with newspaper in a useless attempt to keep warm.

For some reason he still couldn't comprehend, he'd almost told her that.

Of course, he had not done anything so foolish. Instead, he'd kissed her.

"If you can get over your penchant for cold and snow," he'd said, with a little smile, "we can fly to the Caribbean some weekend and you can help me house-hunt. I've been thinking about buying a place in the islands."

Her smile had been soft. "I'd like that," she'd said. "I'd like it very, very much."

Instantly, he'd realized what a mistake he'd made. He'd asked her to take a step into his life and he'd never meant to do that.

He'd never mentioned the Caribbean again. Not that it mattered, because two weeks later, she'd walked out on him.

Walked out, he thought now, his jaw tightening. Left him to come up with excuses explaining her absence at all those endless Christmas charitable events he was expected to attend.

But he'd solved that problem simply enough.

He'd found replacements for her. He'd gone through that season with an endless array of beautiful women on his arm.

On his arm, but not in his bed. It had been a long time until he'd had sex after Taylor, and even then, it hadn't been the same.

The truth was, it still wasn't. Something was lacking.

Not for his lovers. He knew damned well how to make a woman cry out with pleasure but he felt—what was the word? Removed. That was it. His body went through all the motions, but when it was over, he felt unsatisfied.

Taylor was to blame for that.

What in hell had possessed him, to let her walk away? To let her think she'd ended their affair when she hadn't? A man's ego could take just so much.

By Monday, his anger was at the boiling point. When the private investigator turned up at his office, he greeted him with barely concealed impatience.

"Well? Surely you've located Ms. Sommers. How difficult can it be to find a woman in this city?"

The man scratched his ear, took a notepad from his pocket and thumbed it open.

"See, that was the problem, Mr. Russo. The lady isn't in this city. She's in…" He frowned. "Shelby, Vermont."

Dante stared at him. "Vermont?"

"Yeah. Little town, maybe fifty miles from Burlington."

Taylor, in a New England village? Dante almost laughed trying to picture his sophisticated former lover in such a setting.

"The lady has an interior decorating business." The P.I. turned the page. "And she's done okay. In fact, she just applied for an expansion loan at—"

The P.I. rattled on but Dante was only half listening. He knew where to find Taylor. Everything else was superfluous.

How surprised she'd be, he thought with grim satisfaction, to see him again. To hear him tell her that she hadn't needed to leave him, that he'd been leaving her—

"…just for the two of them. I have the details, if you—"

Dante's head came up. "Just for the two of what?" he said carefully.

"Of them," the P.I. said, raising an eyebrow. "You know, what I was saying about the house she inherited. A couple of realtors suggested she might want something newer and larger but she said no, she wanted a small house in a quiet setting, just big enough for two. For her and, uh… I got the name right here, if you just give me a—"

"A house for two people?" Dante said, in a tone opponents had learned to fear.

"That's right. Her and—here it is. Sam Gardner."

"Taylor." Dante cleared his throat. "And Sam Gardner. They live together?"

"Well, sure."

"And Gardner was with her when she moved in?"

The P.I. chuckled. "Yessir. I mean—"

"I know exactly what you mean," Dante said without inflection. "Thank you. You've been most helpful."

"Yeah, but, Mr. Russo—"

"Most helpful," Dante repeated.

The detective got the message.

Alone, Dante told himself he'd accomplish nothing unless he stayed calm, but a knot of red-hot rage was already blooming in his gut. Taylor hadn't left him because she'd grown bored. She'd left him for another man. She'd been seeing someone, making love with someone, while she'd been with him.

He went to the window and clasped the edge of the sill, hands tightening on the marble the way they wanted to tighten on her throat. Confronting her wouldn't be enough. Beating the crap out of her lover wouldn't be enough, either, although it would damned well help.

He wanted more. Wanted the kind of revenge that her infidelity merited. How dare she make a fool of him? How dare she?

There had to be a way. A plan.

Suddenly, he recalled the P.I.'s words. *She's done well. In fact, she's just applied for an expansion loan at the local bank.*

Dante smiled. There was. And he could hardly wait to put it into motion.

CHAPTER TWO

TAYLOR SOMMERS POURED a cup of coffee, put it on the sink, opened the refrigerator to get the cream and realized she'd already put it on the table, right alongside the cup she'd already filled with coffee only minutes before.

She took a steadying breath.

"Keep it up," she said, her voice loud in the silence, "and Walter Dennison's going to tell you he was only joking when he said he'd change those loan payments."

Dennison was a nice man; he'd been a friend of her grandmother's. He'd shown compassion and small-town courtesy when Tally fell behind on repaying the home equity loan his bank had granted her.

But he wasn't a fool and only a fool would go on doing that for a woman who behaved as if she were coming apart.

Was that why he wanted to see her today? Had he changed his mind? If he had, if he wanted her to pay the amount the loan called for each month…

Tally closed her eyes.

She'd be finished. The town had already shut down

the interior decorating business she'd been running from home. Without the loan, she'd lose the shop she'd rented on the village green even before it opened because, to put it simply, she was broke.

Flat broke.

Okay, if you wanted absolute accuracy, she had two hundred dollars in her bank account, but it was a drop in the bucket compared to what she needed.

She'd long ago used up her savings. Moving to Vermont, paying for repairs to make livable the old house she'd inherited from her grandmother, just day-to-day expenses for Sam and her had taken a huge chunk of her savings.

Start-up costs for INTERIORS BY TAYLOR had swallowed the rest. Beginning a decorating business, even from home, was expensive. You had to have at least a small showroom—in her case, what had once been an enclosed porch on the back of the house—so that potential clients could get a feel for your work. Paint, fabric, wicker furniture to make the porch inviting had cost a bundle.

Then there were the fabric samples, decorative items like vases and lamps, handmade candles and fireplace accessories… Expensive, all of them. Some catalogs alone could be incredibly pricey. Advertising costs were astronomical but if you didn't reach the right people, all your other efforts were pointless.

Little by little, INTERIORS BY TAYLOR had begun to draw clients from the upscale ski communities within miles of tiny Shelby. Taylor's accounts had still been in the red, but things had definitely been looking up.

And then the town clerk phoned. He was apologetic, but that didn't make his message any less harsh.

INTERIORS BY TAYLOR was operating illegally. The town had an ordinance against home-based businesses.

That Shelby, Vermont, population 8500 on a good day, had ordinances at all had been a surprise. But it did, and this one was inviolate. You couldn't operate a business from your house even if you'd been raised under its roof after your mother took off for parts unknown.

Tally's pleading had gained her a two-month reprieve.

She'd found a soon-to-be-vacant shop on the village green. Each night, long after Sam was asleep, she'd worked and reworked the costs she'd face. The monthly rent. The three-months up-front deposit. The fees for the carpenter, painter and electrician needed to turn the place from the TV-repair shop it had been into an elegant setting for her designs.

And then there were all the things she'd have to buy to create the right atmosphere. Add in the cost of increased advertising and Tally had arrived at a number that was staggering.

She needed $175,000.00.

The next morning, she'd kissed Sam goodbye, put on a white silk blouse and a black suit she hadn't worn since New York. She'd pulled her blond hair into a knot at the base of her neck and gone to see Walter Dennison, who owned Shelby's one and only bank.

Dennison read through the proposal she'd written, looked up and frowned.

"You're asking for a lot of money."

"I know."

"Asking for it in a home equity loan."

"Yes, sir."

"You understand what would happen if you were unable to pay the loan off, Ms. Sommers? That the bank would have the right to foreclose on your house?"

Taylor had nodded. "Yes, sir," she'd said again. "I do."

Dennison had looked at her for a long moment. Then he'd smiled. "You've got your grandmother's gumption, Tally," he'd said, and held out his hand.

The loan was hers.

She'd made the first payment...but not the second. Or the third. The contractors demanded their money according to the schedules she'd agreed to. Things couldn't get worse, she'd thought...

And the furnace in the house went belly-up.

Pride in tatters, Taylor had gone to Dennison again. If he could see his way clear to lower the monthly payments...

He'd sighed and run his fingers through his thinning hair. In the end he'd done it.

Which brought her back to today's phone call. It had come while she and Sam were having breakfast.

"I need to see you, Ms. Sommers," Dennison had said. "Today."

She'd almost stopped breathing. "Is it about my loan?"

There'd been a little pause. Then Dennison had said yes, it was, and she was to come to his office at four.

"Four," he'd repeated, "promptly, please."

The admonition had surprised her. So had the change from Tally to Ms. Sommers. She'd told herself it wasn't a bad sign. A man who wanted to discuss a six-figure loan was entitled to be a little formal, even if he'd known you since you were a baby.

"Of course," she'd said, all cool New York sophistication. Then she'd hung up the phone and tried to smile at Sam, whose eyes were filled with questions.

"Nothing to worry about, babe," Tally had said airily.

Sam had grinned a Sam-grin, at least until she said she might not be home until suppertime.

"You can visit the Millers," she'd said reassuringly. "You know how much you like them."

She'd smoothed things over by promising they'd have the entire weekend together, doing what Sam liked most: snuggling with her on the sofa, watching videos and eating popcorn.

Dante Russo had probably never watched a video or eaten popcorn in his life...

And what was that man doing in her head again?

Who gave a damn what Dante Russo did or didn't do? He was history. Besides, he'd never meant anything more to her than what she'd meant to him. New York was filled with relationships like theirs. Two consenting adults going out together, being seen together...

Having sex together.

Tally's eyes closed. Memories rushed in. Scents. Tastes. Sensations. Dante's hands, deliciously rough on her skin. His mouth, demanding surrender as he kissed her. His face above her, his silver eyes dark as storm clouds, his sensual lips drawn back with passion...

She swung toward the sink, dumped her coffee and rinsed out the cup.

What stupid thoughts to have today of all days, when she had to be at her best. Still, she understood why she would think of Dante.

Her mouth curved in a bitter smile.

This was an anniversary of sorts. She'd left Dante

Russo a few weeks before Christmas, three years ago. All it took was the scent of pine and the sound of carols to bring the memories rushing back.

She wouldn't let that happen. Dante had no place in the new life she'd built for herself. For herself and Sam.

He was nothing to her anymore.

Or to Sam.

Sam didn't know Dante existed. And Dante certainly didn't know about Sam. He never would, either. She would see to that.

Tally knew her former lover well.

Dante hadn't wanted her and surely wouldn't have understood why she wanted Sam... But that didn't mean he'd simply let her have Sam, if he knew.

Her former lover could be charming but underneath he was cold, determined and ruthless. She refused to think about how he might react if he knew everything.

Tally sighed and turned on the kitchen lights. Night had fallen; it came early to these northern latitudes. The coming storm the weatherman had predicted rattled the old windows.

She'd fled New York on a night like this. Cold, dark, with snow in the forecast.

What a wreck she'd been that night! Pretending to be sick, then packing her clothes and scribbling that final note. All she'd been able to think about was getting away before Dante showed up.

She wasn't stupid. She'd known he hadn't wanted her anymore. He'd been removed and distant for a while and sometimes she'd caught him watching her with a look on his face that made her want to weep.

He was bored with her. And getting ready to end

their affair, but she wouldn't let that happen. She'd end it first. It would be quicker, less humiliating...

And safer, because by then she had a secret she'd never have been foolish enough to share with him.

So she'd made plans to leave him. And she'd done it so he wouldn't be able to find her, even if he looked for her. Not that she thought he would. Why would a man go after a woman when she'd saved him the trouble of getting rid of her?

Even if he had, maybe out of all that macho Sicilian arrogance made all the more potent by his power, his wealth, his gorgeous face and body—even if he had, he'd never have found her. He'd never dream she'd flee to a tiny village in New England. He knew nothing about her. In their six months together, he'd never asked her questions about herself.

Not real ones.

Would you prefer Chez Nicole or L'Etoile for dinner? he'd ask. *Shall I get tickets for the ballet or the symphony?*

Things a man would ask any woman. Never anything more important.

Well, yes. He'd asked her other things. Whispered them, in that husky voice that was a turn-on all by itself.

Do you like it when I touch you this way? And if what he was doing seemed too much, if it made her tremble in his arms, he'd kiss her deeply and say, *Don't stop me, bellissima. Let me. Yes. Let me do this. Yes. Like that. Just like that...*

She was trembling even now, just remembering those moments.

"You're a fool," Tally said, her voice sharp in the silence of the kitchen.

Sex with Dante had been incredible, but sex was all it was, even though lying beneath him, feeling the power of his penetration, his possession, sometimes made her want to weep with joy. But it didn't make up for the fact that he'd never once spent the entire night in her bed or asked her to come to his.

Stay with me, she'd wanted to say, oh, so many times. But she hadn't. Only the once, when the words had slipped out before she could stop them...

Only the once, when she'd forgotten that all her lover wanted was her body, not her heart.

Tally turned her back to the window.

So what?

Why would she have wanted a man to tie her down, give her a baby and then turn his ever-wandering eyes elsewhere as her father had done, as a man like Dante Russo would surely do?

It was the meeting with Walter Dennison that had her feeling so strange, that was all. Once she put that behind her, she'd be fine.

And it was time to get moving. *Be here at four, Ms. Sommers, and please be prompt.*

She smiled as put on her coat and grabbed her car keys. All those years in New York had made her forget how pedantic a true Yankee could be.

AS USUAL, the weatherman had it wrong. Snow was already falling as if someone were shaking a featherbed over the town.

The snow dusting the woods and fields with a blanket of white as Tally drove past would have made a beautiful Christmas card. In the real world, it made for a dangerous drive. The narrow road that led into the heart of town already wore a thin coating of black ice, and the new snow hid stretches of asphalt as slick as glass.

Her old station wagon needed better snow tires. The rear end slewed sickeningly as she turned onto Main Street and her stomach skidded with it, but there were no other vehicles on the road and she came through the turn without harm to anything but her nerves.

Only two cars were parked in the bank's lot, the aged maroon Lincoln she recognized as Dennison's and a big, shiny black SUV that looked as if it could climb Everest in a blizzard and come through laughing.

Dennison would have sent his employees home early because of the storm. The SUV probably belonged to some tourist on his way to ski country who'd stopped to use the ATM.

Tally parked and got out of the station wagon. The double doors to the bank opened as she reached them, revealing Walter Dennison wearing a black topcoat over his usual gray suit.

"You're late, Ms. Sommers."

He whispered the words. And shot a quick look over his shoulder. Tally felt a stab of panic. The black car. The paleness of Dennison's face. His whisper.

Was the bank being held up?

"I'm sorry," she said, trying to peer past him, "but the roads—"

"I understand." He hesitated. "Ms. Sommers. Tally. There's something you need to know."

Oh, God. It was true. She'd walked into a holdup in progress—

"I sold the bank."

She stared at him blankly. "What?"

"I said, I sold the bank."

He might as well have been speaking another language. Sold the bank? How could he have done that? The Dennison family had started the Shelby Bank in the early 1800s.

"I don't understand, Mr. Dennison. Why would you—"

"It's nothing for the town to worry about. The new owner will keep everything just as it is." Dennison cleared his throat. "Almost everything."

His eyes shifted from hers, and Tally's stomach dropped. There could only be one reason he'd wanted to see her.

"What about the new payment arrangements on my loan?"

She saw Dennison's adam's apple move up, then down. He opened his mouth as if he were going to speak. Instead, he shouldered past her, turned up his collar and went out into the storm. Tally stared after him as his lean figure was lost in a swirling maelstrom of white.

"Mr. Dennison! Wait!" Her voice rose. "Will this affect my loan? You said the new owner will keep everything just as it is—"

"Not quite everything," a familiar voice said.

And even as her heart pounded, as she swung toward the open bank doors and told herself it couldn't be true, she knew what she would see.

That voice could belong to only one man.

DANTE SMILED when Taylor turned toward him.

Her face was white with shock.

Excellent. He'd wanted her stunned by the sight of

him. Things were going precisely as he'd intended, despite how quickly he'd had to work. He'd put his plan in motion in less than a week, first convincing the old man to sell and then getting the authorities to approve the sale, but he was Dante Russo.

People always deferred to him.

This morning, he'd phoned Dennison and told him he'd be there at three. Told him, as well, to notify Taylor to be at the bank at four.

Promptly at four.

And, of course, not to mention anything about the bank's new ownership.

Dante's lips curved in a tight smile. He'd figured Taylor would be on edge to start with. A woman who'd put up her home as equity for a loan of $175,000.00 she couldn't pay would not be at ease. Add in Dennison's refusal to explain the reason for the meeting and the warning to be prompt, her nerves would be stretched to the breaking point.

His smile faded. The only thing that would have made this more interesting was if Samuel Gardner was with her, but from the investigator's comments, he'd gathered that his former mistress's new lover didn't stand up to life's tougher moments.

"Why didn't Sam Gardner sign for the loan?" he'd asked Dennison.

The old man had looked at him as if he were insane.

"Buying a bank on a seeming whim, suggesting something anyone in town would know is impossible... You have a strange sense of humor, Mr. Russo," he'd said with a thin-lipped Yankee smile.

Dante stood away from the door.

Dennison was wrong. There was nothing the least bit humorous about this situation. It was payback, pure and simple.

And it was time Taylor knew it.

"Aren't you going to come inside and face me, *cara?*" he said, his tone deliberately soft and coaxing. "Perhaps not. Facing me is not your forte, is it?"

He saw her stiffen. She probably wanted to run, but she didn't. Instead, she raised her chin, squared her shoulders and stepped inside the bank. He had to admire her courage, the way she was girding herself for confrontation.

She had no way of knowing that nothing she could do would be enough. The news he was going to give her was bad, and it delighted him to do it.

"Hello, Dante."

Her voice trembled. Her face had taken on some color, though it was still pale. Three years. Three years since he'd seen her...

And she was still beautiful.

More beautiful than his memory of her, if that were possible. Was it time that had made her mouth seem even softer, her eyes wider and darker?

Still, time had not been completely kind. It had affected her in other ways.

Purple shadows lay beneath her eyes. Her hair was pulled back in an unbecoming knot and he had the indefensible urge to close the distance between them, take out the pins and let all those lustrous cinnamon strands tumble free.

He let his gaze move over her slowly, from her face all the way to her feet and back again. A frown creased his forehead. He'd never seen her in anything but elegantly tailored clothing. Designer suits and gowns, spiked heels that could give a man dangerous fantasies, her face perfectly made up, her hair impeccably cut and styled.

Things were different now. The lapels of her coat were frayed. Her boots were the no-nonsense kind meant for rough weather. Her hair was in that ridiculous knot and her face was bare of everything but lipstick—lipstick and the shadows of exhaustion under her eyes.

He spoke without thinking. "What's happened to you?" he said sharply. "Have you been ill?"

"How nice of you to ask."

She was still pale but her gaze was steady and her words were brittle with sarcasm. He moved quickly; before she could step back he was a breath away, his hand wrapped around her arm.

"I asked you a question. Answer it."

A flush rose in her cheeks. "I'm not ill. I'm simply living in the real world. It's a place where people work hard for what they have. Where you can't just snap your fingers and expect everyone to leap to do your bidding, but then, what would you know of such things?"

What, indeed? It was none of her business, of anyone's business, that he'd started his life scrounging for money, that he'd worked his hands raw in construction jobs when he came to the States, or that he could still remember what it was like to go to sleep hungry.

He'd never snapped his fingers and never would, but he'd be damned if he'd explain that to anyone.

"And your lover? He permits this?"

She looked at him as if he'd lost his mind. "My what?"

"Another question you don't want to answer. That's all right. I have plenty of time."

Tally wrenched free of his grasp. "I'm the one with questions, Dante. What are you doing here?"

"We haven't seen each other in a long time, *cara.*" A slow smile that turned her blood to ice eased across his lips. "Surely, we have other things to talk about first."

"We have nothing to talk about."

"But we do. You know that."

She didn't know anything. That was the problem. What did he know? Did he know about Sam? She didn't think so. Surely, he'd have tossed that at her already, if he did.

Then, what did he want? He wasn't here for a visit. He hadn't bought the Shelby bank on a whim…

The loan. Her loan. Oh God, oh God…

"Ah," he said slyly, "your face is an open book. Have you thought of some things we might wish to discuss?"

She couldn't let him see her fear. There had to be some way she could gain the upper hand.

"What I know," Tally said, "is that we never talked in the past. We went to dinner, to parties…" She took a steadying breath. "And we went to bed."

His mouth twisted. Had she struck a nerve?

"I'm glad you remember that."

"Is that why you came here, Dante? To remind me that we used to have sex together? Or to ask why I left you?" Somehow, she managed a chilly smile. "Really, I thought you'd understand. My note—"

"Your note was a bad joke."

Tally shrugged her shoulders. "It was honest. Or did it never occur to you that a woman is no different from a man? I mean, yes, we can pretend in ways a man can't, but sooner or later, things grow, well, old."

Dante's face contorted with anger. "You're a liar!"

"Come on, admit it. We'd been together for months. It was fun for a long time but then—"

She gasped as he caught hold of her and encircled her throat with his hand.

"I remember how you were in bed," he said, his voice a low growl. "Are you telling me it was all a performance?"

He tugged her closer, until her body brushed his and she had to tilt back her head to look into his eyes. It was deliberate, damn him, a way of emphasizing his strength, his size, his domination.

God, how she hated him! Three years, three endless years, and he was still furious because she'd walked out on him, but she'd done what she had to do to survive. To protect her secret from his unpredictable Sicilian ego.

"You were fire in my arms." His eyes, the color of smoke, locked on hers. She tried to look away but his hand was like a collar around her throat. When he urged her chin up, she had no choice but to meet his gaze. "You cried out as I came inside you. Your womb contracted around me. Would you have me believe you faked that, too?"

"Is it impossible for you to be a gentleman?" Tally said, hating herself for the way her voice shook.

His smile was slow and sexy and so dangerous it made her heartbeat quicken.

"But I was a gentleman with you. Was that a mistake? Perhaps you didn't want a gentleman in your bed." She gasped as he forced her head back. "Is that why you ran away in the middle of the night?"

"I left you, period. Don't make it sound so dramatic."

"Left me for what, exactly? The glory of an existence in the middle of nowhere? A bank account with nothing in it?" His tone turned silken. "I think not, *cara*. I think you left me for a new lover who isn't a gentleman at all."

"I don't know what you're talking about!"

He thrust his fingers into her hair. The pins that held it confined clattered sharply against the marble floor as the strands of gold-burnished cinnamon came loose and fell over her shoulders.

"Is that it? Was I too gentle with you?" He wound her hair around his fist and lowered his head until his face was an inch from hers. "Had you hoped I would do things to you, demand things of you, that people only whisper about?"

"Dante. This is— It's crazy. I don't— I didn't…" She swallowed dryly. "Let me go."

She'd meant the words to be a command. Instead, they were a whisper. He smiled with amusement, and she felt an electric jolt in her blood.

"I said, let go… Or did you come here thinking you could bully me back into your arms?"

His eyes grew dark; she saw his mouth twist. The seconds ticked away and then, when her heart seemed ready to leap from her breast, he thrust her from him, stepped back and folded his arms.

"Never that," he said coolly. "And you're right. Things were over between us. I knew it. In fact, that was the reason I went to see you that night. I wanted to tell you we were finished." He gave a quick smile. "As you say, *cara,* things get old."

She'd known the truth but hearing it made it worse.

Still, she showed no reaction. He wanted her to squirm, and she'd be damned if she would.

"Is that what this is about? That the great Dante Russo wants to be sure I understand I made the first move only because your timing was off?"

Dante chuckled. "Bright as always, Taylor—though you surely don't believe I bought this bank and made this trip only so I could tell you it was pure luck you ended our affair before I did."

Tally moistened her lips with the tip of her tongue. She was dying inside, but she'd be damned if she'd let him know it.

"No. I'm not that naive. You bought the bank because—" Desperately, she ran through the terms of the loan in her mind. Could he do that? Could he cancel what Dennison had already approved? "Because you think you can cancel my loan."

"Think?" he said, very softly. "You underestimate me. I can do whatever I wish, but canceling a loan that already exists would take more time and effort than it's worth." He smiled. "So I'm going to do the next best thing. I'm reinstating the original repayment terms."

Her gaze flew to his. "Reinstating them?" she said stupidly. "I don't understand."

"It's simple, *cara*," he said, almost gently. "As of now, you will pay the amount you are supposed to pay each month."

Tally thought of the four-figure number the loan called for. She was paying a quarter of that amount now, and barely managing it.

"That's—it's out of the question. I can't possibly—"

"Additionally, you will pay the amount that's in arrears." He took a slip of paper from his pocket and held it out toward her. His lips curved. "Plus interest, of course."

Tally looked at the number on the paper and laughed. It was either that or weep.

"I don't have that kind of money!"

"Ah." Dante sighed. "I thought not. In that case, you leave me no choice but to start foreclosure proceedings against your home."

She felt the blood drain from her face. "Foreclosure proceedings?"

"This was a home equity loan. You put up your house as collateral." Another quick, icy smile. "If you don't understand what that means, perhaps your lover can explain it to you."

"Are you crazy?" Tally's voice rose. "You can't do this! You can't take my house. You can't!" Her hands came up like a fighter's, fists at the ready as if she would beat him into understanding the horror of his plan. "Damn you, there are rules!"

"You've forgotten what you know about me," Dante said coldly. "I make my own rules."

He proved it by gathering her into his arms and kissing her.

CHAPTER THREE

HE WAS KISSING HER, Dante told himself, because she'd lied to him a few minutes ago.

Why else would he want her in his arms, except to make her confess to the lie?

Taylor had never faked her responses in bed, and he'd be damned if he'd let her pretend she had.

He was over her, but she knew just the right buttons to push. Well, so did he. He'd kiss her until she melted against him the way she used to and then he'd step back and say, *You see, Taylor? That's the price liars pay.*

Which was why he was kissing her.

Or trying to.

The problem was that he had cornered a wildcat. She fought back, twisted her head to the side to avoid his mouth and pummeled his shoulders with her fists.

When none of that worked, she sank her teeth in his ear lobe so hard he hissed with pain.

"Damn you, woman!"

"Let go of me, you—you—"

Her fist flew by his jaw. Grimly, Dante snared both her hands in one of his and pinned them to his chest. Her knee came up but he felt it happening and yanked her hard against him to immobilize her. She was helpless now, pinned between him and the wall beside the double doors.

"Take your hands off me, Russo! If you don't, so help me—"

"So help you, what? What will you do? How will you stop me from proving what a little liar you are?"

"I don't know what you're talking about. I am not a—"

He bent his head and captured her mouth with his. She nipped his lip, her teeth sharp as a cat's. He tasted blood but if she thought that would stop him, she didn't know him very well.

He would win this battle.

He had the right to know why she'd lied about what she'd felt when he made love to her. And to know why she'd left him.

He wanted answers and, damn it, he was going to get them.

He caught her face in his hands. Kissed her again, angling his mouth over hers, penetrating her with his tongue. He remembered how she'd loved it when he kissed her this way. Deep. Wet. Hot. He'd loved kisses like this, too...

He still did.

Dio, the feel of her in his arms. Her breasts, soft against his chest. Her hips, cradling his erection.

He wanted her, and it had nothing to do with anger.

It was the feel of her. The taste. The scent of her skin. He remembered all of it, everything making love to her had done to them both, and his kiss gentled, his touch turned from demand to caress, and a little sigh whispered from her lips to his.

She was trembling, but not with fear.

It was with desire. For this. For him.

Something began to unlock inside him. Something so primitive he couldn't put a name to it. He only knew that the woman in his arms still belonged to him.

He swept his hands into her hair. All that lush, cinnamon-hued silk tumbled over his fingers.

"Tell me you want me," he said, his voice rough and thick.

She shook her head in denial. "No," she whispered.

But her eyes were pools of darkness as she looked up at him, as her hands spread over his chest.

"I don't," she said, "I don't…"

He took her mouth again and suddenly she gave the wild little cry he had heard her make a thousand times in the past. It excited him as much now as it had then, and when she rose on her toes and wound her arms around his neck, whispered "Dante," as if he were the only man in the world who could ever make her feel this way, he went crazy with desire.

It had been so long. Oh, so long since he'd possessed her. He was on fire…and so was she.

Saying her name, blind to everything but passion, Dante fumbled with the buttons of her coat. When they didn't come undone quickly enough, he cursed and tore the coat open.

He had to cup her breasts or he would die. Had to thrust his knee between her thighs and hear her cry out again as she moved against him. Had to shove up her skirt, slip his hand between her thighs and, yes oh yes, feel her heat, yes, feel the wetness of her desire, yes, yes…

Her head fell back like a flower on a wind-bent stalk.

She whispered his name over and over, knotted her fingers in his hair as she lifted herself to him.

Blindly, he lifted her off her feet. Spread her thighs. Reached for his zipper. Now. Right now. He would be inside her. Lost in her silken folds…

"Mr. Dennison? I didn't finish cleanin' but considerin' the storm's turnin' into a blizzard, an'… Whoa!"

The thin, shocked voice had all the power of an explosion.

Dante whirled around, automatically shielding Taylor with his body. A grizzled old man in overalls and work boots stood next to the tellers' cages, his eyes wide and his jaw somewhere down around his ankles.

"Who," Dante said coldly, "are you?"

Tally pulled the lapels of her coat together and peered past Dante's shoulder, heart thumping in her ears.

"It's Esau Staunton. The janitor," she whispered in a shaky voice.

The old man was also Shelby's biggest gossip. By tomorrow, the whole town would know what had happened here this afternoon. She gave a soft moan of despair, and Dante put his arm around her and drew her forward so that she was pressed against his side. She stiffened and would have moved away but he spread his hand over her hip, the pressure of it insistent.

Was he trying to brand her? Or was he telling her this wasn't finished? Either way, she had to let him do it. Her legs had turned to jelly.

"Is that your name?" Dante said pleasantly. "Staunton?"

The old man swallowed audibly. "That's me." His

eyes danced to Taylor, then back to Dante. "Where's Mr. Dennison?"

"Mr. Dennison no longer owns this bank. I do. And you're right, Mr. Staunton. You should leave now, before the storm gets worse."

"You sure?" Again, the rheumy gaze fell on Taylor. "My boy's just pulled up at the curb in that red pickup, but, ah, if you or the lady wants—"

"Go home, Mr. Staunton," Dante said, his tone still pleasant but now backed with steel.

"Oh. Sure. Sure, I'll do that. Mr., ah, Mr.—"

"Russo. And there's one last thing." Dante spoke softly, in that same polite but unyielding voice. "I'm sure you understand that Ms. Sommers wouldn't want anyone to know about her fainting spell."

"Her fainting—"

"Surely, I can trust you to be discreet. People who work for me always are. And you do want to work for me, Esau, don't you?"

Another audible swallow. "Yessir. I do."

"Excellent. In that case, have a pleasant weekend."

The old man nodded and opened the double doors. The wind filled the room with its icy breath as he scrambled into the red pickup, which disappeared into the swirling snow.

"The old man was right," Dante said. "The storm's turned into a blizzard."

Tally stared at him. How could he talk about the weather after what he'd just done? Forcing his kisses on her. His caresses. If the janitor hadn't turned up, who knew what would have happened?

As for his admonitions to the old man—did he really

think they meant anything here? By tomorrow, this sordid little story would be everywhere.

Not that it mattered.

Without a house, without an income, she and Sam wouldn't be living in Shelby much longer.

"Nothing to say, *cara?*"

She wrenched free of his encircling arm. "You've done what you came to do, Dante. More, thanks to...to that performance just now."

His eyebrows rose. "Is that what you call it?"

Amusement tinged the words. Oh, how she wanted to slap that smug, masculine smile from his face.

"You are—you are despicable. Do you understand? You are the most despicable, contemptible—"

The world blurred. She raised her hand and swung it, but his fingers curled around her wrist.

"Such a temper, *bellissima*. And all because I caught you in a lie." His smile vanished. "You wanted me three years ago and you want me now."

"If you ever come near me again—"

"Don't make threats, Taylor. Not unless you're prepared to back them up."

She wanted to scream. To weep. To lunge at him again—but none of that would change anything. Because of him, her life had almost come apart before. Now, it lay in tatters at her feet.

The only thing left was a dignified retreat.

"You're right," she said, forcing herself to sound calm. "No threats. Just a promise. I don't ever want to see you again. If you come after me, I'll go to court and charge you with harassment. Is that clear?"

He laughed. And, before he could stop her a second time, Tally slapped his face.

Fury darkened his eyes. He reached for her, a harsh Sicilian oath spilling from his lips, but she slipped by him, yanked the doors open and ran.

She heard him shout her name but she didn't look back. The parking lot was a sea of white; the wind tore at her with icy talons as she fought her way to her station wagon, pulled the door open, got behind the wheel and slammed down the lock.

Just in time. A second later, Dante grabbed the door handle, then banged his fist against the window.

"Taylor! Open this door."

Her hands were shaking. It took two tries before she could jab the key into the ignition. The engine coughed, coughed again—and died.

A sob burst from her throat. "Come on," she said, turning the key, "come on, damn it. Start!"

"Taylor!" Another blow against the window. "What in hell do you think you're doing?"

Getting away. That was what she was doing. Dante had destroyed everything she'd built over the last years. He'd taken her home with a stroke of the pen, her pride with a kiss she hadn't wanted, her reputation with an X-rated scene she didn't want to think about.

And all he'd proved was what they'd both already known, that he was powerful and brutal, that he had no heart. That he could still make her respond to him, make her forget what he was and drown in his kisses….

"Taylor!"

She turned the key again. Not even a cough this time. *Calm down,* she told herself. Take it easy. The engine needed work, she knew that, but it had gotten her here, hadn't it?

The car wouldn't start because of the cold, that was all. Or maybe she'd flooded it. You could fit what she knew about cars inside a thimble and have room for the rest of the sewing kit, but wasn't there something about not giving a cold engine too much—

The station wagon rocked under the force of Dante's fist.

"Damn you, woman, are you out of your mind? Get out of that car! You can't drive in a blizzard."

She couldn't stay here, either. Not with him. And there was Sam to worry about. Was Sam safe at the Millers'? Yes. Of course. Sheryl and Dan were Sam's friends as well as hers. Still, she'd worry until she reached home.

If there was one thing life had taught her, it was that anything was possible.

One last try. Turn the key. Touch the gas pedal lightly…

Nothing. Nothing! Tally screamed in frustration and pounded the heels of her hands against the steering wheel.

"Listen to me," Dante said, calmly now, as if he were trying to talk sense to a child.

How could she not listen? They were inches apart, separated only by glass.

"Come back inside until the storm is over. I won't touch you. I swear it."

She almost laughed. What could he possibly know of a New England winter? The storm might last for days. Days, alone with him? With a man who'd just promised not to touch her in a way that made it clear he was sure she was helpless against him?

"Taylor. Be reasonable. We'll phone for help. This town has snowplows, doesn't it?"

Of course it did. But would the phones work? The first thing that always failed in bad weather were the telephone lines.

"Damn you, woman," Dante roared. "Can't you be without your lover for a few hours? Would you risk your neck, just to get back to him?"

So much for logic and reason.

Dante cursed, yanked at the door and it flew open. Tally grabbed for the handle but he was already leaning into the car, gathering her into his arms and striding to the bank through the blinding snow, head bent against the shrieking wind.

When they reached the entrance, he put her down.

"Just stand still," he said grimly. "Once we're inside, I'll call the police. For all I give a damn, you can lock yourself in the vault until they arrive."

He reached for the brass handle and pulled.

Nothing happened.

He grunted, wrapped both hands around the handle and pulled harder. But the doors were locked.

He spat out a word in Sicilian. Tally didn't need a translator to know what it meant. Here was one situation he couldn't control. Neither could she. The doors were probably on a timer. They wouldn't open until Monday.

People died in storms like this, and she knew it.

So, evidently, did Dante.

He picked her up again. She didn't fight him this time. The footing was slippery; he stumbled, recovered his balance and she automatically wrapped her arms around his neck. Snow crunched underfoot as he made his way toward the black SUV she knew must be his. Halfway there, he dug his keys from his pocket, pointed the remote at the vehicle and unlocked it.

He put her in the passenger seat, hurried to the driver's side and got in. For a long moment, they sat without looking at each other. Then he took a cell phone from his pocket and flipped it open.

"It won't work," Tally said wearily, leaning back in her seat.

Dante turned toward her. Her face was pale. He sensed that her anger had given way to resignation. It was an emotion neither of them could afford in a situation like this.

"Well, then," he said briskly, "we'll just have to come up with another plan."

He turned the ignition key so that he could read the instrument panel. The gas gauge, in particular, though he knew what he'd find. He'd been in such a damned rush to get to the bank before Taylor arrived...

One look confirmed what he'd suspected.

"We don't have much gas. Just enough to run the engine for maybe twenty, thirty minutes. After that—" *After that, they'd freeze.* "So," he said, again in that brisk tone, "here's what we're going to do. I'll go for help. You stay here and turn on the engine every ten minutes. Let the car warm up, then shut if off. Do that as long as you can and I'll do my best to find help quickly."

"Don't be a fool! You won't get a hundred yards."

"Why, *cara,*" he said, the words laced with sarcasm, "I didn't think you cared."

She didn't. But she did care about Sam. A moment ago, she'd almost let despair overtake her. Now she knew she couldn't let that happen. She had to live. To live for Sam.

There was only one choice. It was a risk in endless ways, but staying here was worse.

She took a deep breath. "Are you a good driver?"

"Of course."

Such macho intensity! Any other time, she'd have laughed.

"And is there enough gas in the tank to go fifteen miles?"

He nodded. "Just about."

"Then start the car. I'll get us to my house. My neighbor has a truck and snowplow. He can lead you to a place near the highway—tow you, if necessary— where there's a gas station and a motel. You'll be fine there until the storm's over."

"And you? Will you be fine, as well?"

Tally looked at Dante. His eyes were cool, making it clear his was a polite question and nothing more.

"I'm not your concern," she said. "I never was."

A muscle knotted in his jaw. Then he nodded, turned the engine on and headed out of the parking lot and into the teeth of the storm.

THE WORLD HAD TURNED into an undulating sea of white. Shifts in the wind's direction revealed only an occasional landmark, but that was enough.

The heavy vehicle, Dante's skill at the wheel and Tally's knowledge of the roads combined to get them safely to her driveway.

They battled their way to the door. Tally dug out her keys; Dante automatically reached for them as he used to when he saw her home in New York, and they waged a silent, brief struggle until he held up his hands in surrender and let her unlock the door herself.

She paused in the doorway.

The danger of the drive here had deprived her of rational thought. Now she was making up for it with frantic desperation. Were any of Sam's things in the kitchen? She didn't think so. Besides, it was too late to worry about it now.

If there were, she'd come up with some kind of explanation. In the last hour, she'd learned to be an accomplished liar.

She stepped into the room, fingers mentally crossed, with Dante close behind her, and reached for the light switch. The room remained dark. The power was out, as she'd figured it would be. The phone, too. All she heard when she picked up the handset was silence.

"It would seem you're stuck with a guest," Dante said coolly.

Tally didn't answer. She felt her way to the cupboard and took out the candles and matches she kept handy for just such occasions. When the candles were lit, she put one on the sink and another on the round wooden table near the window.

A shudder raced through her. The kitchen was the smallest room in the house but an hour or two without the furnace going had turned it into a walk-in refrigerator.

"Are you cold?"

"I'm fine."

Dante frowned, shrugged off his leather jacket and

draped it around her shoulders. "You'll never be a good liar, *cara*."

"I don't need—"

"You damned well do! Keep the jacket until the room warms up." He jerked his chin at the old stone fireplace that took up most of one long wall. "Is that real?"

"Of course it's real," Tally said brusquely, trying not inhale the scents of night and leather and man that enveloped her. "This is New England, not Manhattan. Nobody here has time for pretence."

A smile twisted across his mouth. "What an interesting observation," he said softly, "all things considered."

She felt her face heat. "I didn't mean—"

"No. I'm sure you didn't." He held out his hand. "Give me those matches and I'll make a fire."

"That's not necessary."

"Nothing is necessary," he said curtly. "Not if it involves me, is that correct?"

He'd come so close to the truth that she was afraid to meet his eyes, but that had been their initial agreement, hadn't it? Their relationship had been based on accommodation, not necessity. No strings. No commitment. No leaning on him for anything...

"Look, I know you want me gone," he said impatiently, "and believe me, I'll be happy to comply, but until then I'll be damned if I'm going to freeze just so you can prove a point. Give me the matches."

He was right, even if she hated to admit it. She tossed him the matches and watched as he knelt before her grandmother's old brick hearth and built a fire. Just seeing the orange flames made her feel better and she moved closer to them, hands outstretched so she could catch some of their warmth.

"Better?"

Tally nodded. All she could do now was wait for the storm's power to abate. At least she wasn't worried about Sam anymore. She'd seen the Millers' lights glowing when they drove past their house. She'd forgotten that Dan and Sheryl had a generator. Their place would be snug. Sam would have a hot meal, a warm bed...

"So. You inherited this from your grandmother?"

Her gaze shot to Dante. Arms folded, face unreadable, he was looking around the kitchen as if it were an alien planet. It probably was, to a man accustomed to luxury.

"Yes," she replied coldly. "And now I'm about to lose it to you."

"And where is your lover? Out of town? Or in another room, afraid to face me?"

"I told you, I don't have a lover. And if I did, why would he fear you? My life is my own, Dante. You have no part in it."

"You made that clear the night you ran away."

"For God's sake, are we going to talk about that again?" Tally marched to the stove, filled a kettle with water, took it to the hearth and knelt down, searching for the best place to put it. "I left you. I was absolutely free to do that. I know it's hard to face, but I didn't need your permission."

"Common courtesy demanded more than that note."

"I don't think so."

"Damn it," he growled, clasping her shoulders and

drawing her up beside him, "I'm tired of you dancing away from my questions. I want to know the reason you left."

"I told you. Our affair was over." She looked straight into his eyes. "And we both knew it."

She was right…wasn't she? Hadn't he come to the same conclusion? That it was time to end things? Not that it mattered. He *hadn't* ended the relationship. She had.

Wasn't that the reason he was here? Except, she was doing it again. Taking the upper hand, and he didn't like it.

"I never gave you the right to speak for me," he said sharply.

"No. You didn't. So I'll speak for myself." She took a deep breath and turned away. "I wanted a change."

Dante's mouth thinned. "You mean, you became involved with another man."

"That's ridiculous! I didn't—"

She cried out as he caught her and swung her toward him. "More lies," he growled.

"For the last time, there is no other man!"

"There is. I know his name." His hands dug into her flesh. "Now I want to know if you respond to him as you did to me a little while ago."

"Respond?" She gave a harsh laugh. "Is that what you call it? You—you forced yourself on me!"

It was a foolish thing to say. His nostrils flared like a stallion's at the scent of a mare in heat.

"You don't learn, do you?" he said softly. "You keep making statements and I end up having to prove that they're lies."

Tally looked up into the face of the man who had once been the center of her universe. How could she have forgotten how beautiful he was? And how cruel?

"We're both adults, *cara*. Why not admit we want each other?"

"Didn't you just say you knew I was eager to see you gone? That you'd be happy to go?" Damn it, why did she sound breathless? "Didn't you say that?"

He didn't answer. Instead, he cupped her face and lifted it to his. "Kiss me once," he whispered. "Just once. Then, if you don't want to make love, I promise, I won't touch you again."

"I don't have to kiss you to know the—"

His mouth took hers captive. Tally made a little sound of protest. Then his arms went around her and she let him gather her into his embrace, let his lips part hers and she knew nothing had changed, not when it came to this. To wanting his touch. His mouth. His body, hardening against hers...

The door flew open; the gust of wind that followed slammed it, hard, against the wall as a small woman cradling a grocery bag in one arm all but sailed into the kitchen.

"Sorry not to knock," Sheryl Miller said breathlessly, "but I don't have a free hand. I brought you leftovers from dinner and a loaf of oatmeal bread I baked this morning. Dan's going to get his mom and I said I'd go with—" Her mouth formed a perfect circle as she peered around the bag. "Oh! Oh, I'm sorry, Tally. I didn't know you had company."

Neither Tally or Dante answered. Both of them were staring at the toddler, round as a snowman in a raspberry-pink snowsuit, who clung to Sheryl's free hand.

"Hi, Mama," Samantha Gardner Sommers said happily, and flew to her mother's arms.

CHAPTER FOUR

FOR A MOMENT, no one moved but the child.

Then, as if someone had pushed a button, the room came to life again. The woman in the doorway, her face a polite mask, put the bag she'd been holding on the counter. Taylor scooped the toddler into her arms, and Dante...

Dante forced himself to breathe.

Mama? Was that really what the child had said? Taylor was staring at him over the little girl's head. Her face had gone white. So, he suspected, had his.

"Who is this?" he said hoarsely.

The woman glanced at Taylor. Then she took a step forward. "I'm Sheryl Miller. Tally's neighbor."

His head swung toward the woman. He thought of saying he didn't mean her, that he didn't give a damn who she was, but that would have been stupid. He needed time to get hold of himself and she had given him exactly that.

Oh yes, he needed time because what he was thinking was surely impossible.

"And you are?" Sheryl said, breaking the strained silence.

"Dante Russo." Dante forced a polite smile. "Taylor and I—"

"We knew each other in New York," Tally said quickly. A little color had returned to her face but it only made her look feverish. "He was in the area and—and he thought he'd drop by."

A horn beeped outside. The Miller woman ignored it. "Funny," she said, "but Tally never mentioned you."

He wanted to tell the woman to get out. To leave him alone so he could ask Taylor who this child was, why she'd called her Mama, but he knew better than to push things. The tension in the room was thick. Taylor's neighbor was already looking at him as if he might be a serial killer.

"No," he said politely, smiling through his teeth, "I'm sure she didn't."

The woman ignored him. "Tally? Is everything okay?"

Tally swallowed a wave of hysterical laughter. Nothing was okay. Nothing would ever be okay again unless she could come up with a story to change the way Dante was looking at her and Sam.

"You want me to tell Dan to come in?"

"No! Oh, no, Sheryl. I mean—" What *did* she mean? "It's as I said. Dante is an old—an old—"

"Friend," Dante said, his tone level. "I thought I'd stop by and see how Taylor was adjusting to small-town life."

The Miller woman looked doubtful but Tally said yes, that was it, and smiled, and finally the woman smiled, too.

"Why wouldn't she adjust? Didn't she ever tell you she's a small-town girl at heart? That she comes from Shelby?"

"No. But then, I'm starting to realize there are lots

of things she didn't tell me." Dante looked at Taylor. "Isn't that right, *cara?*"

Taylor didn't answer. That was good because it meant she knew that whatever she said now would only fuel the fury building inside him.

The horn beeped again. "Dan wants to get going," Sheryl said. She peeled off a glove and offered Dante a brisk handshake. "Nice to have met you." She leaned forward, as if to share a confidence. "Tally can use the company. I keep telling her she needs to get out more but what with Sam, well, you know how it is."

"No," Dante said, forcing another smile, "I'm afraid I don't."

Sheryl grinned. "Men never do. Anyway, it's good to see someone from her old life drop by."

"That's definitely what I am. Someone from Taylor's old life."

This time, the horn beeped three times.

"Okay, okay," Sheryl muttered, "I'm coming. Tally? I was going to say, if you want to come with us, I'm sure Dan's mother wouldn't mind."

For a wild moment, Tally imagined running out into the storm with Sam, getting into the truck, telling Dan to drive and drive and drive until she'd put a million miles between Dante and her—

"Tally?"

What was that old saying? You could run, but you couldn't hide.

"Thanks," she said brightly, "but we'll be fine."

The Miller woman looked unconvinced. Dante put his arm around Tally. When she stiffened, he dug his fingers into her flesh in mute warning.

"Taylor's right. We'll be fine." He drew his lips back from his teeth and hoped the result would still approximate a smile. "The snow, a fire, candlelight…it's quite romantic, especially for old friends. Isn't that right, *cara?*"

The child, thumb tucked in her mouth, looked at him. *Liar,* her round green eyes seemed to say. But the woman's big smile assured him she'd bought the story.

"In that case, I'm off. It was nice meeting you, Mr. Russo."

Dante held his smile until the door closed. *Now,* he told himself, and dropped his arm from Taylor's shoulders.

"Whose child is this?"

No preliminaries, she thought dizzily. No safe answers, either.

"Taylor. I asked you a question. Is the child yours?"

Sam chose that moment to give a huge yawn. Tally grabbed at the diversion.

"Somebody's sleepy," she said, ignoring Dante and the pounding of her heart.

"Am not," Sam said, yawning again.

Despite herself, Tally smiled. "Are, too," she said gently. She buried her face in her daughter's sweet-smelling neck as she carried her to the small sofa near the fireplace and sat her down. She tugged off the baby's boots, zipped her out of her snowsuit but left on the warm sweater and tights beneath it.

"How about taking a nap, sweetie? Right here, by the fire. Would you like that?"

"Wan' Teddy."

"Teddy! Of course. I'll get him. You just put your head down and I'll get Teddy and your yellow blankey, okay?"

"'Kay," Sam said, eyelids already drooping.

Tally rose to her feet and forced herself to look at Dante. "Don't," she began to say, but caught herself in time. Don't what? Go near my child? That wasn't the problem. The questions that blazed in his silver eyes was the problem.

So was answering them.

By the time she returned, Samantha was fast asleep. Tally covered her, tucked the teddy bear beside her, smoothed back the baby's hair…

"Stop playing for time."

She swung around. Dante, standing only inches away, might have been carved from granite. Her heart was beating in her throat but the biggest mistake she could make now would be to show her panic.

"Please keep your voice down. I don't want you to wake Sam."

"Sam?" His mouth twisted. "The child's name. Not your lover's. Why did you let me think otherwise?"

She busied herself picking up the boots and snowsuit from the floor.

"I had no idea what you thought. Besides, why would I care? This is my life. I don't owe you explan—"

She gasped as his hand closed, hard, on her wrist. "No games," he said in a soft, dangerous voice. "I warn you, I'm not in the mood."

"And I'm not in the mood for being bullied. Take your hand off me."

Their eyes met and held. Slowly, he released her. Tally took a last look at her sleeping daughter, then walked briskly into the kitchen with Dante on her heels.

"I'm still waiting for an answer. Is the child yours?"

The million-dollar question. It wasn't as if she hadn't envisioned this scene before and all the possible ways to handle it. Dante would demand to know whose baby this was and she'd come up with a creative reply.

She'd say she was raising the child of a sister or a dear friend. Or she'd tell him that she'd adopted Sam. Any of those explanations had seemed plausible, but now, with his cold eyes boring into hers, Tally knew she'd been kidding herself.

A man with Dante's resources would prove she was lying in the blink of an eye.

"It's a simple question, Taylor. Is the child yours?"

In the end, there was only one possible response. She gave it on a forced exhalation of breath.

"Yes. She's mine."

She steadied herself for what would come next. Anger that she hadn't told him he'd made her pregnant? A demand to claim that which was his? Or perhaps, by some miracle, a thawing of his ice-clad heart at the realization he had a daughter.

Later, she'd weep bitter tears at the memory of those possibilities and how reasonable they'd seemed.

"So, that's the reason you left me. Because you were pregnant."

She nodded and searched his face for some hint of what he was thinking.

"Answer the question! Was your pregnancy the reason you ran away?"

"I didn't run away."

His mouth thinned. "No. Of course you didn't."

"I'm sure you think I should have told you, but—"

"You were quite right, keeping the information to yourself," he said coldly. "However you imagined I'd react, the reality would have been worse."

Tears blurred her eyes. "Yes," she said. "I know that now."

Dante caught her by the shoulders, his hands as hard as his eyes.

"I made myself clear from the start."

She couldn't help it. The tears she'd tried to control trembled on her lashes, then fell. She pulled free of his hands, went to the sink and made a pretense of straightening things that didn't need straightening.

"I know. That's why I didn't—"

"You were my mistress."

That dried her tears in a hurry. "I was never that."

"Don't mince words, damn it!" He came up behind her and swung her toward him. "You belonged to me."

"This jacket belongs to you," she said, shrugging it from her shoulders so it dropped to the floor. "And that vehicle in the driveway." Tally thumped her fist against her chest. "*I* am not property. I never belonged to you."

"No." His smile was as thin as a rapier. "As it turns out, you didn't." His grasp on her tightened. "I knew things had changed between us. I just didn't know the reason."

"I left you. Final answer."

"I thought it was that our relationship was growing old."

Amazing, that such cruel words could wound after all this time, but she'd sooner have died than let him know it.

"You're right. It was. It had. That's why—"

"Now I find out it wasn't that at all." He caught her face, lifted it to him so that their eyes met. "It was this," he said, jerking his chin toward the next room, where the baby lay sleeping. "You had a secret and you were so intent on keeping it from me that you kept yourself from me, too."

"Maybe you're not as thick-headed as you seem," Tally countered, trying for sarcasm and failing, if the twist of his lips was any indication.

"I could kill you," he said softly.

As if to prove it, one cool hand circled her throat. His touch was light, but she felt its warning pressure.

"Let go of me, Dante."

"There's not a court in the land that would convict me."

"This is America. Not Sicily." Tally put her hand over his. "Damn you, do you think I planned to get pregnant?"

He stared at her for a long minute. Then he dropped his hand to his side.

"No," he said. "I suppose not."

He strode away from her, his back rigid, and paced her kitchen like a caged lion.

Her heart thudded.

What was going on in his head? Would he turn his back and walk away? Or would his pride, whatever it was that drove him, demand that he stake his claim to her daughter? She'd do anything to avoid that, anything to keep this heartless man from being involved in raising Samantha.

"Dante." Tally hesitated. "I know you're angry but—but you must believe me. I did what I thought was—"

"You told me you were using a diaphragm."

"Yes. I know. But—"

He swung toward her. "But not with him."

Tally blinked. "What?"

"I want to know who he is."

"You want—you want to know—"

"The name of your child's father. The man you took as a lover while you still belonged to me."

She stared at him in disbelief. He wasn't angry because she'd left him without telling him she was carrying his baby. He was angry because he thought she'd cheated on him.

Was that how little he thought of her? That she'd betrayed him while they were lovers? God oh God, she wanted to launch herself at him. Claw his heart out, except he had no heart.

But then, she'd always known that. It was what had made her weep at night toward the end.

She'd never so much as looked at anyone else while they'd been together. She'd never looked at anyone in the years since, either, because she was a fool, a fool, a fool…

"I am assuming," he said, "that you are not going to tell me I sired this child."

Sired Sam? He made it sound like a procedure performed in a veterinarian's office…but that was fine. Every word he said assured her she'd been right to leave him when she did.

"Damn you," he snarled, catching her by the shoulders, "answer me!"

She could do that. She could do whatever it took, to get this man out of her life.

"You can relax, Dante. I promise you, I'm not going to tell you that you are Samantha's father. If you want that in writing, I'll be happy to oblige."

A muscle bunched in his jaw. "You still haven't said who he was, this man who took you to his bed while you were still sleeping in mine."

Tally wrenched free. "You have it wrong. It was you who slept in *my* bed, remember?"

"Answer me, damn it. Who is he?"

"That's none of your business."

"I told you, you belonged to me. That makes it my business."

"And *I* told *you*, I am not property!" She looked up at him, hating him for what he was, for what he thought, for what she'd once felt in his arms. "What's the matter? Have I wounded your pride? Will I wound it even more if I tell you I was only with him once? That's all it took for him to give me his child."

He grabbed her, his face so white, eyes so hot, that she thought she'd finally pushed him too far, but that didn't matter. She'd wanted to hurt him enough to draw blood and she had…

With the truth.

She knew exactly when their child—when *her* child—had been conceived. On the night of his birthday. She'd learned the date by accident, when he left his wallet open on the nightstand with his driver's license in view. She'd made dinner, baked a cake, bought him a present because she'd—because she'd wanted to.

After, Dante had made such tender love to her that she'd looked into her own heart and come as close as she'd dared to admitting what she felt for him.

"Stay with me tonight," she'd whispered, as they lay in each other's arms.

He hadn't.

After he was gone, she'd felt more alone than she'd ever thought possible. Not just alone but abandoned. Used, not by his heart but by his body.

She'd cried softly as night faded to morning. Hours later, when she got up to shower, she'd discovered that her diaphragm had a pinpoint hole in it. She'd told herself it was nothing. It was her so-called safe time of the month and besides, what were the odds on becoming pregnant after just one night of unprotected sex?

Six weeks later, a home pregnancy kit proved that the odds were excellent.

Tally had considered the life she'd planned. A career, not for her ego but for security. Money in the bank that would guarantee she'd never have to depend on a man the way her mother had.

She'd visited her doctor. Asked tough questions, made tough decisions. And reversed herself on the subway ride home when she saw a young woman with a baby in her arms, the mother cooing, the baby laughing with unrestricted joy.

Her future had changed in that single instant.

Now, it was changing again. If she'd had any last, lingering doubts about her feelings for the man she'd once come close to thinking she loved, they were gone.

She looked pointedly at Dante's hand, encircling her wrist, then at his face.

"I want you out of here," she said softly. "Right now."

He looked at her for a long moment. Then, slowly and deliberately, he took his hand from her.

"I thought I knew you," he said in a low voice.

She almost laughed at the absurdity of those words. "You never knew me," she said.

"No. I didn't. I see that now." He plucked his leather jacket from where she'd dropped it and slipped it on. "Get yourself an attorney. A good one, because I'm going to start foreclosure proceedings as soon as I return to New York."

Panic took an oily slide in her belly. "I can make the payments on the loan. I *have* made them! All you have to do is check the bank records."

"The amount you've been paying each month is a joke. It has nothing to do with the loan agreement."

"But Walter Dennison said—"

"You're not dealing with Dennison. You're dealing with me."

She watched, transfixed, as he strolled to the door. At the last second, she went after him.

"Wait! Please, you can't... My daughter, Dante. My little girl. Surely you wouldn't punish an innocent child for my mistakes. That's not possible!"

"Anything is possible," he said coldly. "You proved that when you took a lover."

"Dante. Don't make me beg. Don't—"

"Why not?" He turned and clasped her elbows, lifting her to him until his empty eyes were all she could see. "I'd love to hear you beg, *cara*. It would fill my heart with joy."

The bitter tears she'd fought to suppress streamed down her cheeks.

"I hate you, Dante Russo. Hate you. Hate you. Hate—"

He took her mouth in a hard, deep kiss, one that demanded acquiescence. Tally fought it. Fought him as he cupped her face, held her prisoner to his plundering mouth until she knew she would kill him when he turned her free, kill him...

And then, slowly, his kiss changed. His lips softened

on hers. His tongue teased. His hands slid into her hair and she felt it again, after all these years, all this anguish and pain. The slow, dangerous heat low in her belly. The thickening of her blood. The need for him, only him…

Dante pushed her away.

"You belonged to me," he said roughly. "Only to me. I could have you again if I wished." His mouth twisted. "But why would I want another man's leavings?"

Then he put up his collar, opened the door and strode into the teeth of the storm.

CHAPTER FIVE

HOW MANY TIMES could a man be subjected to the saccharine nonsense of Christmas before he lost what remained of his sanity?

The holiday was still three weeks away and Dante was already tired of the music pouring out of shops and car radios. He'd seen enough artificial evergreens to last a lifetime, and he was damned close to telling the next sidewalk Santa exactly what he could do with his cheery ho-ho-ho.

New York, his city, belonged to tourists from Thanksgiving through the New Year. They descended on the Big Apple like fruit flies, choking the streets with their numbers, unaware or uncaring of one of the basic rules of Manhattan survival.

Pedestrians were not supposed to dawdle. And they were expected to ignore Walk and Don't Walk signs.

New Yorkers moved briskly from point A to point B and when they reached a street corner, they took one quick look and kept going. It was up to the trucks and taxis that hurtled down the streets to avoid them.

Tourists from Nebraska or Indiana and only-God-knew-where stopped and stared at the displays in department store windows in such numbers that they blocked the sidewalk. They formed a snaking queue around Radio City Music Hall, standing in the cold with the patience of dim-witted cattle. They clustered around the railing in Rockefeller Center, sighing over the too big, too gaudy, too everything Christmas tree that was the center's focal point.

As far as Dante was concerned, Scrooge had it right.

Bah, humbug, indeed, he thought as his chauffeur edged the big Mercedes through traffic.

The strange thing was, he'd never really noticed the inconvenience of the holiday until now. Basically, he'd never really noticed the holiday at all.

It was just another day.

As a child, Christmas had meant—if he were lucky—another third-hand winter jacket from the Jesuits that, you hoped, was warmer than the last. By the time he'd talked, connived and generally wheedled his way into a management job at a construction company where he'd spent a couple of years wielding a jackhammer, he was too busy to pay attention to the nonsense of canned carols and phony good cheer. And after he arrived in New York, earning the small fortune he'd needed to start building his own empire had taken all his concentration.

The last dozen years, of course, he'd had to notice Christmas. Not for himself but for others. Those with whom he did business and the ones who worked for him—the doormen, the elevator operators, the porters at the building in which he lived, all expected certain things of the holiday.

So Dante put in the requisite appearance at the annual

office party his P.A. organized. He authorized bonuses for his employees. He wrote checks for the doormen, the elevator operators and the porters. He thanked his P.A. for the bottle of Courvoisier she inevitably gave him and gave her, in return, a gift certificate to Saks.

Somehow, he'd never observed the larger picture.

Had tourists always descended on the city, inconveniencing everything and everyone? They must have.

Then, how could he not have noticed?

He was noticing now, all right. *Dio,* it was infuriating.

The Mercedes crept forward, then stopped. Crept forward, then stopped. Dante checked his watch, muttered a well-chosen bit of gutter Sicilian and decided he was better off walking.

"Carlo? I'm getting out. I'll call when I need you."

He opened the door to a dissonant blast of horns, as if a man leaving an already-stopped automobile might somehow impede the nonexistent flow of traffic. He slipped between a double-parked truck and a van, stepped onto the sidewalk and headed briskly toward the Fifth Avenue hotel where he was lunching with the owner of a private bank Russo International had just absorbed.

He'd be late. He hated that. Lateness was a sign of weakness.

Everything he did lately was a sign of weakness.

He was short-tempered. Impatient. Hell, there were times he was downright rude. And he was never that. Demanding, yes, but he asked as much of himself as he did of those who reported to him, but the past couple of weeks...

No. He'd be damned if he was going to think about that trip to Vermont again.

He thought about it too much already.

And the dreams that awakened him at night… What were they, if not an indication that he was losing his self-control?

Why would he dream about a woman he despised? For the same reason he'd kissed her, damn it. Because the ugly truth was that he still wanted her, despite her lies and her infidelity. Despite the fact that she'd borne another man's child. Nothing kept the dreams at bay. Each night, he imagined her coming to him, imagined stripping her naked, making love to her until she cried out in his arms and said, *Yes, Dante, yes, you make me feel things he never did.*

And awakened hard as stone, angry at himself for an adolescent's longings, for the frustration that he couldn't lose in another woman's bed though, God knew, he'd tried.

What an embarrassment that had been! *I'm sorry,* he'd said, *that's never happened to me before.*

It hadn't, though he doubted if the lady believed him. *He* could hardly believe it!

He was not himself since Vermont, and he didn't like it. One day in a snow-bound village and he'd discovered he was still an old-world *Siciliano* at heart, reacting to things with emotion instead of intellect.

How could a woman he didn't want ruin his sex life from a distance of four hundred miles?

Taylor had—what was the old saying? She'd put horns on his head, sleeping with another man while she was still his. She deserved whatever happened next.

She *had* been his, no matter what she claimed. So what if she hadn't let him pay her bills? If she hadn't lived with him?

She had belonged to him. He'd marked her with his hands. His mouth. His body.

And she'd let another man plant a seed in her womb. She'd given him a child. A child who should rightly have been—should rightly have been—

Dante frowned, gave himself a mental shake and prepared to vent his anger on the half a dozen idiots who'd come to a dead stop in the middle of the sidewalk.

"Excuse me," he said in a voice so frigid it made a mockery of the words.

Then he saw it wasn't only the people ahead of him. Nobody was moving. Well, yes. The crowd was shifting. Sideways, like a brontosaurus spying a fresh stand of leafy trees, heading for a huge, world-famous toy store.

Dante dug in his heels. "Excuse me," he said again. "Pardon me. Coming through."

Useless. Like a paper boat caught in a stream, the crowd herded him toward the doors.

"Wait a minute," he said to a massive woman with her elbow dug into his side. "Madam. I am not—"

But he was. Like it or not, Dante was swept inside.

A giant clock tower boomed out a welcome; a huge stuffed giraffe gave him the once-over. He was pushed past a tiger so big he half expected it to roar.

Somehow, weaving and bobbing, he worked to the edge of the crowd and found refuge behind a family of stuffed bears. He gave his watch one last glance, sighed and took out his cell phone.

"Traffic," he told the man he was to lunch with, in the tones of a put-upon New Yorker. It turned out the other man was still trapped in a taxi. They laughed and made plans for a drink that evening.

Dante put his phone away, folded his arms over his chest and settled in to wait for a break in the flow of parents and children so he could head for the door.

He didn't have to wait long. A trio of pleasantly efficient security guards cleared the way, formed the crowd into an orderly queue outside. Dante started toward the door, then fell back.

What a place this was!

And what would he have given to be turned loose in it when he was a boy. Just to look, to touch, would have been a time spent in paradise.

His toys had been stick swords. Newspaper kites. And, one magical Christmas Eve, an armless tin soldier he found in a dumpster while he scavenged for his supper.

How could he have forgotten that?

Oh, how he'd loved his soldier! He'd kept it safely buried in the pocket of his sagging jeans, bloodied the nose of a bigger boy who'd tried to steal it.

Was that what Taylor's daughter faced? Improvised toys? If she were lucky, a broken, discarded doll to call her own?

Dante scowled.

Talk about giving in to your emotions! The child—Samantha—was not the Poor Little Match Girl. Neither was her mother. Taylor was perfectly capable of earning a living.

Yes, he'd started the legal procedures that would take her house from her, but she'd reneged on the terms of the loan. It was business, plain and simple. She'd understood the risks when she signed those loan papers.

Besides, she wasn't destitute. She had possessions. She could sell them. She had friends in that town, people who'd help her and the child.

Then, why had her coat looked worn? The house, too. Even by candlelight, he could tell it needed work. The walls needed fresh paint. The wood floors needed refinishing. The furnishings were shabby. And where were the shiny, high-tech gadgets women always had in their kitchens?

Had Taylor deliberately simplified her life...or had fate done it for her?

A muscle flexed in his jaw.

Not that he cared. For every action, there was a reaction. That was basic science. She had deceived him, and he had repaid her.

The child was not his problem. Neither was Taylor. He had no regrets or remorse, and if her daughter didn't have a particularly merry Christmas this year...

Something bumped against his leg.

It was a child. A little girl, older than Samantha, clutching a cloth doll almost as big as she was in her arms.

"What did I tell you, Janey?" A harassed-looking woman caught the child's hand. "You can't see around that thing. Tell the man you're sorry."

"That's all right," Dante said quickly. "No harm done."

The child's mother smiled. "I told Janey that Santa's going to bring her some wonderful surprises in just a few weeks but she saw Raggedy Ann and, well, neither she or I could resist. You know?"

He didn't know, that was just the point. He'd never had surprises from Santa, never fallen in love with a goofy bear, like Samantha, or a rag doll like Janey.

Even if he had, who would have understood how important such a simple toy could be?

Dante watched the little girl and her mother fade into the crowd. He stood motionless, long after they'd disappeared from his sight.

Then he made his way out of the store, took out his cell phone to call his chauffeur… And, instead, called his P.A. to tell her he wasn't returning to the office.

He felt—what was the word? Unsettled. Perhaps he was coming down with something. Whatever the reason, walking to his apartment building on such a cold, crisp day might clear his head.

"You're home early, Mr. Russo," said his housekeeper when he stepped from the private elevator into the foyer of his penthouse.

Dante shrugged off his coat and told her he didn't want to be disturbed. Then he went into his study, turned on his computer and did what he could to further prepare for the meeting he'd have over drinks in just a few hours.

For the first time in his life, he couldn't get interested in the complex facts and figures of an imminent deal.

What kind of Christmas morning would Taylor and her child awaken to? There was a time he'd have assumed Taylor viewed the holiday with as much cynicism as he did. After all, he'd spent six months as her lover. He knew her. He knew her likes and dislikes…

Or did he?

She'd shown him a side of her he'd never suspected. Had she really grown up in a small town? If he hadn't seen her in that shabby little house with a child in her arms, even imagining Taylor in that kind of life would have been impossible.

People didn't even call her by that name in Shelby. She was Tally, not Taylor. A softer, more vulnerable name for a softer, more vulnerable woman.

Dante went to the window and looked down at Central Park. Thanks to the influx of out-of-towners, it was alive with people, even on a weekday afternoon. There were probably more people in the park right now than lived in the entire town of Shelby, Vermont.

If Taylor had stayed in New York, if she'd opened her business here, she'd be turning a handsome profit by now. She had contacts in the city, a reputation.

Dante watched the scene below him for long minutes. Children were sledding down a snowy incline; even from up here, he could see the bright flash of their snowsuits.

Would the little girl in the toy store find a sled under the tree Christmas morning?

Would Taylor's daughter?

A muscle knotted in his jaw.

No. The plan running through his head was clearly insane. She'd made a fool of him, wounded him in the worst way a woman can hurt a man.

But the child was innocent.

It was wrong, that children seemed always to pay for the sins of those who'd given them life.

The muscle in his jaw knotted again. Dante went to the breakfront, took out a bottle of brandy and poured an inch into a snifter. He warmed the glass between his palms, stared sightlessly into the rich depths of the swirling liquid.

And put it down, untouched.

Instead, he went to his desk. Picked up the phone. Made calls to his attorney, to his accountant, to the same private investigator who'd found Taylor for him.

If any of them thought his instructions were unusual, they knew better than to say so.

When he'd finished, Dante picked up his snifter of brandy and went up the spiral staircase to his suite.

The view was even better here. Three walls of glass gave him a vantage point a peregrine falcon would have as it swooped over the city.

Lights glimmered, diamonds sparkling against the pall of encroaching darkness, and he recalled the first time he'd stood here, gazing out into the night, the fierce swell of pride he'd felt at knowing all this was his, that his sweat, his struggles, his fight to get to the top had all been worth it.

Taylor had never seen this view. She'd come here for drinks, for dinner, but he'd never carried her up the stairs to this room.

To his bed.

Dante sipped the brandy.

What if he had? If he'd made love to her while the lights of the city challenged the stars in the night sky? If he'd taken her to these windows, naked. Stood with her as she looked out on his world. Stepped behind her. Cupped her breasts. Bent his head and kissed the skin behind her ear.

She'd always trembled when he kissed her there.

Trembled when he entered her.

He closed his eyes. Imagined entering her now, right now, here, as she looked into the night. Imagined holding her hips, pressing against her, the urgency of his erection seeking the heat, the silken dampness that was for him.

Only for him…

His eyes flew open.

The hell it was.

She'd been with another man, even while she'd been his because, damn it, she *had* belonged to him no matter what she said.

He turned from the window, turned from the images that assailed him.

What he'd just done had nothing to do with Taylor. It was simply an act of charity. This was the season for charity, after all. What he'd done was for a child. An innocent little girl, trapped in a game played by adults.

That the plan he'd set in motion would also bring Taylor back into his life was secondary. Whatever had happened between him and his once-upon-a-time lover was over.

Dante tossed back the rest of the brandy. The liquid burned its way down his throat and, as it did, burned him, as well, with the ugly truth.

Forget charity. Forget pretending that what had happened was over.

It wouldn't be. Not until he slept with the woman who'd made a fool of him, one last time.

CHAPTER SIX

WHEN SHE WAS SIX, Tally stopped believing in Santa Claus.

Her grandmother had taken her to the mall the week before. She'd been terrified of the man with the white beard and the booming laugh, but after a lot of coaxing, she'd sat in his lap and whispered that all she wanted for Christmas was a Pretty Patty doll.

Christmas Eve, she crept out of bed and saw her grandmother putting the doll under the tree.

Even then, she'd understood Grandma had to count every penny. That she'd loved Tally enough to buy the doll meant more than if Santa had brought it.

Now, twenty-two years later, she was close to believing in Santa again.

How else to explain the call from a decorator she'd worked with in Manhattan? He'd been in too much of a hurry to offer details but the bottom line was that he knew someone who knew someone who knew someone who was familiar with her work.

That person had recommended her for the commission of a lifetime.

"The guy's richer than Midas," Aston trilled. "Seems

he just bought out some old-line firm and the digs don't suit him, so he's moving the whole kit and caboodle to that new building on 57th and Mad. You know the one? Baby, this is one plum job! A huge budget, free creative rein… Pull this off, your name will blaze in neon!"

A couple of weeks back, Tally would have been flattered but she'd have turned down the offer. She'd have had no choice, not with a shop to open in Vermont. Now it seemed as if Dante's vicious act of revenge might turn out to be a godsend.

"He wants to meet with you first, of course. See if the synergy's right."

For an assignment like this, she'd do whatever it took to make the synergy right.

She splurged on a haircut, had her black suit cleaned and pressed, charged a new coat which she hated to do but appearance was everything in New York. If things went well, she'd be able to pay for it. If not, she was so broke that the credit card company would have to wait the next hundred years for their money.

She even tried to go back to thinking of herself as Taylor Sommers instead of Tally. Her given name had been the one she'd always used in the city. It suited the image she'd needed, that of a cool sophisticate.

The woman Dante had always assumed her to be. The one she knew he'd wanted her to be.

And yet, today, after leaving Samantha with Sheryl, riding the train into Manhattan, now standing across from the glass tower where she was to meet the Mystery Mogul, she felt more like Tally than Taylor.

Taylor wouldn't have butterflies swarming in her stomach.

Tally did.

She was nervous. Hell, she was terrified about meeting the man who held her future in his hands.

He had no name. Not yet.

"You know how these big shots are," Aston said. "Some of them won't make a move unless a camera's pointed at them, but some guard their privacy like lions protecting a kill. This guy's like that. He wants to stay nameless until the deal is struck."

The Mystery Mogul was meeting her in his new offices. Tally looked up, counting the floors even though she'd already done it twice, head tilted back like an out-of-towner.

The butterflies fluttered their wings again.

She wanted this job more than she'd ever wanted anything. Aston's description of it was almost too good to be true.

Her fee would be—well, enormous. More than she'd earn in five years in Shelby. She'd be able to give Sam everything. New toys, clothes, the best possible nanny to care for her while Tally was at work.

Best of all, she could deal with the loan payments she owed the bank—the payments she owed Dante. So much for his plans to destroy her.

She wouldn't even have to tackle the toughest thing about living in New York. The Mystery Mogul, it turned out, owned an apartment building with a two-bedroom, two-bath vacancy.

"Well, of course he does," Aston had said.

The way he said it made her laugh. It was the first time she'd laughed in weeks.

Since Dante's visit.

Since she'd discovered just how ruthless he could be.

Since she'd found out just how much she could hate him.

"The rent's a perk of the job, can you imagine?"

She could. A picture was emerging of a bona fide eccentric with money to burn. The only thing that almost stopped her was that this meant returning to Dante's city. And that was just plain ridiculous. It was her city, too, or had been for five years. Besides, the odds of running into one person in a city of eight million were zero to none.

And even if there was that eight-million-to-one chance, so what? She'd left Dante so he wouldn't know she was having his baby, but it turned out she needn't have worried. She'd told him Sam wasn't his and he'd been only too willing to believe her.

Tally lifted her chin as she strode through the lobby of the glass tower and stepped into a waiting elevator. She should have spat in his face that night in her kitchen. Given the opportunity a second time, she wouldn't pass it by.

"To hell with you, Dante Russo," she said aloud, as the elevator whisked her to the twenty-seventh floor. "You're a cold, contemptible son of a bitch and—"

The doors slid open.

And the cold, contemptible son of a bitch was standing in front of her, arms folded, face expressionless.

"Hello, Taylor," he said, and that was when she knew she'd been had. All this—the wonderful job, the money, the apartment…

It was all a cruel joke.

A joke only one of them could laugh at, she thought,

and then she stopped thinking, called him a word she had never before thought, much less used, and launched herself at the man she would hate for the rest of her life.

DANTE HAD KNOWN this wouldn't be easy.

Taylor despised him. Well, so what? The feeling was mutual.

And she was proud.

He admired that in her; he always had. She'd never shown the weakness so many women—hell, so many men and women—showed, that of needing someone to lean on. Like him, she was independent and strong.

But things had changed.

She did need someone now. Some no-good SOB had gotten her pregnant and walked away, left her with a child to raise, and that made all the difference.

He'd decided to start by telling her that but she didn't give him the chance. The elevator doors opened, she saw who was waiting for her and she came at him like a tiger.

He got his arms up just in time to keep her from clawing his face.

"Taylor," he said, "Taylor, listen—"

"No," she panted, raining blows on his upraised arms, "I'm done listening, you bastard! Wasn't what you did to me enough? Did you need an encore? You no-good, heartless—"

He caught her hands, yanked them behind her back. "Stop it!"

"Let go. You let go of me or—"

She was still fighting him. Dante grunted, tucked his shoulder down and hoisted her over it like a bag of laundry. She shrieked, kicked her feet and yanked at his hair. What in hell would he say if somebody came running to see who was being murdered?

"Put me down!"

"With pleasure," he said grimly.

The former tenants had left behind a couple of chairs, half a dozen file cabinets and a small black leather sofa. Dante strode to it and dumped her on it. Then he stood back, folded his arms again and glared.

What had made him think helping her would be a good idea?

"Don't even think about it," he warned when she scrambled up against the cushions.

"I hate you, Dante. Do you hear me? I hate you!"

"I'd never have known."

She sat up straight, mouth trembling. "How even *you* could do something like this, you—you—"

"Watch what you say, *cara.*"

"Do not call me that!"

"Is it your habit to attack your clients?"

"If you think I'm going to be party to this—this schoolboy prank—"

"You're so sure you know everything, Taylor. Is it possible you don't?"

"I know what you are. That's all that's necessary."

She rose to her feet, tugged down her coat, smoothed her hands over her hair. She was still shaking and suddenly he wanted to go to her, take her in his arms and tell her everything was going to be all right. That he would take care of her.

Except, that wasn't why he'd brought her here. It was for the child.

And for yourself, a voice in his head said slyly. How

come he'd forgotten his vow to sleep with this woman one last time? That would put her out of his thoughts forever. He didn't need to hear her say she wanted him. Or that she was sorry she'd been unfaithful. He didn't need to hear the words she'd whispered that night three years ago when she'd begged him to stay with her, to stay in her arms, in her bed.

"Get out of my way!"

She was looking up at him as if she wanted to kill him. Fine. The game he'd planned was one that was best played by sworn enemies.

"We'll have our meeting first."

"We've already had it. To think you'd resort to such—to such subterfuge, just so you could make a fool of me!"

"Would you have agreed to this appointment if you'd known I was the man involved?"

"You know I wouldn't." Her eyes filled with angry tears. "Why did you do it? You're taking my house. My livelihood. What more do you want?"

He wasn't going to answer. She could tell by the way he was looking at her but it didn't matter. She already knew the answer. What he'd done to her wasn't sufficient. He wanted to give the knife one more twist.

How? she thought bitterly. How could she have made love with a man like this? How could she have even believed she'd fallen in love with him? Because she had believed it, yes. That was why she'd left him, because she knew he didn't love her, wouldn't love the child they'd created together. She'd left rather than see him look at her as he was looking at her now, as if she had no meaning to him at all.

She took a deep breath, drew what remained of her pride around her like a ragged cloak and started past him.

"Taylor."

She shook her head. She had nothing left to say to him.

His hand closed on her wrist. "You asked me questions. Are you going to leave before you hear the answers?"

She looked pointedly from his hand to hers. "Let go."

"I didn't bring you to New York on false pretenses."

She laughed. "You didn't, huh?"

"Isn't that what I just said?"

"Well, let's see. You got someone to offer me a commission decorating these offices. He mentioned a budget big enough to make my head spin. Oh, and he said there'd be an apartment with the rent a perk of the job." Tally tugged her hand free and put her hands on her hips. "If those aren't false pretenses—"

"The offer is real. All of it. The commission, the budget, the place to live."

Everything from shock to distrust to outright utter disbelief showed in her face. He tucked his hands in his trouser pockets and kept his tone as flat as his eyes.

"It's all yours, if you want it."

She stared at him. "Why?"

"There's an old saying about not looking a gift horse in the mouth."

"I know the saying. Maybe it lost something in the translation. What it means is that an unexpected gift is a gift to beware of."

Dante took a deep breath. "The child," he said.

"What child?" Tally felt her heart beat quicken. Did he know? Had he somehow learned the truth of her pregnancy? "You mean—you mean Sam?"

He nodded. "Yes."

"What about her?"

"I've had time to think." A muscle flexed in his jaw. "And I realized that it's wrong to punish her for your behavior."

He didn't know. Tally almost sagged with relief.

"Your daughter is innocent of all that happened. You deceived me. You left me. But none of that is her doing. The world is filled with children who suffer because of the behavior of adults. I see no reason to add to their number."

She stared at him. Dante Russo, showing compassion to a little girl he thought had been fathered by another man? Why would he show compassion at all? All the months they'd been lovers, she'd waited, she'd yearned to see some show of human emotion in this man.

She never had.

Oh, he supported charities. Smiled at things that were amusing. Frowned at things that were annoying.

But he never lost his composure. Not even in bed.

Not that he wasn't an incredible lover. He was. Alert to her every sigh, her every unspoken desire. He'd given her more pleasure than she'd ever imagined possible.

The way he moved inside her.

The way he brought her to climax.

And yet, he'd always been in control. Always, except that one night when he'd been as tender as he was wild, when she'd asked him to stay with her.

When she'd conceived Samantha.

"Well?"

Tally blinked. Dante was looking at her with barely veiled impatience.

"You asked me why I'd offer this assignment to you and I told you the reason. It's your turn now. Will you accept it? Or will you turn it down because I'm the man making the offer?"

Something was wrong. She felt as if she were looking at a jigsaw puzzle with one piece—the key piece—missing.

"Yes or no?"

She almost laughed. The imperious tone of voice. The straight posture. The cold eyes that said, "I'm in command."

Except, he wasn't.

He couldn't order her around. She wouldn't permit it. She had to think. Nothing was happening the way it was supposed to. She'd worried about being in the same city with this man and now it turned out she'd be working for him.

Impossible.

Better to go home…and do what? Lose the house? Move to a furnished room? Take whatever job she could find? Earn barely enough to live on and, oh yes, impose on Sheryl's kindness by asking her to watch Sam?

"Taylor, I want an answer!"

There was only one answer, but she couldn't bring herself to give it. Not without making him wait.

"I'll call you with my decision."

His eyes narrowed. She tried to move past him as quickly as possible, but his hand clamped down on her shoulder.

"Would you put your pride before the welfare of your daughter?"

"Nice, Dante. Really nice." Tally's eyes blazed with anger. "Don't you try and lay this on me! I never ignored Sam's welfare and I sure as hell never tripped over my own oversize ego! You're the one who came to Shelby, who bought a bank just so you could tear my child's life to pieces."

"That wasn't my intention."

"Maybe not, but it's what you did."

"Yes. And now, I intend to undo it. I will not avenge myself by hurting a child."

"My God, listen to you! So high and mighty. So godlike. Anyone would think you have a conscience. Maybe even a heart."

"Damn you, Taylor!" His fingers dug into her flesh as he pulled her to him. "I want to do the right thing. Why make it so difficult?"

And, in that moment, it came to her. The missing piece of the puzzle. What he'd just called doing the right thing. If that was his intention, there was a much easier way to do it. Why wasn't he taking it?

"If you're serious about not wanting my little girl to pay the price of your revenge—"

"Interesting," he said silkily, "how you manage to misquote me, *cara*. I said I would not avenge myself through her. We both know what that means, that your daughter should not pay the price of your unfaithfulness."

"Put whatever twist you like on it. The point is, if you've suddenly turned into the male counterpart of Mother Teresa, why go through all this? Why not simply stop the foreclosure proceedings?"

There it was, the million-dollar question. The question he'd asked himself a dozen times since coming up with this idea. His attorney and his accountant, each of whom knew only small details of the overall situation, had finally asked it, too, but he hadn't given them any explanations.

A man who answered to no one but himself didn't have to.

That didn't mean it wasn't a damned good question. All he had to do was have the loan payments rescheduled. Or tear up the documents altogether.

End of problem.

Nothing else made sense. Not to his attorney, to his accountant, to him and now to Taylor, who was looking at him with her eyebrows arched.

Dante frowned. She could look at him any way she liked. He didn't owe her an explanation, either.

"It's too complicated to explain."

Her smile was thin. "Try."

"There are banking laws. Rules. And I've already set the foreclosure procedure in motion."

"And I'll unset it by repaying the loan with my earnings from this job." Another thin smile. "Try again."

For a second, he looked blank. "You'd see it as charity. You'd never accept it."

It was a good save. The sudden lift of her eyebrows told him so.

"This way, you'll work for the money," he said, feeling his way carefully through the explanation that had suddenly come to him and knowing it was flawed. Give her too much time, she'd realize that. "I'm simply offering you a practical way out of your dilemma."

Yes, Tally thought. That was how it seemed—but then, the fly that had wandered into the spider's parlor had probably thought she was being asked in for a cup of tea.

And yet, what was the alternative? Could she really say no to his offer and condemn Samantha to financial uncertainty? Besides that, he was right. She'd be working for this money. No favors given, no favors asked.

"Well?"

She looked up. Dante was scowling. Obviously, he had none of her reservations about them being in close contact.

"I can't spend the entire day at this, Taylor. I need an answer. Will you take the job or won't you?"

She took a deep, steadying breath. "I'll take it."

Something flashed in his eyes. Triumph, she thought, but then it was gone, he was smiling politely and holding out his hand. She stared at it. Then, carefully, she extended her hand, too, felt his callused palm against hers as they shook hands.

"I want certain assurances," she said quickly.

"We've already sealed the deal. But go ahead. I'll try and accommodate you. What assurances do you want?"

"Our relationship will be strictly business."

He didn't say anything. His expression didn't change. Was that agreement or was he waiting to hear more?

"Our meetings will occur in public places."

"Such logical choices, *cara*. I'm impressed. Is that all?"

"No. It isn't." She folded her arms. "You're not to call me that."

"What? *Cara?*" He laughed. "You're my employee. I'll call you anything I like."

"I'm not your employee. We'll be working together. Either way, calling me *cara* would be improper."

He smiled, and her heart rose into her throat because everything she'd feared about him, everything she'd adored about him, was in that smile.

"Ah. I understand now." He cupped her elbows.

Slowly, inexorably, he drew her closer. "You're afraid our relationship will become personal."

"It won't," she said stiffly. "How could it, when you're the last man on earth I'd want to become personal with?"

"I used to call you *cara* when you were in my arms. When I was making love to you."

Taylor's breath caught. The sound of his voice at those moments. The feel of his hands on her breasts. The darkness of his eyes as he'd slipped his hands beneath her, as he entered her. Slowly, so slowly, until she cried out with pleasure at the feel of him deep, deep inside her...

"No," she said, "I don't remember. Why would I? It meant nothing. It meant—It meant—"

Dante stopped her lies with a kiss.

Fight him, she thought desperately, *don't let him do this to you.*

But the terrible truth was, he was doing what she had dreamed of. What she ached for. She loved the feel of his mouth on hers. The scent of his skin. The way he moved his hands down her spine and lifted her against him so that his erection pressed against her belly.

"Kiss me back," he said, his voice a rough command, and her treacherous body responded, her lips parted and when they did, he thrust his tongue into her mouth and she felt it happening as it always did, her breasts swelling, her bones melting, her body readying for his possession...

Her heart yearning for what he would never give her.

Tally wrenched free of his embrace.

"No." Her voice was hoarse. "I don't want that from you. Not anymore."

He said nothing for a long moment. Then he let go of her.

"As you wish."

"As I insist."

"Please," he said coolly, "no ultimatums. You made your point. And now…"

He glanced at his watch, then plucked his cell phone from his pocket and made a brief call. It was like a slap in the face, a way of telling her that the kiss had meant nothing to him.

"I've arranged for my driver to come for you."

"That's not necessary. My hotel—"

"I've checked you out of your hotel." His hand clasped her elbow; he moved her into the elevator with determined efficiency. "Carlo will take you to your rooms."

"Rooms?" she said, as the elevator plunged toward the lobby. "Aston said an apartment."

"The rooms for you and your daughter are a separate suite within an apartment."

"Whose apartment?" Tally said, heart suddenly racing.

His eyes met hers. "Mine," he answered.

Before she could respond, the doors swept open on the lobby and Dante handed her over to his waiting driver.

CHAPTER SEVEN

DID HE REALLY THINK she'd live in his apartment?

Not even if the alternative was a tent pitched in the Millers' backyard.

Tally let Dante's driver take her to Central Park West but only because she had to go there if she wanted to reclaim her luggage.

She'd get it, write the imperious Mr. Russo a note telling him, in exquisite detail, what he could do with his contract, phone for a taxi and leave. No. This time, she'd face him. She would not forgo that pleasure.

The driver was new but the doorman was the same as in the past. He greeted her by name, as if three long years had not gone by since her last visit. So did the housekeeper, who added that it was good to see her again.

"This way, miss," she said pleasantly, gesturing not to the library or the dining room or the sitting room, all the places—the only places—Tally had seen when she and Dante had been involved, but to the graceful, winding staircase.

"Thank you," Tally said, "but I'll wait for Mr. Russo in the library. If someone would just bring me my suitcase…?"

"Your things are already upstairs, miss. I'll show you to your rooms."

Arguing seemed pointless. Her quarrel was with Dante, not with his staff. She followed the housekeeper to a door that led into a sitting room as large as her entire house back in Vermont.

"Would you like some tea, miss?"

What she'd have liked was some strychnine for her host, but Tally managed a polite smile.

"Nothing, thank you."

"Ellen's unpacked your things. If you're not pleased with how she's arranged your clothes, just ring."

But I'm not staying, Tally started to say, except, by then the housekeeper had disappeared.

Dante wasn't just arrogant, he was presumptuous. She could hardly wait to see him and tell him so, but where was he? And when was the last train to Shelby? Eight? Nine? She intended to be on it. No way could she afford a night in a hotel now that her prospective job had turned out to be a farce.

Tally took out her cell phone and dialed Sheryl to see how Sam was and to tell her that the plans that had seemed so magical had fallen apart, but there was no answer. What a time to be reminded that cell service in Shelby wasn't always what you hoped.

Was nothing going to go right today?

Twenty minutes passed. Thirty. Tally frowned. Paced the sitting room. Checked her watch again. Damn it, she didn't have time for this! She'd wait another half hour, then give up the pleasure of confronting Mr. Russo and his monumental ego.

Getting on that train, getting back to Sam and the real

world, was more important. In fact, why was she wasting time waiting for Dante when she could be packing? She didn't need a maid to toss things into a suitcase.

Chin lifted, Tally marched through the sitting room, though a light-filled bedroom, to a door she assumed led to a closet…

Her breath caught.

The door didn't open on a closet. It opened on a room meant for a very lucky little girl.

For Samantha.

The walls were painted cream and decorated with murals that spoke of fairy tales, princesses and unicorns. The carpet was pale pink. The crib and furniture were cream and gold. A rocker stood near the window, a patchwork afghan draped over it. Tucked away in one corner, a playhouse shaped like a castle rose toward the ceiling, guarded by a family of plush teddy bears.

The room was a little girl's dream.

For a heartbeat, Tally's mood softened. She could imagine her daughter's excitement at such wonders.

Then she came to her senses and saw the room for what it really was.

Did Dante think he could bribe her into staying?

She turned on her heel. There was nothing she'd brought to the city she couldn't do without. To hell with packing. To hell with confronting Dante. All she wanted was to go home.

Quickly she left the suite, went down the stairs and headed straight for the private elevator…

But it was already there.

The doors slid open just as she reached them and she saw Dante standing in the mahogany and silver car.

Dante, with Samantha curled in his arms.

The blood drained from Tally's head.

Of all the things she'd imagined happening this day, she'd never envisioned this. Not this. Not her former lover, with his daughter in his arms.

Sam was so fair. Dante was so dark. And yet—oh, God—and yet they were so right together. The same softly curling hair. The same wide eyes and firm mouths, curving in the same smiles as they looked at each other, Dante with a softness of expression Tally had never seen in his face before, Sam babbling happily about something in a two-year-old's combination of real and made-up words.

Dante and Samantha. A father and his daughter.

The ground tilted under Tally's feet.

Blindly she stuck out a hand in a search for support. She must have made a sound because suddenly Dante looked up and saw her.

His smile faded. *"Cara?"*

I'm fine, she said. Or tried to say. But the words wouldn't come, nothing would come but another soft sound of distress. Dante barked a command. His housekeeper ran into the room, took Sam from him, and then it was Tally who was in Dante's arms, his strong arms, and he was carrying her swiftly through the apartment.

"Cara," he said again, "Tally…"

He had never called her that before. She thought of how soft the name sounded on his lips. Of how the world was spinning, spinning, spinning…

And then everything went black.

WHEN SHE OPENED HER EYES, she was in an enormous, canopied bed in a softly lit room.

Where was she? What had happened? Something

terrible. Something that carried within it the seeds of disaster.

She sat up against a bank of silk-covered pillows—and everything came rushing back. Dante. Samantha. Her baby in her lover's arms. Her baby, here, in this place, where three years' worth of secrets might untangle like a skein of yarn.

Tally started to push the comforter aside. She had to find Sam. Take her home…

"*Cara.* What are you doing?"

Dante's voice was harsh. He stood in the door between the bath and the bedroom, his tall, powerful figure shadowy in the light.

"Where's my baby?"

"Samantha is fine."

He came toward her, a glass of water in one hand, a small tablet in the other. Tally brushed aside his outstretched hand.

"Where is she?"

"She's in the nursery. Asleep."

"I want to see her."

"I told you, she's fine."

Tally swung her feet to the floor. "Don't argue with me, Dante! I want to see her now."

"The tablet first."

She glared up at him. She knew him well; enough to know he wasn't going to let her get past him until she obeyed his command.

"What is that?"

"Just something to calm you."

"I don't need calming, damn it!"

"The doctor disagreed."

"You called a doctor?"

"Of course I did," he said brusquely. "You fainted."

"Only because—because I was stunned to see my daughter. You had no right—"

"Take the tablet." His mouth twitched. "Then you can tell me what a monster I am, for flying Samantha here so she could be with you."

She glared at him one last time. Then she snatched the glass from his hand, dumped the tablet in her mouth and gulped it down with a mouthful of water.

Tell him what a monster he was? No. She wasn't going to waste the time. You couldn't argue with Dante Russo. He was always right, so why bother? She'd take Sam and leave.

But first, she had to get dressed.

The realization that she was *undressed* surged through her. She was wearing a nightgown of pale blue silk, its thin straps scattered with pink silk rosebuds, the kind of gown only a man would buy for a woman.

An ache, sharp as a knife, pierced her heart. Was the woman Dante had bought it for as lovely as the gown? She must have been, for him to have given her something so fragile and exquisitely beautiful. For him to have made love to that woman here, in his home, where he had never made love to her.

Unaccountably, her eyes stung with tears. Angry tears. What else could they be?

Damn Dante Russo to hell! Who had given him permission to have his housekeeper take off her clothes and dress her in this gown that wasn't hers?

"Well?"

She looked up. Dante was watching her, one dark eyebrow raised.

"Aren't you going to tell me I'm a monster?"

"Get away from me," Tally said, her voice trembling.

"After all," he said, a wry smile curving his lips, "you have every reason to despise me. You pass out, I phone for my doctor.... What woman wouldn't hate a man under those circumstances?"

"I want my clothes."

"Why?"

"Dante. You may find this amusing, but I do not. You seem to think you can—you can take control of my life. Well, you can't. I don't want your job. I don't want your guest suite. I don't want you thinking you can decide what's best for my baby, I don't want your housekeeper undressing me, and I certainly do not want your mistress's cast-offs."

"Such a long list of don'ts," he said mildly, tucking his hands into the pockets of what she now realized were soft-looking gray sweatpants. "Unfortunately, not all of them are appropriate."

"Damn you, I'm not playing games!"

"Let's go through them one by one, shall we?"

"Let's not. I told you—"

"I heard you. Now it's your turn to listen. Number one, I'm not trying to control anything. You agreed to the terms of the job."

"If by 'terms,' you mean me living in your home—"

"Two," he said, ignoring her protests, "I cannot imagine that thinking it best for you and Sam to be together as soon as possible was a mistake."

"I was going home to her. Didn't that occur to you?"

"It did, but I have a private plane. Why would you want to spend hours on the train, only to turn around and make the trip here again when I could arrange to bring her to you tonight?"

"Damn it, who gave you the right to think for me? I was not going to turn around, as you put it, and make the trip here again. I told you, I don't want your—"

"And, finally," he said, "finally, *cara,* you're wrong about the nightgown." He took his hands from his pockets, reached out and trailed one finger deliberately across one rose-embroidered strap, hooking the tip under the fabric, lightly tugging at it so that she had no choice but to sit forward. "I bought it for you, along with some other things I thought you might need to help you settle in." His voice turned silken. "And then there's that final accusation. That my housekeeper undressed you. She didn't."

A rush of color shot into Tally's face. Dante saw it and smiled.

"Why would I have her do that," he said softly, "when I've undressed you myself hundreds of times in the past?"

"The past is dead, Dante. You had no right—"

"Damn it," he said sharply, his smile vanishing, "who are you to talk about rights?" His hands cupped her shoulders and he drew her to her feet. "Such self-righteous garbage from a woman who ran like a coward instead of facing a man and telling him she'd cheated on him!"

"I didn't—"

"What? You didn't cheat? What do you call becoming involved with another man, if not cheating? Come on, Tally. I'd love to hear you come up with a better word."

What could she say to that? Nothing, not without admitting the truth. Telling him he'd fathered Sam would open her to his scorn, his anger and, worst of all, to the possibility he'd try and take her daughter from her.

"That's a fine speech," she said calmly, even though her heart was racing. "But you're only making it because I wounded your ego. You were bored. You were going to leave me. Instead, I made the first move. That's what really bothers you and you know it."

Was it? She'd just told him exactly what he'd been telling himself for three years, but now he wasn't sure it was that simple. Had he planned on breaking things off because he was bored, or was there some deeper reason he hadn't wanted to face?

Was that what had driven her into the arms of a stranger?

Maybe he'd ask himself that question someday, but not now. Not when all his rage at Tally had turned to fear an hour ago, when he'd watched her face whiten as she crumpled to the floor.

Now she stood straight and tall before him, her eyes fixed on his and glittering with unshed, angry tears. Her hair was loose; he'd undone the pins himself, let it tumble to her shoulders in soft, heavy waves. She wore no makeup; he'd washed it away with a cool cloth and it occurred to him that he'd never seen her like this before, that in all the time they'd been lovers, her appearance had always been perfect.

She'd been beautiful then but she was even more lovely like this, he'd thought, her lips naked of artificial color, her hair in sweet disarray. She was what they called her in Vermont.

She was Tally, not Taylor, and something in the softness of the old-fashioned name had made his throat constrict.

Slowly, he'd undressed her, telling himself it was only so he didn't have to ring for Mrs. Tipton or Ellen.

His hands had trembled as he undid the buttons of her suit, as he slid her blouse from her shoulders.

It was so long since he'd seen her breasts. Her belly. The pale curls that hid the sweet folds of flesh where he longed to bury himself. The long legs that had once wrapped around his hips as he lost himself in her welcoming heat.

And yet, despite those images, what he'd felt, undressing Tally, hadn't been sexual desire.

What he'd felt was the desire to protect her. To hold her close. Rock her in his arms. Tell her he was sorry he'd hurt her, sorry he hadn't understood what she'd needed of him, what he'd needed of her all those years ago....

"Even now," Tally said, her voice tinged with bitterness, "even now, you can't tell me the truth."

"You're right," he said quietly. "I was going to leave you." Tally turned away. He cupped her jaw and forced her to meet his eyes. "But I don't know why, *cara*. I thought that I did, but now I'm not so sure." His gaze fell to her lips. "All I'm sure of is this."

"No," she whispered, but even as he lowered his head to hers, Tally didn't pull back. She shut her eyes, felt the whisper of his breath on her mouth, and when he gathered her into his arms and said her name, she moaned and melted against him.

This was the kind of kiss they'd shared on the night that had changed everything. It was a kiss of tenderness and longing so intense she could feel his heart thudding against hers and with a suddenness that stunned her, she knew she wanted more.

"Dante," she said, the word a soft sigh against his lips. "Dante…"

His name, breathed against his mouth. Her breasts, pressed to his chest. Her belly, soft against his. Dante groaned, slid his hands into Tally's spill of cinnamon hair and gathered her closer.

Passion exploded between them.

Tenderness became desire; longing turned to desperate need. Dante's mouth demanded acquiescence and Tally give it, parting her lips so his tongue could seek out her honeyed taste. He groaned, slid down the delicate straps of the nightgown, baring her breasts to his hands and mouth.

"Say it," he demanded, and she did.

Her whispered "Yes, make love to me. Yes, touch me, yes, yes, yes," rose into the silence of the winter night and filled him with ecstasy.

And he knew, in that instant, that taking her to bed once more in a quest for revenge was not what he needed at all.

He needed her wanting him, like this. Crying out as he bent to her and sucked her nipple deep into his mouth. Tossing her head back in frenzied response to the brush of his hand as he dragged up the skirt of her gown, cupped her mons with his palm, felt her hot tears of desire damp on his fingers and sweet heaven, he was going to come, to come, to come…

He scooped Tally into his arms.

"Now," he said fiercely, his mouth at her throat, and she sobbed his name over and over as he carried her through the vast room, heading not to her bed but to his…

A child's voice cried out.

"Sam," Tally whispered.

Dante shut his eyes. Dragged air into his lungs. Turned and carried her to the nursery, where he set her gently on her feet.

He stood back and let her approach the child in the white and gold crib alone.

"Baby," she murmured, "did you have a bad dream?"

"Mama?"

Tally lifted her daughter in her arms. Sam was warm from sleep, sweet from the mingled scents of soap and baby powder. She sighed and laid her head against Tally's shoulder.

"Teddies are sleepin', Mama."

Teddies, indeed. The bedraggled, much-loved bear from home sat in the corner of the crib, side by side with the smallest new teddy from the bear family Dante had bought.

Unaccountably, Tally's heart swelled.

"Yes, baby," she said softly, "I see."

She went to the rocking chair, sat in it and gently rocked Sam back and forth, back and forth.

"'Hush little baby,'" she sang softly, "'don't you cry…'"

Gradually, Samantha's breathing slowed. Tally waited until she was certain she was sound asleep. Then she carried her child to the crib, laid her in it, covered her with a blanket and pressed a kiss to her hair.

When she turned she saw Dante, still in the doorway, watching her, his face unreadable in the soft shadows cast by the nightlight.

Oh, Dante, she thought, *Dante…*

Slowly, she went to him and looked into his eyes. A muscle jumped in his cheek. He lifted his hand and reached toward her and she shook her head and pulled back, knowing that if he touched her—if he touched her…

"What we did—what we almost did—was a mistake."

"Making love is never a mistake, *cara*."

He was wrong. It was a mistake, and Tally knew it. Knew it because she'd finally faced the truth.

She loved Dante Russo with all her heart.

Bad enough she could never tell him she'd borne him a child, but to lie in his arms and pretend it was only sex would be the ultimate travesty.

A heart could only be broken so many times before it shattered into a million pieces.

Tally put her hands lightly on Dante's chest. "Maybe not," she said softly. "But it can't happen anymore."

A smile tilted at the corners of his mouth. "Does this mean I won't have to sue you for breach of contract?"

She smiled, too. "If you mean, will I take the job, the answer is yes. It's a wonderful opportunity, and I thank you for it. And I'll stay here." Her voice grew soft. "This suite is beautiful, and the nursery you created for Sam is a little girl's dream come true." She drew a breath. "But you have to give me your word you won't try to make love to me."

"Is that really what you want?"

No. Oh no, it wasn't. She longed to tell him that, to go into his arms, lift her mouth to his, plead for him to carry her to bed and love her until dawn lit the sky.…

"*Cara?* Is it really what you want?"

She had lied to him already. Now she had no choice but to lie to him again.

"Yes."

Long seconds dragged by. Then Dante took her hand, pressed a kiss to the palm and folded her fingers over it.

It was only hours later, as she lay in bed watching dawn slip over the city, that Tally realized Dante hadn't actually said he'd agree.

CHAPTER EIGHT

TALLY WAS UP at six the next morning.

Sam was still asleep in the next room, sprawled on her belly in her new crib, flanked by both her teddy bears.

Tally smiled, bent down and pressed a light kiss to her daughter's hair. Then she showered, put on a clean blouse but the same black suit and took a critical look at herself in the mirror.

She needed to buy clothes. If you looked successful, people assumed that you were. It wasn't the best way to judge anyone but that was how it went, especially in this town.

Her pay would be based partly on salary and expenses, partly on the cost of the completed project. So far, no one had mentioned when she'd get a check. She hated to ask, especially because it was Dante she'd have to go to, but she'd have to work up to it, and soon.

Tally gave her image another glance, then took a deep breath. Maybe she'd be lucky and Dante would already have left for the day.

No such luck.

He was in the sun-filled breakfast room, seated at

a round glass table with a cup of black coffee in his hand and the business section of the *New York Times* in front of him.

He looked up as Tally entered, and half rose from his chair. She motioned him to stay seated and went to the sideboard to pour herself coffee. It was easier to do that than to think about the fact that this was the very first time they'd had breakfast together.

"Good morning," he said. "Did you sleep well?"

She nodded. "Fine, thank you." A lie, of course. She'd tossed half the night, thinking of him in a room just down the stairs. "Thank you, too, for having that baby intercom installed between my room and Sam's."

"No problem. Actually, I had monitors installed throughout the place. I thought it would make you feel more comfortable, knowing you could hear Samantha no matter where you were."

"That was very thoughtful," she said politely, and sipped at her coffee.

"Sit down and join me."

There was no way to turn down the request, especially since he'd risen to his feet and was pulling out the chair opposite his. She thanked him, slipped into the chair and tried to concentrate on the coffee. It wasn't an easy thing to do.

Dante was a major distraction.

He was—there was no other word for it—he was beautiful. Not in a feminine way but beautiful all the same, wearing what she knew was a custom-made dark-blue suit, a pale-blue shirt from the city's most distinguished shirtmaker, and a maroon silk tie. His dark hair was curling and damp from the shower.

Another first.

They'd never breakfasted together, and she'd never seen him fresh from the shower. They'd had long bouts of incredible sex but afterward, he'd always dressed and gone home to shower. He preferred his own things, he'd told her. His soap, his razor, his toiletries, and she'd understood that what he'd really meant was that sex was one thing but showering was another, that he would only take intimacy just so far....

"Tally?"

She blinked. Dante had pushed a vellum envelope and a leather-bound notebook toward her.

"Sorry." She gave a polite little laugh. "I was—I was just trying to plan my day."

"I've already planned some of it for you. I hope you don't mind, but I want you to get up to speed as quickly as possible."

"Oh. Oh, no. I want that, too."

"There's a check in the envelope. Call it a signing bonus. If it isn't enough—"

"I'm sure it'll be fine. Thank you."

"Don't thank me. You're going to work hard to earn your money. You'll find your appointments for today listed in the notebook. For right now—" Dante glanced at his watch, pushed back his chair and rose to his feet "—I have to get going. Carlo will take you to the office."

"Your driver? Won't you need him?"

"I'm flying to Philadelphia. I'll take a cab to the airport."

Philadelphia. How long would he be gone? Would he be back by evening? It was better if he weren't. Then she wouldn't have to imagine returning here, seeing him, saying something banal as she went to the guest suite and he went out because he would go out, wouldn't he? There had to be a woman in his life. He was too virile a man to be without one.

But if there were, would he have kissed *her?* Would he have said he wanted to make love to her? Would he look at her as he had last night, as if he could almost feel her in his arms, hear her moans, because she would moan if he touched her, and—what was wrong with her today? She couldn't live here and imagine these things.

"Tally?"

"Yes?"

"You seem…distracted."

Heat rushed to her face. "No, not at all." Quickly, to cover her embarrassment, she added, "You said you're flying to Philadelphia?"

"And that my P.A., Joan, will show you around. She took care of furnishing your office. If it doesn't please you, tell her to make whatever changes you wish. Joan's also the one who scheduled your appointments, so if you have any questions—"

"Ask Joan."

Dante nodded and walked around the table to where she sat.

"She's organized meetings for you with half a dozen prospective assistants."

He was leaning over her; his scent drifted to her. Soap, water and pure, sexy essence of Dante. That was how she'd always thought of the smell of his skin. She'd never forgotten it or the memories it evoked.

His taste on her tongue. The feel of him, under her hands.

"I'm right," he said softly.

Tally looked up. His face was close to hers, his eyes a deep, cool gray.

"Something's definitely distracting you, *cara*. What could it be?"

"Nothing. I'm just—I'm concentrating on what you said. My office. Appointments with possible assistants. What else?"

"Did Mrs. Tipton tell you that she and Ellen will be happy to look after Sam, until you've hired a nanny?"

He leaned closer. All she had to do was turn her head an inch and her lips would brush his jaw.

"She told me. That's very—" she cleared her throat "—that's very kind of them. I'll contact an agency first thing and—"

"Joan's already taken care of it. A highly recommended agency is sending over half a dozen women for you to interview. They all have impeccable credentials, but again, if you're not satisfied, all you need do is inform Joan."

His shoulder brushed hers. Was it her imagination, or could she feel the heat of him through all the layers of clothing separating them?

"Tally? Is that acceptable?"

His eyes were on hers. The color had gone from gray to silver. Silver that somehow burned like flame.

"It's—it's fine."

"Because," he said, his voice suddenly low and husky, "because, *cara,* we can always alter the arrangement we made."

He wasn't talking about the office or her appointments, and they both knew it.

"No," she said, "we can't. I want things exactly as we agreed."

"Are you certain?"

The only thing she was certain of was that she had to get herself under control because she couldn't do this. Think about him making love to her, want him making love to her...

She took a deep breath. "Yes."

"In that case, there's nothing left to do this morning." His gaze dropped to her lips. "Except this," he said softly, and brushed his mouth over hers.

"No," she said, hating the soft, breathless quality of her voice.

"You're starting a new career and I'm flying to an important meeting. It's just a kiss for luck. Surely, I'm allowed that?"

"Dante. We can't—"

"We aren't."

He put his hand under her chin, lifted her face and claimed her mouth with his. And she—she let it happen. Let him slide the tip of his tongue between her lips, let him thrust his fingers into her hair, let him deepen the kiss until she was dizzy with wanting him....

Dante let go of her, straightened and took a sleek black leather briefcase from the sideboard.

And then he was gone.

TALLY'S DAY WAS LONG, exhausting—and wonderful.

Her office was a huge, light-filled room, handsomely furnished and perfectly equipped. Selecting an assistant was difficult only because all the candidates Dante's P.A. had chosen were outstanding.

It would have been equally tough to choose one of the nannies but a middle-aged woman with a soft Scottish lilt made things easier when she spotted Sam's photo on Tally's desk and crooned, "Och, the sweet little lamb!"

There was nothing difficult in deciding that Dante's P.A. was the eighth wonder of the world. Joan was fiftyish, elegant, and as warm as she was efficient.

"Just let me know what you need," she said, "and it's as good as yours."

At lunchtime, Tally dashed to Fifth Avenue and did the sort of lightning-fast shopping trip she used to do in the past. Within an hour, she'd bought several trousers, skirts, blazers, cashmere sweaters and a couple of pairs of shoes.

At four, she met with Dante's architect, who showed her the interior changes he was going to make in the new offices. At five, she met with one of her old contacts at the design center. At six, she dismissed Dante's driver and headed for the subway.

Dante would not kiss her anymore, and she would not accept any more favors from him. She was working with him. It was only right that they maintain appropriate behavior.

There was a delay on the subway line. A quarter of an hour passed before the train came and after that, it sat between stations for five endless minutes. When she reached her stop, she went half a block out of her way to buy a chocolate Santa for Sam.

She'd called to talk with her baby half a dozen times and the last time, she'd promised to bring a special treat.

By the time she reached Dante's apartment building,

Tally was feeling wonderful. She was back in the city she loved, involved in a major project, and she'd made peace with the problem of dealing with Dante.

All she had to do was make sure he understood the parameters of their relationship, and—

"Where have you been?"

Dante stood in the entrance to the building, blocking her way. His voice was rough, his face white with unconcealed anger.

"I beg your pardon?"

Mouth set, he clasped her arm and marched her past the doorman to the penthouse elevator.

"I asked you a question. Where the hell were you? You should have been here an hour ago."

She swung toward him, her temper rising to match his as he pushed her, unceremoniously, into the car.

"I should have been here an hour ago?" Tally slapped her hands on her hips. "Are you out of your mind? I don't have to answer to you!"

"You left the office at six. An hour late."

"How nice. You have people spying on me."

"And turned down the use of my car."

"Is your driver a paid informer?"

"And where did you go for lunch? I phoned and you hadn't told Joan or your new assistant where you'd be."

Tally was trembling with anger. "Where I went and why I went there is none of your business. Unless—" The color drained from her face. "Ohmygod, is it Sam? Is my baby ill?"

"No!" Dante stepped in front of her as the car doors opened on his penthouse. "Listen to me. Samantha's fine. This has nothing to do with her."

Sweet relief flooded through her, but it didn't last. She'd accepted a job from this man and moved into his guest suite. If he thought that made her his property, he was wrong.

"Then, get out of my way," she said coldly. "I don't answer to you."

"You damned well will," he said grimly, his hand closing like a steel band around her wrist. "This is New York, not a blip on the map in Vermont. Anything might happen to you on these streets."

"What a short memory you have, Russo!" Tally jerked free of his hand. "I know all about New York. I lived here for five years!"

She had. He knew that. She'd traveled the city's streets, ridden its subways, lived in an apartment alone. Of course he knew that…but things had changed.

He told her so, and she looked at him as if he'd gone crazy.

"Nothing's changed. The city's the same. So am I."

"You're not." His mouth twisted and the ugly suspicions he'd tried to deny while he'd paced the floor and wondered where she was, burst from his lips. "You slept with another man while you belonged to me. How do I know you're not seeing him again?"

Tally's eyes went flat. "You don't," she said coldly, and brushed past him.

Dante let her go. He had to; he was still rational enough to know that if he went after her now, it was a sure bet he'd do something he'd regret.

So he turned his back, strode along the marble floor to the library, flung open the liquor cabinet and poured himself a stiff shot of bourbon. And began pacing again, back and forth on the antique silk carpet before the fireplace, while the hours ticked away.

She'd all but called him crazy.

Hell, maybe she was right.

How come he hadn't thought about this before? All the plans he'd made to bring Tally back to New York and it had never occurred to him that he might be pushing her straight into the arms of her old lover.

The man who'd made her pregnant.

If he wasn't crazy, he was just plain stupid, because the idea hadn't even popped into his head until he'd been at lunch in Philadelphia after a morning of meetings. Somewhere between the salad course and the entrée, he'd suddenly realized he wanted to hear Tally's voice. He'd excused himself, left the table and phoned.

But she wasn't at her office, and Joan had no idea where she'd gone. He'd started to call her on her cell phone, only to realize that he didn't have the number.

He'd gone back to the table. Shoved the grilled shrimps and vegetables back and forth on his plate. Said "yes" and "no" and "how interesting" when it seemed fitting.

And all the while, he'd been thinking, *Where is she? Where did she go?*

That was when he'd first realized that bringing her back to the city might have been a mistake. That even now, while he pretended to pay attention to the details of a billion-dollar deal, Tally might be lying in the arms of the man she'd left him for. She'd slept with the man only once, she'd said, but Tally wasn't like that.

She wouldn't be anybody's one-night stand.

Had she lied about that? Had the bastard been her

lover for weeks? For months? Did she want to go back to him now?

Why would she, when he'd abandoned her when she was pregnant?

He had abandoned her, hadn't he? Because if he hadn't, if something, who the hell knew what, had kept Tally and the SOB apart and that something no longer stood between them—

You are losing your mind, Dante had told himself.

The warning hadn't helped.

Everyone ordered coffee. He lifted his cup, frowned, put it down untouched. He was sorry, he said; he had to leave. And he walked away from three men who stared at him as if they agreed with the silent assessment he'd made of his sanity.

He'd flown back to New York, angry at himself, furious at Tally because it was her fault, all of this, his rage, his distrust, his inability to do anything except think about her. If only she'd never run from him…

Her fault. Entirely.

At home, he'd paced the floor, planning how he'd tell her that if she thought she was going to live with him and take someone else for a lover, she was wrong.

He'd kill the other man before he let that happen.

Then he'd told himself that she wasn't living with him, not in any real sense. Besides, maybe she hadn't gone back to the other man. Maybe she'd told him the truth, that she'd only been with that faceless stranger the one time.

One time had been enough.

The son of a bitch had planted a seed in her womb. He'd given her a child he hadn't helped support, a child who was solely Tally's responsibility. A child who by all rights should have belonged to—should have belonged to—

The clock on the mantel had struck the hour. Seven o'clock. Seven at night, and where the hell was she?

Carlo had no idea. Ms. Sommers had sent his car away. Joan, reached at home, didn't know a thing, either.

And Dante, fueled with a rage he didn't understand, had lost control. He'd paced some more, snarled at his housekeeper when she came in to ask what time he wanted dinner served and, when he was alone again, punched his fist into the wall with such force he was surprised he hadn't put a hole in it.

He went down to the lobby, about to head into the street to find Tally—though he had no idea where in hell he'd start—and saw her come sauntering toward the door, with a smile for the doorman and a blank look for him.

He'd wanted to shake her until her teeth rattled.

He'd wanted to haul her into his arms and kiss her.

In the end, because he knew doing either would be a mistake, he'd launched into a tirade that settled nothing except to prove, once again, he was an idiot where she was concerned.

Dante looked at the clock on the mantel. The hours had raced by. It was two in the morning; the city below was as quiet as it would ever be.

Two in the morning, and he was still ticking like a time bomb while Tally undoubtedly slept peacefully two floors above him.

He tilted the glass to his lips and drained it of bourbon.

Did she get a kick out of this? Out of making him

behave this way? Surely, she knew she had this effect on him.

She did it deliberately.

That was why he'd decided to end their affair three years ago. He hadn't been bored. Who could be bored by a woman who could discuss the stock market and football statistics without missing a beat?

A muscle knotted in his jaw.

He could afford a little honesty now, couldn't he? Admit to himself that the reason he'd wanted to end things was because he'd sensed his feelings for her were becoming uncontrollable?

That night she'd asked him to stay, and he almost had. Other nights when she hadn't asked, when he'd had to force himself from her bed because the thought of leaving her had been agony.

Oh, yes.

Tally was manipulating him. Toying with him and the self-discipline on which he prided himself. The self-discipline that had made him a success.

And he didn't like it, not one bit.

Dante's eyes narrowed. But he knew what to do about it. How to regain that control. Of himself. Of the situation.

Of Tally.

Back to Plan A. He would take her to bed.

He had perfect control there. Holding back, not just physically but emotionally. Exulting in what happened between them, feeling it as a hot rush of pleasure so intense he'd never known it with another woman and yet, keeping a little piece of himself from her.

Emotions were not things to put on exhibit. Control was a man's sole protection against a hostile world.

Control, goddamn it, Dante thought.

His hands knotted into fists. Anger burned like a fire in his belly. Anger, and something far more primitive.

Tally was asleep, satisfied she'd made a fool of him again, and he was here, wide awake, trapped like an insect in a web of rage.

"Enough," he growled.

Dante flung open the library door and headed for the stairs.

CHAPTER NINE

MOONLIGHT SPILLED from a sky bright with stars and lay like fine French lace across the floor of Tally's bedroom.

Some other time, she'd have noticed and admired it.

Not tonight.

Instead, she sat curled in a window seat, her back to the night, focused only on the turmoil inside her, anger and pain warring for control of her heart.

She hated Dante, hated the things he'd accused her of. How could he think her capable of being a cheat and a liar?

Maybe because you told him you slept with another man while he was still your lover, a voice inside her whispered contemptuously.

Yes. All right, but what else could she have done? She'd wanted to protect herself and Sam. Now she knew she'd done the right thing. Dante had shown a side of himself she'd never imagined.

She'd always believed he was a man who suppressed his emotions.

Tonight, he'd been a man out of control, capable of anything.

Tally shivered and drew the silk robe more closely around herself. The night seemed endless, especially without Sam in the next room. The baby had dozed off in her play crib in the little room next to the housekeeper's.

"Let her stay the night, Ms. Sommers," Mrs. Tipton had said. "Why wake her from a sound sleep?"

Now Tally was glad she'd left Sam where she was. Her little girl needed the rest. Tomorrow was going to be a busy day.

She and Sam were going home to Shelby.

She'd scrub floors for a living, move into a furnished flat above a storefront on Main Street if she had to. Better that, better to raise her daughter in poverty, than to raise her here.

Tally rose to her feet and paced the bedroom, the details of her confrontation with Dante as alive as if they'd happened minutes instead of hours ago.

What gave him the right to ask where she'd been? To accuse her of sneaking off to be with Samantha's father? She'd come within a breath of laughing in his face at that, except it really wasn't funny.

Okay. She'd made a mistake, accepting this job. Well, a mistake could be remedied. And maybe some good had come of it. At least now she knew exactly what she felt for Dante Russo.

She despised him.

Tally paused, wrapped her arms around herself and drew a shuddering breath. She had to do something or go crazy. She'd pack. Yes. That was an excellent idea. She'd pack now. That way, come morning, all she'd have to do was take Sam and get the hell out of this snake pit.

Ellen had hung all her clothes in the closet, including the things Saks had delivered this afternoon. Tally dumped her old stuff in her suitcase and ignored the rest. Let Dante give it away. Let him burn it, for all she gave a damn.

She didn't want anything his money had bought.

He was a heartless, manipulative, controlling son of a bitch and it made her sick to think she'd ever imagined that she loved him. Anybody could be guilty of a bit of self-deception, but once you knew it you had to do something about it.

She'd spent years in the city, though maybe she was still a small-town girl at heart, unable or unwilling to think she'd slept with a man, borne his child without loving him.

But no woman could love a man who thought he owned you. Who believed you capable of lies and deceit and—

The bedroom door flew open, the sound of it sharp as a gunshot in the quiet night. Tally whirled around.

Dante stood in the doorway, and her heart leaped into her throat.

This was a Dante she'd never seen before.

His suit jacket was gone, as was his tie. His shirt was open at the neck, the sleeves rolled to the elbows, exposing forearms knotted with muscle.

But it was what she saw in the way he held himself that terrified her. The tall, powerful body poised like a big cat's. The dark intensity of his eyes as they fixed on hers. The cruel little smile that tilted across his mouth.

Tally wanted to run but there was nowhere to go. She had to face the enemy.

"What are you doing here, Dante?"

He answered by stepping inside the room and shutting the door behind him.

"It's late," she said.

"I agree. It's very late. I'm here to remedy that."

"And—and Samantha is sleeping. I don't want to wake her."

"Samantha is with Mrs. Tipton." He took another step forward. "Taylor."

He was back to using her given name. How could he make it seem menacing?

"Dante." Her voice quavered. "Dante, please. You want to talk. So do I. But it can wait until morning."

"I don't want to talk, Taylor."

A sob burst from Tally's throat. To hell with facing the enemy. She turned and ran. Sam's bedroom was empty. If she could get there before he reached her—

Two quick steps, and his powerful hands closed on her shoulders; he spun her toward him and she looked up into eyes that glittered with the desolate cold of a polar night.

"No! Don't. Dante—"

He captured her mouth with his, forced her lips apart and penetrated her with his tongue. He tasted of anger and of whiskey, and of a primitive domination that terrified her.

"No," she cried, and struggled to free herself from his grasp, but he laughed, pushed her back against the wall and yanked her hands high above her head.

"Fight me," he growled. "Go on. Fight! It'll make taking you even more pleasurable."

"Please," she panted. "Dante, please. Don't do this. I beg you—"

"All those months I made love to you and it wasn't enough. Is that why you went to him? Did he do things I didn't?"

"Dante. I never—"

He ripped the robe apart, tore her nightgown from the vee between her breasts straight down to her belly.

"Tell me what you wanted that I didn't give you."

"You're wrong. Wrong! It wasn't the way you make it sound. I didn't—"

She cried out as he captured one breast in his hand and rubbed his thumb across the nipple, his cold eyes locked to hers.

"Was it the way he touched your breasts?"

Tears were streaming down her face. Good, he thought. Let her weep. It wouldn't stop him. He would do this. Pierce her flesh with his and banish her from his life, forever.

"Was it the way he touched you here?"

He thrust his hand between her thighs, searching, even in his madness, for the welcoming heat, the sweet moisture he had never forgotten...

And found, instead, the cold, dry flesh of a woman who was unready and unwilling. A woman who was sobbing as if her heart were breaking...

As she had broken his.

Dante went still. He looked at Tally's face and felt the coldness inside him melting.

"Tally."

His arms went around her; he gathered her to him, his hands stroking her back, her hair. He kissed her forehead, her wet eyes, and as she wept he whispered to her, soft words in his native language, but she stood rigid within his embrace, still quietly crying as if the world were about to end.

"Tally." Dante framed her face between his hands. "*Inamorata*. Forgive me. Please. Don't cry. I won't hurt you. I could never hurt you." He raised her chin, looked into her eyes and saw a darkness and despair that chilled his soul.

He dragged in a deep breath, hating himself, hating what he had almost done, knowing that what was driving him was not hate or anger but something else. Something foreign to his life and to him.

A fear he'd never known gripped him.

He'd fought toughs on the streets of Palermo. Faced down CEOs in hostile boardrooms. Made believers of financial analysts who'd looked him in the eye and assured him he couldn't do any of the things he'd ended up doing.

He was a warrior. Each battle he survived made him stronger.

But he wasn't a warrior now. He was a man, holding in his arms a woman he'd already lost once before. She had run from him and he knew, in his heart of hearts, that she'd run because he had somehow failed her.

She'd turned to another man for the same reason.

If she ran again, if he lost her again…

"Tally."

He held her closer. Rained kisses over her hair. Said her name over and over, and finally, finally when he'd almost given up hope, she lifted her face to his.

"I wasn't with anyone," she whispered. "I never wanted anyone but you, Dante. Never. Never. Nev—"

He kissed her. With all his heart, his soul, with all he had ever been or ever hoped to be, and Tally wound her arms around his neck and kissed him back. They had kissed a thousand times. A million times…but never like this, as if their lives hung in the balance.

Mouths fused, Dante swept Tally into his arms and carried her to the bed.

At first, it was enough. The taste of her mouth. The warmth of his breath. Her sighs. His whispers. The stroke of her hand on his face, of his hand on her throat…

It was enough.

Inevitably, it changed.

Dante could feel the tension growing inside him. The need to take more. To give more. To suck Tally's nipples, put his mouth between her thighs and inhale her exquisite scent.

It was the same for Tally. She needed Dante's mouth on her flesh. His hands on her breasts. Needed to lift her hips to him, impale herself on his rock-hard erection so that she could fly with him to the stars.

"Dante," she whispered.

Everything a man could dream was in the way she spoke his name.

He eased the robe and tattered nightgown from her shoulders, kissing the hollow in her throat, the delicate skin over her collarbone.

She was lovely. As beautiful as he'd remembered.

There was a new fullness to her breasts now. The child, Dante thought, and felt a swift pain at the realization that someone else had given that child to her, but it left him quickly because there was so much more to the woman in his arms than that one moment of infidelity.

He bent his head, kissed the slope of each breast. Brushed a finger lightly over a pale-pink nipple.

Watched her face as he played the nub of flesh delicately between thumb and forefinger, and felt the fierce tightening low in his belly when she sobbed his name as he drew the nub into his mouth.

She tasted like cream and honey; she tasted like the Tally he'd never forgotten, never wanted to forget, and when she tugged impatiently at his shirt he sat up, tried unbuttoning it, cursed and tore it off. Peeled off the rest of his clothing and took her in his arms again.

The hot feel of her breasts against his chest almost undid him. Dante groaned, clenched his teeth, warned himself to hang onto his control.

But she was moving beneath him, rubbing herself against his engorged flesh. She was slick and hot, and the exciting scent of her arousal was more precious to him than all the perfumes in the world.

"Please," she said, kissing his shoulder. "Please, please, please…"

"Soon," he whispered, but she arched against him and he was lost. Nothing mattered but this. This, he thought, and entered her on one long, hard thrust.

Tally screamed. Her hands dug into his hair; she wrapped her legs around his hips and bit his shoulder and he let go. Of himself, of his past, of the restraints that had always defined his life.

Together, they soared over the edge of the earth, two hearts, two souls, two bodies merged as one.

AFTERWARD, they lay in each other's arms and shared soft kisses. They touched and sighed, and then Tally's breathing slowed.

"Go to sleep, *inamorata*," Dante whispered.

"What does that mean? *Inamorata?*"

He kissed her. "It means beloved."

Tally smiled and he kissed her again.

"Go to sleep."

"I'm not sleepy," she murmured.

And slept.

Dante gathered her closer against him. How had he endured three long years without this woman in his life?

Except, he had never really let her into his life. They'd been lovers for six months back then but he'd kept his distance. He always did. Dinners out at the city's best restaurants instead of pasta and vino by the fire. Center row seats at the newest Broadway show instead of an evening of old movies on the DVD. Dancing at the latest club instead of swaying in each other's arms to a Billy Joel CD.

How come?

And how come he didn't even know if she liked old movies? If she liked Billy Joel or maybe newer stuff?

Because he'd never let her into his life. That was how come. It was the same reason he'd called her Taylor, when any fool could see that under all the urban glamour, she was really a girl named Tally.

And he—and he felt something special for her.

His arms tightened around her. He wanted to make love to her again but she was sleeping so soundly…

Okay. He'd kiss her closed eyes. Gently. Like that. Kiss her mouth. Tenderly. Yes, that way. Kiss it again and if she sighed, as she was sighing now, if her lips parted so that he could taste her sweetness, yes, like that… If her lashes fluttered and she looked up at him and smiled and linked her hands behind his neck the way she was doing now, would it be wrong to kiss her again? To run his hand gently down her body? To groan as she lifted herself to him, cradled his body between her thighs?

"Make love to me," Tally whispered.

And he would. He would—but first, he lifted her in his arms and rose from the bed.

"Where are we going?"

"To my room," he said huskily. "To my bed. It's where you belong, *inamorata,* where you always should have been." He kissed her. "Where you will be, from this night on."

HIS ROOM WAS SHADOWED, his bed high and wide.

They made love again, slowly, tenderly, until passion swept them up and Dante brought Tally down on him, impaled her on him, and watched her face as she rode him to fulfillment. They slept in each other's arms and awakened again at dawn, Tally wordlessly drawing Dante to her, sighing his name against his throat as he rocked into her and took her with him to the stars.

When she awoke next, it was to the kiss of the morning sun. Dante lay next to her, head propped on his fist, watching her with a soft smile on his lips.

Tally smiled, too. "Hello," she whispered.

He leaned over and kissed her mouth. "Hello, *bellissima.*"

She stretched with lazy abandon. The sheet dropped to her waist. Dante seized the moment and kissed her breasts.

"Sweet," he murmured.

She smiled again. She might never stop smiling, she thought, clasping his face between her hands and pressing a light kiss to his lips.

"I love it when you kiss me," he said softly.

She loved it, too. She could spend the morning like this, just kissing, touching, locked away from reality....

Oh, God. Locked away from Samantha.

"Tally. What's wrong?"

Everything, Tally thought, and it was all her fault. She moved out of Dante's arms and sat up, suddenly conscious of her nudity.

Dante sat up, too, and caught her in his arms. "Talk to me. What's the matter?"

"Sam's an early riser."

"Is that what's worrying you?" Smiling, he drew her to him. "So is Mrs. Tipton."

"Sam is my daughter. My responsibility. Not your housekeeper's."

"Damn it, Tally, don't look away from me." He clasped her face, forced her eyes to meet his. "Moments ago you were in my arms. Now you're looking at me as if we're strangers. Talk to me. Tell me what you're thinking."

Tell him what? That the long, wonderful night had been a mistake? Because it had been. Yes, he'd brought her to his bed, but nothing had changed. She loved him. Why lie to herself? She loved him, she always would...

And all he felt for her was desire.

It hadn't been enough three years ago. It was why she'd decided to leave him, even before she'd known she was carrying his baby. She'd loved him so much that hearing him say he'd tired of her would have killed her.

Now she'd put herself in the same position. He wanted her because she'd defied him, but the novelty would wear thin. He'd tire of her as he had in the past and they'd be right back where they started, with one enormous difference.

This time, she wouldn't be the only one who'd pay the price for her foolishness.

Samantha would pay, as well.

Her daughter. Dante's daughter. God, oh God, oh God…

"Tally?"

She pulled free of his embrace, plucked his robe from the chair beside the bed and slipped it on.

"Dante." Tally got to her feet. "This was—it was a mistake."

He sat up, the comforter dropping to his waist. "What are you talking about?" he said, his voice sharp.

"I shouldn't have slept with you." She tried not to look at him as he rose from the bed, naked and beautifully masculine. "I—I enjoyed last night." The look on his face made her take a quick step back. "But it shouldn't have happened. I have a daughter. That makes everything different. I can't just live for the moment anymore, I have to think of her. Of how much what I do affects her."

"You're a fine mother, *bellissima.* Anyone can see that."

"I try to be. And that means I can't—I can't sleep with you and then go about my life as if nothing's happened. I can't—" Tally caught her breath as he reached for her. "You're not listening."

"I am," he said softly. Gently, he brushed his lips over hers. "You don't want your little girl to see her mother take a lover."

"That's part of it."

"To live a life with her, and a separate one with him."

Tally nodded. He was more perceptive than she'd given him credit for. "She won't understand. And I can't do something that will confuse her. Do you see?"

"Better than you think, *cara*." He hesitated. "I only wish my own mother had thought the same way."

The words were simple but they caught her by surprise. He had never mentioned anything about his past before.

"She took lover after lover," he said, his mouth twisting, "if that's what you want to call them. Sometimes she brought them home. 'This is Guiseppe,' she'd say. Or Angelo or Giovanni or whoever he was, the man of the hour. Then she'd tell me to be a good boy and go out and play."

"Oh, Dante. That must have been—"

"When I was six, seven—I'm not certain. All I know is that one day, she took me to my *nonna's*—my grandmother's. 'Be a good boy, Dante,' she said. And—"

"And?" Tally said softly.

He shrugged. "And I never saw her again."

Tally wanted to take him in her arms and hold him close, but she didn't. She sensed that the moment was fragile, that it would take little to tear it apart.

"I'm sorry," she said quietly. "That must have been— it must have been hard."

Another shrug, as if it didn't matter, but when he spoke, the tension in his voice told her that it did.

"I survived."

"And grew into a strong, wonderful man."

Dante looked at her. "Not so wonderful," he said, "or you wouldn't have left me three years ago."

This time, she did reach out, even if it was only to touch her hand to his cheek.

"I grew up living with my grandmother, too," she said quietly.

"In that little house in Vermont?"

She nodded. "My mother was—Grandma called her flighty." She managed a quick smile. "What it really means is that she took off when I was little and never came back. My father had already done the same thing, even before I was born."

Dante gathered her into his arms.

"What a pair we make," he said gently.

Tally nodded again. "All the more reason that I can't—why we can't—"

"Yes. I agree," he murmured, tucking a strand of hair behind her ear, "and I have the perfect solution."

"There is no solution. I have to protect Sam." *Sam and me.*

"Of course there is." Dante tilted her face to his. "You'll move out of the guest suite."

One night? Was that all he'd wanted? Tally forced herself to nod in agreement.

"Of course. I'll find an apartment and—"

"And," he said softly, "you'll move in with me. We'll let Sam see that we are—that we are together. That we are part of each other's lives, and that she is, too."

Tally stared at him, her face a mask of confusion. Was she trying to find a way to tell him she wouldn't go along with his plan? It had come to him during the night; he'd been pleased with it until this moment, when he realized that Tally might not want to be with him this way.

"Tally." His hands slid to her shoulders. "Please." His fingers bit into her flesh. "Tell me want to be with me. I don't want to lose you again. Say yes."

Her head whispered of reservations, of questions, of why the arrangement would never work…

But Tally listened to her heart and said, "Yes."

CHAPTER TEN

THROUGHOUT THE AGES, wise men caution that a man who makes decisions in the heat of the moment might very well live to regret them.

Dante had always agreed.

He was not impulsive. He made choices only after he had examined all the facts. If a man did anything less, he might, indeed, live to regret his decisions.

And yet, he'd acted on impulse when he'd asked Tally to live with him.

It should have been a mistake. The worst mistake of his life, considering that he'd never asked a woman to do that before. Living together, spending your days and nights with one woman, was the kind of involvement he'd always avoided. He liked to come and go as he pleased, to spend time in a woman's company only when he was in the mood.

Add a small child to the mix and a man would surely go crazy.

At least, that was what he'd have said of this new arrangement a week ago. A disaster in the making, he'd have called it...

Dante smiled as he stood at his office window and watched the lights wink on over Manhattan.

He'd have been wrong.

Asking Tally to live with him had turned out to be the best decision he'd ever made. Being with her, with Samantha, had already changed his life.

He'd lived in New York for more than a dozen years and most of that time he'd lived very comfortably. As his fortune grew, he'd become accustomed to a certain start and finish to his day.

In the morning, his housekeeper would ask if he'd be home for dinner; in the evening, she'd inquire pleasantly as to how his day had gone. If the doorman made a comment beyond "Good morning" or "Good evening" it was about the weather. His driver might exchange a few polite words with him about European soccer or American football.

Dante's smile became a grin. How that had changed!

Mrs. Tipton regaled him with stories about Sam. Carlo, whose grandson turned out to be Sam's age, was a font of helpful advice. Even the doorman got into the act with details of Sam's latest adventure among the big potted plants in the lobby.

Sam herself, a bundle of energy with big green eyes and a toothy grin, started and ended his days with sloppy kisses.

Amazing, all of it.

But most amazing was his Tally, who fell asleep in his arms each night and awoke in them each morning. She was the most incredible woman he'd ever known, and he wasn't the only one who thought so.

His architect told him she had the best eye for detail

he'd ever seen. His contractor said she made suggestions that were as innovative as they were practical. Even his P.A., a woman who had seen everything and was surprised by nothing, called her remarkable.

His household staff flat-out adored her.

But not as much as he did.

Dante tucked his hands in his trouser pockets and rocked back on his heels. He'd never believed in luck. What you got out of life was in direct proportion to what you put into it, and yet he knew it was luck, good fortune, whatever you wanted to call it, that had given him this second chance with Tally.

He'd lost her through his own callous behavior. He understood that now. He'd treated her like a possession, taking her from the shelf when he wanted to show her off, returning her when he'd finished. It was how he'd always treated his lovers. Kept them at a distance, bought them elaborate gifts, and politely eliminated them from his life when he got bored.

Dante's jaw clenched.

But Tally had never behaved like his other lovers. She'd kept herself at a distance. That was why she'd refused his elaborate gifts and left behind the ones he'd insisted she accept. And she had never bored him. Never. Not for a moment, in bed or out.

At some point, he'd realized it. And it had shaken him to the core. He'd reacted by pushing her away because he hadn't been ready to admit what she had come to mean to him. As recently as a few weeks ago, he'd still been lying to himself about his feelings for her.

That whole thing about wanting to sleep with her to get revenge, get her out of his system…

Sheer, unadulterated idiocy.

It had always been easier to pretend she was just another woman passing through his life than admit his Tally was special. That what he felt for her was special. That what he felt for her was—that it was—

"Dante?"

He swung around, saw her in the doorway and felt his heart swell. And when she smiled, he thought it might burst.

"I knocked," she said, with a little smile, "but you didn't—"

Dante held out his arms. She went into them and he held her close.

"You look beautiful," he said softly.

She leaned back in his embrace. "Not too dressed up?"

He shook his head. "Perfect."

That was the only word to describe her in a softly clinging silk dress and matching jacket in a color he'd have called green but he suspected women gave a more complex name. Her shoes were wispy things, all straps and slender heels, the kind that made a man imagine his woman wearing them with whatever was under the dress and nothing else.

Dante had a pretty good idea of what was under that dress. He'd bought Tally a drawer full of wispy lingerie from The Silk Butterfly, a shop he'd passed on Fifth Avenue.

"Hand-sewn lace," she'd said, her cheeks taking on a light blush. "I'll feel naked under my clothes." And he'd taken her in his arms and shown her just how exciting that would be for them both.

"I know tonight's important to you."

"You're what's important to me."

"Yes, but tonight—the Children's Fund dinner…"

"Tally. We don't have to go. I told you that. We can have a quiet dinner at that little place on the corner and—"

"No. No, I don't want you to change anything because of me. Everyone you know will be there."

"Everyone *we* know. And they'll see how happy we are to be together again."

She nodded, but her eyes were clouded. "There'll be questions."

Dante raised one eyebrow. "No one will dare to ask questions of me." That made her laugh, just as he'd hoped it would. He took her hand, brought it to his mouth and kissed it. "I missed you."

"You saw me an hour ago," she said with another little laugh.

"And that's far too long to be without you." He drew her closer. "It's going to cost you a kiss."

"Dante. Someone will see."

"I don't care."

"But—"

"If I don't get a kiss from you this very minute," he said dramatically, "my death will be on your hands."

She laughed again. He loved the sound of her laugh, the way her lips curved into an eminently kissable bow. He loved everything about her.

The truth was, he loved—he loved—

Dante bent his head and kissed her.

THEY ARRIVED a few minutes late and found five of their dinner companions already at the table. A well-known real estate agent and his third trophy wife. Dennis and Eve. A used-car salesman turned self-help guru, whose latest feel-good book had just gone into its fifth printing.

Tally remembered them all.

And, clearly, they remembered her. She could almost hear their jaws hit the table when they saw her.

Dante had his arm firmly around her waist.

"Good evening," he said pleasantly. "Tally, I think you know everyone here, don't you?"

"Yes," she said brightly, "of course. How are you, Lila? Donald? Eve and Dennis, how good to see you again. And Mark. Your newest book just came out, didn't it? I hope it's doing well?"

Dante pulled out her chair, whispered, "Good girl," as she slipped into it. He sat down beside her, took her hand and held it in his, right on the tabletop where everyone could see. Five pairs of eyes took in the sight. Then someone said, "Well, I see we're going to have chicken for the main course. Surprise, surprise."

Everyone laughed, and that broke the ice.

People began chatting. Wasn't the weather particularly cold for December? Was snow in the forecast again? Wasn't the ballroom handsomely decorated?

I might just get through this, Tally thought...

"DanteDarling," a woman screeched.

And Tally looked up, inhaled a cloud of obscenely expensive perfume, saw Charlotte LeBlanc swoop down to plant a kiss on Dante's mouth even as he jerked back in his chair, saw the woman's hate-filled gaze fix on her before she switched it to a big, artificial smile...

And knew, instinctively, that Charlotte LeBlanc had, probably until very recently, been Dante's mistress.

"Taylor," Charlotte said. "What a surprise!"

"Yes," Tally said, "yes, I—I suppose it is."

"A wonderful surprise," Dante said, squeezing Tally's hand, but he was looking at Charlotte, his eyes cold with warning, and any doubts Tally might have had about her lover's relationship with the LeBlanc woman vanished.

Conversation swirled around her, the polite stuff people discussed when they were casual acquaintances. Eve talked about her new hair stylist. Dennis said he was buying a new yacht. The self-help guru was also buying one. The real estate agent was too busy eating his shrimp cocktail to say anything. His trophy wife was silent, too, perhaps because her face was frozen in Botoxed bliss.

And suddenly, in a lull in the chatter, Charlotte leaned over, her breasts almost spilling from her neckline, and laid a taloned hand on Tally's arm.

"Taylor," she cooed, "you must tell us all where you've been the last few years."

"She's been in New England," Dante said smoothly. "Building a successful business."

"New England. How quaint." Her smile glittered with malice. "And are you here on business?"

"Taylor's working on a project of mine."

"How nice." Her head swiveled toward Dante. "And you, DanteDarling. Are you and I still on for Christmas in Aspen?"

Dante's eyes went black. "No," he said coldly, "we are not. I told you that weeks ago,"

"Oh, but everyone knows how you tend to change your mind, DanteDarling. How fickle you are, well, not about business but about, you know, other things."

There was no mistaking what "things" she meant. Heads swiveled from Charlotte to Tally to Dante, who snarled a word no one had to speak Sicilian to comprehend.

Charlotte turned red. Everyone else gasped. And Tally pushed her chair back from the table.

"Tally! Damn it, Tally…"

Luck was with her. The band was playing and the dance floor was crowded with couples. Tally wove through the mob, pulled open the door to the ladies' room and slammed it behind her. A sob burst from her throat.

How could she have been so stupid? He'd been with that woman. With Charlotte. He'd been with God only knew how many women these last three years. She'd dreamed of him, yearned for him, wanted only him despite all the lies she'd told herself, but Dante…

"Tally!"

His fist slammed against the door.

"Tally! Open this door or I'm coming in."

One of the stall doors swung open. A woman stepped out and stared at her.

"Tally, do you hear me? Open this goddamned door!"

Tally went to the sink, splashed cold water on her face. She would have ignored the hammering on the door but the woman who'd come out of the stall was looking at her as if she'd somehow wandered into the sort of situation that ended in bloodshed.

There was nothing for it but to square her shoulders and walk out of the ladies' room, straight into a muscled wall of male fury.

"Dante," she said quietly, "please, step aside."

He answered by clasping her shoulders and hauling her to her toes.

"If I'd known that bitch would be at our table," he demanded, "do you really think I'd have brought you here tonight?"

"It doesn't matter. Step aside, please."

"Of course it matters! Damn it, she means nothing to me!"

"Dante. Get out of my—"

"Are you deaf?" His hands bit hard into her flesh as he lowered his face to hers. "She doesn't matter."

"She matters enough so you were going to take her to Aspen."

"She suggested it. I said no. In fact, I never saw her after that evening. We were finished and she knew it."

Tally looked into his eyes. They were the color of smoke, and without warning, the pain inside her burst free.

"You slept with her," she whispered.

His mouth twisted. "Tally. *Bellissima…*"

"You should have told me. So I—I could have been prepared to see the way she looked at you. To know you'd been with her, made love to her—"

"It was sex," he said roughly. "Only sex. Never anything more."

She stared into his eyes again. *And what is it with me?* she longed to say, but her heart knew better than to ask.

"How many were there?" Her voice trembled and she hated herself for it. She'd known a man virile as Dante wouldn't live like a monk but to see the proof for herself… "How many women after me?"

His grasp on her tightened. "What does it matter? All

the years we were apart, I never stopped thinking of you. I hated you for leaving me, Tally—and hated myself for not being able to get over you."

Tally looked away from him, certain that her heart was going to break. If he couldn't get over her, how could he have betrayed her with other women? In the endless years since leaving him, she had never even thought of anyone else. She had never betrayed him…

But she had.

Running away had been a kind of betrayal. Even the cold, cleverly worded note she'd left had been a betrayal.

And then there was the cruelest betrayal of all. She'd told him she'd cheated on him with another man, that she'd given birth to that man's child.

"Tally." His voice was thick with anguish. "There's never been anyone but you. You must believe me!"

Slowly she lifted her eyes to his. "What I believe," she whispered, "is that we've both been fools."

He nodded. She could see color returning to his face.

"Yes. We have been, but we won't be any longer." He framed her face with his hands and raised it to his. "I'm not going to lose you again, *inamorata*. I won't let it happen."

Tears gathered on Tally's lashes. Gently Dante kissed them away. Then he wrapped his arm around her shoulders.

"Let's go home."

She smiled. "Yes. Let's go home."

He led her past the curious little group that had been watching them, out of the hotel and into his waiting limousine. Part of him wanted to go back to the ballroom, put his hands around Charlotte's throat and make her pay for what she'd done.

But he was every bit as guilty.

Not for having slept with Charlotte. Tally had been out of his life then. Not even for having not told her about Charlotte. He was a man, not a saint. What man would deliberately tell the woman he cared for that he'd slept with someone else, even if he'd been absolutely free to do so at the time?

He pressed a kiss to Tally's hair as she sat curled against him, her head on his shoulder.

His guilt was over what he'd done three years ago.

He'd let Tally slip away. And he should have gone after her. Should have faced what she meant to him because the truth was he didn't just care for her, he—he—

"Dante?"

Dante cleared his throat. "Yes, *cara?*"

"I'm sorry."

"No! It wasn't your fault."

"Not about tonight. I'm… I'm sorry for…for—" She took a deep breath and sat up straight, her eyes locked to his. "We need to talk. But not here. Someplace… someplace where we can be alone."

Suddenly he knew that was what he wanted, too. A quiet place where they could be alone. Where they could talk—and he could finally confront what was in his heart.

"I have an idea," he said slowly. "Christmas is next week. What if we spend it alone? Just the three of us. You and me and Samantha. We'll go somewhere warm, where we can lie in the sun in each other's arms, where Sam can run around to her heart's content. Would you like that?"

"A place where we can talk," Tally said softly.

Talk about what had really made her run away, she thought as Dante drew her against him, because tonight, she'd finally faced the truth.

No matter what happened, she had to tell Dante that she loved him.

That there'd never been another man.

That he was Sam's father.

CHAPTER ELEVEN

WHAT COULD BE more wonderful than lying in the curve of your lover's arm on a white sand beach under the hot Caribbean sun?

Tally turned her head and put her mouth lightly against Dante's bronzed skin, savoring the exciting taste of salt and man.

How she adored him!

Her Dante was everything a man should be. Strong. Tender. Giving. Demanding. Fiercely passionate, incredibly gentle. She loved him, loved him, loved him…

And it killed her that she'd lied to him.

That she was still lying to him, because she'd yet to tell him the truth about Sam.

Soon, she thought, as she closed her eyes and burrowed closer to his warm, hard body. She'd confess everything to him this evening, after dinner, when they were both tucking Sam in for the night. Or tomorrow morning, at breakfast. And if the time didn't seem right then, she'd wait just another few hours. Another few days…

Tally swallowed hard. *Liar,* she thought, *liar, liar, liar!*

She wouldn't tell him tonight, or tomorrow. Or ever,

at the rate she was going. She wanted to. Wanted to say, *Dante, I've done an awful thing. I lied to you about Sam. About being with someone else. Sam is your child. Ever since we met, there's only been you.*

The problem was, she could see beyond that.

She had let him think she'd been unfaithful.

She had denied him knowledge of his own child.

Who could predict how he'd react?

Some days, she was sure he would understand. Others, she was afraid he wouldn't. She'd thought it would be so easy to admit everything once they were here, on this beautiful island in the midst of a sea as clear as fine green glass, tucked away from the world in a magnificent house on its own long, pristine, private beach. Just the three of them: she and Dante and Samantha. No housekeeper. No maid. No nanny or chauffeur. Just she and the man she loved and her little girl.

Their little girl.

Except, Dante didn't know that yet because she was a coward, because she was terrified of what he'd say, what he'd do when he knew she'd deceived him in the worst way possible—

"*Bellissima,* what's wrong?" Tally's eyes flew open as Dante brushed his lips over hers. "You were whimpering in your sleep, *cara.* Were you having a bad dream?"

"I… I… Yes. Something like that."

Smiling, he kissed her again. "You've been in the sun too long. That's the problem."

Now. Tell him now!

"Dante."

"Hmm?" He bent to her and kissed her again, parting

her lips and slowly slipping the tip of his tongue into her mouth. "You taste delicious."

So did he. Oh, so did—

"Dante." Her breath caught. His mouth was at her throat, her breast, nipping lightly at the rapidly beading tip through the thin cotton of her bikini top. "Dante…"

"I'll bet you taste even more delicious here," he whispered as he slid his hands behind her, undid the top, his eyes shining brightest silver as he exposed her breasts. "Let me see if I'm right."

Tally cried out, arching against him as he drew her nipple into the wet heat of his mouth; even as he began easing her bikini bottom down her thighs, she felt it starting to happen, the shimmering heat building inside her, the hot rush of desire as he stroked her dampening curls, put his mouth to her until she was begging him, pleading with him, to take her.

Slowly, so slowly that she thought it might never end, prayed it might never end, he entered her. Filled her, stretched her, moved deep inside her while he whispered to her in Sicilian, words she didn't know but somehow understood, and she thought, *I love you, Dante. I've always loved you. Only you.*

And shattered like crystal in his arms.

AFTER, HE CARRIED HER into the house, past the room where Samantha lay sleeping, to their bedroom and their canopied bed overlooking the sea.

Gently, he lay her in the center of the white sheets, came down beside her and drew her into his arms. Tally put her face in his neck and sighed.

"I love it here," she said softly.

"I'm glad."

"The house is so beautiful. And the sea… I've never seen a sea this clear."

Dante smiled as he stroked his hand gently up and down her spine. "There's a beach on the Mediterranean where you can stand knee-deep in the water and watch tiny fish swim by like flashes of blue and green light."

Tally tilted her head back so she could see his face. "Is that where you lived with your *nonna?* In a town by the sea?"

"Nothing so postcard-perfect, *cara*. I grew up in Palermo, on a street that was already old when Rome ruled the world."

"It sounds wonderful. All that history—"

"Trust me, Tally. There was nothing wonderful about it. Everyone was dirt-poor, except for us." He gave a self-deprecating laugh. "We were poorer than that."

"Then, everything you have today—you built it all, from scratch?" She smiled. "The amazing Mr. Russo."

He grinned, lifted her so that she lay stretched out along his length.

Well," he said, "if you want to call me that—"

Tally rolled her eyes, brought her mouth to his and kissed him. "Don't let it go to your head," she said softly, "but you really are. Amazing."

Dante framed her face with his hands. "What's amazing," he whispered, "is you."

That brought her back to reality. "Dante," she said carefully, "Dante, do you remember what I said the other night? That we have to talk."

"I agree. We do." His eyes grew hooded. "But not right now."

"Dante. Please—"

"Please what?" He cupped her hips, eased her to her knees above him. "Please, this?" he whispered, and she felt the tip of his erection kiss her labia. "Tell me and I'll do it. I'll do whatever you want, *inamorata*. Anything. Everything…"

Then he was inside her, and words had no meaning. All that mattered was this. This…

This.

AN HOUR LATER, Dante eased his arm from beneath Tally's shoulders, touched his mouth lightly to hers, slipped on a pair of denim shorts and went to check on Sam.

The baby woke just as he peeked into her room. When she saw him, she grinned, said "Da-Tay" and held out her chubby arms. Dante grinned back, picked her up and gave her a kiss.

"Hello, *bambina*. Did you have a good nap?"

"Goo'nap," she said happily.

"I'll bet you need a diaper change."

"Di-chain," Sam gurgled, and Dante laughed.

"You're a regular little echo chamber, aren't you?"

"Eck-chame," Sam said.

Dante laughed again, put her on the changing table and replaced her wet diaper with a fresh one. Then he carried her through the house, into the kitchen, put her in the booster chair at the table while he filled a sippy-cup with milk. She liked it warm so he heated it in the microwave oven, tested a drop on his wrist, screwed the top on, plucked her from the booster, went out on the porch and sat down with her in his arms.

She could handle the sippy-cup herself and he knew

it, but he liked holding her, liked the warm weight of the baby, her sweet smell, the little noises of delight she made as she fed.

He liked caring for Samantha in general. Well, maybe not the poopy-diapers part, which he'd done when he heard her babbling softly to herself early this morning. Why wake Tally when he could change the diaper himself, even if it had been a rather interesting learning experience?

The truth was, he'd never imagined himself with a baby in his arms. Oh, he'd figured on having children someday. A man wanted children to carry on his genes, his life's work, but his thoughts had been of faceless miniature adults and a faceless perfect wife. Now, of course, he knew better.

He wanted a little girl exactly like Sam.

A wife exactly like Tally.

Dante caught his breath.

And, just that easily, came face-to-face with the truth.

He loved Tally. He loved her daughter. He had his family already, right here, the baby in his arms, the woman he adored in his bed.

He rose to his feet, ready to rush to the bedroom, wake Tally with a kiss, tell her what was in his heart—

No. He wanted this to be just right. All the romantic touches he'd always scoffed at. Candlelight. Flowers. Champagne.

The travel agent had given him the name of a respected island family that lived nearby. He waited until Sam finished her milk. Then he kept her safely in the curve of his arm while he made some phone calls. When he was done, he'd arranged for a babysitter, reserved a secluded table at a five-star restaurant on the beach, and ordered a ten-carat canary-yellow diamond in a platinum setting from the delighted owner of the island's most exclusive jewelry shop, with instructions to have a messenger bring the ring to the restaurant promptly at nine that night.

He was about to order flowers when Sam giggled and said, "Mama!"

Dante looked up and saw Tally.

"Hey," she said, smiling.

"Hey," he said softly, smiling back at her.

"You should have woken me."

"Your hear that, kid? Your mother doesn't think we can handle the tough stuff on our own." He paused. "Tally?"

"Hmm?"

I love you. I adore you. I want to marry you and adopt Sam, raise her as our very own daughter...

"What on earth are you thinking" she said, with a little laugh. "You have the strangest look on your face!"

"Do I?" He cleared his throat. "Maybe it's because— because what I was thinking was that I want to celebrate Christmas this evening."

Tally laughed. "Christmas is two days away!"

"You don't think I'm going to permit a little detail like that to stop me, do you?" Smiling, he came toward her. Sam held out her arms and he handed her to her mother. "In fact, I've already made plans for us tonight."

"What plans?" Tally said, hugging her daughter, putting her face up for Dante's kiss, thinking how right all this was, being here together, the man she loved, the child they'd created together. "What plans?" she said again and knew that tonight, no matter what happened, she would tell him everything.

His smile tilted. "It's a surprise. A good one," he added softly, "one I hope will make you happy." He put his arms around them both, the woman he loved and the child he would make his.

The child that should have been his, if he hadn't been so stupid and self-involved.

He felt the dull pain of regret settle over him.

If only Sam really were his. He loved her but some-times—sometimes it hurt to know that Tally had lain with another man. That someone else had joined with her to create this beautiful little life.

"Dante," Tally said softly, "what's wrong?"

"Nothing." He cleared his throat. "I was just thinking about tonight."

"You looked—you looked sad."

"Sad?" He smiled, forced the dark thoughts away. "Nonsense," he said briskly. "I'm just making sure I've thought of everything. Sam's babysitter. Our dinner res-ervations."

"Are we having dinner out?"

"We are. At that place on the beach."

Tally gave him the look women have always given men who are too dense to understand life's basic rules of survival.

"That place? But I don't have anything to wear! You said we'd only need swimsuits. Shorts. Jeans. I can't go there in jeans, Dante!"

He thought she could go there in what she wore now and still be more beautiful than any woman in the place, but this played right into his hands. He still had things to arrange. The flowers for their meal and for the house when they returned to it later. Candles for the bedroom.

More champagne, to drink on the beach once she had his ring on her finger.

"I agree," he said solemnly. "That's why you're going to take my credit card, taxi into town and buy whatever you need for tonight."

"But—"

He silenced the protest with a kiss.

"Find something long and elegant. Something so sexy it will make every man who sees you want me dead so he can claim you for his own." He kissed her again and she leaned into him, the baby gurgling happily between them, and half an hour later, holding Sam in his arms, both of them waving as the taxi and Tally pulled away, Dante knew he was, without question, the luckiest man alive.

HE MADE THE BALANCE of the phone calls, arranged for the delivery of white orchids, white candles and bottles of Cristal. The last call went to his attorney in New York, where he left a message asking him to research the state's adoption laws and to determine the quickest way to effect an adoption.

"I think that about does it, Sammy," he said, grinning at the way Samantha looked when he called her that. It wasn't elegant, but he liked it.

Then he turned all his attention on the child who would soon be his.

He took her into the pool, rode her on his shoulders in the warm water as she laughed and clutched at his hair with her fists.

He held her hand as they walked along the beach, helping her pick up shells, making a show of putting them into his pocket for later while surreptitiously letting ones that were too small for her safety fall to the sand.

He made himself a cup of coffee, handed Sam a sippy-cup of juice and shared an Oreo cookie with her, chuckling as he imagined what all those who trembled at his presence in a boardroom would think if they could see him eating the chunks she handed him, baby drool and all.

Late afternoon, with the sun high overhead, he sat on the palm-shaded patio, Sam playing at his feet. She gave a huge yawn.

"Nap time," he said.

Sam, who was, of course, brilliant for her age, puckered up her baby face and yowled.

"Okay, okay, forget I mentioned it."

The baby smiled, yawned again, put her head down and her rump up, and promptly fell asleep on the blanket at his feet. Dante yawned, too, picked up the magazine he'd been leafing through, wondered if Tally—his Tally—would be as happy as he wanted her to be when he proposed tonight.

She would—wouldn't she?

She loved him—didn't she?

He hadn't really thought about it until now. Yes. Of course she loved him. The way she sighed in his arms. Smiled into his eyes. The way he caught her watching him sometimes, that little smile curving her lips—

What was that? A dark shape, near his foot.

"Dio mio!"

Sam woke up screaming as a thing with eight legs raced across her outflung hand. Dante scooped the child into his arms, stomped on the ugly black thing and saw the bite marks of its fangs on Sam's tender wrist.

"Sam," he said, "Sam, *mia figlia—*"

Her shriek of pain rose into the air. Even as he scooped her into his arms, Dante saw the flesh around the bite start to swell. He paused only long enough to tie a scarf around her arm above the bite and to pick up the dead spider, place it in his handkerchief and tuck it into his pocket.

Heart racing, he ran for his car.

HE PHONED THE HOSPITAL when he was two blocks away. Two physicians and a nurse were waiting outside the emergency room. The nurse tried to take Sam from his arms but he refused to give her up.

"I'm staying with her," he said, and neither the doctors nor the nurse doubted his determination.

They led him into an examining room. Sam clung to his neck, sobbing. He soothed her with words he barely knew, things he'd heard people say to weeping children, things he'd once wished his *nonna* had said to him when he was small and he'd skinned his knee or bloodied his nose, except this wasn't a bloody knee or nose, he thought, as he dug in his pocket and produced the ugly corpse.

The nurse grimaced; one of the physicians barked out a command, and Dante's heart turned over when the nurse appeared with a tiny needle and reached for Sam's hand.

"Shh, *bambina,*" he whispered, "everything will be all right."

But Sam was past listening. Her little body arched; Dante cursed as a convulsion tore through her.

"Do something," he snarled.

"Wait outside," the doctor snapped.

Dante flashed him a look the man would never forget. "I will not leave my baby," he said.

He didn't. Not until Sam finally opened her eyes and looked at him.

"Da-Tay," she whispered, and for the first time since his mother had left him, Dante wept.

IT TOOK TWO HOURS and a dozen calls to the house by the sea before Tally answered the phone.

She was, as Dante had anticipated, frantic.

"Dante! Dear God, where are you? Where is Samantha? I came home and the place was empty and—"

He interrupted. Told her everything was fine, that they were at the hospital, in the emergency room. Lied and said he'd let his worry over a little bug bite get out of hand. He didn't want her to know the truth until he could take her in his arms and hold her and she could see for herself that the crisis was over.

He was waiting at the big double doors of the emergency room when she came flying through them.

"Where's my baby?"

Dante caught her in his arms. "She's fine, *cara*."

"Tell me the truth. My baby—"

"Tally." He held her by the shoulders, brought his eyes level with hers. "I would never lie to you. Never."

She nodded, though he could feel her tremble in his embrace. Slowly, carefully, he explained what had happened. When she swayed, he gathered her against him, rocked her gently until she pushed her hands against his chest and looked into his eyes.

"Where is she?"

He kept his arm around her, let his strength seep into her as he led her to Sam's room. The room was private; so was the nurse who sat beside the baby in the white crib, peacefully sleeping. The danger was past but the IV was still in her arm.

Tally bent over the crib and put her hand on her daughter's back. Tears fell from her eyes.

"My baby," she whispered, "oh, my sweet little girl! I could have lost you."

"Your husband did all the right things, Mrs. Russo," the nurse said softly. "Without his quick thinking, things would have been much worse."

Tally looked at the woman. "But he isn't—"

Dante slid his arm around her shoulders. "Let's let Sam sleep, *cara*. Come into the hall and we can talk."

Bewildered, Tally followed him from the room. "She thinks you and I are married?"

"I don't know the laws here, *cara*. But I remember reading about a child somewhere who died because a hospital wouldn't provide emergency treatment without the permission of a parent." He clasped her shoulders. "I wasn't going to run that risk. Not with our little girl."

Tally swallowed hard. *Our little girl. Our little girl.*

"Don't look at me that way, *cara*. I had no choice. Our Samantha—"

It was her fault, all of it. She had denied Dante knowledge of his child, denied Sam her father. And now, dear God, and now Sam might have died if Dante hadn't thought quickly—

"Tally."

She looked up at him. His face was drawn. He had gone through so much today for a child he didn't know was his, a child he loved.

"Tally." Dante paused. "I know my timing is bad but—*cara*, I want to marry you. And I want to adopt Sam. I want to be her father."

Tears swam in Tally's eyes. "Oh, Dante…"

"I love you. And I love her, as much as if she were my daughter."

Tally began to weep. There was no hiding her secret, not anymore.

"Dante," she said brokenly, "Sam *is* your daughter!"

There was a long silence, broken only by the sound of Dante's breathing and Tally's sobs. When he finally spoke, his voice was without inflection.

"What do you mean, Sam is my daughter?"

"I should have told you. I wanted to tell you—"

She gasped as his hands bit into her shoulders. "Tell me what?"

"There was no other man. I made it up. Samantha is—she's your child."

Moments, an eternity, slipped by. Tally waited, trying to read Dante's face, to see something of what would come next.

"Let me make sure I understand this. You didn't sleep with someone else."

"No."

"You didn't get pregnant by another man."

"I know I should have told you, but—"

"You knew you were pregnant, and you left me anyway?"

"Dante. Please. Listen to what I'm saying. I knew

you'd grown tired of me. How could I have told you I was having a baby?"

"My baby." His voice was like a whip; he caught her wrists and pushed her back against the wall. "*My* baby!"

"It isn't that simple!"

"On the contrary, Taylor. It's brutally simple. You became pregnant with my child and didn't tell me. You were going to raise her to think she had no father."

Tally wrenched her hands free and slapped them over her ears. "Stop it!"

"You were going to raise Samantha—my daughter— as I was raised. Fatherless. Impoverished."

"It wasn't like that, damn it! I did what I thought was right."

"For who? Surely not for Samantha. And not for me."

"Remember when I said I wanted to talk to you? It was about this. About you and Sam. But I had to wait for the right time."

He gave a hollow laugh. "Another lie. How many more will you tell before I know the entire truth?"

Tally stared up into her lover's enraged eyes. He was right. It was time for the truth. All of it.

"No more lies," she said, her voice trembling. "Here's the truth. Sam is yours. There was never anyone else. And I left you—I left you because I knew I'd fallen in love with you."

"Such a pretty story."

"I swear it's true! I still love you. I always will."

"As soon as my daughter is fully recovered," he said, as if she hadn't spoken, "we'll fly back to New York."

"Damn you, Dante! Listen to me!"

"You will move back into the guest suite. I'll permit

that because I don't want my child to be traumatized by too many changes all at once."

A cold knot of fear gripped Tally's stomach. "What does that mean?"

Dante smiled thinly.

"It means," he said silkily, "that Samantha is mine. That you stole her from me. That you are an unfit mother." He paused. "And that I intend to gain custody—sole custody—of her."

"No!" Tally's voice rose in horror. "You can't take her from me. No court will permit it!"

Dante ignored her, walked to the room where Sam lay sleeping and sat down in a chair beside the crib. So much for love. For putting your heart in someone's hands. For being foolish enough to think life was ever anything but a cruel joke.

He took his cell phone from his pocket, called his attorney, cut through the man's perfunctory greeting and told him he'd just learned he was the father of a two-year-old child.

The lawyer, who dealt with several wealthy clients, cut to the chase.

"How much does the woman want?"

"You misunderstand me," Dante said. "I don't want to deny my paternity of the child, I want to claim her. I want full custody. Will that be a problem?"

He listened, answered a couple of questions, then smiled.

There were times having money, power and the right connections paid off.

CHAPTER TWELVE

MOMENTS LATER, TALLY entered the room.

Dante, still seated beside the crib and the sleeping baby, looked at the nurse.

"Please take your dinner break now."

He spoke politely, but that didn't lessen his tone of command. The woman left without a backward glance. Tally looked at him, but he didn't acknowledge her presence.

Anyone looking at him would assume he was angry.

She knew better. He was furious. And it frightened her. Dante was a powerful adversary in any situation. Now he would be formidable.

But he wouldn't win. She would do whatever it took to keep her child and defeat him, and that meant facing up to him, starting now.

She moved the nurse's abandoned chair to the other side of the crib and sat down. Her face softened as she looked at her little girl, so peacefully asleep.

Samantha was hers.

No court in the land would separate a mother from her child, not even to satisfy Dante Russo. None, she thought…and maybe because she wished she really believed it, she spoke the words aloud.

"You won't win," she said.

He looked at her, his eyes empty. "Of course I will."

Her face paled. Good. He was happy to see it. She deserved what would come next. She had brought it on herself with her lies.

His attorney was already earning his million-dollar-a-year retainer, drawing up motions and citing precedents even though the hour was late and Christmas was only a couple of days away.

Dante had no doubt as to which of them would gain custody. Tally had apple pie and motherhood on her side, but he had the things that really mattered.

What a fool he'd been, imagining himself in love. He almost laughed. He, of all people, knew that the word had no meaning. His mother had claimed to love him, right up to the day she kissed him, told him to be a good boy, and vanished. His *nonna* had claimed to love him, too, and proved it by beating the crap out of him at every opportunity until he finally ran away.

Emotion was weakness. Self-discipline was strength. This woman had made him forget that, but he would not make the same mistake again.

The one thing he couldn't understand was why she had kept her pregnancy from him. He was rich. She could have milked him for a lot of money. He knew men who'd had that happen to them. A woman got pregnant, deliberately pregnant, and dipped her manicured hands into a man's bank account.

Anyone could see that Tally could have used the cash. The old house in Vermont, the business she'd attempted... An infusion of dollars would have changed her life.

All right. She had not been after his money. He had to admit that. And he had to admit that she seemed to be a good mother.

Why, then, had she lied? Why had she left him?

Because she loved him. That was what she'd said.

What a joke!

A woman who loved a man didn't run from him. She didn't give birth to his child and tell him the child was someone else's. *Dio*, the anger and pain that had caused him. The nights he'd lain awake, held Tally in his arms, tried not to wonder if she were dreaming of him or of her other lover.

His mouth thinned.

It was some consolation, at least, knowing she had not belonged to anyone else. That she had been his. Only his. That no one else had made love to her, held her close, felt the whisper of her breath against his throat while she slept in his arms.

He'd blanked his mind to the rest. To what she'd looked like when she was pregnant. Now, knowing Sam was his, that was impossible to do.

Her breasts would have been full, the skin translucent over the delicate tracery of her veins. Her belly would have been round, lush with the life they'd created. She had denied him the wonder of those months. The feel of his child, kicking in her mother's womb. The moment of his child's entry into the world.

All those signs, the proof of their love...

Except, it had never been love.

Never. Love was just a polite four-letter word men

and women used in mixed company. Taylor's lies were the issue here, not love.

He'd had the right to know the truth. She should have told him.

He looked up. Tally sat with her head bowed. "You should have told me," he said coldly.

She raised her eyes to his.

"You're right. I should have."

"But you didn't."

"No. I didn't. I've tried to explain, to say I'm sorry—"

"I'm not interested in apologies or explanations."

She gave a sad little laugh. "No. You're only interested in you. That's one of the reasons I didn't tell you I was pregnant. I was afraid you'd react exactly this way, as if our baby's existence concerned only you."

"You're good at making excuses."

"Not as good as you are at feeling nothing for anyone but yourself." Her voice trembled. "I think you do care for Samantha, though. And that surprises me."

"A compliment, *cara*. I can hardly bear it."

"Dante. Don't take her from me. I know you want to hurt me, but you'll hurt her, too."

"Hurt her?" His lips drew back from his teeth. "You have nothing. I have everything. I'll give my daughter a life you can only imagine."

"She's my daughter, too. And what she needs is love. It's what everyone needs. How can you not understand that?"

"*Love,*" he said, his mouth twisting, "is a word without meaning. *Honesty. Responsibility.* Those are words that matter. How can you not understand that?"

Then he folded his arms, fixed his eyes on the sleeping baby and ignored Tally completely.

DAWN HAD JUST TOUCHED the sky with a delicate pink blush when Samantha stirred.

"Mama?"

Tally, who'd fallen into a fitful sleep, sprang to her feet, but she was too late. Dante had already leaned into the crib and lifted the baby into his arms.

"Bella figlia," he said huskily, *"buon giorno."*

Sam grinned. "Da-Tay," she babbled, and wrapped her arms around his neck.

Tally felt her throat tighten. All the time she'd been pregnant, the months and years after, she'd never pictured this. Dante and Samantha as father and daughter. She'd never dreamed of this softness, this sweetness in her lover.

The door opened. The physician who'd treated Sam stepped into the room.

"Well, look at this! It doesn't take a trained eye to see that our patient's made a full recovery."

"Thank you, Doctor. For everything."

"My pleasure, Mr. Russo. Just let me give your little girl the once-over and you can take her home."

"To New York?"

"I'd wait a couple of days, just to be on the safe side." He grinned. "Quite a hardship, having to spend Christmas in the Caribbean, huh, folks?"

Tally made a choked sound. Dante forced a smile.

"We'll manage," he said.

Tally hoped he was right.

COEXISTING in a three-level penthouse, as they'd initially done, was simple.

Coexisting in a one-level house built to take full advantage of the sun was not.

Rooms opened into rooms; doors were almost non-existent. Tally moved her things into the third bedroom, but it was impossible to walk to the kitchen or Sam's room without running into Dante.

"Excuse me," she said, at the beginning.

After a while, she stopped saying it. What was there to apologize for? He was as much in her way as she was in his.

And how did he manage to get to Sam's side so quickly? All the baby had to do was whimper and Dante, damn him, was there.

Tally told herself she'd at least have the pleasure of watching him suffer through the horrors of a full diaper but apparently he'd mastered Diaper 101 on his own. All right, she thought with petty satisfaction, at least he wouldn't know how to mash a banana just the way Sam liked it—and she was right. He didn't.

It didn't matter.

Her sweet little traitor liked Dante's method just fine. She liked everything he did, including taking her for hand-in-hand walks along the beach, the warm water lapping at her ankles.

When Tally attempted the same thing, Sam shrieked with horror.

Dante could charm any woman he set his eyes on, including two-year-old females.

But he couldn't charm Tally. Not that he tried. He looked right through her. That was fine. She'd gone back to hating him. She'd never let her little girl be raised by such a cold-hearted tyrant, never mind the performance he was putting on with Sam, never mind the way his face lit each time the baby toddled toward him…

Never mind the numbing sense of sorrow in her own heart at glimpses of what might have been.

As midnight approached, with Sam sound asleep and the house silent, Tally was close to tears, but it wasn't over Dante.

Never over him.

"Never," Tally whispered, and wept as if her heart might break in half.

TALLY'S SOFT SOBS carried through the walls.

Lying on his bed, arms folded beneath his head, Dante stared up at the dark ceiling. Let her cry, he thought coldly. For all he gave a damn, she could cry enough salt tears to fill the sea.

After a long time, the sound of her weeping grew softer, then stopped. A muscle in his jaw flexed. Good. Now, at least, he might get some sleep.

Half an hour later, he sat up.

To hell with sleep. He was going crazy, trapped in a house that was rapidly becoming a prison. He pulled on a pair of shorts, opened the patio doors and strode over the beach until he reached the surf.

The moon, full and round, was bright enough to carve shadows into the sand. Dante's mouth thinned. It was the kind of night you saw on picture postcards. The endless stretch of sand. The white ruffle of the surf. The dark sea stretching to the horizon under the elegantly cool eye of the moon.

Once, he'd considered buying a house in these islands. He'd even mentioned it to Taylor. The idea had come from out of nowhere...or maybe not. Maybe he'd thought of the beauty of this place because Taylor was so beautiful. Because, fool that he was, he'd imagined he was feeling something for her he'd never felt for another woman.

He'd stepped back from that precipice.

And here he was, three years later, with her in the very setting he'd imagined, except all he wanted was to get away from her and return to New York.

Dio, the irony of it!

Dante kicked at the sand as he walked slowly along the beach.

A beautiful island. A beautiful woman, but what good was her beauty if she had no heart? Not when it came to him.

And why should that mean a damn anyway, when he'd never thought the human heart was responsible for anything more than pumping blood through the body?

Wrong, he thought, tilting back his head and staring blindly at the moon. Dead wrong, and it had taken a two-year-old imp to teach him the lesson.

A painful lesson.

For the first time in his life, he'd begun to think about a different existence from any he'd ever known. A house in the country. A dog, a couple of cats, a station wagon. A little girl to run to the door when she heard his key in the lock and maybe a little boy, too...

And a wife, to step into his embrace.

Not just a wife. Tally. His Tally. Because that was how he thought of her, how he'd always thought of her, even three years ago...

What was that?

Dante cocked his head. Music? Chimes. No. Not chimes. Bells. Church bells. Of course. It must be midnight, and this was Christmas Eve.

He swallowed hard. So what? Christmas was for fools. A holiday that celebrated a miracle, except miracles were in painfully short supply in today's world.

When was the last time he'd seen anything remotely like a miracle?

When was the last time he'd held Tally in his arms?

The sound of the bells came to him again, filled with poignancy and hope that floated on the soft sea breeze. Dante swallowed again but he couldn't ease the constriction in his throat.

"Tally," he whispered, and the name was sweeter than the music of the bells.

Tally was his miracle. She always had been.

And he'd turned his back on that miracle, ruined his one chance at love, at happiness, out of pride, arrogance, all the things she'd accused him of, rather than admit the truth.

He loved Tally. Now, three years ago, forever. He adored her.

And he knew exactly why she'd left him.

He *had* been about to end their affair, just as she'd said, and it hadn't had a damned thing to do with boredom. The truth was the great Dante Russo had been terrified of putting his heart in a woman's hands, of saying, *Here I am, cara. A man, nothing more. A man who loves you and can only hope you love him in return because without you, I am nothing. My life is nothing....*

Dante took a shuddering breath.

"Tally," he whispered, and turned toward the house.

TALLY LAY HUDDLED in her bed, eyes hot and gritty with tears.

Ridiculous, wasn't it? To weep over Dante? He wasn't worth it. Not anymore.

He had shown his true colors today. He was the cold, brutal, arrogant tyrant she'd always called him...

Tally rolled onto her back and stared up at the dark ceiling. No. That wasn't true. Dante had been wonderful today, quick and courageous and tender with Sam, and with her...

Until she'd told him what she should have told him a very long time ago.

She could be honest about this, at least. Dante wasn't a tyrant, he was a man in pain. She had told him a lie that had cut to the bone. Now he was hurting. And a man like Dante Russo knew only one way to deal with pain.

He struck at its cause.

And she—she was the cause.

A sob caught in Tally's throat and she rolled over and buried her face in the already-damp pillow.

If only she'd told him the truth that day in Vermont, when he'd first seen Sam. If only she'd said, "Dante, this is your child. I kept her from you and I kept myself from you, too, because—because I loved you. Because I knew I'd die if you turned away from me."

Would he have laughed? Or would he have opened his arms to her? She'd never know. It was too late. She'd finally told him the truth, that Sam was his and that she loved him, but it didn't matter.

He wanted Sam, not her. And she couldn't blame him for that. Her lies had destroyed everything.

Too late, the beat of her heart said, too late, too late, too—

What was that?

Tally sat up, head cocked. Bells? Yes. Bells, chiming sweetly through the night. Why would bells be...

Of course.

It was Christmas. Christmas! The bells were heralding the start of the holiday, singing of joy, of wonder…

Of miracles.

Tears streamed down Tally's face. She'd had her own miracle. A man. Proud. Strong. Protective and, yes, loving. And she'd let that miracle slip through her fingers out of cowardice. She'd been afraid to tell him about Sam.

And terrified to tell him about herself, that she loved him, that she'd always love him, until it was too late.

Almost too late, she thought, and drew a ragged breath.

Tally threw back the covers and rose from the bed. Her footsteps were hesitant at first but they quickened as she ran from room to room.

"Dante," she said brokenly, "my beloved, where are you?"

The bells rang out again, just as she hurried into the sitting room. A beam of ivory moonlight illuminated the French doors that led to the beach. Tally flung them open—

And saw Dante, just as he turned toward the house.

"Dante," she said, and she began to run across the sand, "Dante…"

Moonlight touched his face. She saw love, understanding, the same hope that burned in her heart, and she flew into his embrace and clung to him.

"I heard the bells," she said, crying and laughing at the same time, kissing his mouth as she rose to him, luxuriating in the racing beat of his heart. "I heard them calling and I thought, I can't lose him again, I can't, I can't, I can't—"

"I love you," Dante said fiercely, cupping her face in

his hands. "I've always loved you, *inamorata,* but I was too proud—and too afraid of needing you—to admit it."

"And I love you," Tally said, "I always have. It's why I left you three years ago. The thought of having you end things between us was more than I could bear."

"I was a fool, *cara,*" he said, tightening his arms around her. "How could a man end what is destined to last through eternity?"

Tally laughed through her tears. "Is that all?"

He smiled, too. And then his mouth was on hers, the taste of her tears was on his lips, and as he lifted her into his arms and carried her to the house, the bells rang out, telling the world that miracles are always possible.

All you have to do is believe.

SOMETIMES, HAVING WEALTH and power and all the right connections really did pay off.

They flew back to New York early in the morning the next day, Tally wearing the diamond solitaire Dante had bought for her in the Caribbean.

"It's beautiful," she whispered, when he slipped the ring on her finger.

"Not as beautiful as you," he said, and kissed her.

All the municipal offices were closed, but such details weren't enough to put a crimp in the plans of Dante Russo.

"I know someone who knows someone who knows someone," he said, laughing when Tally rolled her eyes.

"Such arrogance," she said, but her smile, her voice, her eyes shone with love.

By noon, they had a wedding license and a judge who said he'd be happy to marry them in Dante's penthouse.

By one, the penthouse was filled with Christmas

garlands. Mistletoe hung from every doorway. Dante loved catching Tally under the mistletoe, whirling her in a circle and kissing her.

The enormous sitting room was filled with baskets of crimson and white poinsettias. Holly leaves, bright with berries, lay draped over the top of the fireplace mantel. But the room's centerpiece was a blue spruce so tall its branches reached the ceiling.

The tree was beautiful.

It filled the air with its fragrance; it glowed with what Tally was sure were a thousand white fairy lights. The flames on the hearth in the wall-long fireplace danced on the gleaming surfaces of the gold and silver balls that hung from the tree. Gaily wrapped packages spilled from under the branches, though Sam, squealing with delight, had already opened most of hers.

Champagne was chilling in silver buckets; caviar sat in a silver dish. Everything was perfect...and a little before two, the doorman brought up an enormous white box. Inside was a magnificent gown of lace and seed pearls, straight from the atelier of a world-famous designer.

It was the sort of gown princesses wear in the fairy tales little girls read.

Except, Tally thought when she finally stood beside her gorgeous groom and looked up into his eyes, except, this was no fairy tale.

This was real. It was true love, and it would last forever.

"Do you take this woman," the judge intoned, and Dante short-circuited things by saying "Yes."

The perfect P.A., who was one of the guests, laughed. So did Mrs. Tipton and so did Samantha, who she held against her bosom.

Dante brought his bride's hand to his lips. They smiled into each other's eyes. Then they gave the judge all their attention. Slowly, and with deep meaning, they took the vows that would forever unite them.

Moments later, they were husband and wife. Dante gathered his bride to him and kissed her again.

"I will love you forever, *inamorata*," he said softly.

Tally smiled through tears of happiness. "As I will love you," she whispered.

"Me, too," Sam said.

Everyone laughed as the baby made her pronouncement.

"Down," she told Mrs. Tipton, with all the imperiousness of a two-year-old. She toddled to her parents and held up her arms. "Up," she commanded.

Dante, a man who never took orders from anyone, happily took this one and settled his daughter into the curve of his arm.

"Mama," Sam said, touching a chubby hand to Tally's cheek.

She looked at Dante, who smiled and waited for her to call him Da-Tay.

But she didn't.

Instead, she put a little hand on each side of his face and said, "Dada."

Dante's eyes filled. He looked at his wife, and Tally smiled.

"Merry Christmas, beloved," she whispered.

"Buon natale, inamorata," he said softly.

Their daughter laughed, and flung her arms around them both.

The Boss's
Christmas Seduction

YVONNE LINDSAY

Dear Reader,

I've always considered myself extremely fortunate to have the unquestionable support and love of my family and have striven to re-create that sense of belonging with my own children. While growing up, I couldn't imagine how the holiday season must feel to those who have no one, especially those who don't even know where they come from.

From that flipside of my life Holly Christmas was born. Trying to imagine her unspeakable losses since babyhood, the steps to adulthood she could never share with family and her struggle to come to terms with who she is, combined with her determination to discover her background, reduced me to tears at times while writing this story, but I trust you'll find her path to happiness with Connor Knight as rewarding as she eventually does.

Of course, one passionate Knight brother is never enough, and I sincerely hope after reading Holly and Connor's story you'll look out for my next title, *The CEO's Contract Bride* (on sale in January 2008), where Connor's eldest and very sexy brother, Declan, meets his match.

With very best wishes,

Yvonne Lindsay

New Zealand born, to Dutch immigrant parents, **Yvonne Lindsay** became an avid romance reader at the age of thirteen. Now, married to her "blind date" and with two surprisingly amenable teen-agers, she remains a firm believer in the power of romance. Yvonne balances her days between a part-time legal management position and crafting the stories of her heart. In her spare time, when not writing, she can be found with her nose firmly in a book, reliving the power of love in all walks of life. She can be contacted via her website, www.yvonnelindsay.com.

For Bron,
my mentor, my friend,
and
in memory of Delia Bridgens,
who introduced me to the joy of
reading romance.
Thank you both for the impact you
have made on my life.

One

Bile rose in his throat. Hot, bitter, acrid bile.

Connor Knight dashed the investigator's report violently across the mahogany surface of his desk, scattering papers like giant confetti through the air where they hovered briefly, before floating to the thickly carpeted study floor.

Through the open French doors behind him he heard the drone of the launch's engines as it pulled away from his private jetty, taking the bearer of bad tidings back across the harbour to Auckland city.

The vile taste in Connor's mouth rivalled the malevolence of his ex-wife's actions. He swallowed against it, but the irrefutable proof of her betrayal could not be as easily diminished.

As if her insatiable partying and gambling hadn't been enough, now he knew that six months into their marriage she'd knowingly destroyed their baby—the child she knew he'd wanted—and had then been sterilised rather than ever bear another child again.

If not for a careless comment from one of her friends at a recent fund-raiser he'd have been none the wiser. Yet the throwaway remark had been all he needed to start the investigation and to confirm that she'd lied about the miscarriage.

A tearing pain clawed at his chest.

The proof of her treachery now lay scattered on his floor—information that had come at a hell of a price, but which was worth every last cent.

A copy of her admission to a private hospital four years ago, the bills from the anaesthetist, the surgeon, the hospital. The procedures. *Termination. Sterilisation.*

And through it all he'd been oblivious.

So now she wanted more money? He'd have paid it just to be rid of her—until he'd received today's information.

It had been bad enough to realise back then that she'd emasculated him with her deceit, her avaricious need to grasp at everything in her path during their brief union, but this? This went way further than that.

The grandfather clock chimed the hour. Nine o'clock. *Damn!* The meeting had made him later in to the office than he expected.

He punched the quick dial on the speakerphone on the desk, connecting immediately to his office in the city.

"Holly, I'm running late. Any messages or problems?"

"Nothing urgent, Mr. Knight, I've rescheduled your conference call to New York." His personal assistant's gentle, well-modulated voice washed over him like a calming wave of sanity in the madness of his morning. Thank goodness he could still rely on some people.

Connor slipped into his suit jacket, adjusted his tie and,

oblivious to the crunch of the report underfoot, stalked out the open French doors and towards the chopper waiting to take him from his island home and into Auckland's central business district.

If Holly Christmas received one more tartan-beribboned poinsettia she would scream.

So what if her birthday fell on Christmas Eve? She was used to that. After all, it *was* the same day every year. She blinked back the unbidden rush of tears that pricked her eyes, and gave herself a mental shake. Toughen up, she growled silently. Self-pity was so not her style. Survival—whatever it took—that was her key. Then why did she feel different this year? Empty. Alone.

At least her colleagues had remembered today was her birthday, and not just the last day of work before Knight Enterprises closed for the Christmas break. She straightened her shoulders, stiffened her spine and, with the plant clutched tightly to her aching chest, summoned a smile.

"The poinsettia is beautiful, thanks. I really appreciate it." The words sounded normal, thank goodness, coloured with just the right amount of enthusiasm.

"See you at the party tonight, Holly?" one of the girls asked.

"Oh, yes, I'll be there," she confirmed with a wry twist of her lips. Someone had to see to it that the annual bash ran smoothly, that the grossly inebriated were tactfully withdrawn from the proceedings and inserted into taxis and that spills and breakages were swiftly dealt with. For the third year in a row she was that someone.

She loved her job and she was darned good at it. No, she was better than good. She was the best. And that's why, after working her way through the secretarial pool here at Knight

Enterprises she'd risen to Executive PA to Connor Knight, head of the corporate law department.

A "ping" from the elevator bank down the hall heralded the tall, imposing figure striding along the carpet-lined corridor, and sent the small group of women scurrying back to their respective workstations. Holly turned and put the lush red-leafed poinsettia on the credenza behind her desk—next to the one from the finance department and the two that had come up from security and personnel. She caught her lower lip in between her teeth, tugging at its fullness. How on earth was she supposed to get them home on the bus?

"Good morning, Holly." His voice, as rich and dark as sinful chocolate, made the hairs on the back of her neck stand up. From the day she'd interviewed for her position as his personal assistant, her reaction to him had always been this painfully immediate, although she'd schooled herself to hide it well.

She'd given up asking herself why his presence made every nerve ending in her body stand on full alert, and learned instead to knuckle down and do her job, masking the flush of warmth that suffused her body. Some people didn't believe in love at first sight, but Holly knew from sudden and lasting experience that it happened.

She clenched her jaw slightly then slowly released it and the tension that bound her muscles, and turned to face him secure in the knowledge he'd never have an inkling as to the thoughts that raced through her mind or the sharpened awareness that brought her senses to screaming attention when he was around.

"Mr. Tanaka from the Tokyo office called about the negotiations. He sounded tense."

Connor didn't break his stride on his way through the open polished-rimu double doors that led to his corner office. "He must be. It's about five-thirty in the morning there. Get him on the line for me."

For the briefest moment Holly allowed herself the luxury of inhaling the lingering scent of his cologne—crisp, fresh and expensive yet with an underlying hint of something forbidden, especially to someone like her. With a mental shake she lifted the receiver of her phone, automatically punching in the numbers that would connect his private line to Japan. She waited until he picked up, then she stood to unlatch the hooks that held the doors open to his interior office. Absorbed in the conversation, his Japanese flawless, he didn't so much as acknowledge her.

Holly indulged in a tiny sigh. Well, love at first sight on her part or not, Connor Knight was oblivious. Newly divorced from his socialite wife when Holly had started working for him, he'd looked right through her, and every other woman who'd crossed his path since, as if she didn't exist. She was a highly dependable machine to him, period.

Confident the call with Mr. Tanaka would tie him up for some time, she made one last check through the details for the staff and children's Christmas parties. This year she'd excelled herself. The cafeteria, transformed into a fairy grotto, looked stunning, and at six-thirty Connor would be playing Santa Claus.

A wry smile played around Holly's lips as she eyed the glaring red Santa suit that hung on the antique brass hat stand in the corner. Mr. Knight, Sr. had insisted Connor play Santa this year, claiming his arthritic knee made it difficult for him to attend to the task, and saying how important it was someone from the family took on the role. Oh, Connor had argued against it, but once his father made up his mind there was no denying it—especially not from his youngest son.

It was probably the only time she'd witnessed her boss at a total disadvantage.

"Hell." A deep voice from behind made her spin around in her chair. "He doesn't really expect me to wear that, does he?"

"I think you'll make a wonderful Santa, Mr. Knight."

The disgust on his face was self-evident. He thrust a dicta-tape at her together with a clutch of papers. "Transcribe this for me straight away. Oh, and before you do, check the boardroom is free and tell the team we need to meet in half an hour."

"Trouble?" Holly enquired, mentally shifting his appointments to free him up for the rest of the morning. It had to be serious if the whole legal team was being called in.

"Nothing we can't handle. Timing's a bit of a blow, though." He cast a baleful glance at the Santa suit, draped limply on the hanger. "I don't suppose…"

"He's not going to let you get out of it." She shook her head sympathetically.

"No, he won't." Connor huffed out a breath and pushed a hand through his immaculately cut and styled hair, sending several strands into unaccustomed disarray.

Holly stifled another smile. This whole Santa thing had sent the cool, calm and sophisticated Connor Knight for a loop, and this from a man she'd seen face down battalions of international lawyers over land and property deals.

She'd never have dreamed that the prospect of a steady procession of children queuing to take their turn seated on his knee would elicit such a nervous response. Still, who was she to ponder? Children made her nervous, too, and, unlike so many of her peers, Holly had put her biological clock firmly on hold. At twenty-six the rest of her life stretched long and lonely ahead of her. There'd be no kids in her future, at least not until she had some answers about her past.

She hated this time of year. All the fun and gaiety of the

festivities served to remind her of everything she didn't have—had never had. Knowing she'd ensured everyone else's fun tonight would have to be sufficient to buoy her through the harrowing, bleak emptiness of the holiday break until she could bury herself back in work.

Holly sighed again, and bent to the task at hand. Regretting her decision was not a possibility. Maybe she'd grow old in this chair, or one just like it in another office in another city, but she'd be the best executive PA on the planet. That would have to be enough.

Shrieks of laughter echoed around the room as the clown she'd hired made a fool of himself yet again. Holly took a quick look at her watch. Five minutes until Santa time. He should be here by now. Maybe he was having trouble with the suit.

She turned to her assistant, Janet, a quiet young woman not long out of business college but already showing every sign of making a great PA herself in time.

"If I'm not back in five minutes with Mr. Knight, give the clown the nod to carry on a little longer, will you?"

"Is there anything else I can do to help?"

"No, I'm sure we'll be fine. Santa probably got a phone call."

In the elevator Holly mentally ticked off the order of the evening, everything *had* to run like clockwork. Irritation drummed at the back of her mind. As much as she sympathised with Connor's reluctance to play Santa tonight, he had an obligation to the kids. An obligation he had no business putting off. If he'd bailed on those excited children downstairs she'd be giving him a piece of her mind, boss or not.

She covered the distance from the elevator bank to his corner office in record time and knocked sharply before pushing through the doors. The head of anger she'd built up propelled her into his office with a flurry. But her words stalled in her throat, and she halted midstride.

Connor Knight stood, half-dressed, in the middle of his office. The garish red trousers of his suit hung loosely on his hips, threatening to drop lower if he so much as moved a muscle.

Holly dragged her eyes upwards, her throat as dry as the Sahara, and a deep-seated throb pulsed through her body. Lord have mercy, she thought as her gaze swept across the disturbingly bare tanned expanse of his chest, to the powerful width of his shoulders above it and to the strong column of his neck. It was amazing what Armani could hide, she thought as she forced herself to look him in the eye, hoping the surge of energy that rocketed with heated awareness through her wasn't apparent on her face. If her internal temperature was anything to go by, she should be glowing like a beacon.

She took a steadying breath. What was she here for again? Oh, yes, that's right. Santa.

"Five minutes, Mr. Knight."

"Yeah, I know. Damn suit's too big. Help me stuff some cushions in here. I'm sure the kids of today still expect a bit of meat on their Santas."

"I imagine so," she agreed, and swept up an armful of cushions from the sofa in his office. "Will these do?" she asked.

"As good as anything. Here," Connor slid his hands behind the band of the trousers and held them away from his waist. "You stuff, I'll hold."

He had to be joking. Holly hesitated and swallowed against the constriction in her throat.

"What are you waiting for?" He shot her a glance, a tiny frown pulling his dark brows together briefly, his impatience clear.

Of course he had no idea of his effect on her. To him she wasn't a woman with needs and desires. She was just his PA.

Besides, as his PA, why wouldn't she be called upon to stuff cushions in her boss's trousers?

"I suppose this is what you meant in my job description, when you said 'and other duties as required from time to time.'" Keep it light she told herself. Just keep it light.

Surprise skated over his features at her words. Holly inwardly groaned. Why on earth had she said that?

His eyes suddenly crinkled at the edges and he laughed—a rusty sound, as if he didn't do it often enough. "Yeah, something like that. Although, I don't think HR had this scenario in mind."

Holly returned a nervous smile and forced herself forward. Warmth radiated from his bare torso, or was that just the flush of heat in her cheeks? She fought to quell the tremor that threatened to vibrate through her and, with a stern silent warning to herself not to look down, she carefully eased the first cushion between his ridged abdomen and the red satin.

"It's okay, Holly. I won't bite."

Oh, great. Now he was laughing at her. Fine, she'd show him she wasn't scared. She shoved in the next cushion with more haste than finesse, her fingers accidentally grazing against the fine row of dark hair that feathered from his belly button and down. She heard the hitch in his breathing as she touched him and snatched her hand back as goose bumps rose on his skin.

"That should do the trick." Darn, was that a quaver in her voice? Worse, had he heard it?

"I need more."

More? Her hand still burned from its fleeting touch against his skin—the texture of the hair beneath his belly button a tactile impression against her fingers—she needed more, too, although she knew with painful honesty they weren't thinking about the same thing.

With her lower lip caught between her teeth, Holly edged

another cushion into the waistband. The urge to let her fingers linger against the heated surface of his belly tempted her like a candy shop window did a sugar addict. Determined not to give in to her baser instincts she gave the padded mass a gentle, dehumanising pat. "There, that's it."

She reached for the red jacket, yanked it off its hanger and held it out for him. She allowed herself the brief luxury of letting her gaze stroke across his back and shoulders, mesmerised by the play of his muscles as he shrugged into the garment and cinched the broad, black belt around his now-expanded waistline.

He grabbed the hat and beard from his desk and hastily arranged them before turning to face Holly again.

"So, how do I look?"

Her breath caught. How did he look? She blinked, searching for the words to describe him. He certainly wasn't like the Santas that had filled her with terror as a child, and caused her to drag free of her caregiver's hand to tearfully hasten as far away as she could get.

Despite the padding at his waist and the ridiculously fluffy beard that obscured the strong lines of his jaw, she couldn't erase the half-naked picture of him that burned on her retinas. She barely trusted herself to speak.

"You've forgotten the eyebrows," she eventually managed. Well done, she congratulated herself, that almost sounded like her usual cool, composed self.

"I don't have to wear those white caterpillars, do I?"

"Of course you do, you wouldn't be Santa without them."

Holly clenched and unclenched her fingers in a vain attempt to stem the trembling that threatened to give away her nerves before she peeled the stick-on brows from the backing paper. She leaned nearer and reached up to smooth them above his eyes, trying desperately not to let her fingers linger on his face. He bent his head slightly to assist, and suddenly his lips were level with hers—the warmth of his breath caressing her cheek.

So close, yet so far. All she had to do was step in, just one tiny step, and press her lips against his. To give life to the dreams that invaded her sleep and caused her to wake, tangled in her sheets, filled with a want she could never assuage.

Hastily she quelled her rampant thoughts and concentrated on applying the strips of white fluff. She'd be on the fast track to unemployment if she gave in to her desires, and no way could she afford that. Not with Andrea's medical fees to consider. The reminder was as chilling as an Antarctic winter.

Finally, the job done, she stepped away to safety—to where she couldn't give in to impulse. "You look great," she said softly.

"Well then, that's all that matters. Let's go."

They travelled in silence to the eighth-floor cafeteria where Holly put a steadying hand on his red sleeve. She tried to ignore the waves of heat that emanated through the fabric to her fingers.

"Wait here," she ordered, although her voice came out like a strangled croak and earned her a strange look from the dark eyes that burned under bushy white brows. "I need to let your warm-up act announce you first."

Was it her imagination or had he suddenly become paler? Surely he wasn't scared? Not Connor Knight. Under the fluffy beard, she discerned small lines of tension bracketing his lips, and the urge to comfort him stilled her in her tracks.

"You'll be fine," she murmured softly, as reassuringly as she could. "The kids will love you."

"You're staying, aren't you?"

His question caught her by surprise. She hadn't planned on

sticking around for this part of the proceedings. Seeing a line of children waiting to sit with Santa still had the power to fill her with dread.

"No, I have some other things to attend to. I'll be back just before the party finishes."

"Stay."

Holly looked away. He had no idea. But then, of course, why should he? Everyone loved Christmas. Everyone but the little girl who'd grown up saddled with a surname chosen by Social Services that linked her irrevocably to the most traumatic experience of her life. It was one of the reasons she never disclosed her background or years in foster care. No one wanted to admit they'd been abandoned. As far as Holly was concerned, her life had begun the day she'd turned eighteen and been released from the state's control.

"Holly?"

Her teeth were clenched so hard she was amazed they didn't shatter in her jaw, and her throat ached with years of suppressed tension. She couldn't explain, not even to him. Some things you kept buried. She gave him a tight nod. "Let's get it over with."

The children didn't give him the slightest opportunity to be nervous. Their vigorous excitement and squeals of pleasure energised the room to such an extent Holly felt as though her nerves would shred into ribbons and scatter all around her. Why on earth had she agreed to stay? It was madness.

Seated on his special throne, Connor lifted a little girl with a gleaming cap of dark hair onto his lap. The child, no more than three or four, scanned the room, her bottom lip starting to tremble.

Despite the constant temperature of air conditioning, tiny beads of perspiration prickled along Holly's spine. A wave of dizziness made her press her body against the hard wall behind her—trying to connect with something solid, something real. Anything other than the dread that built within her and threatened to swamp her mind. She dragged a deep breath into deflated lungs, struggling to push the fear back down—down to where she could control it—but it was too late.

An image flashed, sharp and clear in her mind, and in a heartbeat she was lost. She was that little girl. Sitting on Santa's knee, her eyes nervously—futilely—raking the crowd of shoppers for her mother. Nervousness becoming fear. Fear becoming absolute terror when she couldn't find her mother's face anywhere in the swirling mass.

The authorities had been summoned as soon as someone could make any sense out of her hysterical sobbing. But not quickly enough to find her mother in the crowd of stunned onlookers. Even now the overwhelming sense of desertion and loss left Holly shocked and vulnerable.

Resentment lanced through her, swift and searing, before she determinedly crushed it. She'd given up trying to work out what kind of mother walked away from her child the night before Christmas—abandoning a three-year-old to strangers and an uncertain future.

She forced herself to find an anchor, something she could focus on and that would help her bring her rapid breathing back under control and calm the tremors that shook her frame. That anchor was Connor Knight as, with infinite patience, he pointed out the little girl's parents in the crowd and cajoled a smile from her worried wee face.

Holly uncurled her fisted hands, feeling the sharp sting of sensation as blood eked its way back to her fingertips. Across the room the little girl was smiling and waving to her mother. And Connor, instead of paying attention to the child on his lap, was staring straight back at her. She watched as his lips, outlined by the absurdly fluffy beard, framed the words, "Are you all right?" Had he noticed her panic? She gave a weak smile and lifted her chin with a small nod. He held her gaze a moment longer, then turned his attention back to the child in his care and handed her a cheerfully wrapped gift.

This was how it was meant to be for kids. Each one with their own special gift and a chance to impart their deepest desires for Christmas morning to Santa, and the steady assurance of a loving parent waiting in the wings. Hadn't she wished that for herself so many times?

When the last parcel was distributed, it was time to call the children's party to an end. Santa had other obligations, and Holly's half-hour window between the children's party and the staff party was closing.

With a small announcement she brought the celebrations to a close and judging by the overwhelming round of applause, from both parents and children, Connor was a hit. As everyone filtered out, Holly finally allowed herself to relax, the knot of tension that kept her operating at maximum performance efficiency all day, all year for that matter, slowly untangling. Only one more party to get through, then it was all over for another year, she consoled herself.

"What was that all about?" Connor Knight's voice slid through her like a hot knife through butter.

She drew in a long breath before answering. "I think it went well, don't you? The children certainly loved you."

"You looked like you'd seen a ghost."

Holly sighed. Evasion wouldn't work. Tenacity was one of the many talents that had driven him to being one of the most-respected men in his field—worldwide. He wouldn't give up until completely satisfied with her answer.

"Just catching my breath. That's all. It's taken a bit of work, getting this all organised." She tried to assure him, and for a moment thought she'd succeeded.

A tiny flash lit the onyx depths of his eyes and grew into the hot glow of challenge. "Looked like more than that to me. I thought you were going to keel over."

"Oh, good heavens, no." Holly forced a smile on her face.

"Are you okay now?" he persisted.

"I'm fine. Just fine."

"You've been pushing yourself too hard. Janet will take over for this evening."

"No, I'm okay. Truly."

Connor gave her a hard look. "We'll see about that. Come on, we'd better get ready for the next onslaught."

"You go on ahead. I'll meet you back down here."

She watched as he left. What had made him notice her during that dreadful moment of weakness? Had anyone else seen it? She should never have agreed to stay on. Never.

Holly quickly glanced around. The cleaning staff were busy completing the transformation of the children's party to a more sophisticated reenactment of a Christmas fantasy. It had been a brainwave to carry through the same delightful childlike theme to the staff party, and such a simple solution, given the time constraints. She wasn't needed here any longer.

Back upstairs in her office, Holly opened the coat cupboard and lifted a long dry cleaner's carrier from the rail. It was a simple matter to slip into the ladies' room to change and touch up her makeup. She took a brief minute to loosen her hair, combing through its thick dark length so hard her scalp tingled. She studied her reflection a moment. How long had it been since she'd let her hair down, literally or figuratively?

Too long. But time was not a commodity she could afford to waste. Not when so much depended on her.

She twisted her hair back up again, softening the tight twist that she usually wore by securing the silky black length in a fuller, softer knot at the nape of her neck. Finally satisfied when not a hair dared stray out of place she slicked on a ruby-coloured lipstick. The sales assistant had been right, Holly acceded with a small grimace, the rich colour did bring life to her faintly olive-tinted skin. She preferred softer, more understated colours that wouldn't draw attention to the fullness of her lips, yet knew that she needed something striking for this evening. Besides, she'd reminded herself, today was her birthday. A girl had a right to look good.

A swift glance at her watch reminded her she had little time left. Holly slipped out of her sombre businesslike suit and carefully unzipped the carrier to remove the ankle-length crimson sheath cocooned within.

The high, straight, boat neckline of the sleeveless gown belied the deep vee cut away at its back. Holly unhooked her bra and stuffed it in the bottom of the carrier bag before stepping into the gown and shimmying the silky lined fabric up over her body. Surveying her reflection in the mirror, she wondered if she hadn't gone too far this year; normally she hired a black dress, but there was something about this gown that had beckoned to her like a promise of hidden treasure. She'd hesitated at the cost, mindful of her financial commitments, but it wasn't as if she'd be deluged with gifts from family or a lover. She had neither.

So for once she'd splurged. This was her gift to herself, and she would bask in the pleasure of wearing the gown all evening.

The minute Holly stepped from the ladies' room she heard a raised female voice through the open door to Connor's office.

She would have recognised his ex-wife's shrill tone anywhere. Before the divorce the secretarial pool had been at her beck and call to assist with her charity work—Carla Knight was nothing if not demanding. The girls would draw straws before anyone would set foot on this floor to take her instructions. Holly sent a silent wish skywards that whatever the situation was, and it sounded intense, it would be resolved quickly.

As silently as she could, she stowed her things back in her cupboard and turned to leave when suddenly Connor's voice vibrated through the air, disgust lacing his words with a sharpness Holly had rarely heard from him.

"You don't deny it then?"

"How dare you have me investigated? Those records were private!"

"Everything has its price, Carla. Unfortunately I never realised yours until it was too late. You can tell your fancy overpriced divorce lawyer you won't be getting another cent beyond the settlement you've already received. Ever. Now, get out of my sight."

"Gladly!"

It was too late to retreat now. Holly straightened her shoulders. There was nothing else for it but to meet the former Mrs. Knight face on.

"Slumming it with the staff tonight, Connor?" Carla spat, vitriol poisoning her exquisite features as she pushed her petite frame past Holly. She slanted a spiteful glare at Holly. "I might have known you'd be hovering around. But of course, I forgot, you don't have anyone to go home to, do you?"

Speechless, Holly stood back and let the other woman through, leaving behind her a cloud of expensive French fragrance and the air crackling with ill humour.

"I'm sorry you had to bear the brunt of that, Holly."

She drew in a calming breath and turned to face him. Connor stood at the door to his office, the usual resonance in his voice flat, his eyes glittering and fired with anger.

"It's all right, sir." She reached across her desk and extracted her evening bag from the top drawer, determined not to acknowledge the barb Carla had flung. She refused to submit to the other woman's cruel taunt; she'd grown up with worse. While such sneers had the power to inflict pain, Holly had learned the hard way to never let it show. She straightened from her desk. "Are you ready to go back downstairs?"

He let out a breath, slowly and carefully, as if he'd been holding on to his control by a thread.

"Yeah. I'm ready." He took a step towards her and let out a low whistle. "And so, it appears, are you." A feral flash of hunger blazed and died in his eyes so quickly Holly wondered if she'd identified it correctly. "Holly, you look…amazing."

She forced herself to remember to breathe as he raked her body with his eyes. It was one thing being the target of a few harshly spoken words, but quite another to be the target of a gaze that stroked her body like a silk scarf over bare skin. It was as if he saw her through new eyes. She instantly pushed the idea away for the foolishness it was.

"Thank you, sir. You look pretty amazing yourself." Formal dress should make a man look more distant, she decided distractedly, not make him look so wickedly sensual. With his dark hair and eyes, and dressed in a tailored black suit with a crisp white shirt and black bow tie at his tanned throat, Connor Knight looked like he'd stepped out of a dream fantasy. *Her* dream fantasy. The one where they stood at an altar and he promised to love and cherish her, forever. *Enough!* Holly snapped her thoughts back into the present. To reality.

She turned her back on him and began to walk towards the

door before she did or said anything foolish. Her emotions had already taken a battering tonight, and the way he looked, not to mention the way he looked at her, scrambled her senses so badly she could barely think let alone walk straight.

"Hold on a minute, Holly." His voice came from close behind. "Shall we?" He offered his arm and, with only a tiny hesitation, she threaded her hand through the crook of his elbow and laid her fingers on his sleeve. He was a solid wall of strength next to her, his hip brushing against hers with each step as he matched his pace to hers. Holly's nerves wound tighter and tighter, like a spring about to snap.

In the elevator she found respite by removing her hand from his arm and stepping slightly away to press the button to take them back downstairs. She let her hand drop back down to her side, where it rested momentarily before Connor's strong fingers grasped hers and replaced them on his sleeve.

"Mr Knight?" Her voice caught on a tiny gasp.

His eyes burned with an emotion she couldn't quite tag. One corner of his mouth tilted, almost as if he mocked himself. "Humour me, Holly. Maybe I need a beautiful woman on my arm tonight."

Two

Lost for words, Holly tried to school her features into their usual calm. Yet when her eyes met his, she couldn't hold his gaze, and they flicked nervously instead to her fingers lying, starkly docile, against the black cloth of his tuxedo. He needed her? That was an entirely new and unexpected development. One she wasn't sure how to handle.

Beneath her hand she sensed the play of muscles in his forearm. Suppressed tension shimmered off him in waves. Okay, so he was stinging after his meeting with Carla, and maybe he was using her for whatever reason tonight—she could accept that—but try as she might, it was difficult to subdue the answering call of her body to the leashed power of his. Heat flickered deep inside her, tiny flames taking hold and sending burning liquid through her veins.

Need? She knew all about need.

As short as the elevator ride was, to Holly it felt like

forever. If they didn't make the distance soon she was certain she'd melt, lose her inhibitions and press herself against his tensely held form.

The cooling air of the cafeteria was a breath of sanity as the doors opened. Staff and their partners had already begun to arrive and were drifting around the room in a hum of conversation.

Connor wondered how long it would be before he could shuck his duties and slink back to his flat. A couple of hours, tops. Holly needed to take it easy, too. She'd scared him tonight when he'd looked across the room and seen her face, as stark and white as the wall behind her, during the children's party. Despite her denial, it was obvious something was wrong.

It didn't stop you using her to make yourself feel better, a cynical voice from inside remarked with scathing honesty. The admission brought him down a notch. No, he hadn't hesitated. Holly was the antithesis of the vicious blazing fury of Carla's indignation—the constant epitome of calm in his storm. An influence, he freely admitted, he'd always taken for granted.

Until he'd seen her tonight, and been hurriedly and disturbingly reminded she was most definitely a woman. A sensuously beautiful woman.

He looked at the slender bow of her neck as she fussed with something in her evening bag and wondered how her skin would feel, would taste. Connor clamped a lid on the thought before it had time to flourish and grow into something more than a tingle of awareness. She was his PA. And she'd be horrified if she knew the rampant slant of his thoughts. No doubt she'd be a darn sight paler than she'd been earlier tonight.

There was a flush on her cheeks now, he noted with some relief, and her eyes, as they darted about the room checking everything, had a sparkle in their blue depths that had been missing before. He was glad he'd made the decision earlier to put Janet in charge of tonight. Holly deserved the break, and her assistant had been thrilled at the chance to show off her training. It was a win-win all round, and it would keep Holly at his side—all night.

Connor bent his head close to her ear. "Relax, Holly, you're officially off duty as of now." Her faint scent teased his nostrils with its hint of warm summer nights and fresh linen, and enticed him to linger before his own hands-off rule, lit in neon signs across the back of his eyes.

"But someone has to oversee—"

"I've instructed Janet to take over for you tonight, she'll manage fine. You've organised the party to within a nanosecond of perfection, anyway. Let her take care of whatever crops up."

"Really, I must—"

"Relax," he urged her quietly.

With his dark head still bent to hers so intimately, he realised they were getting speculative glances from a few of the staff around the room. The office buzz needed little to fuel it, although most wouldn't dare get caught out in gossip about one of the Knights. He needed to get things back on an even footing, although for some indeterminate reason he didn't want to.

"You must let me do my job," she protested again, taking a tiny step away.

Connor fought back a frustrated retort. He elegantly snagged two glasses of champagne from a passing waiter and pressed one into her fingers. "Your job is done, Holly. Here, celebrate. Another brilliant year, thank you." He clinked his glass gently against hers in his own personal toast.

"You know I don't drink at company functions."

"Quit arguing and lighten up, hmm?" He scanned the room. "Try to look as though you're having fun. I insist." He lowered his voice and gave her a mock-stern glower. For a moment he thought she'd taken him seriously, until a welcome spark of rebellion flared in her eyes, darkening and deepening their intense blue.

Had he ever noticed the colour of her eyes before tonight? He must have, surely. The negative response, as he dredged his memory, reminded him of his position, and hers. Of course he hadn't paid attention to her features. Then why, he wondered, did he want more detail tonight?

A perverse, devilish urge made him shift closer to her as the revellers swirled about them, and he placed his free hand against her exposed lower back. Under his fingers her spine straightened, ramrod stiff, as he stroked lightly across skin that felt astonishingly heated. The contrast between his cool fingers and her intense warmth reminded him yet again of their differences, their positions, urging him to desist while sensation burned an enticing brand across his fingertips. He sensed, rather than heard, Holly's breath catch in her throat. This was getting out of control. *He* was getting out of control, and way overstepping the mark.

Reluctantly he withdrew his hand. Just in time it seemed, as Janet came over, gushing with pride. "You don't need to worry, Holly, I have it all under control. I think Mr. Knight's idea to let you enjoy yourself tonight was great, don't you? For once you can be one of the guests and really have a good time."

Holly's lips peeled back from her teeth in what approximated a smile but inside she was on the verge of shattering.

"Thank you, Janet. I…I appreciate you stepping into the breach like that. But don't hesitate to—"

"You're doing a marvellous job, Janet. Thank you." Connor's fingers stroked another delicious line across the small of her back, sending a cascade of goose bumps rippling beneath the seam of her gown and shocking the words she was about to utter into silence.

She couldn't stand it anymore. She stepped forward and turned so he could no longer reach her bare skin. 'Mr. Knight—"

"Connor. And let it go for one night, okay. Orders from the boss." He stared down the final protest that hovered on her lips, a taunting slant to his smile. "Speaking of the boss, let's work our way over and see mine." He nodded to where his father, Tony Knight, the founder and president of Knight Enterprises stood, like the patriarch he was, his erect posture exuding strength and pride as he gazed about the room.

The steady gentle pressure of Connor's hand returned against the base of her spine, a pressure that sent wild spirals of warmth unfurling through her body. She barely acknowledged the greetings and festive wishes from the staff as they cut a swathe through the crowd, the minglers parting like the Red Sea as they moved across the room.

As they neared the gathering of senior executives, she struggled to regain her composure, to ignore the imprint of Connor's proprietary hand against the small of her back and to settle the butterflies that fluttered every time she had to deal with the senior Mr. Knight. She worked with men of his position and power on a regular basis, but there was something about Antony Knight that commanded respect. A respect that, for Holly, bordered on something closer to awe. She certainly didn't want to dissolve like an idiot at his feet because his youngest son was sending her senses into meltdown.

A first generation Kiwi, born to Italian immigrant parents who'd anglicised their name to better fit into their adopted country, Tony Knight had built Knight Enterprises from the ground up. Holly had no doubt he could still swing a hammer with the best of them, but that wasn't what made her admire him the most.

No, she acknowledged as she fought to bank the fire burning in her veins, it was his unstinting devotion to his family. His abiding love for his long-dead wife. He'd raised three sons while building an empire, and yet, even though she had no doubt that the past had been rocky, he'd maintained that solid thread of familial connection between them. Despite his setbacks he hadn't given them up to strangers to raise, like her mother had when she'd discarded Holly, as if she'd been unwanted baggage.

Holly would give just about anything to be a part of a background like that. A background she could call her own. The sobering thought did its work with chilling accuracy and she stepped clear of Connor's reach to greet his father.

Her face ached with the effort of keeping a smile pasted on.

Connor had stayed close to her all evening, shepherding her as she mingled and chatted sociably with their colleagues, ensuring she constantly had a glass of champagne in her fingers and that she stayed well clear of administrative responsibilities for the evening. For once she knew what it felt like to be the one being looked after—the sensation was totally foreign to her and strangely unsettling at the same time.

She lifted her drink to her lips and took a tiny sip of the wine. Darn, warm again. She'd barely drunk a full glass all evening. Mind you, that was probably a good thing. Her stomach had been so knotted with tension she hadn't eaten, either. While the food on the buffet and circulating on trays looked wonderful, and as usual she'd ensured there was plenty of it, she simply couldn't bring herself to take a bite.

She flicked a glance to the wall clock by the door, and her shoulders sagged gently in relief. Things would draw to a close soon. Mr. Knight, Sr. would make his usual end-of-year speech, thanking the skeleton crew who would keep the business ticking over in its usual efficient fashion during the three weeks while most staff took their holiday break, and wishing everyone a happy Christmas.

Happy Christmas indeed, for those who had family and friends to share it with. Holly felt a tiny frown pull at her forehead, and the beginnings of a headache prodded behind her eyes.

Would Andrea even be aware it was Christmas Day tomorrow? The staff at the nursing home had recommended that Holly not come in, and that her foster sister wouldn't worry if for once she spent a holiday with her other friends. Except Holly had no one else she wanted to spend the day with. Andrea was all she had—her one positive link to her past.

Maybe she'd call into the home, anyway, and take Andrea the filmy new nightgown she'd bought her—a soft mossy green, to match her eyes.

"Hey, smile. It's Christmas, remember? No need to look so sad." Connor's warm breath caressed the side of her neck, his voice lowered to a sensuous hum that stroked along her nerve endings like fingertips over plush velvet. A rush of awareness prickled all the way up into her scalp.

"Was I?" She turned to face him. "I'm okay."

"Are you sure?"

"Of course," she responded in her usual brisk tone.

"Good to see you're feeling better." Connor grinned back at her. "You've got your 'office voice' back again. Come on, let your hair down. Enjoy yourself."

"I am." Oh, Lord, she sounded so darn prim and defensive.

To offset the prudishly proper tone of her voice she lifted her wine again to take another sip, but was halted when a warm hand grasped her wrist. A shock of electricity raced up to her hand, causing a wild tremble as Connor took the glass from her suddenly nerveless fingers.

"Here, I'll get you another. That one must be warm by now. You *are* supposed to drink it, you know."

She shook her head slightly, but he ignored her and signalled to a passing waiter for a fresh glass. She grasped the slender stem, sloshing a bit of the wine over the edge.

"Are you sure you're all right, Holly?" Connor stepped closer, his arm slipping supportively behind her back. "You still look a bit shaky, there."

"I'm fine. Just a little tired, that's all. If you don't mind, perhaps I could slip away early."

"Great idea." Connor scanned the room. "I think we've done our dash tonight. Let's go."

Together?

"No, truly," she protested, "you stay. I'm sure your father—"

"Will excuse me this time. He owes me for that Santa episode. He knows how I feel about kids." Even though he was smiling, there was a hard glitter in his eyes. The urbane mask he'd worn all evening slipped, and bleakness hardened his face to marble.

"You don't like children?" Holly couldn't keep the surprise from her voice. He'd been so natural with the little ones, so patient.

"On the contrary." His voice was clipped. "He knows exactly how much children mean to me. Let's make our goodbyes." He slipped her hand in the crook of his arm, and they moved to where his father was holding court with a bunch of his cronies. She felt every eye in the room surreptitiously staring at them as they cut through the crowd.

What on earth was he talking about? If he liked children, why the big deal about being Santa? Unless, a thought occurred to her with sharpening clarity, it had served as a painful reminder of what he didn't have. That might explain his reluctance earlier tonight, not to mention his irritation with his dad.

Another gulf of difference between them. He wanted kids; she didn't. So don't go getting any ideas about his behaviour tonight, she warned herself firmly.

"I see the two of you are off, then." Tony Knight sent a sharp look at Connor, which Holly read quite clearly as admonishment. She watched the silent interplay between father and son, neither backing down, yet an undercurrent so strong flowing between them no one would dare get caught in their crossfire. Holly knew Tony Knight frowned on relationships between staff, and for the life of her she couldn't understand why Connor was giving his father the impression they were leaving together.

"Yes, Papa. *We* are."

Connor's subtle emphasis on the word *we* made the older man's lips thin somewhat in response, and his eyes flicked assessingly between her and his youngest son. A frisson of disquiet trickled down Holly's spine. He thought they were a couple? She had to dissuade him from that idea straight away.

Before she could interject, he bent down and bussed Holly's cheeks in his extravagant Italian fashion. Her shock at his action burst through her cool reserve, painting a warm stain of colour on her face. For all that his family had done their best to adopt the "Kiwi way", he was, and would always remain, Italian to the soles of his handmade shoes.

"You did a marvellous job again tonight, Holly." He smiled,

although it didn't quite reach his eyes. They remained sharply tuned to her face—watching as intently as a hawk, and making her feel about as vulnerable as a field mouse exposed on an overgrazed paddock.

"It's my pleasure, sir," she eventually managed, her own smile frozen on her face.

He gave a sharp nod in acknowledgement, then fired his gaze back at Connor. "I'll still be seeing you tomorrow morning, then? Remember my cousin Isabella and her daughter will also be attending."

"Of course." She felt Connor's arm tighten beneath the fine cloth of his suit as if he was holding himself in check.

"Good." His father turned slightly, dismissing them both.

"I thought I'd invite Holly to join us. You don't mind, do you?" Connor's challenge hung in the air, and he faced down the shocked expression on his father's face. He turned to Holly. "You don't have any plans for the morning do you?"

"But I—" she began to protest.

"I'm sure Holly—" Tony Knight spoke simultaneously.

Connor raised an eyebrow at Holly. "Well?"

"I can't intrude."

"So you have no plans, then, for tomorrow?"

"No." Her response was barely a breath on the air. She hated having to admit it. Hated it, and the unwanted sympathy it always engendered, with a vengeance.

"Fine. We'll be there at ten-thirty, Papa."

Holly felt as though she'd been hijacked. At what point had Connor decided to use her in some game he was playing against his father? And why? The older man's eyes were spitting chips of ice although he reined in his anger well. If she hadn't already been so finely attuned to the atmosphere between the two men, she might not even have noticed.

"Don't be late." Tony Knight bit off the command, acceding he'd been outmanoeuvred.

"We won't be."

Before she could further analyse their veiled animosity, Connor was guiding her towards the door.

In the elevator Connor released a deep sigh and leaned back against the wall, closing his eyes briefly. He was sick of playing his father's games. Tony Knight had tried to control each of his three boys at some time or another. Connor had always counted his blessings that he'd been last in the queue. But tonight, especially tonight, he'd resolved not to play his father's game any longer. There was no way he'd be put on parade for yet another matchmaking attempt with yet another distant cousin. The pressure his old man had been exerting, initially subtle and then later not so, for Connor to get over Carla and find a new woman to make a home—a family—with, had been the last straw. Especially today.

He shouldn't have used Holly like that, though. It was shameful. He'd seen the questions flinging around in his father's mind as if they were graffiti, starkly spray painted on the boardroom wall. What was he, Connor, thinking? Christmas had always traditionally been for family. Only family. The last woman he'd brought had been Carla, as his wife. He knew he'd be in for a grilling tomorrow. What the hell? It'd be worth it. Maybe he'd even get around to telling his father about the grandchild he'd never get to know or love.

He glanced at Holly. The slender line of her throat arched slightly as she held her head tilted, staring at the numbers as they lit consecutively on the overhead console. A man could dream about making love to a neck like that. Feathering gentle kisses along the pale-blue pulse that beat beneath her ear.

Stroking his tongue down the feminine cord of her neck, lower and lower until he bit softly at the curve of her shoulder.

Heat flooded his groin, driving his body to full, pulsing life. What the hell was he thinking? Holly wasn't some potential conquest to reignite the flame of hunger his wife had annihilated with her deceptions. Yet, for some reason he couldn't tear his eyes from her throat, and his mouth dried as he imagined living out the fantasy of the image playing in his mind.

At their floor, the doors slid smoothly open and she stepped out ahead of him, affording him a delectable view of her smooth straight back. Her skin glowed with a hint of colour that made him wonder if she'd be that colour all over.

A jolt of need struck him, deep and hard. Suddenly, Lord help him, it was crucial to find out.

Three

"It always feels weird being here when everyone's gone home." Holly retrieved her suit carrier and handbag from the cupboard in her office.

"Yeah," Connor agreed from where he leaned against the wall, his hands thrust into his trouser pockets.

Holly turned, startled by the odd note to his voice. He watched her, his dark black-brown eyes unblinking. The burning heat in them made her stomach lurch with a nervous flip-flop.

She needed to get this business about Christmas Day sorted now. "About tomorrow—"

"I'll pick you up in the morning. I'll need your address."

He pushed off the wall and came to stand closer. The fresh citrus scent of his cologne together with the underlying spice of pure male filled her nostrils. They flared involuntarily, as if trying to inhale his scent deeper. Instantaneously she shut down the urge to breathe in deep, switching instead to short, shallow intakes through her mouth. It was one thing to believe yourself in love with your boss but quite another to believe he was interested in return. Somehow he must have unconsciously picked up the message that she was attracted to him, more than attracted if her wildly chaotic hormones were anything to go by. He was strong, he was male, no doubt he was reacting instinctively to whatever signals she'd been sending. The signals had to stop here and now.

"Look, it won't be necessary. I'll call your father in the morning and make my apologies. You don't need me gate crashing your family's special day."

"Nonsense. You're coming." Connor strolled towards his office, loosening his tie before discarding it on the couch against the wall. "And speaking of special days, how come you never told me it was your birthday?"

He knew? "It's not important," Holly responded sharply.

"All birthdays are important. Besides, I got you something. Come in here for a minute."

Holly's heart hammered in her chest like a woodpecker at a tree trunk. *He'd bought her a gift?*

She placed her things carefully on her desk and stepped into his office. The door swung silently to a close behind her as he turned from his desk, a large cellophane-and-tissue-wrapped parcel in his hands.

"I noticed today how much you seem to like these things, but I wanted to get you something a bit different. Here, happy birthday."

Connor stepped forward and placed the white poinsettia in her hands. She didn't know whether to laugh or cry until weary emotion got the better of her and sudden tears sprang to her eyes. She blinked, hard, and kept her head tilted down, not trusting herself to speak. She would *not* break down in front of him.

"It's beautiful, Mr. Knight. Thank you."

"Hey, I thought we'd agreed you'd call me Connor." He lifted a long finger and tipped up her chin so she couldn't avoid drowning in the concern reflected on his face.

Her breath hitched, and she blinked again. Except this time she couldn't stem the acidic burn of moisture in her eyes.

"Tears, Holly?" His eyes narrowed as one fat tear hovered for a brief second then spilled off her lower lashes and tracked its inexorable path down her cheek to the corner of her lips. She turned her face, pulling away from the tenderness of his fingers, the pity in his gaze.

She'd had a lifetime of pity and she couldn't bear to look up and see more from him. Not now. Not ever. She swallowed against the lump in her throat, instinctively reaching for the anger she knew she needed to shore herself up and carry through with the rest of this farce.

"It's nothing. Just a headache, that's all." She held the gift with numb fingers, the crunch of the cellophane rippling in the air over her laboured breathing.

Connor stepped forward and removed the plant from her hands. "It doesn't look like nothing to me."

He put the plant back on his desk, then turned and caught her hands in his, drawing her closer until her breasts brushed against the fine-textured cloth of his suit. Beneath the fabric of her gown her nipples tingled and tightened almost painfully.

Her reaction to his nearness, to him, didn't go unnoticed. His eyes gleamed like black fire, his pupils dilating, almost consuming the rich dark brown of his irises.

For an infinitesimal moment Holly allowed herself to dream, to believe he might want her. To believe he might return her love. In that moment, she was certain, her heart laid itself bare to his scrutiny, her own eyes the shimmering window to her feelings.

But then the smouldering anger flamed back into life. Love, ha! He didn't love her. He pitied her. Otherwise why would she be here, pressed up against the hard wall of his chest, feeling the rise and fall of his breathing as it matched her own. She couldn't allow herself to be so vulnerable. Vulnerability was an indulgence she simply couldn't afford. She pulled free of his hold, her body mourning the loss of his heat even as she did so.

"I must go. Thank you for the plant." She wrenched the poinsettia back off his desk and swivelled on her heels to leave, silently castigating herself for a being a fool to want more than she had a right to.

Three weeks away from work, away from Connor Knight, would be a godsend right now. She wanted distance and she wanted it now. Yet a tiny chink in her rapidly assumed armour whispered, *Liar. You want him.*

"Holly—?" He caught her by her elbow and swung her around to face him.

Refusing to make eye contact, she stared blindly past his shoulder at the sparkling vista of the Auckland city lights, dazzling like a pirate's treasure against the skyline and inky black harbour beyond. He could keep his wretched pity and he could keep his blasted plant along with it.

He brushed another errant tear from her cheek with the back of his hand, his touch igniting the banked embers of desire she was working so hard to contain.

Contain it be damned.

She'd probably regret this in the morning. Heck, probably, nothing. Regrets were for the weak. If life had taught her anything it was how to be strong. To grab what you wanted and hold on tight. And right now, more than anything, she wanted Connor Knight.

The poinsettia dropped, unheeded, to the soft carpeted floor. The crinkle of cellophane as it rolled to one side, spilling a little dark soil on the pristine grey wool surface, barely registering against the roaring sound in her ears.

Holly reached up and laced her fingers at the back of Connor's neck and drew his head down to hers. She parted her lips, drawing in the taste of him before she pressed her mouth to his.

A jolt of shock shuddered through him. Shock and desire. Hot, hungry and hard. It had been years since he'd felt like this. Since he'd *allowed* himself to feel like this. Tonight Holly had struck at something deep within him. Something he'd held encased in ice, since desire and trust had been eviscerated from him by his ex-wife. Something that was now beginning to thaw.

Connor angled his head to taste her more deeply. While she'd led, he now took control. It was what he did best, and his body had been dormant for far too long. His tongue probed the moist recess of her willing mouth, stroking, tasting and wanting more. He slid his hands around to the small of her back, tilting her hips forward, drawing her closer towards his heat, his very need. A groan wrenched from deep in his throat at the contact—the warmth of her body igniting a fever in him, making him want with a savage hunger that ached through his entire frame.

He stroked one hand along the length of her exposed back, drawing her closer until he could feel the softness of her breasts pressing against his chest. And it wasn't enough. Right now, he felt like it would never be enough.

His hand travelled further, upwards to the nape of her neck, where tiny strands of fine dark hair had fanned out and escaped the confines of her formal hairdo. Tiny strands that had enticed and goaded him all evening to feel their soft-ness—a hint of the woman beneath the touch-me-not armour.

Her skin tightened and reacted to his touch, much as his had earlier this evening when she'd helped him transform into Santa Claus. But he felt anything but jolly and benevolent right now. He was like a dormant geyser, coerced into boiling, surging life. A geyser about to erupt.

His lips left her mouth. He had to taste her skin, to feel its texture against his lips, his tongue. He relished her sudden gasp as his tongue traced along the base of her hairline and he welcomed her weight as she sagged bodily against him.

Yet still, it wasn't enough, he wanted more of her. To touch. To see. To explore.

"Stay right where you are," he instructed, his voice nothing more than a husky growl.

Connor moved swiftly behind her and skimmed both hands under her dress to coax the fabric over her shoulders until with a 'shoosh' of lining it dropped forward. In the reflection of his privacy-tinted floor-length office window he watched, mesmerised as the falling fabric exposed the delicious line of her collarbone. The dim lighting of the office lent ethereal mystery and shadows to the creamy caramel of her skin.

"Lift your arms," he instructed, and slid the fabric down further as she did so.

A groan of approval, husky and raw, escaped him as he exposed the full roundness of her breasts, her dark rose-tinted nipples tight and distended.

"So beautiful," he murmured.

Holly felt a moment's panic as his warm breath sent flickers of dancing flame across the nape of her neck. She watched their reflection as his strong hands cupped her breasts, taking their weight, testing them. Then panic was overwhelmed by sensation as his thumbs stroked the aching peaks. Tension swamped her body, and her legs began to tremble as sensation arrowed to the core of her body, tighter and tighter until moist heat gathered then pooled in her panties.

She shivered and sucked in a breath as Connor nipped gently at the tender skin below her ear. The tiny pleasure-pain the pressure of his teeth left against her skin was foreign, yet deeply addictive at the same time.

She uttered a tightly strangled sob when his hands left her breasts. She wanted more with a desperation she'd never known. Not even when she'd been a child, wanting and needing a family to call her own. A family to belong to. She might not belong to Connor Knight forever, but she could belong to him for now—this moment—couldn't she? For this one exquisite moment?

She sighed as his hands trailed gently down her back to where her dress had arrested at her waist. The movement of his wrist was slight, but sufficient to send her gown cascading in a pool of crimson to her feet, exposing her matching lace bikini briefs and the length of her bare legs.

In the window she watched, mesmerised, as his hands slid over the gentle curve of her hips and the tension at the apex of her thighs ratcheted up another notch.

"Do you like what you see?" His voice was a tantalizing whisper in the shell of her ear.

Holly trembled as his hands slid around to the front of her body. One hand stroked upwards to caress her breast, and the other down where it slid inside the sheer lace of her panties and dragged them away to expose the dark coils of hair that led to her private core.

"Y-esss," the word hissed past her lips as he parted the folds of her flesh and gently stroked the centre of tension that wound her body hard against his like a bow. Unaccustomed sensation cascaded through her, building in undulating waves, but riding on the crest of those waves surfed a flicker of fear. She was losing control, surrendering absolutely to him.

"So do I."

His words were almost her undoing, yet she clenched her body tight—holding on, holding back, trying to regain some measure of restraint.

Connor slid one finger inside the liquid heat that threatened to send him over the edge. He struggled to meet the challenge of maintaining an intellectual distance from the vision in the glass and the waves of heat and passion that emanated from the woman shaking in his arms—against his insistent body.

Their reflection only served to incite him to a higher plane of need. Her glowing creamy skin fractured by the scanty line of red lace and framed by the darkness of his black suit behind her. The total contrast in their state of dress did nothing to lower the raging want that almost threatened to undo him, to send him uncontrollably over the edge in a way he hadn't experienced since his early teens.

He focused on Holly's face and noted, with powerful pleasure, how her eyes glittered. No longer with tears, but with a dark intense blue flame of passion.

With a slick finger he circled the hood of swollen flesh concealing the sensitive bud of nerve endings he knew would send her over the edge. Her breath quickened and the luscious swell of her breasts tightened and lifted as he gently increased pressure.

Her cry of release was a trophy to his ears, and he supported her body against the screaming responsive demands of his own as she shuddered to completion. He felt all-powerful. For the first time in forever, he felt like a man who had it all.

Well, not quite all, he acceded as he slid her underpants

further down, exposing the globes of her buttocks, buttocks that as they'd pressed against him had been driving him closer and closer to losing control.

He bent her forward, placing her hands to rest on the surface of his desk, and swiftly released himself from the confines of his trousers. He guided himself forward until his tip nestled at her entrance. He was acutely sensitive, still feeling the tiny tremors that pulsed through her, waiting, holding back until he could hold back no longer.

The guttural cry that ripped from his throat as he thrust forward was as foreign to him as the concept of making love to his PA on his desk, yet for some reason—here, now—it all seemed perfectly right.

She was tight, almost unbearably so, and from somewhere he miraculously found the strength to hold back until he felt her mould to his length, to sheath him with her wet heat until instinct overrode sensibility. Her body stiffened as he drove his full length into her and he reached around again to caress her sensitive nub. Taking the time to bring her to climax again was excruciating, until the rhythmic pull of her inner muscles took him suddenly, gloriously, over the edge.

Spent, mentally and physically, and breathing in great gulps, Connor collapsed over Holly's back. Bit by bit he became aware of their surroundings. Of the way his body pressed against hers, the feel of her silky smooth buttocks against his groin, her knotted fists beneath the spread of his fingers where he'd imprisoned them against the polished surface of his desk.

His desk.

The distant "ping" of the elevator returning to their floor rudely brought him to his senses. Someone was outside in the main office.

Reluctantly he withdrew from Holly and hastily rearranged his clothes before bending to assist her with the twisted swathe of her gown from where it lay about her feet.

As she slid her underpants back up, Connor caught sight of a telltale stain on her inner thighs. Blood?

"Here," he said, retrieving a handkerchief from his pocket, "You have your period."

"No." Her voice was strained. "It's not my period." She shimmied back into her gown, hiding the luminescent glory of her skin behind the rich glowing fabric.

"What?"

"I said I don't have my period." Holly smoothed her gown with shaking hands.

"You mean…" Connor was lost for words. *She was a virgin?* Or at least she had been until he'd taken her like a rutting stag. He grabbed her hand and stopped her as she started to walk away.

"Holly, you can't just leave. We need to talk."

A knock sounded at his inner office door.

"I think we've just said everything we needed to say for tonight." Holly lifted her chin and summoned every ounce of poise she'd worked so hard to develop. "Merry Christmas, Mr. Knight."

As an exit line she knew it was sadly lacking, but her mind was so scrambled she could barely think straight. She slid from his grasp and walked over to the door, swinging it open.

"Yes, Janet?" Holly dragged every scrap of composure she could garner. No mean feat when her heart still pounded like a marathon runner's and her legs were the consistency of jelly.

"I, um, I came upstairs to get my things, and I thought I heard something in Mr. Knight's office. I didn't realise you were still here." A flush of pink dusted the younger woman's cheeks, emphasizing the unsettled look in her eyes as her voice petered out. Holly only hoped her own embarrassment wasn't as visible.

Connor had drawn in behind her and stood like a shield at Holly's back. She stiffened at the sudden sense of heat and latent strength that emanated from him. A tiny quiver of pleasure rippled through her at the physical memory of his hard body behind her, within her, driving her past her prim and proper exterior and onto an entirely new level of living. She fought to control the urge to lean back against him and relive their lovemaking all over again.

"Is that all then, Janet?" Connor asked.

"Yes, sir."

"Then I think you should go, don't you?"

"Yes, sir."

"Merry Christmas, Janet."

"Merry Christmas to you too, sir, and you Holly."

"Thank you, Janet. Have a good holiday." Holly suppressed a hysterical bubble of laughter that rose in her throat. She couldn't believe how normal their exchange sounded. Inside, her heart was hammering a crazy tattoo, while on the exterior she felt like ice. She allowed herself a small sigh of relief when her assistant gave them both a weak smile and left them.

Alone, again.

Holly remained frozen where she was until rationality kicked in and she made for the door. She couldn't stop in case she threw herself at him again. Already she wanted more of him, more than she could ever ask for.

"Don't go. It's not over, Holly."

"Yes, it is. It has to be." With swift simple movements she gathered her garment bag and handbag and made it to the elevator before even taking another shaking breath. With each step she'd expected to hear Connor's footfall on the carpet behind her, yet when she stepped inside the elevator and turned to push the ground-floor button he remained silhouetted in the door to his office, his face inscrutable.

Behind him, his office appeared normal, unchanged—the clock on the wall giving evidence to the passage of but half an hour. Only half an hour? It felt like a whole new lifetime. Holly knew she would never feel normal again. But whatever happened after tonight, she would always be able to lock the memory deep within her to take out and examine and cherish at will.

The elevator doors took forever to close but finally they began to draw together. She bit back a cry of alarm as a dark-suited arm wedged between the closing elevator doors sent them springing wide apart again.

"What are you doing?" she asked, her voice high pitched and foreign to her ears.

"It may have escaped your notice but we didn't use protection. We need to talk. Besides which, that was your first time, Holly. For whatever reason, you chose me, and now I owe it to you to make tonight memorable and not just some denigrating experience."

Denigrating? He thought that had been denigrating?

"You don't need to—" Her protest was cut short by an implacable sweep of his hand.

"No, that's where you're completely wrong, Holly. I do need to. And, I will."

Four

Holly watched as Connor swiped his key card through the internal controls that permitted access to the penthouse apartment on the top floor of the tower that he used during the week when late nights didn't make it practical for him to fly back to his home on the island.

She knew she could stop him, if she really wanted to. He was nothing if not a gentleman. But she didn't want to. Not at all.

Despite the climate-controlled temperature in the elevator, a shiver ran down to the base of her spine. She'd only wanted to belong to someone for a moment, to have a connection, albeit fleeting. She hadn't dared dream for any more than that. From the time she'd been old enough to understand what had happened, that her mother was never coming back for her and there was no one else out there who cared enough to try and find her, Christmas Eve had always been the hardest day of the year.

It now struck her as ironic that despite all those years of conditioning, the one time she'd weakened and sought comfort had turned into her first sexual experience. A tug of heat reminded her that Connor had intimated there was more to come.

Was that why she hadn't put up any argument? Was she so pathetic that she'd take whatever he could hand out to her and be grateful? *Yes.*

Suddenly his comment about not using protection struck home. She'd acted purely on instinct, on basic need, and been so swept away by both the man and the moment that the possibility of pregnancy hadn't even occurred to her.

Stupid! Of anyone, she should have known better. There was no way she could have a baby. *No way.*

She silently counted back to the days of her last period. If all the overheard conversations in the staff cafeteria from the women desperate to become pregnant were any measure, she should be safe.

Well, there was always the morning-after pill. Provided, of course, she could find a dispensing pharmacy open on Christmas in the suburb where she lived. Yes, that's what she'd do. As soon as she could get back home she'd source the nearest one.

She stood to one side of the small enclosure as it raced to the top of the building, unsure about where this evening would end. For three years she'd been of no more interest to Connor than a fixture in his office, yet now he chose to spend the night with her? Her skin tingled—*the whole night?*

What had triggered this change in him? Carla! Of course, that was it. He'd been behaving out of sorts ever since his meeting with his ex-wife this evening. Anger and passion were both powerful, strong emotions. Holly knew, from her own tempestuous teenage years and the frustrated anger that had led her into so much trouble and seen her caseworker throw her hands up in surrender, how intrinsically mixed the two emotions could be.

So, he'd spent his anger on Carla, then he'd slaked his passion on her.

The realisation flayed her like a whip. Holly mentally squared her shoulders, absorbing the pain. She was a big girl, and well used to looking after herself. If he wanted to find comfort in her, so be it. They could each have their own agenda, fooling themselves for however long it took to burn out. And burn out it would, Holly had no doubt. On Connor's part at least.

For her, however, the physical act of love had only heightened her senses as far as he was concerned. The intimacy they'd shared in his office now made her more aware of him physically and emotionally.

And more in love with him than before.

The realization was as agonizing as it was hopeless. They were oil and water. The silver-spooned rich boy and the girl from the wrong side of town. The man who wanted children and the woman who swore she wouldn't.

Connor took her things as they stepped into the sumptuously furnished apartment and tossed them onto a leather-covered sofa. In silence he walked over to the bar and poured two glasses of wine before returning, like a panther on the prowl, to where she stood, waiting and unsure of what he expected.

He watched as she tilted the wineglass to her mouth and took a sip, his eyes drawn to the movement of her slender throat as she swallowed. He could still taste her, he realised. And he still wanted her with a fierceness that made his hand tremble slightly as he lifted his own glass in a silent toast.

"Could you become pregnant?" His stark question obviously startled her and she fought to regain her composure.

"That's impossible." She was emphatic.

"Nothing's impossible, Holly. What if it happens?"

She stared at him across the room, her eyes shooting sparks of blue fire. "I'm never having children."

Her words were like a knife twisting deep into his gut. They were harsh words from a woman her age and, ironically, words his treacherous ex-wife had never uttered, even though that had been her intention all along. The knife gave another sharp turn.

"So you're saying you'd terminate a pregnancy?" It was hard to keep anger from his voice, to maintain a rational, conversational tone.

"I didn't say anything of the kind. Don't put words into my mouth."

"Then what are you saying, Holly?" he demanded. "It might already be too late."

"If the worst did happen, I'd take care of it," she replied flatly.

"Take care of it," he repeated. "Why don't I get the impression you're discussing love and nurturing here."

"Look, I'm safe. I already told you that."

"So you say. Nothing's infallible, Holly. And I doubt you're on any form of contraception. Are you?" He gazed at her over the rim of his glass as she responded with a fierce shake of her head. Such fire, such passion. And all this over a conversation. What would she be like when she assumed that passion in the luxury of a large bed? There had been no denying her response to him earlier.

Heat, hot and heavy and clawing with need, engulfed his body.

One thing was for sure. Holly Christmas wouldn't be "taking care of it" if she was pregnant. Nothing would happen to another child of his ever again.

Grief tore at the ragged edges of his mind. He determinedly forced the crushing strength of the emotion aside. He'd take his time to grieve, later. The loss was still too new, too raw to even acknowledge. He needed to lock it away inside and deal with it on his own terms.

For now he intended to lose himself. To focus on the energy that seethed inside of him and turn it into something positive. Something that would surpass the loss and replace it with physical, pleasurable sensations.

Connor reached across and took her wineglass, placed it on a coffee table then reached to take her hand.

"I'd take care of you, Holly." It was a promise. If she carried his child he would ensure they both had the best of everything medicine and money had to offer.

"I can take care of myself." She lifted her chin in defiance of his words, yet her voice, tellingly, wavered. Her vulnerability cut him to the quick, and stark realization dawned. Take care of her? What the hell was he thinking? Had he been so addled by the intoxication of making love to her that he'd forgotten his position as her employer?

He forced himself to question his motives and, for the first time in forever, he didn't like the answers. Had he been so driven by the detestable evidence he'd been presented this morning that he'd subconsciously grasped at the next available opportunity? The thought was anathema to him, yet even so, he couldn't categorically state that in some dark and wounded corner of his heart he hadn't been provoked into manipulating the situation, manipulating Holly, to his own ends.

He dropped her hand as if her touch burned him. "Holly, I—" For the life of him he couldn't do it. He couldn't apologise for making love to her—especially when he wanted to do it again.

She lifted her hand and pressed her fingers gently to his mouth. "Shhh. Don't say it. Don't say you're sorry."

She knew him that well? Shock robbed him of speech, even more than the warm gentle imprint of her fingers against his lips.

"We're both adults," she continued, her voice slightly hesitant at first but growing stronger with each syllable. "We both know what we want. I'm not asking for forever, Connor. Just tonight. Only tonight."

Her fingers traced the outline of his lips and his body leapt to rock-hard attention at her touch. The sound of his name on her lips hung in the air, crashing through the final barrier of indecision. Intently he examined her face, her eyes, searching for the tiniest hint of reluctance, and could barely suppress his elation when he found none.

"Tonight, then." His throat felt raw as the words strained from him in agreement.

Sizzling anticipation shot scorching sparks through her. Her body felt taut, like a runner at the starting blocks, every nerve, every particle on alert. Waiting. Wanting.

"Ready?" Connor murmured as he lifted her hand to his lips and gently pressed them against her knuckles.

"Yes." Her voice was strong. There was no hesitation now. This was what she wanted. Her lips parted on a gasp of pleasure as his warm tongue stroked a hot, wet line between her fingers.

"Let's go, then."

In the softly lit bedroom he let her hand go. Holly stood on the threshold, seeing, but not really taking in, the lush draperies at the window and the hand-crafted armoire and matching dresser. Connor hit a switch on a remote and the curtains drew closed.

"Come here," Connor commanded from where he stood, next to the impossibly wide bed.

Shivering with nerves, Holly did as he bade.

"Undress me."

Where to start? Holly thought for a frantic second, then, almost of their own volition, her hands reached for the lapels of his jacket and pushed them wide, sliding the tailored garment off his broad shoulders and letting it drop to the floor.

She pulled his shirt free of his trousers and painstakingly undid each button from top to bottom until the fine white cotton hung free from his body. She reached for his hands, one at a time, and undid the cuffs on his sleeves, then pushed his shirt away to expose him to her.

He was beautiful. The latent strength of his body evident in the swell of his shoulders and the depth and breadth of his chest. She watched as a quiver ran over the taut muscles of his stomach, the same skin she'd barely grazed with her touch earlier tonight, yet could still feel searing her fingers.

She heard his swift intake of breath as she reached out and trailed her fingers across his belly before fumbling for the catch at his waistband.

"Stop." His voice was a deep-throated growl.

Her fingers halted their activity. Now she wanted to finish what she'd started. He knew already how painfully inexperienced she was, had he changed his mind?

"Touch me."

"Like this?" Her question was tentative. While she'd dreamed of touching him, the reality was hugely different. His skin tightened beneath her feather-light caress as she trailed her fingers over his chest and traced his nipples. To her surprise, and delight, they tightened into hard peaks, much like her own at this very minute. Did he ache for more, like she did?

With a groan, he grabbed her hands, halting them on their path as they trailed down past his belly button. "It's your turn."

"But—"

"But, nothing." He drew in a shuddering breath. "Undo your hair."

Holly lifted her shaking hands to slide out the pins that bound her hair, letting them scatter on the carpet at her feet and allowing the thick black swathe to uncoil and drape past her shoulders and down her back.

Connor ran his hands through the weighty length and she felt his fingers twist and curl in the tresses, gently tilting her head back. He lowered his head and captured her lips in a fierce sweep, demanding she surrender her mouth to him.

At first hesitantly, and then with increasingly more courage, Holly met his onslaught, giving as good as she got. Sucking at his tongue and swirling her own around his in a tango that turned her legs to water and her blood to molten lava.

She could feel how much he wanted her in the marble-hard lines of his body, and even though she knew it wasn't in the same way she wanted him, she would accept everything he had to give her. Her breasts ached to be touched, to be suckled as he suckled her tongue.

His hands skimmed down, pushing her dress over her waist to slide unhindered to the floor. The irony of how easily he'd undressed her wasn't lost, considering her inexperience in undressing him, yet she couldn't have cared less. She needed him holding her, touching her, inside her. Finally his lips were at her breast and a new tension built deep within her. A tension she was learning to identify. The rhythmic pull of his teeth and tongue over her sensitive nipples wrought a tiny scream of pleasure from her lips.

He swooped her off her feet, lifting her from her shoes and leaving a pool of clothing where she'd stood. She felt the fire of his skin as her breast pressed against his bare chest before he placed her on top of the fine, cool sheets of his bed. There had to be an acre of cotton, she thought wildly before she felt the depression of his body next to her. The finely woven fabric felt like a caress against her sensitised skin and even in the dazed heat of passion its quality wasn't lost on her. She had to hoard every memory, every sensation, and hold it fast to her forever.

He'd removed his clothes, and the rasp of his legs along her own made her squirm against the sheets. The hard dry heat of his erection nudged her body, causing a deep-seated contraction to ripple wildly from her core—a prophecy of what was yet to come.

"I won't hurt you this time, Holly," he whispered, his voice laden with more promise than mere words could imply.

"But you didn't—" She stopped on a gasp as he traced her lips with his tongue.

"Don't make me eat your words." A tiny smile played around his lips as he nibbled across her jaw and over her neck.

The laugh that fought past the constriction in her throat surprised her. Humour, when she'd never felt more serious in all her days? Life was full of contradictions.

She pressed against the bed as he gently licked and nipped a line down her body, between her breasts, stopping to lave at her belly button before dropping lower.

Propped as she was on a mound of pillows, the shadowed view of his dark head against her skin made an erotic picture. She could almost separate her mind from what was happening. Almost. But when she felt his warm breath against her, through her panties, thought and reason fled on the building waves of delight that undulated through her body.

She gripped wildly at the sheets, almost too afraid to draw breath, as his tongue traced the leg line of her panties. His fingers tugged the scrap of fabric away from her to be discarded onto the thickly carpeted floor.

Holly almost sprang off the bed when he replaced her panties with the hot wet pressure of his mouth. The surging waves of pleasure built and built inside, until she hovered so close to the brink of release she thought she might shatter.

His weight shifted just before she toppled over the edge, leaving her trembling, craving for more. He slid over her, stroking the line of her body with his hands. She felt him reach past her head and heard the tear of a foil packet. He held himself away from her momentarily and then he was nestling between her thighs. Hot, heavy and totally male.

"Open for me."

At his bidding she lifted her hips and let her legs fall open. He slid within her in one slick delicious movement. Her inner muscles tightened and released against the length of him as he pushed deeper until he was buried inside her. She luxuriated in the sensation of oneness with him, the deep sense of rightness in how they fit together. He'd had her heart for far longer than he knew, or would ever know, and now he had her body. She'd never felt drawn to another human being the way she was pulled to this man. Admitting how much she needed him both thrilled and terrified her. How would she cope when it was all over?

She sighed, the breath erratic, as he slowly withdrew before resettling back so deeply in her body she thought she'd pass out from the exquisite fullness of him. This was nothing like their first encounter where everything had been driven by the heat of the moment. This was making love on a completely different level. She could almost feel his heartbeat, hear his blood rush through his veins, breathe each breath he drew through his lungs.

Spirals of pleasure increased in intensity and urgency as he moved and she moved with him, sensually lifting to meet his every thrust, tilting away as he withdrew only to lift again to welcome his return.

The transition of time suspended, they were the only two people who existed. Locked in a cocoon of pleasure and need and, finally, satisfaction as they cleaved together in a joining that left them depleted yet still alive with exhilaration. Intimately locked together, Holly wrapped her arms about him as he rolled onto his side. She nestled against his chest, inhaling his male scent, committing it to memory as with a deep sense of sadness she remembered this could never last.

The persistent buzz of a telephone finally penetrated the fog that enveloped his brain. Who on earth would ring at such an hour? It couldn't be morning yet, Connor thought irritably as he attempted to roll over. Yet his mobility was impeded by a warm, lush body curved against him, by a swathe of black hair over his shoulders and by long silky legs entwined with his.

Gently he extricated himself and padded, naked, to where his suit jacket lay discarded on the plush navy carpet. He extracted his phone and flipped it open. He found the remote for the curtains and as they pulled open he stretched his back and noted the dull overcast sky.

Typical, he thought irritably. Another muggy, wet Christmas morning. *Christmas morning!* Remembrance dawned with sharp clarity just as his father's voice bellowed in his ear.

"Connor! You're on your way soon, yes?"

"Merry Christmas to you too, Papa."

"You're still bringing that secretary of yours?"

"Holly. Yes, I am. See you soon. *Ciao,* Papa."

He disconnected the call and looked across the room at the

enticing sleeping form draped across his bed. What a shame he couldn't take his time in waking her as he wanted, despite his body's instant reaction. He shook her bare shoulder gently, enjoying watching awareness dawn in her denim-blue eyes as he chased sleep away.

"Come on, my father is expecting us and we still need to stop by your place so you can change."

A wry smile twisted his lips as she shyly pulled the sheets about her, obscuring her breasts from view.

"Just give me a couple of minutes to gather my things." Her voice, husky and thickened with sleep, lit a flame within him he knew only one thing could extinguish.

"Shy?" He tugged persistently at the sheet until it fell away, exposing her. Already she was like a drug invading his senses. With damning clarity he knew one night with Holly would never be enough. So what if they were late, he decided as he pushed her back against the rumpled bedclothes.

They were running more than a little late when they drove out to her home she could change into more suitable clothing. As they turned a corner into her street, Connor managed to hide his surprise when he saw the rundown housing area that Holly had reluctantly given as her address. Sure, in a few years, developers would be renovating the old state-built houses and making a killing, but right now that future seemed a million miles, and several million dollars, away.

"You can pull in here." She indicated a driveway on the cold, southern side of the road. Exposed as the dreary house was, it would get little natural sunlight through its tiny windows, he noted. He couldn't imagine why anyone would want to live like this. Certainly she could do better.

"How long have you owned this place?" he probed.

"I rent."

She *chose* to live here? Connor mentally reviewed the well-above-average sum he knew he paid her. Surely she could have rented somewhere more up-market. Or at the very least, he thought, as he cast a doubtful eye at the large party carrying on a few doors away where even at this hour patched gang members already spilled drunkenly onto the footpath, somewhere safer.

"I'll only be a minute."

"I'm coming in with you."

"Really, it's all right."

"Don't argue with me, Holly. You know you won't win."

Inside, the tiny house was no better. The fact she had to turn on the lights when it was only late morning spoke for itself. Naked bulbs in the ceiling fixtures cast stark light over meagre threadbare furniture. He tried not to curl his lip at the Formica-topped table and two vinyl-covered tubular steel-framed chairs standing askew on the cracked linoleum floor in the kitchen.

"Is this your furniture?" He couldn't help but ask.

"No, I rent the place furnished. Take a seat, and I'll get changed."

Not that it was any of his business, but what on earth did she do with her money?

"Don't I pay you enough?" The question dropped like a bomb in the room, and Holly halted in her tracks.

"You pay me very well." She held herself tightly coiled, as if she was hiding something and was afraid he'd find it. It was a side of her he'd never seen before, and he didn't like it.

"So what the hell do you do with it?" He swung out one arm, gesturing at the miserable conditions.

"Are you dissatisfied with the way I do my job?" Her voice was cold, yet vibrated with suppressed anger.

"Of course not. If I was, you'd know it."

"I'm glad that's settled, then. Because that's where we begin and end. What I do with my money is my business." With that she stalked from the room and into what he assumed was her bedroom. He could hear her moving about—slamming drawers, clattering coat hangers as if she had to vent her anger somehow.

She was right. He didn't like it one bit, but he had no right to push. There were ways and means of getting to the bottom of this. Connor shoved his hands deep into his trouser pockets and rocked on his heels, loath to sit on the sagging sofa positioned in front of the small television.

Through the paper-thin walls, the racket from the party down the street suddenly rose in volume and foul-mouthed jeers rang out through the air against the accompaniment of shattering glass bottles.

"Holly!" he shouted. "We need to go, now."

She reappeared in the doorway. She'd changed into smart pale-grey trousers with matching heeled sandals and a hot-pink short-sleeved blouse that lent a soft glow to her skin and served to detract from the faint shadows under her eyes. Shadows he himself had put there.

Connor urged her down the hallway. He guarded her back impatiently as she took the time to double lock and dead bolt the front door. Probably a total waste of time, he observed cynically, given the fact that it had glass panes that could easily be broken. He ushered her into the front seat of his 5-series BMW and pulled away from the driveway, the slight squeal of his tires as he planted the accelerator eliciting several one-fingered salutes from the partying throng.

Why did she live there, he asked himself again. Were there financial problems that necessitated it? Or some vice perhaps?

It occurred to him that he knew very little about her at all. But whatever secrets she was hiding, he would find them out.

Holly slammed her front door closed behind her and listened as the taxi sped away up the broken-glass-littered street. The day had been interminable. The polite smiles, the conjecture Connor's family couldn't quite hide from their eyes.

Certainly they'd been polite and friendly, his two brothers especially so. But all the while she felt as though she was being judged—and found wanting. Maybe they'd thought he'd bring someone more like Carla—social, outgoing and supremely confident.

She'd been a cuckoo in the nest. Again. The knowledge clutched like a fist around her heart. She should be used to that by now, yet the pain still had the power to bring her to her knees. Still, she was an old hand at hiding her pain deep inside, and that's where the memories of the past twenty-four hours would be firmly lodged.

Leaving hadn't been as difficult as she'd expected. In the end, she'd pleaded a headache to one of Connor's brothers and asked that he make Holly's apologies to everyone. For some stupid, foolish reason, she'd half expected to hear Connor come after her. Why, she didn't really know, because he'd been strategically monopolised by his father's other guests the whole time. He certainly hadn't noticed when she'd slipped from the front portico of Tony Knight's palatial Epsom home and into the waiting taxi she could ill afford.

Maybe he'd accepted that she didn't really belong. Or maybe he'd simply had his fill of her and made his point, whatever that was, with his father. She didn't know which hurt the most.

She dropped onto her bed, half the size of the one she'd slept in last night. The paradox was a joke—a bad one—and her hollow laugh echoed in the scantily furnished room. Deep down she had to admit that there was a tiny piece of her that still wanted the Cinderella finish—the knight in shining armour taking her to his castle to love her forever.

She gave herself a brisk mental shakedown. What had she been thinking? No, the sooner she put last night firmly in the past, where it belonged, the better. Difficult, though, when her body still hummed from the aftermath of Connor's lovemaking this morning and tiny twinges reminded her of the unaccustomed exercise she'd indulged in. And no matter which way she looked at it, it had been an indulgence. One she couldn't afford. After seeing him with his family, the close-knit group, the children, she'd realised with damning clarity that she'd never belong there. And nor could she when she was in no position to offer Connor what, she'd evidenced with her own observations today, he most wanted.

Children of his own.

Moping about the house wouldn't change anything, so Holly did what she did best—got on with things. First order of the afternoon was to find where the nearest urgent pharmacy was, then she'd call and see how Andrea was doing.

Bang, bang, bang! Holly all but leapt out her skin as a fist battered at her front door. Apprehensive, given the flavour of the neighbourhood, she peeped around her doorway and down the hall to the front door. An unmistakable figure loomed through the frosted glass panes.

"Holly, open up. I know you're in there."

She covered the distance to the door reluctantly, taking her time to unbolt the flimsy door and swing it open. He filled the open frame like a dark avenging angel.

"You left without saying goodbye." He stepped inside,

forcing her to flatten herself against the wall to avoid contact. Her shredded nerves couldn't take any more. "Are you okay?"

His hand lifted to her cheek. Holly flinched and pulled her head back. She couldn't bear it if he touched her again. She was strong, but not *that* strong. Challenge lit his gaze as his hand dropped down to his side.

"I'm fine. I thought it was better if I didn't make a fuss about leaving." Her heart pounded in her chest, and she took another step back. "Look. What we did last night was crazy. I was emotional because it was my birthday and you…well, I don't know why you wanted me, and I don't need to know. Let's not make life complicated by turning it into more than it was."

"And what was it, exactly?"

"We fulfilled a need, scratched an itch if you like. That's all."

"An itch?" His expression was deadpan, his voice level. Cool and calm, Connor Knight was formidable, and at this minute he scared Holly far more than if he'd developed a sudden rage at her words.

"For want of a better term, yes."

"What if I want more?"

"More?" her mouth dried and a bolt of desire shot with pulsing heat to radiate through her body. "There can be no *more*. It'll make working together impossible. People will talk…your father, you know his policy on office relationships." Frantic, Holly clutched at every reason she could—no easy feat with her mind just about fried from the dangerous heat in his coal-dark eyes.

"And that's it." His voice grew hard, cold.

"Yes. That's it. We're both adult enough to handle it, aren't we?"

Connor stood still as a statue. Bit by bit she saw a bleak coldness quench the fire in his gaze. His lips thinned in a tight line. A taut coil of tension emanated from him like a palpable thing. *Please, please, please,* she begged silently. *Just go!* Go before I change my mind. His jaw clenched and released as if he'd been on the verge of saying something then thought the better of it.

Down the hall her phone started to ring—the shrill sound grating through the atmosphere that hung thick between them.

A shiver of fear ran the length of her spine. The only calls she ever got were from Andrea's hospital. Something must be wrong for them to be calling now.

"I need to answer that. You can let yourself out." She turned to walk away but his arm snaked out to halt her in her tracks. He spun her back, and suddenly she was pressed against him, her body already willingly forming to the hard lines of his.

"Just one more thing," he growled.

Connor pinned her against the wall, pressing his lips against hers in a hard, possessive move that left her in no doubt of his anger. She pushed the flats of her hands against the wall behind her to stop herself from reaching out to touch him. Yet, despite her best intentions, she couldn't help but respond to the commanding sweep of his tongue, and her lips parted in reluctant welcome.

The instant she surrendered, he broke away and turned to stalk down the cracked, uneven concrete path. Away from her house and away from her. Holly could only watch, helpless yet thankful he'd done so before she threw herself back at him, plastered herself against his body and begged him to stay.

Five

At the private convalescent hospital nestled quietly in vast lawns on the northern-facing slopes of one of Auckland's prestigious suburbs, Holly brushed her foster sister's fine hair against her pillow. It was the only thing to soothe Andrea today.

"Sorry to have disturbed your Christmas," the nurse at the foot of the bed remarked. "She just seemed worse today. We tried earlier to get a hold of you to let you know."

"I know. I'm sorry," Holly answered with a worried smile. "You did the right thing to call me in."

"I hope we didn't interrupt anything important."

"No," she managed through stiffened lips, "nothing that couldn't be left."

"Maybe next Christmas there'll be someone special to sweep you off your feet," the nurse continued with a wink. "You never know just what's around the corner."

Heat suffused Holly's cheeks. No, you never did know

what was around the corner and that was precisely why she was never sleeping with Connor Knight again. The nurse didn't know quite how close she'd struck to the bone. Holly smiled a brief response and put the hairbrush down, looking at Andrea's tragically uncommunicative twitching form in the bed. She was a far cry from the exuberant adolescent who'd egged her on to believe in herself when no one else would. Fate had finally smiled on them both when they'd been placed in a home together.

While it was highly unlikely Holly carried the juvenile Huntington's gene that slowly and painstakingly stole her dearest and closest friend from her, who knew what time bomb she could pass onto her children? And for as long as Holly was responsible for paying for Andrea's care, she couldn't afford the investigators necessary to try and trace her own parents.

So it was simple. No children. Ever. Andrea was far more important than anything else right now. Including Connor Knight.

Back at work just over a month later, Holly was grateful she'd had no other demands on her time. Andrea's deterioration over the break had been marked, and Holly had been forced to request to use up the balance of her accrued leave so she could spend every available minute with her. It had taken some juggling, but Janet had happily returned early from her holidays to fill in.

The emotional demands of remaining positive for Andrea had left Holly totally wrung out by the end of each day, and now the onset of a mild yet persistent tummy bug meant that she'd have to restrict her visits until she was better again. At first she'd panicked, terrified she was pregnant, but the light period she'd had two weeks ago made that impossible. Thank God.

Holly's feet dragged as she stepped down the corridor to her office. The poinsettias hadn't suffered for the lack of natural light at her workstation, she observed ruefully. Obviously, someone had kept them watered during her extended break, although they did seem a bit washed out for colour. How symbolic, she thought, cynicism twisting her lips, just like her.

She'd lost weight and her appetite had been reduced to nil. How she'd contracted this wretched stomach bug was beyond her, although she had her suspicions about the efficiency of her ancient refrigerator, with its damaged door seal, combined with Auckland's high summer humidity. The mix was bound to have wreaked havoc on the food she'd managed to force past her lips.

In response to the thought of food, her stomach heaved slightly. Holly took a deep levelling breath and waited for the nausea to subside.

The white poinsettia was nowhere to be seen. She supposed the cleaners must have disposed of it when they'd cleaned up the mess it had left after landing ignominiously on the carpet on Christmas Eve. That night seemed so long ago.

She hadn't heard from Connor. He'd been away at his family's holiday home on the Coromandel Peninsula during the two weeks immediately after Christmas, and HR had handled her request for additional time off in his absence. Even if he had tried to call her once he was back in Auckland, she'd been at the hospital most of the time, only going home to sleep late at night, then racing off early to catch the succession of buses that took her back to Andrea. Besides, it was exactly what she'd wanted. No fuss, no complications and certainly no recriminations to interfere with her ability to do her job and earn her desperately needed income.

"Good morning, Holly."

Connor stood in the doorway to his office. It was all she could do not to jump at the sound of his voice. She hadn't allowed herself to realise, until now, how much she'd missed the timbre of her name on his lips. How much she'd missed *him*.

"Good morning, Mr. Knight."

Holly busied herself putting her handbag away and checking the papers in the in-box on the corner of her desk. She heard Connor sigh from behind her.

"I think we've gone past you calling me Mr. Knight, don't you?"

"Yes, sir. We did. But that was last year."

"So we're to pretend it never happened?" Was it her imagination or had the liquid velvet in his tone suddenly turned to molten steel?

"I had a wonderful birthday. Thank you." She kept her head averted. There was no way she could meet his gaze. He'd see too much. He'd see how much she loved him, how much his lovemaking had meant to her. She couldn't do that. Not now, not ever.

She would never be a part of his world, just as he could never understand hers. She'd learned that particular lesson when she'd been placed in a home more affluent than most. A budding adolescent already with the attitude from hell, she'd appealed just a little too much to the teenage son of her caregivers. They hadn't believed her claims when she'd finally drummed up the courage to tell her new foster mother of his unwelcome attentions. They'd closed ranks, snapping together like a gilded trap, telling her caseworker that her behaviour was uncouth at best and that she'd never fit in. Perhaps she'd be more comfortable with a different family. One on the other side of town. Holly had learned that "like stuck with like."

Pushing back the pain of past hurts, Holly jerked her mind

back to the present. Andrea needed her now, more than ever before. A relationship with Connor Knight was a luxury she couldn't afford.

Her phone rang and she lifted the receiver. "Connor Knight's office, Holly speaking."

"Holly, it's Miriam Sanders."

The administrator at Andrea's hospital. Icy-cold fear shrouded Holly's body. Her fingers gripped the phone, squeezing so tight it hurt. "Yes?"

"Look, this is difficult for me to say, but Andrea's needs have been reassessed in light of her recent deterioration, and I'm afraid we've had to revise the cost of her care."

Holly slumped in relief issuing a silent prayer of thanks it wasn't the news she'd been dreading.

"How much more?" She held her breath. When the administrator mentioned the sum it was all she could do not to scream "No!" into the receiver.

"So as you can see," the woman continued, "we need your guarantee of payment."

Holly did a quick mental calculation. With a bit more juggling she could meet the increase, just. "Yes, I'll pay. I'll find the money from somewhere." She hung up the telephone with a wrenching sigh.

"Problem?" Connor's voice made her jump. She'd forgotten he was there. Listening. How much had he heard?

"Nothing I can't handle." Her stomach pitched again uncomfortably, and she blindly started to sort through the mail on her desk, willing him to turn away and go back into his office. Willing him, against everything her mind and her body cried out for, to just leave her alone.

The almost silent swish of his door closing gave her the answer she sought, yet cut her to the quick. Stop being an idiot, she rebuked silently. What did you expect? That he'd sweep you in his arms and tell you he'd make everything all right? That he loved you? Ha! Not in this lifetime.

The printed words on the correspondence she gripped tightly between her fingers shimmered and swirled. Holly blinked back the tears that threatened to fall. Since Andrea's condition had declined so severely her emotions had been such a mess.

The day passed in a blur. A blur peppered by Janet's excitedly related story about how she had met some wonderful holiday squeeze at New Year. Holly tried to summon the energy to be happy for her, but failed miserably. Instead, she struggled to focus on the work at hand—a particularly sensitive contract that Connor had dictated specific alterations to.

She worked long into the evening on the document, heedful that Knight Enterprises expected to close this deal with a major public fanfare and had courted both print and television media for some time about releasing the details. Her head and neck ached with the strain of sitting at her computer station without a break. While Janet had brought her several cups of tea during the day, more often than not they'd cooled in the mug unnoticed as her fingers continued to fly over the keyboard.

"Here you are, Miss Christmas. I know you've hardly taken a break today so I thought you might need something to eat."

Holly lifted her attention from the bundle of papers on her desk to smile her thanks to Janet. Her words hovered precariously at the edge of her lips as the smoked mussel salad, a specialty from the restaurant in the complex at the base of the tower and enticingly presented on the boardroom's best china, sent her stomach on a sudden looping roller-coaster ride.

"How thoughtful. Thank you, Janet." She managed, swallowing against the nauseating metallic taste that flooded her mouth. She hastily averted her eyes. "Will you excuse me? I think I need to freshen up a bit first."

"Are you okay? You've gone awfully pale."

"Yes—yes. I'm fine. I'll be back in a minute." Her ears roared, and the back of her neck felt as though it was encased in a cold, clammy grip as she forced the words past her lips and swept around the side of her desk.

Stay down, stay down, stay down. She said the words over and over in her mind, praying the silent mantra would help her maintain her equilibrium until she made it to the ladies' room.

Thankfully the stalls were all empty, and Holly slammed and locked the door behind her and dropped to her knees, her hands clutching the cold porcelain as if her life depended on it while she dry-retched over the bowl.

With watering eyes and shaky hands, she tore off a few squares of toilet paper and wiped at her face. When would this end? She'd have to see a doctor soon. If she didn't get on top of things, she couldn't visit Andrea, and as much as she'd wanted to deny the specialist's report and ignore the sorrow in his eyes as he'd delivered the latest news, she knew she wouldn't have her precious friend much longer.

Holly's chest tightened painfully at the admission before she resolutely pushed the thought aside. She couldn't deal with that now. Some things were just too much to bear. She hauled herself upright and leaned back against the door while she waited for the dizziness to subside, which finally, thankfully, it did.

Janet had returned to her own desk by the time Holly re-emerged on the scene. Without looking too closely at the contents of the plate, she lifted it from her desk and took it to the kitchenette off their office suite, hastily dumping the contents in the plastic-lined bin and throwing a few paper towels over the top for good measure.

She settled herself back at her desk, trying to make sense of the scattered words on her screen.

Connor came out of his office and leaned against her desk. "Are you okay? Janet said you weren't looking too well a minute ago."

"She's exaggerating, really. I'll be fine."

"Whatever, it's time you called it a day. You look shattered."

"The contract's almost complete. If you're sure you don't need me…?" The words she'd left unspoken trailed away into nothing at the fire that blazed dark and hungry in eyes that all day had been as cold and glittering hard as obsidian.

"Need you, Holly?" Cynicism curled his lips, and she futilely wished her words unsaid.

"Right, I'll be off then." She severed eye contact, hastily gathered up her things and switched her monitor off.

"Before you go, come into my office." He didn't wait for a response.

All the remaining energy she had left within her sagged from her body in a whoosh. Holly steadied herself against her desk struggling to summon the reserves she needed to face him again.

"Yes?" she enquired as she hovered in the doorway.

"Come in and close the door."

Her nerves jangled as she did as instructed and came further into his office. She averted her eyes from his desk and the view beyond it. Holly didn't think she'd ever be able to walk in here again and not see the two of them, their reflections as starkly painted in her mind's eye as they'd been in the glass reflection that night only a few weeks ago.

"Take a seat," Connor instructed firmly.

"I'd prefer to stand. This will only take a minute, won't it?"

"That all depends," he answered.

"Depends? On what?" Holly clenched the straps of her handbag so tight her fingers hurt.

Connor came closer and took her by the elbow, leading her firmly to the long sofa at the end of his office. "Sit."

She sat, perched at the edge, and pulled her legs away slightly as Connor loomed over her.

Holly looked about as frightened as a deer caught in a hunter's sights, Connor realised. What was she hiding? He'd tried several times during her holiday to contact her, but she didn't answer her phone at home and when he'd driven by she hadn't come to the door.

There was nothing for it but to cut straight to the chase, he decided. "Why are you sick?"

"What?"

"Are you pregnant?"

"No!" Holly shot to her feet and swayed slightly, her face bleached white at the sudden movement.

Connor pushed her back down in the chair and lowered himself next to her. He could see her pulse fluttering in her neck, like a trapped bird, against the alabaster of her skin.

Most people came back from their summer holiday tanned and rested. Holly's skin, usually filled with a warm glow that had nothing to do with sunshine was now wan and sallow, and unhealthy shadows underscored her eyes.

"Are you sure? You've seen a doctor?"

"Of course I'm sure. I would never make a mistake about something like that. *Never!*"

Her vehement response took him aback. He rose from the couch and went to pour a glass of water from the cut-crystal carafe on the antique sideboard against the wall. Their fingers brushed as he handed it to her, sending a surge blazing up his arm. The weeks apart hadn't dulled the edge of his hunger for her. If anything, the aching need to be with her again was even stronger.

"What's wrong then?" he pressed. "You haven't been sick once in the three years you've worked for me."

"Something I ate this week hasn't agreed with me. That's all."

"You've been sick for a week?"

"I've only been feeling a bit off colour for a day or two. I'm sure it'll pass soon."

"Take tomorrow off."

"That's quite unnecessary, it's just a mild tummy bug. Now, if that's all you wanted me for…?" Holly stood, more slowly than before, and walked towards the door. There was no legitimate reason he could keep her here any longer.

"Have dinner with me."

She stopped and turned. "I beg your pardon?"

The words had sprung from his mouth before he'd had time to consider them fully, but now he'd had a second or two to turn the idea over in his mind it sounded like a good one.

He rose and walked over to her. "Have dinner with me. I know you've barely eaten all day and you must be starving. Just something simple, okay?"

Holly's stomach growled in response. She grimaced and placed a hand over her abdomen, a movement that caught Connor's eye. Quickly she let her arm drop. It wouldn't do to give him any further ridiculous ideas.

"I should get going, I'll miss my bus."

"Damn it, Holly. I'll take you home. What kind of man do you think I am? I'm not asking you to leap into bed with me!" Although the prospect of doing just that painted a vivid image of the two of them—naked, together—with such sharp clarity his entire body tensed. He held his breath waiting for her to reply. Her determinedly obvious inaccessibility had made him begin to question why it was so important to him that she say yes. All he knew was since that night, here in his office and upstairs in his bed, he'd wanted more of her in every way. It wasn't enough to have her working at her desk outside his office. He wanted her by his side. In his bed.

"Yes, all right."

Just like that? He had to put his libido on hold and double take on what she had agreed to. With unaccustomed sluggishness his brain finally caught up and overcame the raw desire that surged with a seething hunger.

"Great. Let's go, then."

Traffic was light along the Auckland waterfront at this time of the evening. Hundreds of walkers, joggers and families on their bikes were still out enjoying the warm summer evening despite the encroaching night. Connor pulled his car into a car park that fronted onto the beach at Mission Bay.

"Let's take a walk along the beach before we have dinner," he suggested, and took Holly's hand, guiding her towards the promenade.

It was a gorgeous evening. The last of the sun's rays spread in a flash of darkest red through to the palest orange. The light reflected across the gentle sea in the harbour. Seagulls wheeled and dived through the air, shrieking their strident cry as they scouted out for the nearest scrap of food. Mission Bay was easy pickings for any bird, including the fat pigeons that cooed and strutted along the path by the sea wall.

Bit by bit Holly began to relax and started to feel a lot better. The fresh air and gentle exercise seemed to be doing her good, and her appetite had quadrupled by the time they'd meandered past the massive fountain at the centre of the domain and crossed the main road towards the plethora of restaurants on the other side.

"How do you feel about Italian? If you'd prefer, we can take a table on the pavement."

"That'd be great, thank you." Without realizing it, he'd given her the perfect opportunity to avoid the aromas that permeated the interior of the restaurant. Outside, the light breeze would ensure her sensitive stomach didn't overreact.

Either they were extremely lucky, or Connor Knight had a way with the maître d' because miraculously, and despite being very busy, a table for two was available.

"White wine or red?" Connor asked as he perused the wine list.

Her taste buds soured at the thought of drinking wine. "I'll stick with water tonight."

"Good idea. Me too. We'll have two of these." He pointed to the New Zealand branded bottled spring water on the list and handed it back to the waiter.

"So, do you come here often?" Holly broke the silence that had settled between them.

Connor laughed, the spontaneous sound lighting a warm ember deep inside her chest. "I think that's supposed to be my line."

Holly smiled weakly in response. Okay, as conversation starters went it had been a bit weak, but there was no rule book to cover polite conversation with your boss over a late dinner—especially when one heated look from him was enough to set up a chain reaction inside her that had nothing to do with pain. Except, perhaps, the pain of denial.

Connor continued, "It's been a while since I've been here, but the food's always been very good. What do you feel like?" He flicked a glance at her over the top of his menu.

You. Holly suddenly put her fingers over her mouth. Oh, God, she hadn't said that aloud had she?

"The fish looks good. If your stomach's still a bit weak you might find that light enough."

She heaved a sigh of relief. "Yes, that sounds great. I'll have the poached terakihi and a salad."

The waiter rematerialised to take their orders, Connor placed her order and chose scaloppini for himself.

"You used to work in the typing pool, right?" His question, out of the blue, startled her.

"Yes," she replied cautiously.

"You were such an earnest young thing."

Surprised he'd even noticed her back then, Holly just nodded. Connor stroked the condensation from the side of his glass with one long finger. She couldn't tear her eyes away from the movement, nor bring herself to take a sip of her water to relieve her suddenly very dry throat.

"What made you decide to become a PA? I would've thought you'd have gone for a degree at the university. Law, maybe."

As idly curious as his comment was, all Holly's shutters came racing down. She'd held her cards so close to her chest for so long now it had become second nature. If you shared nothing, you couldn't lay yourself open to ridicule or worse, pity. While part of her ached to tell Connor more about her past, the lines, as she knew them, had been clearly delineated many years ago. In life there were the "haves" and the "have nots." Those lines weren't made to be crossed.

"I thought about it," she admitted, pushing a piece of fish around her plate with her fork, "but I decided I'd rather get my teeth into a job where I could start earning straightaway."

She would have given anything to complete a degree at Auckland University, but in her world there had been no well-heeled parents to supplement a student loan. If she was to get anywhere in life it would be on her own, just like she'd been since the day her mother had left her.

"Money's that important to you you'd give up doing something you really wanted?"

Holly's throat closed. Something she really wanted? All her plans—*what she'd wanted*—to save enough money to start an investigation into who she really was and where she'd come from—had come unstuck with the onset of the latter stages of Andrea's illness when Holly had assumed responsibility for the financial maintenance of Andrea's care. She owed it to her foster sister, and more. Andrea had been the one person who'd stuck up for her and who'd forced her to take a long hard look at what had become self-destructive behaviour. She owed her foster sister her very existence. Looking after Andrea, for however much longer she lived, was something Holly was bound by both love and honour to do.

"You can't deny that money is important. Look at your own family." She attempted to deflect his attention from herself. "I've heard the stories about how hard your dad worked when you were just a boy. You don't build a corporation like Knights without a lot of hard work. He never had any degree."

"True. But it came at a far bigger cost than just money. He was a stranger to us while we were growing up. When our mother died, it was like he'd died, too, for all we saw him. Believe me, Holly, money isn't everything."

"And so says the man who has everything." Holly couldn't stop the bitter words from escaping her mouth and desperately wished them unsaid when she saw his face. His eyes glittered darkly and his lips settled in a straight line.

"Not everything, Holly. Some things you can't buy."

"I'm sorry, I shouldn't have said that."

"Come on, it's getting late and you look like you've done about ten rounds in the boxing ring. I'll take you home."

Six

Connor stared out the window of his penthouse apartment, watching as the world hurtled by regardless of the late hour. Try as he might, he couldn't get Holly out of his mind. What was it with him and women that it always came down to money? She'd made no bones about how important money was to her, yet, if that was the case, why did she live where and how she did? She was a conundrum. One he had every intention of figuring out even though logic told him he should just forget their night together, as she had so conveniently managed to do.

Logic could take a hike.

He turned from the window and flipped open his cell. One press of a quick-dial would take him a step closer to the answers he needed.

The summarised report, when it came through to his private fax line in the morning, did little to calm his disquiet. It was clear Holly had major financial issues, not least of which were large sums of money being paid out on a very regular basis—most of her wages in fact. No wonder she lived in such squalid conditions. Something, or someone, drained every dollar she earned. The only savings account she'd had was well in the past, and it had been cleared out completely several months ago. But all the financial information aside, the report did nothing to shed any light on exactly *who* she was.

The memory of the conversation he'd overheard between Holly and another person yesterday tickled at the back of his mind. She had financial pressure from somewhere, but where? Was it gambling, or worse?

He called his private investigator again.

"I need you to go deeper. Find out who she is, where she's from. Everything. I don't care how long it takes."

Holly let herself into the house and locked the door behind her before making her way to the bathroom. The past week had been interminable. Wearying queasiness still plagued her and kept her from visiting Andrea. While the staff at the hospital understood, it didn't help assuage the guilt she felt at not being able to be there herself.

To make matters worse, not only had she been sick at work again but this time Janet had seen her and had been full of overwhelming fuss. To gain some respite, Holly had agreed to Janet's suggestion that she should go home for the day. Connor was tied up in a video conference call when she'd gathered her things and headed for the door. The last thing she'd needed had been his concern, as well.

As she'd searched for change for the bus in the bottom of her bag she'd come across the emergency sanitary items she kept in a small cosmetic purse. Connor's question from last week rung hollowly in her ears. She'd been adamant at the time that she couldn't be pregnant, but could she? Really? She couldn't hide from the possibility any longer.

Holly put the pharmacy packet she'd brought home onto the vanity of her tiny bathroom and removed its contents. The instructions were simple. Too simple really, when it was something so terrifyingly important. She followed the steps to the letter, then paced the tiny confines of room like a caged animal, an analogy that rang a little too close to the truth for her comfort.

She forced herself to calm down, to take stock of the situation. To breathe. And started to pace again. Her mind whirled in ever-diminishing circles—bringing her back to the same conclusion every time.

She couldn't be pregnant. She just couldn't. Life couldn't be so unfair as to twist its jagged blade into her so cruelly. Not with so many questions unanswered and certainly not in her current financial position. Never in her worst nightmares had she ever imagined this happening to her. She'd promised herself never to have a baby until she knew she wouldn't be bringing ill health and unhappiness to another life and, even then, only if she could provide it with the things she'd never had—a background, the unconditional love of two parents and the financial security to meet all its needs.

The sound of a car pulling up outside her house brought her pacing to an abrupt halt. There was only one person it could be. A bolt of queasiness hurtled from her stomach. She swallowed against it and willed her body back under control.

Footsteps echoed on the path—pounding inexorably closer to her front door. A heavy knock made the flimsy door rattle angrily inside its frame. Holly dragged a steadying breath through tightened lips.

"Holly!" Connor Knight shouted through the glass.

Her legs trembled as she walked down the short narrow hall and cautiously opened the front door the scant few inches the security chain allowed.

"Let me in, Holly." His voice was liquid velvet, soft and sensual and spoke to her on a physical level that made her heart leap skittishly in her chest, yet despite the virtual stroke against her psyche there was an underlying steel in his tone that demanded he be obeyed.

Holly took a small step back. "No."

"Open the door." His voice grew louder.

"You can say what you need to from where you are and leave."

"Janet said you were sick—again. Don't think you can fob me off this time, Holly." He bit the words out, and they ricocheted around the barren front porch.

A young boy riding past on his skateboard, stopped on the sidewalk. "Hey, miss, you wan' me to go get my uncle? He'll get rid of the suit for ya!"

Holly recognised the boy from the house a couple of doors away, and she had no doubt that one of his many "uncles" had been members of the throng that had partied hard on Christmas Day.

"Holly?" Connor stared at her through the gap, his brows pulled together in a forbidding line. "Would you like the young man to get his uncle? Go ahead, I'm in the mood."

She swallowed against the lump in her throat and raised shaking fingers to the door, closing it enough to slide the chain back off then pulling it wide open.

"It's okay. I know him." She gave a weak smile over Connor's broad-suited shoulder and watched as the boy gave a cheeky grin before boarding further down the street. "You'd better come in." She gestured to Connor to follow her down the narrow hall.

"Thank you."

Who'd have thought two simple words could have been laced with such fury? For a minute she wondered if she'd done the right thing. Maybe having one of the heavies from up the street "take care of him" for her might not have been such a stupid idea after all. Holly discarded the thought immediately. No. She had to face this, as she'd had to face every crossroads in her life. Somehow, she'd make it.

"Can I get you coffee or tea? I'm sorry I don't have milk, though." The fridge had totally given up the ghost during the night, and Holly had tipped out the gelatinous remains of her milk before heading to work in the morning.

"No. I don't want anything except a few honest answers."

"I've never been anything but honest with you," Holly retorted, stung at the implication.

He pushed his hands in his pockets and looked around the room. "That's good. So there's no need to stop now, is there?"

What on earth was he getting at? Did he know about the pregnancy test? Holly didn't have to wait long to find out.

"When Janet told me you'd been sick, I thought you might prefer a ride home rather than catch the bus. I sent her after you this afternoon when you left. I was surprised to hear you took a little shopping detour before going to the station." He removed his hands from his pockets and caught her upper arms, his fingers tightening slightly. "So have you taken the test yet, Holly? Were you going to tell me the result?"

She tried to twist free, but he held her firm. The heat of his fingers imprinted on her skin and, damn it, she couldn't help but want to feel them touching other parts of her. She was nuts. Only a crazy woman reacted this way with so much at stake.

"I can't believe you made her spy on me." She turned her head so he couldn't see the flare of desire she knew reflected in her face. "Let me go."

"Tell me." The demand was no less forceful than the glare in his eyes.

"I don't know."

"Which—the result, or if you'd tell me?"

"Neither! Both! I…I don't know!" Holly wrenched herself loose from his intoxicating hold. "I was taking the test when you arrived."

"Where is it?" He demanded.

"On the bathroom vanity," Holly replied in a tiny voice, frozen to the spot, as he strode past her, headed straight for the bathroom.

His footsteps halted in the bathroom, and her stomach clenched as she waited. A sound, like a muffled groan, filtered through the hallway, then silence. Eventually she heard the pipes clank in protest and water run in the basin. One look at his face and his slightly reddened eyes when he returned, and Holly's world tilted sharply. Disoriented, she grabbed the back of one of the tubular steel chairs Connor had eschewed so disdainfully during his last visit.

"No!" The wail broke from her throat. "Tell me it isn't true!"

Cold fury glistened in his eyes. "Oh, it's true all right. You're pregnant with my child."

Another wave of nausea, more persistent than before, rose with a surge of determination she couldn't disregard.

"Oh, God!" With her hand clamped to her mouth, Holly made short work of the distance to her bathroom.

Spent with exhaustion a few minutes later, she dimly became aware of Connor's presence behind her, of his strong, warm hand gently stroking her back. Tremors of shock rippled through her as she leaned weakly against the porcelain, the hard floor pressing against her knees.

"You all done?" He sounded distant, emotionally removed.

"I think so."

"Then wash your face and come with me."

"Come with you?" Holly was confused. "Back to work?"

Connor offered his hand and helped her to her feet, a line of tension between his brows as he turned the taps on at the stained basin. Holly grabbed a flannel and dashed it under the trickle, scrubbing at her face before scooping up some water with her hand to rinse her mouth. Connor handed her a towel and stood silent as a statue while she mopped her face dry.

"No. To a doctor."

Seven

"She's pregnant, early days, but definite."

Connor looked up at the softly spoken words as the doctor, one of his female cousins, closed the door to her examination room behind her allowing Holly some privacy to get dressed.

"Hell." Connor stopped his pacing and dropped into the seat across from Carmen's desk.

"She's the one you brought to Christmas brunch, isn't she?"

Connor nodded.

"I thought Uncle Tony had strict rules about office romance."

"It was an aberration."

"Unprotected sex is some aberration."

"She assured me she was okay." Connor couldn't meet her gaze, or read the reproach he knew would be there.

"Well, looks like you have some rethinking to do, cuz."

"Yeah." More than Carmen could ever realise. Connor flung a look at the still-closed door. "Will she be okay?"

"Once she starts to eat properly and gets plenty of rest. I'll give you a list of supplements to help build her strength up. She hasn't been looking after herself that well. If you two are going to have a healthy baby, that has to change."

A healthy baby. Connor's head spun. *He was going to be a father!* Moisture sprang to his eyes. He blinked it away as emotion cascaded through him, tightening his chest and setting a fire of hope burning low in his gut.

"Don't worry, I'll make sure she takes care of herself."

Holly remained on the examining table, the doctor's parting words still ringing in her ears. "No doubt you and Connor will need to talk."

Holly couldn't even acknowledge her. Her hand slid to her lower belly and pressed against the flat surface. Disbelief raged through her mind. Pregnant.

In all her worst nightmares she'd never imagined this could happen. Not to her. Never to her. She'd always been so careful never to let anyone close enough. The one time in her life she'd let go of reason and given in to impulse, to admit to the need for another—a need she'd guarded against for so long—and fate threw this savage twist at her.

Holly shuddered. She couldn't afford to bring up a child. She could barely afford to support Andrea, let alone herself. The financial demands of a baby didn't bear thinking about. She drew her knees up and curled into a protective ball. What the hell was she going to do?

Holly's heart twisted sharply in her chest. If she'd had the luxury of normal circumstances, the news would have sent the blood in her veins singing with joy to know she carried Connor's child, yet the fearful weight of responsibility paralysed her. What if there was something wrong? She couldn't bear to watch another person she loved die a slow and painful death.

Her breath caught in her throat. Love? She couldn't love the baby already. It was far too soon. In fact, never would be too soon. Holly pulled down the shutters on her emotions. She couldn't afford to feel anything for this new life growing inside her. Not when there was so much at stake.

Slowly she uncurled and pushed away the sheet the doctor had draped over her for privacy. *Privacy*—the term was completely incongruous after an internal examination.

The muted murmur of voices filtered through the door. She had to get moving. She didn't put it past Connor to be making plans with the doctor. Plans *she* should be making.

At least this meant she wouldn't have to restrict her visits to Andrea because of her assumed stomach flu. The weighty responsibility of another life rocked her again. *What on earth was she going to do?*

The door across the room opened.

"You okay?" Connor asked, his lips a grim line, and expectation shining in his eyes she couldn't quite identify.

The strangled sound that dragged itself from her throat could have passed for a laugh any other day of the week but failed miserably right now. "Okay? No. I'm not okay. I couldn't be worse." She couldn't hold back the bitterness from her words, nor did she want to. She wanted to run from the room, from Connor. From the truth.

Connor's face hardened, his eyes darkening to blackest granite. "Come through. We need to talk about your care."

"Care? What's that got to do with you?"

"Everything," he challenged, his voice no more than a growl.

Connor held the door open wider, and Holly swept through, driven by helpless anger. How dare he think he could discuss her care with a stranger? She'd had enough of that in her lifetime—of other people making all her decisions. She wasn't a child any longer, she was an adult. A strong and capable woman, with responsibilities. A woman who didn't need anyone else.

The doctor sat at her desk, eyeing Holly carefully, as if weighing her words before speaking.

Biting the inside of her lip, Holly sat on the chair Connor indicated, sweeping her legs away to one side when he sat in the seat beside her.

"According to Carmen you need supplements to rebuild your strength, and you need more rest, too. Whatever you've been doing to drive yourself to this state, it has to stop."

"Stop? You can't dictate to me."

"Watch me."

"You have no right. This is my body. My choice. I don't want to bring another unwanted child into this world." Holly felt Connor's body go rigid beside her.

Carmen looked up, a startled look on her face and a hint of censure in her eyes.

His tone was unmistakably feral. "If you think this baby is unwanted, you're wrong. Completely and utterly wrong." Connor rose to his feet. "I'm sorry, Carmen, but Holly and I have some matters to discuss—privately."

"Sure, I understand." Carmen gave him a worried smile before looking at Holly. "Don't rush into any decisions. Obviously the news has come as a bit of a shock—for you both. Connor, I think you have all you need from me today."

"Thanks, Carmen. Yes. I'll call the specialist in the morning."

"Specialist? I can't afford a specialist." Holly wanted to scream—anything to make them pay attention to her. Didn't her opinion matter at all? Her entire childhood people had talked around her as if she didn't exist and, when they couldn't ignore her, as if she didn't matter. She'd fought hard for control of her life—she wasn't about to give that up now.

Connor's strong hand caught at her elbow, urging her from her seat and propelling her towards the door. In his car, Holly sat glowering mutinously out the front window. Instead of starting up the engine, Connor gripped the leather-wrapped steering wheel and turned to her. But for the whitening of his knuckles she would probably never have realised how angry he was. Now tension undulated from his body in waves.

"I'm going to make this perfectly clear right here and right now. You're not handling this by yourself, understood?"

Holly faced him, the burning determination in his eyes making her mouth dry and the words she'd been about to utter in denial fade into obscurity.

"Holly?" He ground out her name as if holding himself in check.

She wasn't going to win this war. Not today. She gave a curt nod. "All right. I understand you."

"Good." Without another word, Connor twisted the key in the ignition and fired the BMW to throbbing life.

She didn't pay a lot of attention to the route he'd chosen to take her back to her house, until she had to flip the sun visor down to block the late-afternoon sun now shining in her face. If they were heading to her place, the sun would be at their backs, not blinding them as it was now.

"This isn't the way to my place. Why aren't you taking me home?" She demanded.

"I am." Connor's hands tightened on the steering wheel.

"This isn't the way to my house," she persisted.

"No."

"Then where are you taking me?"

"To mine."

"To the apartment?"

"No, to the island."

"What?"

"You heard me." Connor turned the wheel of the car, and they swooped down the ramp leading to the basement car park of the Knight Enterprises Tower.

"Why?"

"Holly, be reasonable. You don't even have enough food in your house to eat a decent meal, let alone enough money in your account to go out and buy one."

"You don't know that!" Holly stared at him in horror. How could he know?

He slid the car to a halt in his designated park and turned and raised one eyebrow. While he didn't so much as murmur, he told her in no uncertain terms he knew far more about her than she was willing to say.

"And we need to talk about the baby, and how long you can keep working, if at all." Connor reached across and unclicked her seat belt when she made no move to do it herself.

Shock sent a tremor of fear through her. Her job! She couldn't afford to lose her job. Holly slumped deeper against the expensive upholstery, helpless in defeat.

Connor knew the instant she gave up. It was there in the slump of her shoulders, the droop of her lips, the incline of her delectable, slender neck. All fire, all life, all hope extinguished. A flicker of compassion ignited briefly before he ruthlessly quelled it.

He couldn't afford compassion now, not when his mind still reeled in disbelief. She might never have told him about the baby if he hadn't pushed her. Who knew what crazy decisions she'd have reached on her own, especially given her precarious financial state. Anger roiled violently inside him.

By all that defined him, there was no way anything was happening to his child. The truth had been hidden from him before with disastrous consequences. No way on this earth would he let that happen again.

He exited the BMW, barely managing to resist the urge to slam his door, and walked around to her side to help her from the car. She was about as responsive as a rag doll, a far cry from the woman who'd argued with him at the doctor's surgery—even further from the woman whose passion had ignited in his arms and who'd since invaded his dreams and virtually every waking thought.

As he guided her towards the elevator, Connor flipped his cell phone from his pocket and punched in a few digits. "Thompson, could you arrange dinner for two on the pool patio please." He paused while Thompson, his general factotum at his residence responded. "No, the guest suite won't be necessary. We'll be there soon." He snapped his phone shut.

"I'm coming back tonight?" Holly lifted her head, hope flaring like a struggling beacon in the depths of her dark-blue eyes.

"Why would you think that?"

"Well, you said no extra room." Her voice trailed off, sounding suddenly unsure.

"You're sleeping with me, where I can keep an eye on you." He baled her up with a glare. "At all times."

Like it or not, she'd be sleeping with him. He wasn't taking any risks. Not with something as precious as his baby. He couldn't help the involuntary blistering flood of desire, that pervaded his body. Sharing a bed with Holly would bring its own gruelling brand of torture, but each night his son or daughter would lie secure in his arms. That was a promise.

"I don't recall agreeing to come and stay with you. We're supposed to be talking." She paused, giving emphasis to her next words. "Just talking."

"We'll be talking all right. Don't worry on that score."

"But I still have to stay with you?"

"Yes." He wasn't prepared to negotiate on that one.

He watched as Holly nibbled at her lower lip.

"One night, then. So we can sort things out."

Connor let go of the breath he didn't realise he'd been holding, relieved that he didn't have to answer his own question about what he might have done if she'd refused. But one night wouldn't be enough to satisfy his concerns. He'd do his best to ensure that he was there to protect his child at all times.

Their silent journey to the helipad on the rooftop was uninterrupted. At this late hour of the afternoon most of the staff had already gone home. Holly tried to settle the cascading fear that threatened to tip her over the edge as the elevator sped to the top of the building.

Why couldn't he just leave her alone? The plea rose within her, sharp and powerful, but never made it past the obstruction lodged in her throat. She knew darn well the reason why. Her hand fluttered to her lower abdomen, settling there briefly before dropping back to her side. The baby.

Her baby.

Life couldn't get any worse.

The corporate chopper, a sleek shining black Agusta, custom detailed for Knight Enterprises, crouched with ominous intent on the helipad. The pilot was already at the controls, the rotors swinging in an inexorable circle and boiling up a wind that buffeted stinging dust into Holly's eyes.

Connor drew her close to his side, sheltering her from the worst of the wind with his body, and guided her to the open chopper door. Inside, she clipped her belt, then sat still in her seat, hardly daring to move as her heart began to race and her stomach lurched a fierce warning that it'd had about enough excitement for one day. Although she'd travelled in the Agusta before, she'd never made the short hop to Connor's private sanctum.

"To the island now, sir?"

"Thanks, Dave. Thompson will be waiting for us."

In the darkened cabin Connor levelled a shadowed stare in her direction and a tentative frisson of anticipation licked at Holly's body. He adjusted his headset and gestured to Holly to do the same. She shook her head in denial. She had no desire to hold a conversation with him in this shining display of wealth and prestige, not now while her nerves were so raw. It would take every last ounce of composure to gather her thoughts together for the coming discussion.

To her knowledge Connor had never brought a female guest, who wasn't family, to the island he'd bought after his divorce. A short flight from the central business district, she knew the island was his oasis of peace and tranquillity—a haven he guarded fiercely.

By the time they circled the island and landed Holly felt about as brittle and tightly strung as overstretched fencing wire. One touch, one word, and she'd splinter into a million shattered pieces. She eschewed Connor's assistance to exit the chopper, preferring to make it on her own, albeit unsteady, legs. She ducked and walked as quickly as she could towards the looming two-storied silver-grey stone house several yards in front of them.

Holly counted no less than three chimneys reaching into the twilight sky above the steeply peaked slate-shingled roof.

"This is your home?" she asked, annoyed that she couldn't keep the awe from her breathless voice.

"It's my house. It takes a family to make a home." Connor's jaw tightened as he ejected the words from tensely drawn lips.

Family. How cruelly ironic they both seemed to want what they didn't have. Although, given her current disposition, he'd have his family within the next year, but where would she feature in all that? And did she want to feature anywhere?

Holly clenched her fingers into tight fists, welcoming the physical pain of her nails as they embedded in her palms. The sharp contrast of the tangible discomfort balanced the mental torment that battered at her senses. She didn't want to go down that road. Too much remained unanswered in her life— far, far too much. Right now she had to get a grip on controlling her own destiny—whatever that might be.

Eight

A tall gentleman with silver hair waited at the edge of the patio to greet them.

"Thompson, this is Miss Christmas, who will be staying with me."

"Certainly, sir. I'll take Miss Christmas's things up to the master suite—"

"I don't have a bag." Holly interrupted, adding silently, *I don't have anything. No possessions. No choice. Nothing.*

"I'm sure we can accommodate your needs for one night," Connor gave Thompson a look that demanded an affirmative answer.

"Certainly we can," the other man carried on smoothly, not even a wrinkle of curiosity or concern marring his expressionless features. "I've prepared drinks on the patio for you. Dinner will be brought through in about fifteen minutes if that's all right with you, sir."

"Sounds fine, Thompson. Thank you." Connor pulled out a comfortably cushioned patio chair, "Sit down."

It was more of a command than an invitation. She accepted the chair he offered and gazed around her apprehensively. This really was some place. A subtly lit pool glimmered deep turquoise green over to her left, while cleverly positioned uplights cast a glow over rough-hewn stone blocks, making the house seem more like a living thing than a building. Subtropical native palms and ferns clustered in the garden while hints of colour could be picked out in the soft night light from lush red begonias and bromeliads strategically planted for effect.

"The garden is beautiful," she blurted, as she accepted a flute filled with sparkling golden liquid. She lifted the glass to her lips, then hesitated. Should she even be drinking alcohol? Lord, she had no idea what she should be doing. While she denied wanting the child, and would do anything to undo the fact that she'd fallen pregnant in the first place, some instinct halted her hand.

"It's sparkling grape juice, no alcohol." Connor sipped his own glass as he leaned back in his chair. "Do you like gardening?" Connor tilted his head to one side. Shadowed as he was, she couldn't make out his expression.

"Well, if I had time I'm sure I would."

Connor forced himself to hold his tongue at her stilted response. Time? She'd have plenty of time in the coming months, he'd make certain of that.

He suddenly realised that even though, as his PA, she'd basically run his days, and many of his weekends, for the past three years, he still knew little about her. Nothing bar what made her eyes deepen and darken in exquisite pleasure and how the cool satin of her skin heated to his touch and flushed a delicate rose in the height of passion.

His groin tightened in flaming response—a response he ruthlessly quashed with sudden loathing at his own unbridled reaction.

"Well, Thompson won't mind a bit of company in the garden if you want to test your green fingers." A sardonic smile played at his lips as she shot daggers of fury from her eyes.

"I hardly think that one night will make any difference to your Mr. Thompson."

The subtle sound of rubber-soled shoes on the slate-tiled patio announced Thompson's return. "Here's our meal. I'm sure you're ready to eat."

"I'm not hungry." Her voice distant, stilted, Holly leaned back in her chair and folded her hands on her lap.

"You *will* have something."

"I can look after myself. Thank you."

"I don't know where you got the misguided idea that you can look after yourself. Look at you. You're nothing but skin and bone. Keep this up and you'll hurt the baby." Ah, now that generated a response. He watched as blue fire flickered in her eyes and she leaned forward, placing her hands flat on the table in front of her, challenge glowing fiercely on her face.

"Well, maybe that's up to me."

Connor bit back the retort that sprang to his lips and forced himself back in his chair. Damn difficult when all he wanted to do was tie her down and force feed her. So, she wanted to jeopardise his baby? If she did, it would be over his dead body.

He needed to try a different tack. He hadn't made his reputation by being bullheaded and intractable. Silently he dished up a small portion of the steaming fluffy white rice onto a plate, then ladled the sweetly scented Thai chicken sauce onto it and set it in front of her, before serving a larger portion for himself.

"Do you remember when you last had something to eat?"

He lifted her fork and scooped up a small bite, holding it in front of her lips. "Go on, try it. It's very good."

He watched as Holly's nostrils flared ever so slightly, inhaling the aroma of the perfectly prepared meal. She moistened her lips with the tip of her tongue and swallowed. Tracking the small movement of the muscles in her neck shot a bolt of electricity through him—an unnerving reminder of another time when he'd felt the play of those muscles beneath his lips, his tongue.

Disgust swamped him, swift and fierce. He didn't need this, or the constant reminders of what they'd shared. She didn't want to eat. So be it. He'd have her hospitalised if necessary. He didn't need to wait on her hand and foot. And then, miracle of miracles, she parted her lips and accepted the food he held poised in front of her. He lowered the fork back to the plate and watched as she methodically chewed, then swallowed.

She dipped her head, not meeting his eyes. "I'm sorry, you're right. The food is lovely. I can manage for myself."

They ate without speaking, accompanied only by the lap of gentle waves in the distance, stroking back and forth on the silver strand of sandy beach visible only a few hundred yards away, and the chirrup of crickets' unobtrusive accompaniment in the background. Enchanting scents swirled around them, borne on the gentle summer night air: Queen of the Night, rich and heady, and the salt tang of the sea a short distance away.

The irony of the beauty of the setting and the romanticism of the night wasn't lost on Holly, who'd surprised herself by finishing the serving Connor had dished for her.

Thompson came to clear away their dishes and replaced them with a slice each of a light and tangy passion-fruit cheesecake, topped with fresh whipped cream and drizzled with mango sauce. Holly had devoured her portion, her taste buds savouring the delicate flavours. Now replete, she sat back and barely managed to stifle a yawn. She looked around with a heavy heart and tired eyes. This would be paradise under any other circumstances.

"You're tired. I'll show you our room."

She jumped at the sound of his voice and looked up to find his eyes still burning into her. Had he taken his gaze off her once this evening? Holly couldn't be certain, but she doubted it.

"We haven't discussed what we're going to do about the…the…." She couldn't bring herself to even say the word *baby* out loud.

"Do, Holly?" Connor spun his coffee cup in his strong capable hands, hands that had driven her to heights of pleasure she had never dreamed imaginable. Hands in which her future now lay.

Holly stifled a shudder. "Yes, we need to talk about it."

"There's nothing to discuss. You're pregnant with my baby. I'll ensure you're accorded the best care possible, and I'll be there when he or she is born."

"What if something goes wrong?" She had to ask. She had heard, somewhere, one in four pregnancies miscarried. Maybe she'd be that one in four. After all, it was early days yet. She had no idea whether there was some abnormality, some genetic predisposition, that would prevent a normal healthy pregnancy. A chill prickled over her skin. She had no idea at all.

"I will do everything I can to make certain nothing goes wrong." Connor pushed his chair away from the patio table and rose to his feet, looming over her in a manner that brooked no argument. "So will you."

"And after the baby is born, what then? What if it's sick, or has some defect or abnormality that you didn't know about. Will you want it then?" Her voice rose uncontrollably as fear of the unknown tore through her like the jaws of a voracious shark.

"Family is everything to me." Connor looked at her as if she'd crawled out from under a particularly slimy rock. "In my opinion only the lowest kind of parent wouldn't want and love their child no matter how perfect or imperfect they are."

"There are some that don't." Holly replied, a tremor belying the emotion that ripped her apart. Parents like her mother, who'd abandoned a perfectly healthy child without reason.

"Some like yourself? Is that what you're saying?" Connor reached up and loosened the knot of his tie. "Well, don't worry, Holly. I will happily bring up my child on my own. I have more than enough love for both of us."

"And what then? What about me?"

"Good question." His face hardened like granite, his eyes bottomless in their hooded darkness. He continued in a voice colder than the Arctic Circle, "You'll be free to go, won't you? That *is* what you want, isn't it?"

Free to go. A shard of ice lodged deep in her chest. She hadn't had a chance to stop to think about what would happen once the child was born. What did she know about motherhood? She'd hardly had a sterling example in her own mother. And what about extended family? As far as she knew, she had none.

The prospect of trying to raise a child terrified her. In the deepest recesses of her memory she had shadowed pictures of a smiling face, an impression of the warmth of another's arms, snatches of a tune hummed in the dark to chase the night terrors away. But the memories were so few and so ephemeral, they may have merely been wishful thinking. And moneywise, even after Andrea died it still wouldn't be easy. Babies cost money, there were no two ways about it. To keep the child, she'd have to work anyway to support day care, leave her baby to a stranger to be raised. To abandon her baby daily to what she'd spent the last eight years trying to forget. Connor could offer this child everything she'd never had, everything except its own mother. With sudden clarity Holly understood what she had to do.

"I take it I still have a job at Knights?"

"Well, we'll have to see about that." Connor sat back in his chair and rubbed his chin with one long-fingered hand. "Why don't you get your strength back first, then we'll discuss it further."

"Oh, really? And tell me, how am I supposed to support myself in the meantime? I've used up all my leave and sick days."

"I'll see to it that you continue to receive your pay. Until the baby's born you won't want for anything. Obviously, I'd prefer you stay here instead of that excuse for a house you've been living in. You'll have everything you need."

A short sharp bark of laughter ejected from her throat. Need? What did he know about need? He had it all in spades. A family, a home. A job. And now this baby. All she had left was her pride and a whole lot of expenses, and her pride was about to take a long walk off a short pier. She had to tell him about Andrea, risk more of his pity. If he didn't understand why the money was so important, she didn't know what to do next.

"This is about more than my comfort. Have you ever heard of juvenile Huntington's disease?"

"Vaguely." His face blanched in the evening light. "Are you saying you're a carrier?"

"No. I don't even have a medical background to check. But my sister—my foster sister—Andrea, has the disease. She's in the last stages and requires full-time care. Very expensive care. That's where my money goes. I can't afford to lose my job.

She'd have to be moved into the public system. I promised her when she was still well enough to understand I would never let that happen. She's all I have. I won't let her down. Not now."

"And you never told me this before. Why exactly?"

"It's my problem. I handle my problems myself. My way." She took a deep breath, filling her lungs with the scents that lingered enticingly on the night air, knowing that with her next words she'd no doubt be damning herself in his opinion of her. Somehow she had to keep her promise to look after Andrea, no matter what. "Her disease is incurable, but there are things she could have to make her more comfortable. Things I can't afford. I'll agree to have this baby for you, on condition that you continue to pay me so I can cover Andrea's fees."

Her words fell like lead pellets on a tin plate, and across the table Connor flinched. He leaned back in his chair, eyeing her as if she'd escaped from a lunatic asylum.

"You're kidding me, right? You want me to pay you, like some surrogate?" His tone implied he expected her to withdraw her words, but Holly wouldn't take them back even if she'd wanted.

She settled more comfortably in her chair, forcing her fingers to relax, to project an aura of calm. "I think I made myself clear."

A muscle worked on the side of his jaw. Clench, release. Clench, release. Holly knew she'd crossed some invisible line to a point of no return. If he'd had an ounce of respect left for her, she'd splintered it beyond redemption.

"I can see why you'd want to help Andrea. But, Holly, you only had to ask me. I'm not a monster."

No, he wasn't a monster, and that was the problem. She was the monster with her hazy past and unnatural feelings about motherhood. Holly felt trapped, vulnerable, exposed.

"Well, like I said. I deal with my problems my way." She fought to remain still in her seat. If she backed down on this, she was terrified she'd lose everything. "And while I'm on the subject of Andrea, if I agree to stay here, I'll still need to see her regularly."

"Fine. I'll see to it that Thompson takes you over to the city in the launch each day, weather permitting. I'll even continue to pay your salary for as long as you're here, with a lump-sum payout after the baby's birth. Give me the details of Andrea's hospital, too. I'll make the necessary arrangements to take over her bills."

Relief flowed through her. With her income unencumbered by Andrea's fees she'd be able to start the investigation into her background she'd always promised herself. After the baby was born maybe she'd even have enough saved to hire someone to find out who she really was, instead of stabbing around in the dark searching public records for any information.

"So, is that everything tied up to your satisfaction? You'll stay?" Connor interrupted her thoughts.

She meticulously refolded her napkin and placed it back on the table, amazed that her fingers weren't shaking. "Actually there's one other thing."

"Really, just the one?" Sarcasm twisted his lips into an ugly line.

"I want a written contract." Holly lowered her hands to her lap and clenched her fingers together until they started to go numb.

"A contract to have my baby. What? You think I'll renege on the deal?"

"That's right." Her mother had, after all, reneged on her. By whatever means possible, Holly would ensure that this baby had at least one parent that could continue to look after it.

He sighed and closed his eyes briefly before opening them wide again and impaling her on the hot anger of his glare.

"A contract to have my baby and then leave."

Leave? She hadn't had a minute to even think that far ahead, but if that's what it took... "Yes." Her voice quavered.

"To never have anything to do with the child again?"

"Yes." Her reply was nothing but a whisper on the sultry evening air.

His expression changed to one of complete and utter disgust. Had she gone too far? Holly felt regret bloom in her chest; wasn't she just as bad as her own mother? She ruthlessly quashed the thought as it gained momentum in her mind, reducing it back into that dark part deep inside where her hurts remained locked away. She wasn't like her mother. She wasn't abandoning her baby to the unknown. Connor and his family would love and cherish this child in ways she'd never known nor knew how to.

"It's a deal." He sounded as though he'd aged twenty years in twenty minutes. "I'll have the papers drawn up immediately."

She looked at him, seeing the man she'd secretly given her heart to—the man she'd given her innocence to—and saw a stranger. Holly inclined her head in acceptance and pushed her chair away from the table, rising onto surprisingly steady legs. She lifted her chin and raised all the composure she could find within her. "I'd like to go to bed now."

Connor's chair scraped roughly across the tiled patio as he, too, rose from the table. "Follow me."

In silence Holly followed Connor inside the house. They passed through French doors into a vaulted-ceilinged room, the high walls lined with bookcases and a highly polished antique partner's desk claimed pride of place on a vibrant, jewel-hued carpet. While modern office equipment, including the latest discreet flat-screen computer, proved this was a working office, there was an elegance and permanence about the fittings.

Only the best adorned his house—his whole life in fact, she reminded herself as the sliver of ice slid deeper into her chest. The baby would want for nothing. She'd made the right choice.

Holly, however, belonged here about as much as a speck of dust on the immaculately polished sideboard in the formal dining room. She was a castoff. Unwanted, unloved and definitely surplus to requirements once she'd completed her duties. But Andrea would be secure in the hospital. With the best of everything Connor Knight's money could buy for as long as it still mattered.

She barely noticed the rest of the house as they passed through a wide, carpeted hallway and through to a sweeping curve of stairs leading to the second floor. She gripped the satin-finished handrail as though it was a lifeline and dragged herself up the stairs in his wake.

The master suite upstairs, which included a private sitting room to one side, overlooked the pool area. Someone, Thompson presumably, had dimmed the exterior lights so only the blue-black hue of the sky, littered with diamond bright stars, was now visible through the open deep bay windows. Filmy net filters, drawn back from the glass, drifted softly on an imperceptible breeze.

The stark contrast of her position, having only the clothes on her back, to his immense wealth and privilege widened the gulf in her mind. Her love for Connor was even more futile now than ever before. Aside from producing his child what use could she possibly be to him once the pregnancy was over? It wasn't as if they would be able to continue to work together. Not even she was that naive.

They had nothing in common. Not background, not education, not position. Somehow she had to rediscover her dignity, her self-respect. Finding exactly how seemed about as insurmountable as her ability to scale Mt. Ruapehu in high heels and a corporate suit.

Connor's voice interrupted her thoughts.

"The bathroom's through there, and beside it the wardrobe." He gestured one arm across the spacious room to panelled doors on the other side. "We can gather your things tomorrow. Thompson will find space in the closet for you. Get some rest. You look shattered." He took a step closer to her, his hand lifting to her face, one finger gently tracing her cheekbone, an unreadable expression locked in his eyes. Holly's pulse jumped in her veins at the tenderness of his touch. She held her breath, too afraid to exhale in case it destroyed the insubstantial sense of intimacy between them. But the intimacy was as far from the real thing as a cubic zirconia from a Kimberly diamond. His hand dropped back down to his side, breaking the tenuous thread of closeness. "We'll talk in the morning."

"You're not coming to bed now, too?" The words blurted from her before she could think.

"I have work to do."

Holly watched Connor go, feeling strangely lost until she reminded herself of her reasons for being here. Any hope she'd harboured that he might still want her in some way, no matter how minute, disintegrated in the face of the harsh reality. She was little more than a baby incubator for him.

The room, huge compared to anywhere she'd slept before, was cavernous without him there to fill the massive space with his presence. She drifted across the floor to the window and looked out at the city twinkling far, far away in the distance.

Weariness dragged desolately at every atom in her body, yet she couldn't bring herself to pull away from the window. It was as if she'd lived a lifetime in one day. Had it only been this morning she'd arrived at work, determined to start the day fresh? She wrapped her arms around her torso in a futile effort to seek comfort from the helplessness that permeated her mind.

Eventually, she wasn't sure how much later, she made her way to the en suite bathroom. A folded white towelling robe had been placed on the large marble vanity next to feminine toiletries, obviously placed there for her use.

Holly peeled away her clothing, letting it drop to the floor in a heap. She didn't care if she had to wear it creased tomorrow. Right now, that was the least of her worries. She gave a longing glance at the deep oval spa bath, big enough for two. She hastily pushed aside the mental image of Connor and her bathing together and tried to quell the heated flush of desire that fought through her exhaustion and struck like an arrow of need from deep within her. It would be foolish to dream, or even imagine, such a thing would ever happen.

Holly thrust open the glass panel door that opened to the shower and twisted the mixer on. Without even waiting for the water to heat she stepped inside the tiled stall and under the cascade of water. Finally she let go the wrenching emotion she'd held banked since Carmen had delivered the news of her pregnancy. The pulsing jets sluiced away her tears until she was empty and could cry no more.

By the time Holly had dried herself and wrapped the soft terry cloth robe around her frame, all she craved was unconsciousness. She didn't want to think anymore. She didn't want to feel. Tomorrow would be soon enough to face her demons.

Some time in the night a sound penetrated her sleep, rousing her enough to open her eyes.

Connor.

She'd left the drapes open, to give her some sense of contact with the familiarity of the city she'd left behind. Now she could see him clearly as he stood, framed in the window, naked. Her body clenched at the beauty of him as moonlight caressed his form. His muscles, like sculpted marble, were thrown in deeper definition by the silver light cast through the window.

Holly squeezed her eyes shut. She couldn't bear to look at him and not want to mould her fingers over each perfect line. To touch him as she'd always dreamed of doing. Yet she knew her hopes and desires were futile. He would no more welcome her attentions than he'd allow her the freedom to return to her house. She was ensnared by her own foolish love. A love that lay in tatters—barren of hope.

She held her breath as she heard him move across the floor and slide in between the divinely soft and faintly scented cotton sheets. All her senses screamed to full alert as he moved across the wide expanse of no-man's land in the centre of the bed, to where she'd curled up far on one side.

His arm, hot and heavy, hooked around her, pulling her to him until, through the towelling robe, her back was infused with the hard heat of his body. She felt the tie at her waist slide loose and the fabric part as he gently pushed his hand past the cloth barrier to her skin.

Her nipples tightened and tingled as his fingers stroked her, cupping the almost nonexistent curve of her belly as if cradling the new life that grew deep inside of her. He was aroused; she could feel the pressure of his erection cradled by her buttocks. Flames licked from her core, setting a hot throb of desire through her. Would he make love with her? Did he know she was awake? Wanting him? Feeling him want her? All she had to do was shift her hips and the short robe would ride a little further and she'd feel him against her.

His hand at her stomach stilled. No longer stroking. Just there. She felt his body relax against hers and heard his breathing settle into a deep even rhythm. *He was asleep?*

Her nerve endings shrieked their disbelief. Her body was on tormented full alert and he'd gone to sleep. It was another slap in the face. Emphatic proof that his interest lay in the baby, and only in the baby.

Gently, then with a little more pressure, Holly tried to push his arm away from across her waist. His breathing didn't alter but she felt the corded muscles in his arm bunch beneath her fingers as he pulled her harder against him.

He wasn't letting go. His strength should give her comfort. She tried to rationalise her fractured thoughts in an attempt to calm the need that spiralled in coils of tension throughout her body.

Instead, pain carved to the depths of her soul—it wasn't her he wanted.

Nine

Connor straightened his tie and slipped into his jacket. The rustle of the lining didn't even disturb Holly as she lay sprawled across the bed.

It was a week since she'd made her outrageous demands reducing herself to nothing but a surrogate bearing his child. A week since he'd learned he'd be a father and watched his child's mother sign away all rights to her natural state. It had sickened him to his heart to see her do so. He'd given her every opportunity that night to argue for her position in their baby's life. But she'd been almost thankful to accept the terms he'd stated, never believing for a minute that she would rescind all rights to him like that or that she'd be just as driven by money as his ex-wife had been.

Once he'd discovered Holly's financial problems were based in her obligations to Andrea, he'd relaxed a little on pressuring the investigator. The dearth of information had been frustrating, anyway. It was as if she'd been born at the age of fifteen, when she'd finally been placed with the family where she'd met Andrea.

Connor reached out his hand and touched Holly lightly on the shoulder. "We have an appointment with an obstetrician this morning. It's time you got up."

She sat upright, her disoriented state lending a charming dishevelment to her normally aloof air. Then the expression on her face, at first slightly puzzled, changed as her skin paled. Her eyes were deep-blue lakes in their sockets. She muffled a tiny moan of dismay behind fingers pressed to her mouth, and he watched, helpless, as she bolted for the bathroom. What had started as afternoon sickness, now dominated her whole day, and he worried incessantly that she wasn't getting enough nutrition.

Connor waited until he heard her rinse out her mouth at the basin a few minutes later. Frustration rippled through him. Every morning for the past four days had been the same, and he hadn't the faintest idea of how to handle it. It galled him to feel so helpless.

He hovered at the bathroom door. "We need to be ready to go in about forty-five minutes. Would you prefer to have breakfast upstairs?"

In the mirror he watched Holly grit her teeth in staunch determination. "I'll be okay. Just give me a minute or two to get dressed."

She lifted her eyes from the highly polished chrome taps and met his stare in the huge bevelled mirror above the vanity. The angry flare of heat reflected there seared him like a brand. His gaze dropped. Bent, as she was over the basin, the generous neckline of her nightgown had fallen open, exposing one creamy swell of breast tipped with dusky rose.

His libido, still stinging from the denial he'd rigorously implemented, clawed at his insides like a starving, roaring beast. His mouth dried and he felt his lips part, almost in remembrance of the night, just over two months ago now, when he'd tasted the intoxicating sweetness of her skin. He should move, say something, do something—anything but stand here, a helpless victim to the siren call of her body.

She swayed slightly, and her knuckles whitened as she gripped tighter at the marble surface, as though that was the only thing holding her up. "Seen your fill for the morning?" she asked acerbically, lifting her chin and watching as his eyes flicked up to meet her angry stare in the mirror.

"Be ready to leave on time." He snapped, mad as hell that, like some hormone-driven teenager, he hadn't been able to control his voyeuristic tendencies and in doing so he'd allowed her the upper hand.

Connor stalked out of the bedroom suite. Holding her to him each night was sweet torture. His hands clenched into fists and unclenched again. As uncomfortable as it was proving to be, she had to remain hands off. He didn't want to crave her like this. He would overcome the incessant desire she'd loosed in him, even if it took every last ounce of control he had left. Denial was nothing new in his life. It made him who he was.

Connor pounded down the staircase and made his way to the breakfast room. His cell phone buzzed in his pocket and he frowned as he identified the number. Euminides Investigations.

"Yeah," he barked.

"I thought you might like to know that your Miss Christmas has put a request into our office."

"A request? What the hell? What sort of request?"

"One identical to yours, mate. Since the file's still active, I wasn't sure if we should take her on."

"Thanks for the heads-up." Connor thought for a minute. Why on earth would Holly be investigating herself? "Keep the enquiry open, and keep me posted on the results."

"And Miss Christmas?"

If Connor told them not to take her on as a client he knew they wouldn't, but then she'd probably go elsewhere and for some reason that filled him with unease. No, he wanted to find out why she was doing this. "Keep her on, too, but I want to see whatever you find first, okay?"

"Sure. I understand."

Connor snapped his phone shut and pushed it back in his pocket. What the heck was Holly up to now?

"Coffee, sir?"

"Thanks, I need it. Miss Christmas will be down shortly. She's a little indisposed."

"Ah, yes, good morning, miss." Thompson stared over Connor's shoulder, a polite smile of greeting pasted on his face. "Your usual tea and dry toast?"

Holly stood at the door, wearing a suit Connor recognised from the office. The stark navy blue, broken only by the slash of her soft cream blouse at the lapels, drained her of colour. She'd scraped her hair off her face in a tight twist that would probably leave her with a headache by lunchtime. Still who was he to care? So long as the baby was okay, that was all that mattered. At least, that's what he told himself. He refused to consider that anything or anyone else mattered as much.

"Thank you, Thompson," Holly answered as she skirted around to the far side of the small, circular table in a clear attempt to put as much physical distance between them as she could, given the cosy bay-window setting of the breakfast room.

"Might I suggest water crackers, miss?"

"Pardon?"

"Water crackers?"

Holly's response only just beat his own. What was Thompson on about?

"I've been doing a little reading. It might give you some relief if you eat a dry cracker or two when you first wake. I'll arrange for a container by the bed for you."

"Thank you." Holly looked uncomfortable. A tiny blush of colour stained her cheeks.

"Don't worry, Miss Christmas, we'll look after you." With a pointed look at Connor, Thompson slid a plate of dry toast onto the table in front of Holly.

Connor snapped open the pages of the daily newspaper loudly enough to make her flinch. Fine, if they wanted to be buddies, so be it. He had one agenda and one agenda only. A strong and healthy child. This time there would be no mistakes.

Holly resolutely munched her way through the dry toast and tea, pleasantly surprised that it seemed to want to stay down. She took her empty dishes to the kitchen bench with a grateful smile. "That was just the ticket, thank you."

"Let me know when you're up to eating something else and 'll make sure it's ready for you. My late wife was quite the treat when she was expecting. Went from one extreme to the other."

If she wasn't mistaken there was a little more than an answering smile on Thompson's face. Compassion now lit his severe features, instead of the frigidly aloof demeanour she'd been subjected to since she'd arrived. A tiny spark of warmth kindled in the pit of her stomach. For what it was worth, she had discovered an ally in hostile territory.

"When you two have finished playing happy families, we need to get on our way." Connor's voice intruded into the atmosphere of the kitchen with the chill factor of a southerly blast of wind direct from Scott Base.

"I'll freshen up and be back down in a few minutes. We have plenty of time," Holly answered defensively. She would show him he didn't call quite all the shots.

Connor had barely said a word during the entire visit to the obstetrician, who'd confirmed Carmen's diagnosis and concurred with her recommendations. They'd set up an appointment schedule, at first monthly, then later fortnightly, for Holly's checkups, but the details had swirled past her like wisps of fog on a winter morning. She couldn't afford to be too interested in what was happening within her body. She couldn't afford to care. She'd take no active part in the procedure for as long as she could help it.

Holly twisted her handbag strap between restless fingers as they approached the helipad where the Agusta waited to fly her back to the island while Connor returned to his office. He was acting like her gaoler, escorting her to the chopper as if he expected her to run away.

She barely acknowledged him as he handed her the headset, then with a curt nod walked back to the building. She caught a tiny glimmer of his silhouette behind the glass, backlit by the door to the elevator, and then the elevator doors slid shut and he was gone. She knew she shouldn't feel so suddenly bereft, it was exactly how she'd insisted it be. Yet for some strange reason tears pricked at her eyes.

The rotors were putting up more vibration than normal, she thought as she gripped her handbag tightly in her lap. Realisation dawned. It wasn't the chopper blades. It was her bag that was vibrating. Her pager. A cold shiver racked her body. There was only one reason that pager would be buzzing. She shoved shaking fingers deep into her bag, her breath catching in her throat as they finally closed around the small, oblong box. She identified the number on the small screen. *Andrea's hospital.*

The whine of the rotors began to change in pitch. It was now or never.

"Dave! Stop!"

"Are you all right back there, Miss Christmas?"

"No, I need to make an urgent call. Can you wait a few minutes?"

"I'll call Mr. Knight back."

"Don't bother him just yet. I won't be long."

"I'll be waiting."

She ducked and raced from the chopper the instant Dave came around to open the door.

"Are you sure you don't want me to call Mr. Knight?" he yelled at her retreating back.

Clear of the helipad, Holly waved in response and headed straight for the elevator, punching the call button as if her life depended on it. Her heart pounded as the doors opened down in the lobby less than a minute later.

"Miss Christmas, can I help you?" Stan, one of the day security guards rose from behind his console at the side of the foyer.

"Stan, I need to use a phone. It's urgent. Do you mind?"

"Not at all, miss. Do you know the number?"

"Off by heart." She gave him a small tight smile and took the handset off the cradle, pressing in the numbers in swift succession.

Two minutes later, Holly replaced the receiver. A knot tightened in her chest. The doctor had come to the phone immediately. He'd been waiting for her call, in itself a bad sign. He'd imparted the news Holly had dreaded most since Christmas. Andrea was slipping away.

"Is there something wrong?" Stan's voice penetrated the silent case of shock that enveloped her.

"I need a taxi." Her voice wobbled as tears threatened to choke her throat.

"Come with me, miss. I'll get one for you from the rank outside."

A belt of hot, humid air hit her like a wall as they left the air-conditioned sanctuary of the lobby and approached the taxi rank outside. Stan pulled open the taxi's door, pushing a validated, prepaid taxi voucher into her hands, and Holly slid into the back seat. As the Knight Enterprises Tower disappeared behind her, she murmured the private hospital's address to the driver, then began to pray as she'd never done before in her life.

Please, please let me not be too late.

"What do you mean she isn't there?" Connor paced his office, shouting at the speaker phone on his desk as if that would refute Thompson's calm information that Holly wasn't back at the island.

"They haven't arrived yet, sir."

"Arrived? Dave should have returned here by now. I'll call you back." Connor buzzed down to the front desk security in the lobby.

"Did you see Miss Christmas leave the building a short time ago?... You did? Find out what taxi company and call them to see where they took her."

What the hell was she up to? Why hadn't she called him? He slapped his hands on his desk and fought the urge to swipe everything off its cluttered surface and to the floor. Their agreement had been quite specific. She wasn't to go anywhere without his okay. He should have known better than to trust her. Once he found her, he wasn't letting her out of his sight

If he found her.

He sank into his chair. She couldn't go missing completely, he rationalised. He would find her. He would find his baby. No matter what. She didn't have the means or the support to disappear for long.

"What?" he roared as Janet peeked her head around the doorway. A pang of guilt punctured his foul temper as she flinched. "I'm sorry, what is it?" he asked in a level tone, banking the fury that roiled inside him.

"Security didn't get the name of the cab company that you wanted, but Stan said she made a call on his phone before she left. No one's used it since. Do you want him to redial it?"

"I'll do it myself. Make sure nobody touches that phone."

Who could she have called? Dozens of possibilities, none of them making any sense, raced through his mind before he arrived at the ground floor and covered the short distance to the front desk.

"I'm sorry, sir. I didn't know she wasn't—" Beads of perspiration stood out on the elderly security guard's forehead.

"Don't worry, Stan. It wasn't your fault." He reached across the desk and pulled the telephone toward him. "This was the one she used?"

"Yes, sir. No one has used it since."

"Haven View Hospital." The disembodied reply at the other end brought him up sharply. She'd gone to her foster sister? But why? "Hello?" The voice enquired down the telephone line.

He gathered his thoughts together, relieved it had been so easy to track her down. "Has Holly Christmas arrived yet?"

"Yes, she has. Would you like me to bring her to the phone?"

"No, don't worry. I'll be there as soon as I can."

He swiftly replaced the receiver and bolted for the emergency stairwell that led to the basement car park. The BMW's tyres squealed in protest as he roared up the garage ramp.

Haven View was Auckland's most exclusive hospital, he knew that from his own personal experience. After all, the last time he'd set foot in there had been to say a final farewell to his mother when he was eight years old. Despite its lavish surroundings and the expansive gardens outside, it was first and foremost a place where people went to die. He thought he'd forgotten the smells, the atmosphere, the fear. Yet it all came rushing back, as current and clear as if it had been yesterday.

Snap out of it! he growled fiercely at his reflection in the rearview mirror. You're thirty-one years old—not a boy of eight filled with terror. Not some little kid who'd cried to be allowed to go outside and play in the sunshine rather than stay with his father and brothers in the room with a mother he barely knew as anything more than a frail bedridden woman. He'd been too young to understand the cancer that had destroyed the vibrant woman she'd been. He could still see the look on his mother's face, of compassion tinged with sorrow the sweet smile she'd given him as he'd run from the room the instant his father had given him reluctant permission to go

His oldest brother, Declan, had found him in the garden a short time later, and the look in his brother's eyes had told him it was too late to ever say goodbye. He'd lost his chance forever. His mother was gone.

An air horn sounded a strident warning from in front snapping him from the past with an urgency he couldn't ignore Connor swore and swung his car to one side, narrowly missing the container truck headed through the intersection towards the docks. Focus. He had to focus. He had to find Holly.

The entrance to the hospital had changed, and he almos overshot the driveway in his haste. As he got out of his ca and walked up the path to push through the front doors, he fought down the memories that rushed back through him of that other day. He'd never dreamed he'd have to set foot in here ever again.

His unexpected presence commanded immediate attention as the two ladies at reception both approached him at the same time.

"I'm looking for Holly Christmas, I understand she's here?"

"Oh, yes, in the Rose room, second down the hall to your right. Are you family?"

Before Connor could reply, a keening sound struck his ears—so inconsolable it cut through to his nerve endings and made the hairs on the back of his neck rise. A shiver ran the length of his spine. Holly!

He flew down the short hallway, coming to an abrupt halt at the door to a room where Holly lay, sobbing, across the inert form of a young woman. The painfully thin figure in the bed, although clearly ravaged by illness, bore a serenity on her face that gave evidence to the battle she'd borne, and finally won, with her release from life.

The room was cluttered with photo frames on every available surface, yet Connor couldn't tear his eyes from Holly's grief-stricken form as she wept—her sorrow a physical force in the room. Desperate helplessness slammed into him with the power of a freight train. He didn't do emotion. Not this kind. Every muscle in his body tensed with the effort not to leave. One way or another Holly needed him right now. He had to stay. He couldn't walk out on this—on her.

A sudden flurry of activity at the door saw the hurried entrance of two other people, a doctor and a nurse. They spared him a cursory glance, their attention on Holly and Andrea's lifeless form. The nurse gently pulled her away, wrapping Holly in strong arms and holding her tight, while the doctor swiftly examined the dead woman.

"Holly, I'm so sorry," the doctor said in a voice that cracked with emotion. "She's at rest now."

"She was all I had left. *All I had.*" A fresh wave of tears swamped Holly's face as she lifted her head from the nurse's shoulder. Suddenly she became aware of Connor standing by the bed. "*You!* What are you doing here?" The words shot from her mouth like gravel from beneath a spinning tyre. "Can't you ever leave me alone? You don't belong here. Get out. *Get out!*"

"Sir, if you could wait outside for a moment, and give Holly a little time to say goodbye to her sister?" The doctor guided him back out the door, closing it gently behind him, a sympathetic look on his face.

Connor stared at the closed door as helplessness seeped into every cell in his body. He should be in there, with her. Providing comfort. Yet he was the last person on earth she wanted to see.

His acknowledgement of that fact scored deeper than he wanted to admit.

Ten

Wherever Holly turned he was there. At night he held her close to him and cradled her in his arms as she cried herself to sleep, despite her every attempt to remain apart.

Through the mind-numbing fog of loss, she sensed his strong quiet presence behind her, acting as a shield, a support, whatever she needed at any given point in time. Ensuring she had everything.

Everything except Andrea.

The funeral arrangements had been taken care of with the precision of a military engagement. Even Thompson had attended the brief but poignant graveside service, his presence swelling the scant number of staff from the hospital who could make it, together with herself and Connor.

The unfairness that Andrea, who'd been so full of life as a teenager, should be so forgotten emphasised with driving, painful clarity just how alone Holly now was.

Somehow, in the past couple of days, she had learned to lock in the pain of saying goodbye to Andrea. It was better not to love. Not to need. Not to want.

She was alone. Utterly and completely alone.

She thought fleetingly of the child she now carried. Not her baby…Connor's. Under the circumstances it was for the best. It was easier not to flay herself open again.

At the island, Holly drifted aimlessly through the house, before wandering upstairs to the bedroom. In the private sitting room off the master suite, she curled up in a deep armchair that faced the window looking back out to the sea. She'd never thought she'd ever feel so abandoned again, yet the pain and the suffering continued. Andrea's illness had cut her to the bone, but it was nothing compared to the raw screaming pain inside her now.

"Holly?"

She turned at the uncharacteristic hesitance in Connor's voice. He carried a large archive box under his arm. Surely he didn't expect her to work now? He'd assured her that she could take up her duties when she felt ready but that Janet was managing brilliantly in the meantime. With her visits to Andrea and the overwhelming tiredness the pregnancy had wrought she hadn't been in any hurry to take on any more.

"I thought you might like these. You know, to have around you. You can put them around the house if you like."

He put the box in her lap and lifted the lid. Inside, wrapped in layers of tissue, were the photo frames that had filled Andrea's room with the history of their all-too-short time together. Slowly Holly extracted each one and stood them on the long coffee table in front of her.

"Thank you," she whispered.

Connor shifted uncomfortably, his hands thrust deep into the pockets of his trousers. "Do you want to talk about her?"

"What's to tell? She's gone."

He squatted down in front of her, taking the frame she clutched in numb fingers and setting it beside the others before wrapping his hands around hers. The heat of his skin enveloped her chilled hands, warming them through and sending the heat in a slow gentle wave up her arms. She didn't want to feel. It was better to stay numb. Holly tried to pull her hands away, but his hold on her firmed.

"Tell me," he coaxed. He hated seeing her like this—empty of fire, of life. It was as if she'd given up on everything. He'd already spoken at length to the obstetrician, concerned about the effect of her mental distress on the baby, and despite the specialist's assurances, he had to do something to chip her out of the frozen block of ice she'd locked herself into.

He pulled a clean monogrammed handkerchief from his pocket and gently mopped at the tears she hadn't even realised she'd shed. "You never listed her on your company profile as a contact in lieu of next of kin. Why?"

Holly sighed and leaned her head back against the cushioned fabric, casting her mind back to the first time she'd met Andrea. It was so unfair that, aside from herself, there was no one left to remember what Andrea had been like before she'd become ill. Maybe if she could share some piece of her past, instead of locking it all inside, it would help keep Andrea alive in someone else's memory for a little longer. Holly drew in a deep settling breath.

"I was fifteen when I was fostered by the Haweras. I thought they'd be like all the others, happy to help until I got into trouble more times than they could cope and then wash their hands of me. But no. They kept coming back to bail me out of trouble, until one night Andrea, who'd been with them already for about a year, told me how much it was hurting them all, her included, to see me trying to destroy myself.

"I'd never seen it through anyone else's eyes before, but she made me believe that they saw something in me that was worth something. Worth keeping. No matter what I threw at them, they stayed right there beside me, until eventually it was easier to want to please them than to make them angry."

"When did she get sick?" The hospital doctor had explained to him the nature of Andrea's illness and its insidious, slow progression. He'd been stunned when he realised Holly had borne the financial and emotional burden alone for so long. It showed a side of her he'd suspected lurked beneath the aloof surface she presented the rest of the world. But why, then, had she given up all rights to her baby? For someone who'd so obviously clung to the one person who had loved her in return, why would she relinquish the chance to share that with a child of her own?

"She started showing early symptoms when she was about sixteen. She went from being a happy girl to having massive mood swings, and her grades at school started to slide. At first I thought it was my fault for being a bad influence, or for not being supportive enough. But then we realised it was more than that. Bit by bit over the years, we lost her. The Haweras did what they could, but it was far more than they could handle financially. Soon after I started work at Knight's, they were killed in a car accident. I took over everything for Andrea at that point. But it was never enough."

Holly pushed up from the chair and stood in front of the picture window, staring at the rolling lawn that stretched to the small private golden beach and the sparkling blue water that lay beyond. "Did you know that if you carry the Huntington's gene there's a fifty percent chance of passing it on to your children?"

"No, I didn't. Is that what's bothering you about the baby? Do you think you might carry the gene?"

"I don't know."

"She was your foster sister, not your blood relative. You probably don't even have the disease in your family."

"But that's the problem." She spun away from the window, pain and fear etched on her face, in her eyes. "I don't *know.* If it's not that disease it could be any one of hundreds of others. Have you any idea of the number of genetic disorders people face every day? I have no idea about my background. Nothing. I don't even know my real last name. I'm terrified I'm about to bring a child into this world only to watch it suffer like Andrea suffered!" Holly's voice grew more frantic with each syllable.

So that's why she'd started her own investigation. Suddenly it all made perfect sense. The wretched fear in her eyes ripped at Connor like a physical threat as the enormity of her dread became more real with every word. This was his baby they were talking about. His flesh and blood. The concept of bringing a child to life—a precious young life— then watching it slowly die while you stood helpless on the sidelines was as foreign as it was abhorrent to him. After watching her foster sister die no wonder she was so frightened, so opposed to bearing a child.

"The baby will be okay." He forced the words out like a mantra. If he said it with enough strength, enough belief, it would be so. Fate wouldn't be so fickle as to take another baby away from him. It wouldn't dare. They'd undergo every test available to be sure.

To lend weight to his words, Connor stepped closer and deliberately cupped his hands on either side of her neck and drew her closer. Face-to-face. Her eyes were still awash with tears and a tiny frown furrowed between her eyebrows. He leaned forward and pressed his lips against the puckered skin.

"Don't worry," he murmured. "Nothing will happen—to either of you. Trust me."

"You can't be sure of that. No one can." Her voice wobbled with uncertainty.

"I protect what's mine." He rested his forehead against hers and slid one hand down to press gently against her lower abdomen. "And this *is* mine."

"Andrea was my life. Don't you understand? I don't know how to go on. I can't do this." The plaintive cry in her voice struck him at his heart.

"You have to go on. One second…one minute…one day at a time. You're alive. You have a new life growing inside you." He spread his fingers possessively across her belly.

"It doesn't seem real. I don't want to believe it's real."

"Believe it, Holly. You. Me. The baby. Very real."

Suddenly words were not enough. He needed to imprint the truth on her. To make her see, to feel, to finally understand, that to distance herself from their baby was useless. He tilted his head and captured her lips, teasing her mouth open, and swept his tongue inside—plundering, imprinting himself upon her. Need burned through him like a flash fire, and he slid his arms around her still-slender waist, pulling her closer until she lined up against the hardness of his body and the softness of her breasts pressed against him.

It wasn't enough. A shudder rocked through her body as he kissed her, and a surge of triumph swelled from deep inside as her arms crept around him, her hands sliding up his back, her nails digging into his shoulders as he suckled on her tongue.

He reached for the buttons that fastened the front of her blouse, fumbling in his desperation to feel her without any barriers, to taste her creamy softness. As the panels swung free he reached behind to unfasten her bra and pushed the lace fabric up—groaning against her mouth with delight as her breasts filled his hands. He rubbed against her tightened nipples with the flats of his palms and felt her lips tremble beneath his.

"Too much," she protested, her legs buckling. "I…feel… too much."

Connor swept her into his arms, and in a few short strides laid her on the bed. Her skirt worked its way up around her hips as he settled his body gently between her legs feeling the cradle of her hips cup his sex. He'd read that her breasts might be more sensitive, that she might even recoil from his touch.

"Tell me to stop," he whispered against her nipple.

He twirled his tongue gently around the darkened aureole then blew gently and watched as it tightened and peaked even harder, goose bumps prickling on her pale skin. He repeated the movement, first warm and wet, then a soft cool breath, wrenching a sound from her that was half plea, half sigh. His lips teased into a smile as he shifted his attentions to her other nipple. She squirmed against him, pushing her hips up to strain against his erection and sending a shaft of desire so deep he had to halt his ministrations to catch himself, to slow down.

But she wouldn't let him slow down. She pulled his head down to her breast and ground her hips against him as, at first gently, then with a steadier pressure, he began to suckle at her sweet flesh. He felt her body wind tighter and tighter, until she bowed against him, her head thrown back in supplication. He tilted his pelvis against her, pressing his aching shaft against the apex of her thighs, against the dampness and heat that shimmered from her core.

He lifted himself away from her before he lost control completely and gently slid his thumb inside the elastic leg of her panties and further until the pad of his thumb rested against the heat of her soft hood of flesh. Slick with her wetness, his thumb swept a lazy circle around her, increasing in pressure as he decreased the tiny spiralling journey.

He laved his tongue again around one nipple before closing around the taut peak and pulling it gently past his teeth and deeper into his mouth. He felt the ripples of climax begin from deep within her, radiating out until she shattered against him before collapsing back into the mattress. Alive. Real.

He released her nipple from his mouth and pressed gentle kisses against her rib cage, trailing down to her waist, her belly. The skirt had to go. It was entirely too much clothing for what he needed now. He dispensed with the zip fastening and slid the black fabric from her and pulled her panties away from her limp body, throwing them both to the floor in a heap.

If he never saw her wear black again it would be too soon.

He pulled up onto his knees and wrenched his shirt off, sending buttons flying in his haste to bare his skin, to feel hers. In seconds he'd discarded the last of his clothing, freed at last. She lay still on the bed. Her eyes glazed, not with tears but with satiation. Her skin flushed a soft delicate pink.

Holly's heart was beating nineteen to the dozen. Her entire body zinged with energy. With life. Connor had rent open the floodgates of feeling, of need and desire, and she wanted more—she wanted him.

She watched as he ripped away his clothing with little attention to care. She pushed herself upright and onto her knees and shrugged off her blouse and bra, letting them slide off the side of the bed to the floor. She didn't want to think. She simply wanted.

Holly reached out and trailed her fingers across the expanse of his chest, intrigued to watch the muscles beneath the surface of his bronzed skin ripple and tighten in answer to her touch. His reaction lent her power. She did this to him. She governed how hard, or soft, she touched him.

She let her nails scrape across his nipples, at first gently, then stronger, harder. At his sharply indrawn breath she looked up, the expression on his face reminding her he was a man, not merely a body. Their eyes linked as she circled his nipples with her nails, bearing closer and closer to the tender, puckered discs. He held his arms rigid at his sides, and she sensed the restraint he employed in keeping them there. In allowing her this discovery of him.

She parted her lips and ran her tongue first along the bottom, then the top. Then slowly, deliberately, she leaned forward and pressed them, swollen, hot and wet, against him. She felt his reaction in the tremors he fought to control. She dropped her hands to his fists, gently imprisoning them against his hips while she kissed his nipples and trailed a moist line of heat down the crease between his rib cage, then lower to his belly.

The dark hair that circled his belly button matted under the onslaught of her lips and her tongue, and again she felt that surge of power, of energy, of life. Reluctantly she pulled away and dropped one leg over the edge of the bed, bearing her weight on it before sliding the other to the soft carpet on the floor.

"Lie down," she commanded. Was that her voice? That husky, sultry, sexy demand. Desire arrowed sharp and true to her centre and radiated out starbursts of fire.

To her surprise he did so without argument, and she climbed back onto the bed, placing one knee on either side of his thighs. A tiny burst of insecurity bloomed inside her. What was she doing behaving like a wanton?

His dark eyes narrowed to slits, and he watched her as she hesitated, his sensual lips immobile as she gazed upon his body. The mute challenge in his eyes dared her to go further, to touch and take him as *she* wanted to. Without severing visual contact she arched her back and lifted her arms to loose the final strands of hair that remained caught in the twist she'd restrained them in.

The long, dark length of silk swung free, and she leaned forward, letting the strands stroke along the inside of his thighs and higher to where his arousal jutted hungrily. Lowering her head, she caught a hank of hair, wound it softly around his shaft and pulled gently upwards watching, intrigued, as the hair tightened around his swollen head before sliding, teasingly over the tip. She repeated the action, suddenly feeling more wanton and far more aroused than ever before.

A pearl of moisture appeared at the tip of his penis. Without thought, driven purely by sensation, she lowered her mouth to him and flicked her tongue across his straining flesh. The taste of him sent a thrumming pulse through her body. She could barely believe her daring. She could barely believe his restraint.

Between her thighs his legs vibrated with tiny tremors. She could feel the suppressed power in him even as he allowed her to play her sensual game with his body. The fact that he even permitted her this supremacy over him burned like a white-hot catalyst, and Holly lowered her mouth again, this time closing her lips over his erection, her tongue playing against the very tip, swirling, tasting, suckling him. His passion-filled groan empowered her even further as she took him deeper into her mouth, amazed at her boldness, terrified by her might.

"Stop!" he demanded, and his hands slid to her hair pulling her gently away from him.

"Did I hurt you?" she asked, instantly remorseful.

"No. But not being inside you is killing me." He swept her off his body and rolled, tucking her beneath him, settling the hard and heavy length of his sex against her. "Open for me," he demanded, his voice as rough as gravel, his eyes consumed by darkness.

He didn't need to ask twice. Holly parted her thighs and lifted her hips to meet him, quivering as he entered her and tightening against the strength of his body. If she thought she had any control now she was seriously kidding herself, she realised, as Connor withdrew slowly from her before sinking to the hilt again, grinding his hips against her, inflaming her body. Saturating her mind with sensation after sensation. He pulled away and plunged again, this time lowering his lips to hers and parting her mouth, taking her tongue inside his mouth and pulling against it in the same rhythm.

Her entire body tensed, aflame with feeling and sharply aware of the taste of him, the feel of him, her complete and utter acceptance of his right to be inside her, to be part of her.

Pleasure built with increasing force as his hips ground against her again. No, it was too soon, too much. And then there was nothing but the sensation of intense satisfaction as it rolled through her body, building and building until she cried out with the intensity and bowed against him, cleaved to him, became part of him as he was a part of her.

Deep in the recess of supreme satisfaction, she felt his body grow taut as with a final thrust he breached his own peak and spilled himself into her body until finally, shaking, he lowered himself against her, taking them both into the softness of the mattress and the limbo of the aftermath of their passion.

The late-afternoon sun slanted through the window, bathing them in a golden glow and drying the perspiration on their bodies. Holly didn't know that she'd ever felt so complete. Connor shifted slightly, taking his weight off her, and tucked her into his side. It struck her in that moment, she was nothing against his will. It didn't matter what he said or what he did. She loved him, and compounding that love she now carried his child.

Instead of the usual terror rising inside her at the thought of bearing a baby, a sense of warmth and wonder permeated her mind as for the first time she allowed herself to wonder, to dream. What would their baby look like? What would it be?

Languidly she curled into Connor's body, relishing the warmth, the security. She was no fool. She knew it wouldn't last. It couldn't. But for now she could allow herself to pretend.

She drifted off to sleep, locked in the curve of his arms. Maybe, just maybe, she could cope with tomorrow and the day after that.

Connor stirred and opened his eyes slowly. The sun had long since begun its traverse to the other side of the world, and now the bedroom was dark, with long moonlit shadows drawn across the carpet. He inhaled deeply, taking in the scent of Holly's hair, her skin, the residue of their carnal fervour, and felt his body rouse all over again.

Not yet, he commanded, willing his body to submit to his command, but it was useless. She'd invaded his senses like an aphrodisiac, feeding the craving he'd duelled with, and lost against, since the first addictive taste of her body.

Beside him, she slept deeply, her whole body relaxed for the first time since he'd brought her here. She needed rest far more than she needed to be woken right now. Connor forced himself to ease his body away from hers and to slide from the bed, pausing to pull the covers over her delectable body, then he padded quietly to the en suite. Closing the door behind him, he flicked on the lights before reaching into the shower stall and wrenching on the faucet, leaving the setting at cold. He couldn't afford to indulge in his baser needs again tonight.

Even though it had been his choice, looking after Holly in the past few days since her sister had died had eaten into him in a way he'd never expected. He had no desire to explore how devastated she was at losing Andrea or how her loss had reminded him of his own desolation at his mother's death. The only way he'd known how to manage her grief, and his own, was to keep going. To force, to cajole—to place one foot in front of the other to get through every day.

Until today. Today she'd passed a boundary he hadn't even realised existed. In some ways it was as if by actually letting Andrea go, in saying goodbye, she'd allowed herself to move forward, albeit with unrelenting encouragement from him.

He stepped into the shower, hissing through clenched teeth as the stinging cold spray assaulted his body, chilling his ardour, and tried to focus his mind instead on the files he'd brought home. He needed to toughen up. To put her back into that corner of his mind where reason mastered sensation and where logic beat attraction. Connor snapped off the stream of cold water with a determined twist of his hand. He had to get back to work.

And yet he still craved her like an addict needed a fix.

Eleven

Holly heard the chopper blades agitating the air. Connor was home. She hadn't even heard him leave for work. After their lovemaking yesterday she'd slept soundly in their bed, right through until morning. The rest had done her good and she didn't feel anywhere near as unwell when she'd risen, although the flask of hot weak tea and the dry crackers she'd found on the bedside table this morning had probably helped, too.

She'd spent the day sorting through the pictures Connor had brought, reliving happier days when she and Andrea could laugh together. Most of the frames she'd wrapped in tissue and put away, until later. Until a time when she'd have her own place again. Only one picture stood on her bedside cabinet under the lamp—a joyful remembrance of Andrea and her at the beach before the symptoms of the disease had begun to show, both of them smiling and full of good health and dreams of the future. It suited Holly that it would be the last thing she saw at bedtime and the first thing she saw when she awoke.

For the rest of the day Holly had wandered around the gardens and taken a swim in the pool. It had been so long since she'd taken some exercise, the swim had left her feeling enervated and she'd drifted off to sleep in a deck chair on the patio. On waking, a couple of hours later, she found that Thompson had positioned a sun umbrella to protect her from the sun's biting force, and a light cotton throw rug now protected her from the gentle sea breeze that blew in from the ocean.

She'd woken feeling deliciously decadent. Never in her life had she ever had the luxury of doing simply nothing. Although it certainly had its appeal, and was allowing her to catch up on much needed rest, she knew she'd be driven crazy with boredom before long. As far as the house was concerned that was entirely Thompson's domain. He saw to the cleaning and the cooking. She hadn't even done so much as her own laundry since she'd been here. She had to talk to Connor about being allowed to do something, anything, to keep her mind active and alert.

He looked tired, she thought as she watched him alight from the Agusta and walk towards the house, his briefcase buffeting against his legs from the wash of air from the rotors. Even looking as tired as he did, he still made her heart race. Their lovemaking last night had sated her senses, yet just one look at him now and she wanted to press herself against him and peel away the corporate layers that turned her lover into the aloof and sophisticated lawyer he was.

She forced herself to ignore the tingling in her breasts and the heat that uncoiled slowly between her thighs and stepped forward to welcome him home.

"Bad day?" she asked, handing him a glass of chilled water with a twist of lime juice.

He looked hot and bothered and downed the drink at once. There was something very sensual about watching a man drink with such thirst, Holly realised, her own throat growing dry in response. The muscles in his strong brown throat drew her gaze, working in a steady rhythm as he pulled at the liquid and drew it down deep into his body. He took the glass away from his mouth, leaving a shining film of water slicked across his lips. She accepted the glass back from him, trying desperately not to stare at his lips or to wonder what they would taste like right now, this minute.

"Thanks, yeah, you could say that. I have a lot of work to get through before tomorrow. Can you ask Thompson to serve my dinner in my office?"

His dismissive rejection of her presence couldn't have been more emphatic. Hadn't last night meant anything to him?

"Surely you can stop to eat. You'll need to take a break to stay fresh."

"Can't afford to." He walked across the patio towards the house.

"Connor!"

He stopped in his tracks and turned slowly, his black eyebrows pulled together in a forbidding frown. "What is it, Holly? I told you I have a lot of work to do. Can't this wait?"

She baulked for a moment; very few people dared press him when he wore that particular look. But she dared. She had to or she'd go mad with boredom. "Maybe I could help you?"

His right hand fidgeted, always a give away when he was irritated. "No. You need to rest. You're still too pale."

"Rest?" Anger swirled like a red haze through her mind. "I've been resting all day. I want to do something. I *need* to do something or I'll go crazy."

"Go read a book, watch a movie."

"I want to help you." He just didn't get it, she thought in frustration. After spending her day wandering around like a lost soul, she'd looked forward to him coming home. The prospect of an endless evening with only her own company stretched before her like an echoing void.

"I said no. Look, if you really want to do something to fill your days, pick a room upstairs and turn it into a nursery. We're going to need it eventually. Maybe the turret room, since that's closest to the master suite, then the nanny can have the room next to it."

"Nanny?" The word *nursery* had been enough to turn her blood to ice in her veins, but *nanny* elicited a gut deep response she didn't want to identify.

"For when you're gone, Holly." Connor explained with pseudo patience. "I'm going to need a nanny."

He turned and went inside. His exit hit her like a physical slap, and Holly sank to the chair behind her. Hearing him speak of a nanny in such cold and clinical terms brought the reality of this pregnancy back to her in spades. A cold clammy shiver ran down her back. She was only here to have his baby and then move on, he'd reminded her quite succinctly. He neither expected nor, obviously, wanted her to stay. And why would she? She hadn't the faintest notion of how to be a mother. Her own had abandoned her so she had no role model here, nor had the succession of foster mothers over the years touched her heart.

The risk of pain was just too great. Losing Andrea had proven that. It was much better to lock those feelings down. Look at what loving Connor had given her. Only more heartache, and now a child she didn't want to love—just as her mother had so obviously not wanted her.

But wouldn't she be doing the very same thing as her

mother? Wouldn't she be just as wilfully neglectful by walking away from her baby? No, it wasn't the same. Not the same thing at all. She propelled herself out of the seat and hurried back inside. Her baby would be loved and would be cared for. It would lack for nothing. *Nothing but a mother's love,* the insidious voice in the back of her mind taunted.

She didn't want to deal with this, not now, not ever, she thought irrationally even while knowing that at some stage she was going to have to. Nature had its own way of making a person sit up and take notice. So Connor wanted a nursery for his baby. Well, she'd give it to him. It would be the best nursery on the planet, just as she'd been the best PA he'd ever had. She'd show him it didn't matter to her. She'd show him she could do this and then walk away. No matter what.

Connor leaned back in his chair and looked through the closed French doors to the patio where Holly still stood, her face partially obscured by the long late-afternoon shadows. He tilted his chair and rested his head against the high leather back.

Why had he baited her like that? What had he expected? That she would suddenly develop overwhelming maternal instincts and demand that *she* be the one caring for the baby and not some nameless faceless stranger? And what did it matter to him, anyway? It wasn't as if he expected her to stay. To be a mother. To be a real family. Life was complicated enough without that.

Truth be told he'd been looking forward to coming home tonight, to seeing Holly. Yet, when he'd seen her all he could think about was her absolute rejection of the child she carried. This morning, before work, he'd almost toyed with the possibility they could have a normal relationship. Be a couple.

But it was hopeless—the mere thought ridiculous—that

was as clear as the nose on his face. Her expression when he'd suggested she create the baby's nursery had been filled with horror. There was no way she'd take on the task. Regret tinged with an emotion even more intangible, knotted in his gut.

He sat upright and flicked open his briefcase. Caring for Holly, beyond seeing to her good health and welfare was not an option. Going down any other road, unthinkable. He'd cared about his mother and she had gone. He'd cared about his wife, and she'd betrayed his deepest trust, totally and irrevocably.

They said you couldn't control who you loved or who loved you. Well, maybe the latter was true, but he had news for the former. He could and would control whom he loved, and right now that began and ended with his baby.

When Connor arrived home the next evening Holly wasn't waiting on the patio with an ice-cool drink. Even Thompson, instead of being in the kitchen putting the finishing touches to the evening meal, was nowhere to be found. Connor flung his briefcase behind his desk in his office and sank down into his chair when a loud hollow thud sounded from the second floor—a thud that sounded sickeningly like someone falling. He hurtled from his seat and headed up the stairs, taking them two at a time.

"Holly!" he shouted as he rounded the landing at the top, his heart hammering in his chest. He tried to tell himself it was just the baby he was worried about, but he had to be honest with himself. It wasn't. Not anymore.

"Holly!" he shouted again, and sagged in relief when he heard her muffled voice.

He raced towards the turret bedroom, the one he'd suggested as a nursery the night before. The door was closed and another thump echoed under the door. As he reached his hand to the doorknob he heard something he hadn't heard before. Surely that wasn't Thompson laughing? The door opened abruptly beneath his hand and swung inwards.

The carpet had been rolled back from the polished floor and the heavy carved wooden furniture in the room was all shoved in the centre and draped in dust covers. Thompson, wearing a baggy set of coveralls, was on his hands and knees, sanding the foot-high moulded skirting boards.

Holly, to his horror, stood on a makeshift scaffold, a scraper in her hand, and balanced precariously on a plank that to his eyes looked far too narrow. A strip of wallpaper hung drunkenly from the wall. She turned, twisting to see him, simultaneously losing her balance and sending the narrow plank skittering to the floor. Connor leapt forward to catch her in his arms and held her against him before lowering her feet to the floor.

His heart beat double time. "What the hell are you doing?" he demanded. A fierce wave of anger swiftly replaced the fear that had torn through him when he'd seen Holly lose balance.

She pushed away from him and free of his hold. Her eyes sparkled and colour flushed her cheeks. A strand of long dark hair had worked free of the crooked ponytail she wore. A smudge of paint dust streaked across her forehead. Connor lifted a hand and wiped it away and watched as her expression froze and changed from one of relief to defensiveness.

"What do you mean, what are we doing? You have eyes in your head don't you?" She turned and defiantly replaced the plank and stepped back up onto it. "We're preparing a nursery."

"Not now you're not." Connor stepped forward and lifted her back down off the makeshift trestle. "It's too dangerous."

"Oh, don't be so ridiculous. If you hadn't burst through the door and startled me like that I would never have fallen. Besides, Edgar is here with me."

"Edgar?" Did she mean Thompson?

"Yes, sir. I offered to do the wallpaper, but in light of my frozen shoulder, Miss Christmas insisted she do it." Thompson levered up from his knees and stood as he spoke, brushing clouds of dust off him as he did so.

Thompson had a frozen shoulder? He'd never so much as complained once. What the hell was going on?

"Well, whatever the two of you have decided to embark on together it stops right now. I'll get contractors in." He spun Holly around to face him. "And the most risky thing you will do from now on is choose paint and fabric swatches."

"Excuse me, I think I'd best go and finish dinner while you discuss this." Thompson edged past the bristling pair and disappeared down the hall.

"There is nothing further to discuss," Connor said through clenched teeth. He wheeled around and stalked from the room, fury building up inside him until he felt as if he'd erupt into a seething, spitting cauldron of molten metal.

The solid thump of the wooden-handled scraper hit him square between the shoulder blades and stopped him in his tracks.

"How *dare* you dictate to me like that?" Holly's voice followed with equal force.

He turned slowly, his hands fisted on his hips. "I dare because you endangered my baby. Remember? The one I'm paying you to have."

"You can't wrap me in cotton wool! Make up your mind for goodness sake. First you tell me to decorate a nursery, now you tell me I can't. Well I have news for you, Connor Knight, and it's all bad. I'll decorate that room if it kills me. You've taken my job from me. You've taken my home from me. You will not take my will away from me, too."

Her eyes flashed, burning blue like heated cobalt. Connor closed the distance between them, aware of the emotion that poured from her, of the way her breasts heaved under an old T-shirt he thought he'd discarded years ago. The worn white cotton draped over her, shaping to her gently rounded shoulders—the sleeves coming halfway down her arms. She looked soft and feminine and extremely desirable. Rigidly he slammed the brakes on his thoughts before they further roused his disruptive libido.

"I don't want to take your will away from you. I just want to keep the baby safe."

"That's all I am to you, isn't it? Just some damn incubator for your blasted baby! What about me? Me?"

She raised her hands and pressed against his chest, vehemently emphasizing each word, and pushing him back a step. Connor caught her wrists before she wound up for another push.

"Stop! Holly, stop!"

"No! I don't want to stop. I can't live like this with you dictating everything I do. I can't wait to get away from here—away from you!"

Her eyes washed with tears. They were his undoing. Maybe he'd been too dictatorial. But she didn't understand what was at stake, or why this child was so important to him. But she was wrong, he realised with damning clarity. She was more than just an incubator for his baby. Somewhere along the line she'd inveigled her way into a crack in his heart. A crack that was opening to let her into a piece of him he fought to hold apart.

If he wanted to be totally honest with himself right now, his first thought had been about the potential danger to her. He hadn't even been thinking about the baby when he'd seen Holly twist and begin to fall. Even now, just thinking about it—the startled look in her eyes, the position of her body—made him feel sick to his stomach.

As he held Holly's hands and looked down into her face, tears pooled in her lower lids and one by one spilled over her lower lashes to track twin trails down her smooth cheeks.

He didn't want to admit that he cared for her, nor the vulnerability it would leave him open to. Loving his unborn baby was simple. There could be no lies between them, no trust broken. Loving Holly was not an option.

Warily he let go her hands and took a step backwards. Anything that created some barrier between them had to be good, even if it was only a short, air-filled distance.

"Okay, I admit it. I overreacted. But I mean it about the contractors. I will get them in to do the basics." He saw her stiffen, and rushed on before she could interrupt. "To do the basics only. The rest you can do yourself."

"Define the rest."

"Anything that you can safely reach without requiring assistance like ladders or that wretched scaffolding you put up. Is that completely clear?"

"Yes."

He turned to walk away, pulling his jacket off and tossing it onto the bed. The evening sun glinted on the metal edge of the wallpaper scraper where it had landed on the floor. He bent to pick it up and turned to face Holly. "I believe this is yours?"

A wash of pink coloured her neck and upwards to her cheeks. She put out her hand to accept the scraper. "I'm sorry. I overreacted, too."

Connor held onto one end of the scraper even as she held the other. "Truce?"

"Yes," she whispered again, this time with her eyes fixed on the carpet between their feet, as if she was ashamed to meet his eyes. She'd caught her lower lip between her teeth, biting down hard enough that all colour fled their usual rosy fullness.

Connor tugged gently on the scraper, pulling her slightly off balance and into his arms. Her surprise at being pulled off centre made her let go her lip, and he watched as colour returned to the soft membrane.

He had to taste her.

He lowered his head and drew her more firmly into his hold. She tasted of a heady combination of salt and dust. But more than that, she tasted of her incredibly individual and enticing sweetness and spice that left him constantly craving for more.

Reluctantly he let her go. Any more of this and it would get to be a habit. He had to remember why she was here and how temporary it was. Remember who she was and the fact she was prepared to walk away from their child without so much as a backward glance. A man didn't love a woman like that.

Love?

A wave of denial swamped him. No way. There was no way he'd let himself love Holly. His son or daughter, no matter how perfect or imperfect, would see the light of day. Would feel the warmth of its father's arms, would know—every single day of its life—the love that was for his child and his alone. He had no room in his heart to love another.

He turned away abruptly, wrenched off his tie and yanked at the buttons on his shirt on his way through to the en suite. It had been a day of pure chaos in the office. Janet was good at her job, but she wasn't Holly. The calm and controlled order he'd taken for granted each day had gone to hell in a hand basket, and it didn't look as if it would improve anytime soon. He needed a stiff drink and dinner, and then enough work to ensure he'd fall asleep exhausted, immune to the temptation of wanting to slide inside her body and slake the hunger she set alight in him.

As he'd driven himself to the top of his field, he'd learned to recognise weakness in all its forms and to identify his opponent's Achilles' Heel. He'd honed the ability into a sixth sense and become a master at capitalizing on it, using it to his advantage, then driving home an unbreakable deal.

Now, suddenly, he identified weakness in himself. And he hated admitting he'd allowed himself to become vulnerable to the one woman he couldn't love.

Twelve

Holly stepped back from the curtain she'd just straightened—her heart swelling with pride. She'd painstakingly learned to sew and she'd made them herself, just like she'd made the comforter for the crib and the layette for the bassinette right down to the miniature sheets. She reached forward and gave the drapes a tiny flick, smoothing an imaginary hitch in the fall of the fabric.

Seven months ago she'd never have imagined she could turn into such a homebody let alone furnish an entire nursery. Once Connor's contractors had finished wallpapering and painting the room, she'd had carte blanche to use whichever interior designer she wanted to create the baby's room. Yet, for some reason, it had become more important than she'd ever imagined to leave an indelible print behind her. To leave a piece of her heart.

She reached for the framed picture of the baby's first

sonogram that Connor had placed on the tallboy, trailing her finger across the tiny form captured in black and white. She could still see the wonder that had spread across his face when he'd caught his first glimpse of his child, still see the unsettling and uncharacteristic shine of tears in his eyes. Up until then, she'd hardly had the nerve to look at the radiographer's screen, yet the love that shone from him as he viewed his baby had forced her to turn away from him and look for herself. It was easier to look at the object of his love than to admit that love could never be shared with her.

Holly took a final look around. While she'd been oddly loath to finish the room, taking her time on small details no one but herself would notice, Connor's reluctant yet urgent departure for the States a week ago had been the catalyst that drove her to complete it.

This would be the last time she would come in here. Her end of the deal was all but finished. As if to acknowledge her hard work a tiny foot pressed against her rib cage. Absently she massaged her swollen belly.

With the baby's due date only three weeks away, the days now stretched emptily before her. Holly turned and walked out. A ragged sigh dragged past the sudden tightness in her chest as she closed the door behind her. The day she'd have to leave the island, leave Connor, permanently drew closer with every cross on the calendar.

He'd miss her checkup tomorrow she realised with a pang. He'd made all her doctor's visits thus far, hovering like a worried shadow at every stage of the pregnancy. The baby was everything to him. She'd given up hoping he'd forget for just one moment that she was carrying his baby and see her as a woman with needs and desires again. Sleeping with him every night was fraught with hopes of what might have been, but still he made no attempt to touch her, unless it was to feel the baby's vigorous reminders of its existence. Now, more than ever before, Holly felt incredibly and desolately alone.

She missed him. Even as remote as he'd been, he'd imbued a sense of security—made her feel protected. Now she felt vulnerable. Afraid. She shook her head and sighed. Must be hormones, she reasoned. Either that or she was going completely nuts, as she'd been to think she could ignore the life burgeoning within her.

Tears pricked at her eyelids as Holly hung her head. She was a useless overemotional wreck. Her feet were swollen, her figure nonexistent, even her moods swung as wildly as the New Zealand flag atop of the Auckland Harbour Bridge. She was about as attractive as an overblown blimp. No wonder Connor didn't want her. Although why he still insisted on sleeping with her she couldn't understand. Maybe she'd move her things into the nanny's bedroom while he was away, she thought, then cast the idea out of hand. She no more wanted to sleep without Connor's solid presence behind her in the bed than she suspected he'd let her indulge in her fit of pique.

The constant ring of the telephone downstairs interrupted her miserable soliloquy. She waited for Thompson to answer it but obviously he was busy elsewhere in the house. She didn't feel like talking to anyone right now. But what if it was Connor? She reached out again and lifted the receiver, at the same time hearing a breathless Thompson pick up from downstairs. She knew she should hang up, but when she heard the caller identify himself as the private investigator she'd engaged, she stayed on the line waiting for him to ask for her.

A flash of hope lit inside her at the sound of his voice. Finally he had some information. The investigation had remained at a frustrating stalemate for far too long, with little more information available other than what she'd grown up knowing. How someone could give birth and raise a child for three years then disappear should have been impossible in a country the size of New Zealand, but somehow, her mother had managed it.

When Holly replaced the receiver a few minutes later she was shaking. The call hadn't been for her. It had been for Connor—to let him know a final report was on its way by boat and, more important, that it held urgent information that Connor had been waiting for.

Holly drew in short sharp breaths through her nose, feeling her chest rise and fall with each intake and exhalation and willed herself to calm down. Had Connor had her investigated as he'd investigated Carla, his ex-wife? Why? And since when?

Anger lit within her, burning with a steady glow. It stood to reason that he'd want to know some background for his baby's lineage. But to order an investigation behind her back? And all along the investigator had been working for both of them—had even deliberately been stonewalling her own repeated requests for more information.

She felt invaded. Violated. And fiercely determined to get to the report before he did. For the first time in days she was glad Connor wasn't around. In fact, right now she wondered if she ever wanted to see him again.

Later, instead of taking her usual afternoon nap, Holly anxiously watched and waited from the master suite's sitting room as Thompson met the courier at the end of the private jetty and accepted a large white envelope. Her heart plummeted. It wasn't very thick. It didn't seem right that something that possibly held the key to her past—her life—could be so insignificant as that single large envelope.

As Thompson made his way back to the house, she shot

silently down the back stairs that led to the informal sitting room. Beyond that lay Connor's office. She hid, poised behind the open door, and listened as Thompson came back inside. He went straight into Connor's office where she heard the telltale snick of a key in a lock and the faint slide of wood as he opened then closed a drawer.

That was it? She listened carefully as Thompson left the office again. She replayed the sounds she'd just heard in her head. There'd been no sound of a key being turned in the lock to secure the drawer. Connor would have to beef up his home security if he thought one little drawer would keep her from finding out what secrets lay inside that envelope. A new and more startling thought occurred to her. Had he even planned to share his findings with her? She seriously doubted it.

For an infinitesimal moment she wondered how different her life would be now if she hadn't made love with Connor that night and, even if they had, if she hadn't fallen pregnant? She'd still be at her desk, doing her job better than anyone else could. Still being his trusted right-hand person, instead of someone he now endured only for as long as completely necessary. Holly sighed and pushed her hand against the ache in the small of her back. All the what-ifs in the world wouldn't change anything. She wasn't good enough for Connor Knight. She never would be.

The sound of the French doors being pushed closed caught her attention. Thompson was stepping out for his afternoon walk—a trip she knew would take him at least thirty minutes. Now was her opportunity.

Her heart pounded as she retraced Thompson's steps. If he came back sooner than expected, she'd be clearly visible through the French doors. Holly's hands trembled as she opened the drawer. To her surprise, there was not one, but two identically addressed envelopes. She frowned as she tried to remember exactly what she'd seen from the window upstairs. No, there was nothing wrong with her eyesight. Thompson had definitely received only one. That could only mean one thing—Connor already had a report on her. Holly swiftly removed both envelopes and jammed them under her loose, long-sleeved shirt before heading for the stairs.

On the day bed in the baby's room, she slid her finger under the flap of the already open envelope. Now she had it in her hands, she almost dreaded what the news would disclose, but she had to know. Her hands shook uncontrollably and her heart thundered in her chest, filling her ears with the cacophony, as she tipped the papers from the envelope where they fanned haphazardly onto the lemon-coloured bedcover. She gathered up the loose-leaf typewritten sheets.

The report dated back to just after Christmas and listed, in minute detail, her financial dealings including the regular payments she'd made to the hospital for Andrea. How dare he? He'd obviously requested this information before they even knew she was pregnant. What had he been playing at? She wanted to scream and rant and hit something. Preferably Connor Knight. Holly threw the information back down on the bed in disgust.

All his concern for her when Andrea had died suddenly rang unbelievably false. All along he'd been playing her for a fool. There was only one thing on his mind and that was the baby. Right now, she hated him more than she could have believed, and deep inside, her heart splintered into bleeding shards. Holly's anger drove her to snatch the sealed envelope from the bed. What other secrets had been exposed? Her eyes scanned disappointedly through the first few pages. It was nothing she didn't already know. Summaries of social workers' reports detailed how difficult she'd been to place in a foster home after the incident with the Mitchells' son. Was this all he'd been able to find out?

Holly turned to the next page and instantly her heart shuddered erratically in her chest as she saw the faxed copy of a Police report, dated the twenty-seventh of December nearly twenty-four years ago. Three days after she'd been abandoned.

She sank to the bed, her throat choked with trepidation, and forced herself to continue to read the investigating officer's coldly clinical description of the discovery of a teenage girl's body, dead from a suspected drug overdose, under a motorway overpass. She'd been found wrapped in a bunch of newspapers. A low-resolution copy of the crime scene photo brought a cold metallic taste to Holly's mouth. The dead girl couldn't have been more than seventeen or eighteen. What a waste of a life.

Apparently she'd been found wearing a locket which, when the photo inside was publicised, lead the police back to her family. A family she'd run away from three and a half years earlier.

Fingers shaking, Holly flicked to the report. It was believed the dead girl was Holly's mother—the clue lying in the newspapers that had surrounded the body, many of which shouted the headlines of Holly's abandonment on Christmas Eve in the downtown shopping complex.

Holly pored over the photo again. She could faintly distinguish the headlines he referred to. A gaping sense of loss penetrated her chest and with it a sense of hopelessness. She would never know her mother—could never ask her the million and one questions that had plagued her as a child.

This bereavement felt different from when Andrea had died. This time her sorrow was threaded with frustration and anger at the young woman who'd taken her life and left Holly to a future no one could have known. And yet, the young woman's desolation was painted clear and strong in the picture. Alone and wrapped in the evidence of what had probably been the hardest thing she'd ever done. What could have driven her to such a lonely death? She must have used support services when Holly was born—why hadn't she called for help when she could no longer cope on her own? How had she slipped through the cracks?

No matter what the answers, it was all too late now.

Holly swallowed hard against the lump in her throat. She would not cry. Not again. She'd shed a lifetime of tears for her mother already.

She continued to read, damming all emotion behind an invisible wall, until finally she reached the end and put the papers back into the envelope. Hope flickered like a timid ember in her mind. A woman named Queenie Fleming lived at a coastal holiday spot, about half an hour north of Whangarei. If the investigator's deductions were correct, she could be Holly's grandmother. Her sole surviving relative.

How long would Connor have kept this information from her, Holly wondered. Would he *ever* have told her?

She had to meet Queenie Fleming, although she knew Connor would never sanction such a meeting. Finally, she thought with grim realization, fate was on her side. With Connor away she'd have no difficulty slipping away after her obstetric appointment tomorrow. She could withdraw the money that had been accumulating in her account over the past few months and pay untraceable cash for a rental car. A quiver of excitement ran up her back. Tomorrow she had a date with her past.

"You look tired this morning, miss. Didn't you sleep well?"

"A bit unsettled," she admitted, stifling a yawn.

With forced steadiness, she reluctantly accepted the cup of tea Thompson had poured for her, taking it over to the bay window to look out on the early spring morning. Last night she'd been too excited to sleep, fearful with every creak of the house that Connor had returned. By the time the sun breached the horizon, she'd already been up and dressed and made a last-minute check on the few toiletries and personal items she'd stowed in her bag.

While she'd waited for the next hour to tick past on the bedside clock, she wondered how Connor would react. He'd be livid. By leaving him she was effectively kidnapping his baby. He'd be after her as soon as he could, which was why she had the reports rolled up and secured in the bottom of her bag. Once he discovered she had them, he wouldn't have a leg to stand on. He couldn't force her back here if he tried, and with luck she'd gain a head start of at least a few days.

She didn't doubt he'd come after her, well the baby at least. He loved the baby already with a single-minded intensity she envied. How could he be so certain that he wasn't opening himself up to heartache?

Holly put the cup on the breakfast table and stretched her lower back. She'd been so achy these past couple of days and the baby felt as though it sat lower than before. She'd have to watch her fluid intake today or she'd be forever stopping at restrooms on the way up north. She had to be as invisible as possible. Every stop would leave another imprint of where she'd been and make her easier to find. She'd go light on the liquids.

"The usual toast today?" Thompson asked.

"Yes, please, but I feel like something a bit more substantial. Some scrambled eggs would be lovely." Who knew when she'd next stop to eat?

Thompson hid his surprise well. Since the early days of her

pregnancy when she'd suffered with all-day morning sickness so violently, she'd barely stomached anything heavier than a slice of toast or some fresh fruit for breakfast. But instead of questioning her, he only smiled.

"Coming right up. The helicopter will be here at nine to collect us for your appointment. Mr. Knight will be sorry he missed it."

"He's been busy. I'm sure he'd have been back by now if he could have."

"For certain," Thompson agreed vigorously. "He's so looking forward to the baby."

The enormity of what she was about to do today shafted through her. She couldn't wait until after she'd had the baby, even though she'd given her word to stay until after the birth. In doing what she was about to, she was not only burning her bridges, she was systematically destroying all the roads that led to them, too. Roads that could never be rebuilt at any price. He would never trust her again.

It was a price she was prepared to pay.

Thirteen

Holly swung the car gently around yet another winding curve, her knuckles white, her fingers clenched around the steering wheel.

It had been years since she'd driven, and this road was certainly taking it out of her. Her shoulders sagged in relief as she reached a short straight stretch of road. To the right, a general-goods and fast-food store perched on the corner of an intersection. That must be her turn. She forced her fingers to relax and turned off to the right. As she wound down the hillside, she left banks of green bush behind her as the manuka and native ferns gave way to pasture and the occasional house.

Her back was killing her from sitting so long, but she'd been too scared to pull off the road and take a walk. Driving straight through had been the most sensible thing to do, if not the most comfortable. It had taken three hours by the time she'd deciphered the map and had had to turn back a few times, but finally she was here.

Butterflies buffeted at her stomach as she drove down the main road and straight towards the beach. The road curved to the left, and a tall stand of ancient pohutukawa trees guarded a reserve on the right-hand side. Holly grimaced as a cramp started in her calf muscles. She had to stop and stretch it out before she crippled herself. Thankfully, there were plenty of places to park.

Despite the sunny day, a cool wind blew in off the ocean. Unintentionally she compared the strand of beach, stretching from left to right for a couple of miles, with Connor's secluded private beach on the island. They were nothing alike.

Just as she and Connor were nothing alike, she reminded herself forcefully.

The cramp was getting worse. Holly climbed out of the car and turned to lean against it, stretching out the aggrieved muscles. Despite his aloofness, Connor had taken to massaging her lower legs before bed when he'd realised it helped to prevent the painful cramps that sometimes had her shooting out of bed at night.

She missed him.

God, where had that thought come from? She needed her head read and her mind shrunk. They were poles apart and always would be. She was the daughter of a drug-addicted street kid; he was used to wealth and privilege. Once the baby was born he'd cast her off as easily as he would a shirt with a frayed cuff, although probably with a better reference. There, that felt better. She was angry again.

But her anger didn't last. Holly looked around the reserve and the beach that bordered it. Breakers rolled in, big and fat and just perfect for body surfing. Even at this time of year the place was a miniparadise. In summer it would be magnificent. Why had her mother left? She could only have been a child herself—certainly no more than fifteen.

A group of teenagers burst from the takeaway store across the road, laughing and fooling as they crossed to the reserve and settled at a table where they eagerly started into fresh fish and chips wrapped in newspaper.

Had her mother done this with her friends? Would Holly have done the very same thing if she'd been allowed to grow up here? It was so unfair. She'd been cheated of so many things— a carefree childhood, happy memories, a sense of belonging.

She'd thought she was done with empty questions, but now, here where her mother had been born and raised, she felt them peck at her mind like seagulls picking at a sandwich on the beach.

The reality of actually being here, of walking on a path that her mother had trod was suddenly more overwhelming than Holly had ever imagined—and more frightening. Another flurry of questions, like the swirling sand lifted and cast around by the on-shore breeze, battered at her brain. What if she found her grandmother, and the woman wanted nothing to do with her? What if her mother had had good reason to flee her family and home?

What if she was just setting herself up for rejection again?

A part of her was tempted to get straight back in the rental car and drive flat-out back to Auckland. But she couldn't run away now. She needed to know, for her own sake.

A walk, she needed a walk to clear her head and put some distance between herself and the car that would tempt her to take the easy way out. Besides, a walk would give her a few more minutes to pull her ragged nerves together. Finding her grandmother's house wouldn't be difficult. To the right there weren't more than twenty houses along the beachfront, and the house photo in the report was quite distinctive. She felt sure she'd recognise it from the waterside just as easily as from the road that ran parallel to the beach.

Holly lifted her bag from the front seat, swiped her keys from the ignition and locked the car. At the edge of the beach she kicked off her runners and, balancing against a large park bench, she slipped off her socks and shoved them into her bag. The sand felt cool and soft beneath her feet and she sank a little in the loose granules before she reached the firmer base where the outgoing tide had left its mark scattered with seaweed and pieces of driftwood.

With the setting sun at her back, she headed off down the beach, peering intently at each of the houses she drew level with. The houses were an eclectic collection in various states of size and repair. At a glance it looked as if the traditional Kiwi baches, or holiday homes as they were becoming more widely known, were being superseded by palatial homes that wouldn't have looked out of place in some of Auckland's highly sought-after eastern suburbs. Each one built to face the sea. Holly easily identified her grandmother's tidy cottage from the photo in the report and fought to stem the rush of adrenaline that flooded her body and propelled her up the sand to the wide grass berm that separated the houses from the beach.

Her heart hammered against her ribs as Holly placed a shaking hand on the front gate and gently pushed it open. This side of the house was built to enjoy the vista of the bay, and wide French doors were flung open. Holly determinedly placed one foot in front of the other until she was standing on the weathered deck and raised her hand to knock firmly on the doorjamb.

Her heart skipped a beat as she heard a noise from inside,

but still no one came at her knock. She banged against the door frame again.

"Hello?" An elderly man's head popped up from the other side of the fence that bordered the property. "If you're looking for Queenie she's coming up the beach now."

"Yes, yes, I am. Thank you."

"Say, you look familiar. Have I seen you before?"

Holly's breath caught in her throat. "No, I've never been here before." She swiftly descended the shallow stairs that led off the deck and walked back down to the beach, scanning the shoreline for the figure that was in all probability her only living family.

All at once she felt the earth tilt. The woman walking towards her was older than the photo from the locket that had been printed in the paper, but the likeness was unmistakable.

Queenie Fleming. Her grandmother.

Holly's shoes dropped unheeded from her hands as she stopped and stared, unable to speak. Unable to even think.

"Hello? Were you looking for me?"

For longer than you can ever know. "Yes, I am." Holly managed to force the words past lips that quivered as they stretched into a welcoming smile.

As she drew nearer, the woman's smile became more set and her face, weathered by sun and wind and marked with lines of sorrow, paled as she fixed her gaze on Holly. "Giselle? No, you can't be…" Her voice trailed away weakly.

A shiver rippled through her—Giselle, her mother. It was all she could do not to throw herself in the other woman's arms, yet one remaining ounce of caution—a lingering fear of being brushed aside if she identified who she was—held her in place.

"I'm sorry, dear, you startled me. You look such a lot like

my late daughter. Don't worry about a silly old thing like me." She gathered herself together and gave Holly another smile. "You look worn-out, dear. Long trip? Why don't you come and have a cuppa with me. I'm Queenie Fleming, but the young ones around here call me Nana, you may as well, too."

Queenie's chatter washed over her, and Holly felt herself nod, not even believing it could be so simple. *Nana.* Her stomach did a little flip. If she'd grown up here she'd have had every right to call her Nana.

"Wait, please?" She put a hand out to the woman's arm, her fingers curling gently around it ever so briefly before letting go. Her grandmother. It still seemed unreal.

"Am I going too fast for you, dear? Oh look, you've left your shoes in the sand. The tide'll take them if you're not careful." She bustled back and collected Holly's shoes. "Come on with me and I'll sit you down and get you a nice hot cuppa. Gee, this wind has some bite in it, doesn't it?"

Without hesitation Nana hooked an arm around Holly's expanded waist, helped her over the loose sand and towards the old but well-maintained house that squatted amongst the larger architecturally designed homes.

"They call it progress, dear." Her grandmother sniffed and waved a disparaging hand towards the two-storied home to the side, leaving no doubt as to what she thought of it, and led Holly across the deck and into the cottage. "I call it a shame."

"I can see why. It's so beautiful here."

"I've lived here over sixty years, was born and grew up in the area. I never thought I'd see the day when my neighbours would be city folk weekending at the beach. Ah well, one thing you can't control and that's time. When I'm gone, no doubt this place will be bowled and another place built—it's not like I've any family to leave it to. Sit down there, dear. You'll be comfortable on the firm chair."

"Thanks." Holly sank gratefully into a roomy and blessedly comfortable wicker chair. "You're on your own?"

"Yes, just me left. That's why you'll have to indulge an old woman who doesn't get a lot of company. I tend to talk far too much when I do." She laughed and slapped her hips at the joke. "My husband, Ted, passed on five years ago. It's been a bit lonely since then." She gave a wink and tenderly patted Holly's belly. "You won't be alone for long. You look about fit to pop anyday."

Holly smiled, trying not to dwell on another loss—the grandfather she'd never know. "I'm supposed to be another three weeks yet."

"You'll be early, you mark my words. Have you thought of any names yet?" Nana filled the kettle and put it on to boil, before clattering about in a cupboard and getting cups and spooning tealeaves into a pot.

"No, I haven't." She hadn't let herself. She didn't dare to.

"Don't worry. You'll think of something perfect when the time is right. Now, my Giselle, she was a determined one. So set in her thoughts. Nothing could sway her. She always said that if she had a little girl she'd name her Holly." Queenie sighed sadly. "She died twenty-four years ago this coming Christmas and I still don't know what we did wrong there."

"Wrong? Why?" Ice traced a nervous finger down Holly's spine.

"We were older parents. She came as a late bonus in our marriage, and as a result we probably overindulged her. At least Ted said *I* did. He put his foot down when she started to hang out with a young larrikin from further up the coast. Nice family, shame about the boy. Mind you, he settled down some in later years. Anyway, Ted made it quite clear that he disapproved of young Matt and forbade her from seeing him again. One night, soon after, she ran away from home. She was just shy of her fifteenth birthday. We did our best to locate her, but the police said some kids simply don't want to be found. We never did find out what drove her away in the end. It broke my Ted's heart. He was never the same."

Holly felt faint and forced herself to drag much-needed air into her lungs. Her voice shaking, she replied. "Maybe I know."

"You know? Why would you know, dear?" Nana gave Holly a puzzled smile before turning back to the whistling kettle and filling the teapot with hot water.

"I think I know why she ran away." Holly gripped the cane arms of her chair so hard she thought she'd snap them into matchsticks. "I'm Holly."

"That's nice, dear. Born at Christmas were you?" Slowly realization dawned on the older woman's face, and shock replaced her friendly smile. Her skin paled, driving the lifetime of sunshine from her weathered visage, and her eyes rounded in disbelief.

She should have been more careful, Holly thought, more considerate of the older woman's feelings. But she'd waited so damn long that suddenly even another second was forever.

Queenie lowered herself carefully into a chair opposite Holly. She opened, then closed, her mouth a few times before one word shuddered past her thin lips. "H-Holly?"

"Yes." Holly's voice was barely a whisper as it fought past the tears that constricted her throat. "I think Giselle was my mother."

Nana clapped her fingers to her mouth in a futile attempt to stifle the moan that escaped. "A baby? She had a baby?

That's why she ran away?" Tears began to track down her wrinkled cheeks. "But how did she cope? What did she do? Oh mercy, why didn't she tell us?"

Holly could only shake her head. "I don't know. Somehow she looked after me. Then on Christmas Eve, my third birthday, she left me where I'd be found and cared for. I suppose she didn't really know what else to do. I don't remember her face, but I remember a tune she used to sing." Holly started to hum the song she'd sung to herself over and over again at night to keep fear away, until one night she'd realised that no one was ever coming to get her and she'd locked the tune down deep in her memory. She stopped when Nana rose abruptly from her chair and left the room, coming back a few seconds later, a music box in her hands.

"It was my mother's. Giselle always loved it." Slowly she turned the key on the side before opening the box. Holly's skin prickled as the tune swelled through the air. *Her tune.*

The music box ran out and silence filled the room before Holly slid from her chair and knelt, wrapping her arms around her grandmother's waist and placing her head in her lap.

"I thought I'd never find you," she whispered brokenly against the soft fabric of her Nana's dress, finally giving way to the decades of loneliness that could now, finally, begin to be assuaged.

Her grandmother rested a hand on Holly's head, stroking trembling fingers soothingly through the long dark tresses, her voice awash with emotion. "I'm so glad you did, my darling. I'm so glad you did."

The next morning Holly awoke to the sound of seagulls calling across the beach and waves crawling up the sand. Although she'd slept deeply, she still felt exhausted. After dinner last night she and her grandmother had walked back to her car together, and Holly had garaged it at the cottage. Then they'd talked into the small hours of the night, piecing together the life they'd been cheated of. And yet, despite all she'd never had a chance to know before now, Holly couldn't blame her mother. She'd been young and foolish, following a dream of love with a boy she knew her father didn't approve of. How she'd hung on to Holly for as long as she did was a miracle in itself.

On Nana's part, while she couldn't come to grips with the fact that her daughter had never asked her family for help, she was so incredibly happy to have Holly here with her. Finally Holly had somewhere she belonged, someone of her own to love. And Nana was so excited about the new baby, Holly hadn't had the heart, or the courage, to tell her the truth last night. But she would have to do it today.

When she finally summoned the courage, her grandmother's eyes had filled with tears of compassion.

"But you love this Connor Knight, don't you?" Nana asked, confusion clear in her eyes.

"Yes." It was the simple truth, and Holly couldn't deny it to the woman who deserved honesty from her above all else.

"Does he know?"

"No, I've never told him."

"Well then, maybe you should think about that."

"I couldn't. If I told him now he'd only think I'm doing it to stay with the baby." Holly looked down at her hands. "I didn't want this baby. Not at the beginning. Not even a week ago. Not knowing my family, and with Andrea—I've been so scared."

"Well, now you know. There are no hidden nasties amongst our lot. You have to let go of the things you can't control, dear. Your baby will be fine. You'll see."

"It's too late." Holly's voice was flat, devoid of emotion as if the past twenty-four hours had stripped her bare.

"What do you mean? How can it ever be too late? Look at us. Yesterday I didn't even know you existed, yet I love you as if I'd been a part of your life since the day you were born," Queenie argued passionately.

Dread filled Holly's heart. How would her grandmother take the news? How could she understand? "I've already signed away all parental rights to Connor. Under the agreement, I won't even see it after it's born." Her voice cracked on a sob as the truth rammed home. She would never see her baby. Never be a part of its life, never hear its first words, or see its first hesitant steps. Never be party to her baby's first day at school, or its first wiggly tooth. *What had she done?* She didn't think she could hurt any more, but now she felt as though she'd scraped away the very lining of her soul.

Queenie's face dropped and she gathered Holly into the comfort of her arms. "Oh, my darling. My poor, poor girl. Don't you worry—we'll sort something out. You have family now. I might not be much, but I'm yours and we'll fight this together."

"It's hopeless, Nana. The contract is unbreakable. He's made certain of that. It's what he does. Who he is." Holly pulled away and stood apart, her shoulders slumped, her head low. She could hardly bear the truth herself—the bitter and cruel irony—that she should want this baby now more than anything she'd wanted before. "There's nothing we can do."

"You're wrong, Holly. You can't give up. I won't let you. You haven't waited all this time to be a quitter now. Why don't you go out and enjoy that sunshine and take a walk along the beach before the rain comes. I have some phone calls to make."

"I'll wait for you." Holly didn't want to be alone with her thoughts. Not now.

"No, dear, you go on. Once I've made those calls I'm going to look out some old photos of Giselle you might like to keep."

"I can stay and help you."

"No, no, dear. This is something I have to do for myself. Now hurry on before the rain, my old bones never lie."

Understanding dawned. In meeting her, her Nana finally had some of the answers she'd sought, and while neither of them would ever know the full story, it was time for her to make her peace with her daughter. And time for Holly to try and make peace with her own choices, she realised with hollow truth sounding a knell deep inside.

The tide was full out on the beach, and Holly was amazed at the width of firm damp sand. Her feet felt invigorated as the ground shells crunched beneath her feet and, in the damper spots, squelched up in between her toes. She wished her back felt as good. The nagging ache from yesterday had escalated into a dragging dull pain. Maybe her bones were becoming a weather forecaster like her grandmother's. She smiled softly to herself at the thought of having a familial link for the first time.

In the distance Holly saw a flock of birds scatter off the point. She laughed aloud as they wheeled in the air, their angry cries at being disturbed carried down the beach. Then, suddenly, her laughter died on her lips. A familiar sound beat at the air, drowning out the birds and sending deepening dread from her heart all the way to the soles of her feet.

The dark shape of a helicopter swooped over the hills at the end of the beach.

"No!" she shouted. "Not yet. It's too soon."

She turned and struggled through the sand, desperate to get back to her grandmother's. Desperate to find sanctuary.

She flung a look over her shoulder. A short distance away

the Agusta set down on the hard-packed sand and an all-too-recognizable figure stepped down.

"Holly! Stop!"

"No-o-o!" she cried. "Go away. I don't want you here. Leave me alone."

Connor was at her side quickly. She felt his presence before he stepped around her, halting her in her frantic flight.

Strong. Powerful. Angry.

"What the hell did you think you were doing?" he demanded.

"How can you even ask me that? Like you were going to tell me and bring me on a family visit? I don't think so. How could you keep something that important from me? I had a right to know! Oh!" She heard a soft pop and a warm gush of fluid rushed between her legs.

"Your waters?" Connor scooped her into his arms. "Don't worry. I'll get you to the chopper. I'll have you back in Auckland in no time."

"No! Put me down." Holly struggled against him, forcing him to let her feet back down to touch the sand. "Ahhhh." Holly clutched at his forearms and groaned as the dragging pain in the small of her back intensified and spread around the front of her belly, tightening and tightening, then slowly easing off. "I'm not going anywhere."

"Holly, you have to." For the first time in her life, Holly saw Connor at a disadvantage. Her groan of pain sent fear rushing into his eyes.

"I've waited a lifetime to be here. I'm not leaving now."

"You can bring my granddaughter back to my house, young man." Queenie strode down the beach towards them, a fiercely protective expression on her face.

"Nana! It's too early. What if there's something wrong?"

"My point exactly." Connor interjected. "Look, I can have

you at Auckland hospital in close to half an hour." Connor rested his hands on Holly's hips, looking her straight in the eye. "Please, Holly. Let me take you back."

"You don't need to be frightened, my darling," Nana interrupted. "We've birthed many a baby here." She turned and fixed a stern look at Connor. "Bring her to the house and then make yourself useful. You can call the local doctor for me."

"She's coming back to Auckland." Connor looked from one woman to the other. This was his baby they were talking about, and this woman—Holly's grandmother, he corrected himself—expected him to simply let them have the baby here? They were out of their minds.

"It's starting again." Holly clutched hold of his arms again, this time breathing through the contraction.

"You really don't have time, Mr. Knight. The women in our family have our babies mighty quick."

In the face of her testimonial and Holly's frighteningly quick onset of labour, Connor couldn't argue any longer. He lifted Holly back into his arms and followed her grandmother.

Half an hour later he paced back from the beach after reluctantly sending the helicopter off to the nearest grassed landing area, hopefully to await his call to return and take Holly and the baby back to Auckland. He let himself into the house and strode into Holly's room. "Where's the damn doctor?" he growled. "I rang him ages ago."

"It hasn't been that long," Holly answered, her hair already beginning to mat against her forehead as perspiration built up on her face. "Here comes another one. Ahhhh."

"Come here and rub her back like this, nice and firm." Nana took Connor's hand and pressed it against Holly's back. "No, no, lad. Not like that. That'll never give her any relief. Firm, like this."

Finally he seemed to be doing something right in the old woman's eyes. Holly sat back to front on a tall wooden-backed chair, her arms resting along the top rail, her legs spread on either side. He sensed her body tighten and spasm, could feel the moment she separated her mind from her surroundings and focused one hundred percent on the process that wracked her body.

This wasn't as simple as negotiating a contract. Nothing quantified how helpless he felt. He was responsible for what she was going through right now.

As she sighed a moan of relief, Connor acknowledged he should have cared a lot more. Should have listened to his inner voice when it urged him to let himself love her.

He'd been coming through Auckland Customs when his cell phone had buzzed with the frantic call from Thompson, who'd discovered Holly's flight from the obstetrician's rooms yesterday. He hadn't had time to be angry. All he'd felt was fear. Fear that something would happen to Holly.

On the periphery of his thoughts he heard another man's voice. The doctor, at last. Connor stepped aside to let him introduce himself to Holly.

"How're the pains?" the doctor asked.

"Awful," Holly replied with a weak grin, before closing her eyes and breathing through the next wave.

"I think it's time we got you up onto the bed so I can examine you."

"Oh!" Holly gasped, "I feel like I need to push."

"Hold back as much as you can. We need to check you first."

Connor and Queenie swiftly helped Holly onto the bed while the doctor slipped away to wash his hands and glove up. Once back he quickly examined her before giving her a smile and a nod. "You're all set to go."

"Connor!" Holly shrieked his name. He was at her side in a second, and she gripped his hand so tight his fingers lost all feeling. But the discomfort was minor as he became lost in another more miraculous event. The birth of his baby.

He couldn't tell later if it had been minutes or hours, but the incredible rush of seeing his son slide from Holly's body beat all description. The doctor lifted the squalling infant onto Holly's stomach, and Connor reached out to touch his son.

His son! The gift of life he'd never thought would be his.

Tears coursed down Holly's cheeks as she looked at the child, but she didn't reach to hold him, instead she turned her cheek against the stack of pillows bunched behind her and closed her eyes.

"Look at him, Holly. He's perfect. We have a son." His voice broke with emotion.

"No. Take him." Her voice shook.

"Wh-what?" Had he heard her correctly?

"Take him. He's yours. You have what you wanted. Take him now." The harsh whisper that dragged from her throat slashed him to his core. "Take him before I can't bear to let him go."

The doctor and Holly's grandmother exchanged worried glances as they attended to the final stages of the birth.

"Now, now, girl. That's no way to talk," her grandmother admonished gently. "Look at him. He's beautiful."

"I don't want him. Please, take him away." Her voice rose in pitch, and the doctor reached forward to swaddle the baby in a receiving blanket and gave Connor a troubled look.

Connor nodded in reply. "Take him out of the room. We need to talk."

Tremors shook Holly's body as the doctor handed the baby

to Nana, who cradled him close, then swiftly covered his patient with a sheet and woollen blankets. "Keep her warm, she's in shock. We'll be just outside the door."

As they closed the door behind them, Connor lowered himself carefully on the bed. Still Holly kept her face pressed against the pillows, away from him.

"Why don't you just take him and go?" Her voice, muffled against the pillow, wrenched a gaping hole in his chest.

"I can't go. Not without you."

"You don't need me. You have him now. It's what you wanted isn't it?"

"Did you think I'd just toss you a cheque, pick up the baby and go? What kind of man do you think I am? It's not about the baby anymore, Holly. I want *you,* and I'm not leaving here without you."

She turned back to face him, her mouth a twisted line. "No-o-o! You can't do that to me. You can't demand any more from me. I've done everything you asked. Now go, and leave me alone."

"Holly, you can't abandon him like this. Don't do this to yourself. Don't do this to our baby." Maybe shock tactics would work, he thought, grasping at anything he could to shake her from her resolve. "I read the report on your mother; it was faxed it to me in the States. Haven't you wondered if she died that way because she couldn't bear to be without you? Didn't you learn anything from her death? Don't you see? You're doing exactly what she did, except she was too young and too alone to know how it could be any different. Give yourself a chance. Give our son a chance."

"How dare you. She had no choice. I made mine," she whispered, her face paling. "I pity the poor woman you fall in love with, Connor Knight, I hope she never knows how low or how mean you're prepared to go." He barely made out her words through the thickness of her tears.

"Then pity yourself," he answered, finding her hand beneath the covers and holding it firmly in his.

"Don't! Don't lie to me."

"I mean it, Holly. I love you." He reached forward and brushed her damp hair from her face, his fingers tingling at the softness of her skin. "I've been a complete fool. I didn't tell you about the investigation because I didn't want you to have an excuse to leave. I wanted you to need me. I wanted to be the only one there for you, even though I fought it and fought it and treated you abominably every step of the way. I couldn't even admit it to myself until last week. I knew I needed to talk to you before the baby arrived but I couldn't do it over the phone. How could I tell you from thousands of miles away that I love you? You have every right to never want to forgive me."

She remained silent; her eyes boring into his as if she could see right through him, as if nothing he said mattered. Connor held her gaze and felt his heart skip a beat. He'd missed her with a physical and emotional ache that he hadn't wanted to identify when he'd first arrived in the States. He'd thrown himself into business and meetings, but in the back of his mind, and during every quiet moment, he'd wondered and worried about Holly. What kind of day she'd had. How she was feeling. Did she miss him as much as he missed her?

Bit by bit, he'd recognised that his motivation to close the deal and get home was no longer the imminent birth of his baby.

He wanted Holly. He wanted her like he had never wanted any woman.

It shamed him to realise it had taken the distance of several thousand miles to allow himself to admit he loved her. Right now, nothing he'd achieved in his career, in his entire life, meant a thing if he couldn't convince Holly of that too.

"Do you know why I wanted this baby, our baby, so much?" he asked, leaning forward to gently rest his forehead against hers. When she didn't respond he continued, regardless. "On your birthday last year I discovered Carla had terminated a pregnancy in the early stages of our marriage. It doesn't excuse what I did, but when you became pregnant all I could see was that I had another chance. A chance to do it right this time. Maybe, in the back of my mind, I even wanted you to fall pregnant.

"I put you through months of hell for my own selfish reasons, to replace the baby she killed. I couldn't let another child of mine die like that. When you talked about 'options' at Carmen's office that day, I was incensed. What if you'd insisted on a termination? My fears made me pretend you were just like her, when deep down I should have known better. Known you could never be anything like her."

"She had an abortion?" Holly asked, her voice hushed and filled with disbelief.

"Without ever telling me—then she was sterilised to make certain it would never happen again." Connor drew back and looked deep into her eyes, relieved to see the anguish had begun to fade, that the tears had finally dried. "Holly, you were right. I did treat you like nothing more than an incubator. By dehumanising you I didn't need to face my own feelings or inadequacies. I couldn't help my first baby, couldn't stop its murder. I was prepared to do anything to make sure that never happened again. Can you ever forgive me? Can you ever love me?"

"Love you? I've loved you forever, Connor Knight. It was killing me slowly inside working with you, then living with you, and knowing you were unattainable. I felt so alone, so unwanted. That night we made love? I wanted you so much. Making love with you gave me a chance to pretend that you wanted me, too."

"Holly, you didn't need to pretend. I needed you that night more than I'd ever needed another human being in my entire life. You were so real. So giving. So beautiful."

"And so wrong for you. When I saw you with your family the next day, I knew I could never be good enough for you. I had no background, no family. And at the office party, you obviously loved children. It was there in every movement, every gesture you made with the children. I couldn't give you that. My fear made that impossible."

"Nothing is impossible. Not for us. Not anymore. I love you, Holly Christmas. Will you marry me?"

"Marry you?" Her breath squeezed tight in her lungs. Her hands shook. "You don't need to marry me. What will your father say? What about your brothers?"

"They'll tell me again what a fool I was not to have married you before our child came into this world. In fact, they're barely speaking to me, they've been so disgusted with my actions. So, do you have an answer for me, my beautiful Holly?"

"Nothing would make me happier." She reached for him, a burst of pure joy blooming deep in her chest, chasing away the last pockets of darkness, of fear, of loneliness.

"So what do you say you reintroduce yourself to our little man." Connor tipped his head towards the door through which the newborn's demanding cries could be heard. "Something tells me he wants to meet his mama."

"Please! Bring him back."

Connor rose from the bed and swung open the door, putting his arms out to take the baby, his heart filled to bursting at the feel of this tiny adorable infant in his arms. Gently he gave him to Holly and watched, a lump forming in his throat as the baby settled in her arms and she pushed away the blanket and checked his long slender fingers tipped with perfect nails and his tiny pink toes, before gathering him to her and pressing her lips against his little face.

"He is perfect, isn't he?" Her voice was full of wonder.

"Yes, yes he is. And so are you. Thank you for the gift of my son."

"Poor little guy, he needs a name," she said softly, a gentle smile of wonder curving her lips as she gazed upon his tiny face.

"Why don't we call him André, for his aunty."

"André." Holly tested the sound of the name on her tongue. "Thank you. Andrea would have loved that."

Epilogue

"Have I told you how beautiful you look today, Mrs. Knight?"

"Only about three dozen times." Holly smiled as she leaned into her husband, relishing the hard strength of his body against hers and feeling the embers of desire stir deep within.

Their wedding guests had departed on Tony Knight's luxury yacht and into the crisp clear winter night, and with them, André. It would be their first time without him. She'd objected, but his doting grandfather had insisted that he and Queenie, who was staying at his house for the weekend, could manage just fine.

She still couldn't believe the chubby little boy was theirs, or that he'd been an active and demanding part of their lives for nine months now. Soon he'd be walking, no doubt making Thompson's life far more complicated than he'd ever bargained for.

But tonight wasn't about André. Tonight was about Connor and her.

She reached up and pulled her husband's face closer to hers, inhaling his scent, making it a part of her as much as she was now a part of him.

"Have I told you today how much I love you, Mr. Knight?"

Connors lips parted in a smile. "Only about three dozen times."

He closed the gap between them, taking her lips with a fierce possession Holly savoured with soul-deep satisfaction and the embers flamed into urgent need.

As they drew apart and slowly walked back to the house, Holly looked up at him, her eyes aglow with the joy of the truth that filled her heart every day.

Finally she had her very own family.

Finally her life was complete.

* * * * *

Don't miss The CEO's Contract Bride, *Declan Knight's romance, available in January 2008 from Yvonne Lindsay and Mills & Boon® Desire™!*

Happy Birthday

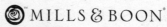

MILLS & BOON®

Celebrate our 100th birthday with the Mills & Boon® Annual 2008!

- Includes ten short stories from your favourite authors including:
  Rebecca Winters
  Jane Porter
  Elizabeth Rolls

- NEW diary section with useful tips all year round

- Plus...fabulous festive recipes, bumper puzzles, your 2008 horoscope, gardening tips and much, much more...

Available 21st September 2007

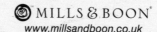

MILLS & BOON®
www.millsandboon.co.uk

1007/THE ANNUAL/2008

1107/009/MB112

Beautiful brides, rich and gorgeous grooms...
...magical marriages made at Christmas

Three festive weddings from our bestselling authors:

His Christmas Eve Proposal
by Carole Mortimer

Snowbound Bride
by Shirley Jump

Their Christmas Vows
by Margaret McDonagh

Available 19th October 2007

www.millsandboon.co.uk

1107/25/MB114

From Nora Roberts, the first lady of romance, come two stories to warm your heart this Christmas season!

Featuring the classic Christmas stories:

Gabriel's Angel

and

First Impressions

Available 2nd November 2007

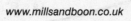

www.millsandboon.co.uk

M&B

1207/009/MB116

Every child wants a family at Christmas...

A Child's Christmas Wish

Susan Meier, Julianna Morris
Janet Tronstad

Three heart-warming festive stories for the holidays!

Snowbound Baby
by Susan Meier

Meet Me Under the Mistletoe
by Julianna Morris

Stranded with Santa
by Janet Tronstad

Available 16th November 2007

www.millsandboon.co.uk

✳ *Two Victorian Christmas Treasures*

Wicked Pleasures by **Helen Dickson**
Betrothed against her will, innocent young Adeline
Osbourne is resigned to a loveless marriage. Then dark,
dashing Grant Leighton comes along. Can the festive
season lead to pleasures Adeline thought impossible?

A Christmas Wedding Wager by **Michelle Styles**
Lovely Miss Emma Harrison has dedicated
herself to helping her father. But this Christmas,
ruthless and unforgettable Jack Stanton is back!
And Emma can't help but wonder if she made the
wrong choice seven years ago...

Available 16th November 2007

www.millsandboon.co.uk

1207/24/MB118

Cosy up to the fireplace with these two classic tales of love beneath the mistletoe...

New York Times bestselling author

DIANA PALMER

Heart of Winter

Woman Hater

Having been burned in the past, Winthrop Christopher was wary of women. But when Nicole White had to visit his home, what she found was the most roughly masculine man she'd ever met. Could she ever teach this woman hater to love again?

If Winter Comes

Charismatic mayor Bryan Moreland was on his way to getting Carla Maxwell's vote – until she found out he might be a fraud. As a reporter, Carla had to get to the bottom of it; as a woman, she wanted to lose herself in the sexy mayor's arms. Or was that exactly where he wanted her?

Available 7th December 2007

www.millsandboon.co.uk

M&B

1107/41/MB115

A collection of
short, period
regional sagas
– especially for
Christmas

Bride at Bellfield Mill
by Penny Jordan

A Family for Hawthorn Farm
by Helen Brooks

Tilly of Tap House
by Carol Wood

Available 19th October 2007

www.millsandboon.co.uk

1007/24/MB110

There's no better gift than the gift of love this Christmas-time...

A very special collection of stories, each sprinkled with seasonal delights!

The Mistletoe Kiss
by Betty Neels

Outback Angel
by Margaret Way

The Christmas Marriage Mission
by Helen Brooks

Available 5th October 2007

www.millsandboon.co.uk

M&B

Romantic reads to
Need, Want

**...*International affairs, seduction
and passion guaranteed***
8 brand-new books every month

Pure romance, pure emotion
4 brand-new books every month

**Pulse-raising romance –
Heart-racing medical drama**
6 brand-new books every month

**From Regency England to
Ancient Rome, rich, vivid and
passionate romance...**
4 brand-new books every month

Scorching hot sexy reads...
4 brand-new books every month

*Mills & Boon® books are available from WHSmith,
ASDA, Tesco and all good bookshops.*

MILLS & BOON
Pure reading pleasure

M&B/GENERIC 2 a

satisfy your every
and Desire...

**Two passionate, dramatic love
stories in every book**
3 brand-new books every month

Life, love and family
6 brand-new books every month

Breathtaking romance & adventure
8 brand-new books every month

**Enjoy the drama, explore the
emotions, experience
the relationships**
4 brand-new books every month

*Mills & Boon® books are available from WHSmith, ASDA,
Tesco and all good bookshops.*

MILLS & BOON
Pure reading pleasure

M&B/GENERIC 2 b

1107/10/MB111

Share the warmth and happiness of

A Regency Christmas

with three award-winning authors!

A *Soldier's* Tale by Elizabeth Rolls

A *Winter Night's* Tale by Deborah Hale

A *Twelfth Night* Tale by Diane Gaston

Available 5th October 2007

www.millsandboon.co.uk

M&B